Whispers & POISON

MANDY RAE WYLIE

First published in Australia in 2018
by Mandy Rae Wylie

www.mandyraewylie.com

Print US edition ISBN 9780994580702
Print Australian edition ISBN 9780994580733
Epub ISBN 9780994580719
Kindle ISBN 9780994580726

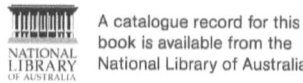

A catalogue record for this
book is available from the
National Library of Australia

For my children, my greatest gifts

And for my grandmothers - Ruby and Doris -
my earth angels

Thank you for your love

Prologue

Nell spun around and around, peering wildly into the darkling woods. The full moon, still low in the sky, cast an eerie glow through fishbone clouds coloured charcoal. Beyond the patchy moonlight, the woods were shadowed and sly, keeping their secrets, stealing hers. He could be hiding within a few yards of her and she'd never see him, not until he'd moved into the open, which was nothing more than a treeless track. She strained her ears, listening for his footfalls, his breathing, the snap of a twig, but couldn't hear much over her own panting and the thrum of blood in her head.

Forcing herself to stand still, she held her hands up and outwards, as if to sense on the air the ripples of any movements he made. Her fingers trembled as they touched the dampness settling around her. Nothing.

A sound. Muffled. Indistinct. Had he called her name?

Unsure of where the sound had come from, but knowing that she needed to move fast, she ran towards a narrow break in the thicket, and then along an overgrown path where tree roots snaked out to trip her and dangling branches snatched at her hair. Her threadbare cloak snagged on vicious thorns, bringing her to an unexpected and jerky standstill. Unable to free the cloth without shredding her hands, she leaned back and tugged until it tore free.

The sound came again, from somewhere just ahead.

~

The full moon looked down and wept. Through churning clouds –
the tail end of a storm – it caught fleeting glimpses of the forest and
kept watch over the clearing. Some things should not go unnoticed.
On nights like this, when the moon witnessed the suffering of the
innocent, it longed for the power to influence the lives of men.
Instead, it could only observe their deeds, both good and bad, and
light the way for the eventual passing of their souls.

Reaching through the still dripping trees, the moon touched the
young woman's lifeless body with ivory light. She lay slumped on
her back in a wooden barrow that tilted to one side on the uneven
ground. Her arms and legs dangled awkwardly over its edges, giving
her a neglected air that nothing could now mend. Strands of damp
hair fell across her face, and bruises darkened the fair skin of her
neck. The light was gone from her lovely eyes.

Steadying his boot on the slippery spade, the man beside her cut
into the wet ground again. Water seeped into the knee-deep grave
and lapped at the muddy hem of his cloak but he appeared not to
notice. He paused to wipe his face with a woollen scarf and the
moon couldn't tell whether sweat or tears coursed down his face,
whether the slump of his shoulders was from fatigue or misery, or
both.

Without looking at the young woman, he returned to digging, his
grunts loud, almost beastlike. He was safe from prying eyes in this
unfrequented part of the forest. When the hole was large enough
to hold her body, he lined its sodden base with a piece of sackcloth,
then crossed the soggy ground to where she lay.

He held a horn lantern aloft but didn't seem able to look at
her face. Instead, he stared into the dark woods and grasped the
barrow's splintery edge with his other hand until his knuckles turned
white. Eventually, as one day passed into the next, he put the lantern

on the ground, uncurled his fingers and reached out to touch her. His hands hovered over her waist while his breath came short and fast, white puffs that disappeared into the wandering mist. Then he groaned, thrust his hands under her armpits and pulled her forward. Her head flopped against his chest.

Crouching low, he heaved her from the barrow and carried her to the grave's edge. He kneeled and arranged her body in the hole, carefully straightening her legs and folding her arms across her chest. He picked the finest blooms from the bluebells that grew all around and placed them in her hands.

He then ran his fingers beneath the neckline of her bodice and pulled out a crescent of polished shell threaded onto a thin leather lace. The man closed his eyes and pressed the necklace to his lips, then placed it in a pouch hanging from his belt.

He drew the sackcloth over the girl's face and returned the soil to whence it came, and covered the mound of earth with leaves. Then he fell upon his knees, his whole body trembling, and buried his face in his soil-stained hands. A dreadful moan swelled from his chest and he cried the grim song in his heart to the moon.

The soul of the young woman rose from her unhallowed grave. She was relieved – and troubled – to find that she wasn't alone. Her sisters-in-death – three of them – gathered around her, their ghostly feet treading softly upon the air. They had been missing for months, and she longed to ask them how they'd come to be buried in these woods.

One Month Earlier

Chapter One

The Boar's Den

Nell hitched her skirts and sprang up onto the end of the bar, cursing under her breath when her bare feet landed in a sticky puddle of ale. She jigged up and down on her toes and peered around the overflowing tavern. A spate of gales had forced many merchants and fishermen to extend their stay in Stonhard's port and at least forty of them, along with the regular patrons, had come to the Boar's Den for a night of entertainment. If Nell could ignore the jitters that had plagued her since old Nancy Wilkes's death two days ago, she'd a good chance of adding a few coins and pilfered trinkets to the bag of treasure she'd buried in the back alley, ready for the day when she left the tavern and Stonhard far behind. And that day needed to be soon, now that Nancy, the smelly, coarse old cow, wasn't there to prevent her son and daughter-in-law forcing Nell to seduce the patrons with her body as well as her tales.

William Wilkes, scruffy and swaggering with self-importance now that he no longer had to defer to his mother, stepped into the bar room and clanged two pots together. 'Boar and sow,' he bellowed, 'I present our very own minstrel, Nell Brannerly, with another of her titillating tales, *The Masked Lady of Shadow*!'

Nell caught her breath behind the grey felt mask she was wearing.

What was Wilkes doing here? He'd been called away that morning and wasn't due back until tomorrow. As she stepped into a pool of lantern light, she wondered how she was going to explain to him her song choice for tonight, especially its surprise ending that was intended to make men feel guilty for cheating on their good wives. Since Wilkes's unexpected appearance, some of the wenches were now looking as nervous as she felt. But it was too late to back out now. Wilkes would want to know why.

A drumroll of fists on tables and wolf-whistles cheered Nell on as she swept the faded brown cloak from her shoulders to reveal a low-cut russet dress that had a few too many moth holes. She flung her arms overhead, then trailed her fingers lightly down the silhouette of her body until they rested on her generous hips. She posed, head held high, allowing the patrons' excitement to build.

In a dimly lit corner, huddled around a brazier of glowing charcoal, a trio of musicians struck up a jaunty tune. Nell unhooked a tambourine from her belt and rattled it overhead in time with the flute, lute and pitter-patter of a small drum. She skipped to the centre of the bar and moistened her dry mouth. The stench of sweat and unwashed bodies was overpowering, and the rancid smoke billowing from tallow candles didn't help. She longed to flee this stuffy room that was thick with men's rank need, and huddle on her bed and cry.

Behind her mask, she swallowed past the lump in her throat and wondered what was happening to her. Her stomach had been twisted in knots for months – ever since Nancy's poor health had worsened – and even when she was dry-eyed, a part of her continued to weep. She didn't need to see herself in a mirror to know that her hold on life was weakening daily. She still washed herself morning and night, but rarely combed her hair and couldn't be fagged mending the holes in her cloak and gown. Most disturbing of all though was the way she was beginning to welcome the dazed detached feeling that came when she skipped a meal or two. Living was easier when her thoughts were fuzzy and adrift.

She needed to get away while she still could, before her will shrivelled and died, but she was terrified of what might happen once she did. Leaving the place where she'd lived in constant fear for the past seven years filled her with dread and kept her awake most nights into the wee hours until she was utterly exhausted.

Aside from the lack of escape funds and the hold the Wilkeses had over her, she'd remained living among the scum of Stonhard because she'd been more afraid of being alone with herself and thoughts of her past, which had a way of rushing forth and swamping her in quiet moments. There was no time for idleness and solitude at the Boar's Den; its only redeeming benefits.

The here and now, the 'known', wasn't pretty, far from it, but she'd learned to survive, to hold herself tightly together so the patrons' lecherous hands and the Wilkeses' conniving gazes barely touched her, or so she liked to believe.

Realising that the musicians were waiting for her, Nell cleared her throat and, in a husky voice, began to sing:

'From the shadows came forth a Lady
Of Mystery – a mask she did wear.
Men opened their fickle hearts to her,
Forgetting their wives without care.

The blacksmith left his young wife at dawn,
A babe in her arms a-bawling.
Sweet breakfast he shared with the Lady,
In love, in love, he was falling.

'And when her gown slipped from her shoulder,
A horseshoe of gold he promised her.'

Nell opened her arms to the crowd and asked, 'Would ye, would ye forsake your wife, and give all to the Lady of Shadow?'

Cheering and whistling, the men stamped their approval while the serving girls and wenches hissed and booed laughingly – and a touch nervously now that Wilkes was watching. Nancy Wilkes had gone along with her son's plan to use Nell's story-telling talents to write songs for herself and the other women to perform, and Wilkes insisted that Nell begin each night with a light-hearted bawdy song to loosen the men's purse strings, before the other wenches presented the vile and disquieting fetishes that Nancy had delighted in coming up with – usually while Nell was massaging the old woman's useless legs or cleaning her bottom.

From her perch on the bar, Nell spied a well-dressed fellow of middle years playing a game of dice at one of the greasy trestle tables in the centre of the tavern. He leaned back to laugh and the jewelled hilt of a dagger at his belt twinkled in the lantern light. Nell's fingers tingled. Such a fine weapon would fetch enough on the sly-market to buy passage on a ship to the mainland of Lanbricke as soon as the seas calmed.

Nell jumped off the bar, landed on sodden straw stinking of stale ale and urine, and danced through the crowd towards the hog with the jewelled dagger. With shoulders shimmying and hips swaying, she nudged the fuzzy-haired occupant of a bench aside and stood on the bum-warmed seat. The man with the dagger was sitting at the table behind her.

The candle-maker kissed his old crone
On the cheek, then scurried down the lane.
Midday wine he shared with the Lady.
"Oh, my love!" he cried, "soothe my pain."

And when her red lips sucked his finger,
A bejewelled pricket he promised her.

The tailor patted his wife on the back

As she farewelled him with a smile.
Dusk delight he shared with the Lady,
"Oh, love, must I wait such a while?"

'And when she tickled his thigh and purred,
A gown of fine silk he promised her.

'Would ye, would ye forsake your wife
And give all to the Lady of Shadow?'

Nell placed a hand to her ear and leaned forward to receive the crowd's raucous reply, pushing her bottom towards her intended victim and giving her hips an extra *flickety-flick*.

In less time than it took to say *oink-oink*, the well-heeled man with the dagger appeared beside her. He bowed and offered her his arm. She hopped down from the seat and, arms entwined, they danced a merry jig as the crowd clapped them. Nell stood just over five feet, so she suppressed a twitter of amusement when she realised the man's nose only reached her bosom. His eyes remained fixed on those creamy quivering mounds as they completed a twirl; and when she curtsied and returned to her tale, he clung to her hand.

From each man she received a promise
(Each believing he was alone)
To bring their gifts to her at midnight
And stand naked beneath the moon.

To each, a heartfelt promise she made
To unveil her face and her soul.
Into their arms she'd willingly fall
If they promised to love her whole.

'Eager to please, each arrived early

And scowled at the other two men.
Bare bottoms aside, each pretended
He was out exploring the glen.

The midnight bell tolled — lo and behold,
From the shadows she did appear.
Her naked beauty — achingly rare
And each man shed a longing tear.

Preparing to fight for her favour,
Each man placed his gift at her feet.
Then he cooed and crowed his love for her,
Certain he had the others beat.

Would ye, would ye forsake your wife
And give all to the Lady of Shadow?'

The man with the dagger grabbed Nell around the waist and pressed his paunch against her hip. Swallowing her revulsion, she put a hand on his shoulder and steered him towards the most enthusiastic revellers. Folk rarely felt a hand slide into their pocket when they were jostled in a crowd. She fluttered her eyelashes at her eager companion and tilted her head so the lantern light was reflected in her amber eyes. It was a distraction that worked wonders on most occasions and kept men's thoughts from their purses, or in this case the belt where the dagger was fastened.

Her pudgy suitor was far from handsome but had taken care with his appearance. His face was freshly shaven and he'd oiled his sparse gingery hair. His fingernails were long and well-tended, and he wore a thick gold chain around his neck. No amount of careful grooming or flashy baubles could distract from his nose, however. It was meaty and red, and looked as if someone had mashed it against his face. He truly was a squat, ugly piggy.

He tickled Nell's cheek and poked two coins down her cleavage. To distract him, she rattled her tambourine close to his ear and slid her other hand towards his belt. She touched the hilt of the dagger; it was cold against her fingertips.

Piggy was watching every look that crossed her face. She wondered who he was. What sort of man felt safe enough to wear fine jewels to the Boar's Den?

Over Piggy's head, she watched another man, bald except for a plaited rat's tail, drag her friend Emily, a petite wench of fifteen years, by her hair towards a curtained alcove at the back of the tavern. Emily, her face scrunched with pain, knew better than to scream or complain. No one batted an eyelid, even though the men with darker desires usually slithered out of the shadows much later in the evening, after most other folk had gone home. For things to be turning nasty so early in the night seemed like a warning to Nell, an ill-favoured omen telling her to accept her lot and whatever Wilkes had in mind for her future without kicking up a stink, for things could be a whole lot worse.

She only had to look at Emily to know how deep his cruelty went. About a year ago, Emily had escaped the tavern and found work as a servant a day's ride north of Stonhard. Wilkes, enraged by the loss of one of his most desired girls, tracked her down and punished her by burning half of her face with a hot poker. Now Emily was reserved for well-paying patrons who revelled in rough handling and didn't mind an already scarred victim. Her light-brown eyes were dull and lifeless; she'd lost the will to save herself from further harm. Nell feared the day when they found the girl choked to death on the cobblestones beside the scraps pile. She hoped to persuade Emily to sail with her to Lanbricke, where they could both start life anew.

Nell snatched her hand away from the dagger and fear sliced through her. If her escape plan failed, what would Wilkes do to her? He'd hated the way his mother had claimed Nell as her nurse and companion, forcing him to put aside his and his wife's plans to sell her, a fresh girl of ten years, on the sly-market. Now that Nancy was dead and Wilkes was in charge, it was only a matter of time before he got his own back. And if Nell allowed that to happen, her own eyes would soon become dull and lifeless, just like Emily's.

Even though it was foolhardy to steal something so valuable, she pulled Piggy's dagger from its leather sheath and slipped it between the folds of her skirt and into a deep pocket that rested against her inner thigh. Rattling her tambourine with vigour, she twisted out of Piggy's embrace, pretending not to notice his scowl, and gave him a cheery wave as she skipped away to the other side of the room.

Nell wiped her sweaty hands on the back of her skirt as she realised she'd have to leave the Boar's Den tonight, as soon as she'd finished her performance. Piggy would soon notice the loss of his dagger, and Wilkes would tear the tavern apart until he found it.

If she left immediately, she hoped to get a good head start before Wilkes and his henchmen realised she'd gone. Stonhard port would be the first place they'd look for her, so she'd have to change her plans and travel north to the next port instead. Besides, she didn't trust any merchant or fisherman to hide her aboard his vessel until the wind died down.

She resumed her song with a slightly quavering voice:

'She received their gifts with heartfelt thanks
And, surrendering, kneeled and bowed.
Slowly, slowly she removed the mask
To reveal her fair face, as vowed.

The men gasped in horror and affright
As she laid her many scars bare.
Her beauty and wit they could not see
Their love vanished into the air.
Pfft!'

Feeling an unsettling mix of anticipation and dread, Nell jumped onto a table and pulled the mask from her face. The crowd erupted with cries of disgust and howls of laughter. She'd rubbed berry-stained oatmeal over her cheeks, turning them a gooey shade of blue, and poked a few strands of black horsehair up her nose.

Pretending to laugh, she plucked the hairs from her nose and finished her tale. The sooner this was over, the sooner she could collect her things, find Emily and leave.

'"You despicable whore! You have lied
And cheated us out of riches.
You promised us false and left us with
Nothing, not even our britches!"

'"I did not lie or steal," she whispered,
'My face and soul I bared to three.
And each of you rejected my whole.
Will no one declare love for me?"

'"Not I," said the candle-maker,
His wick withering in reply.
"Not I," cried the blacksmith,
His hammer a shrinking tool.
"Not I," snivelled the tailor,
His needle shrivelling through its eye.

'"Oh, but three promises will be kept,
Faithfully and soon," she declared.
With ghastly smile, she bade them farewell
Leaving them bereft and despaired.

'From the shadows stepped three angry wives
Broom, horsewhip and poker held high.

As they thrashed their husband's bare backsides,
Each shouted his love for his wife.'

Nell pulled a small broom from inside her cloak and twirled it overhead, a prearranged signal to the serving girls and wenches to grab their own spanking weapons and join in the fun. Ululating, she leaped from the table to chase the men closest to her and whack them with the broom.

Most of the men gave mock squeals and hid behind their companions or ducked under tables, but some weren't amused – including Piggy, who backhanded a young serving girl.

Already planning what she and Emily would need to pack, Nell made for the back corner of the room to find her, then came to a sudden standstill. Three identical men appeared to be hovering over a bench seat. Each had short-cropped hair that shone blue-black in the lantern light, skin of dark gold, and glinting almond-shaped eyes. Simple black robes covered their slight frames and she had a fleeting impression of birds of dark wing, ravens or crows. They appeared to be praying, for each held his palms pressed together over his heart. A strange sight at the Boar's Den. Why was no one heckling them? Was she the only one to have noticed them?

The three men nodded in unison, their eyes intent upon her. Nell felt faint. Had they seen her steal the dagger? She tried to turn away, but they whistled an eerie tune that held her in place somehow, and then she was tumbling backwards, backwards through time …

She was holding another knife and it felt as cold as snow in her small, shaking hand. Warm urine ran down her legs as she gazed at a fly flitting over the remains of an unfinished meal …

William Wilkes grabbed Nell's shoulder and pulled her away from the now empty seat. The three strange men had disappeared. Nell looked wildly around the room – where could they have gone?

Chapter Two

Hobgoblin

Wilkes steered Nell towards the bar, shouting to the patrons that Exotic Lola and her Feathered Tickler was about to perform. He shoved her through the door into the back passage and said, 'Wait here, you stupid little bitch. Edmund's watching the alley so don't move.'

Nell felt her hastily eaten supper of bread and watery pea soup flip-flopping in her belly as she looked for somewhere to hide Piggy's dagger. She couldn't duck outside and bury it with her other treasures because Edmund was guarding the alley. Why had Wilkes ordered him to do that?

She dashed over to a sack of boots and burrowed into them with her hands to make a hiding place, but shouts from the bar startled her just as she was about to take the dagger from her pocket. Fearing that Piggy had raised the alarm, she darted to the back door. If she surprised Edmund, she might have a chance to elude him before he gathered his meagre wits. He was as dumb as dog shit, but also mean and strong.

She fumbled with the door latch.

'Where are you off to in such haste, my girl?' said Wilkes. He'd opened the bar door without her hearing.

Fear squeezed her throat like two giant hands. 'The privy,' she muttered, adding a couple of coughs to give him the impression that something other than a lie was stuck in her throat.

He laughed, not a cheery sound.

Whistles and laughter sounded from inside the tavern and she realised with relief that the patrons were only making a commotion because Exotic Lola had unwound the first of her veils. Wilkes hadn't come to accuse her of stealing the dagger.

Wilkes sucked on his moustache with his bottom lip and moved closer to her. He picked up a handful of her wavy chestnut hair and flicked it back and forth under her nose, then tugged on it hard. 'Folk come here to be aroused and fulfilled, not mocked and judged. Are you weary of telling tales?'

She kept her eyes on his clean-shaven, rather babyish chin and shook her head. 'I thought some playful spanking might warm them up for Annie's performance of the song you told me to write about men whipping –'

He held up a finger to silence her and wound her hair around her throat. 'Remember your first days with us, when you sat on the bar entertaining my guests with riddles and songs?'

Nell immediately pictured the bucket, as he knew she would. If it was heavy with pennies after she'd finished charming the patrons, he patted her cheeks and fed her supper. On the nights it weighed light, he made her lift up her skirt and show off her knees. If she whimpered or cried, he'd threatened to sell her to the hobgoblin that loved to drink of little girls' sweetness until they died. Some of the men had snuck their hands up Nell's skirt with half-closed eyes and quickened breath, then sniffed their fingers as they dropped coins into the bucket.

Wilkes pulled on the hair around her throat until it felt uncomfortably tight, then mimed wiping tears from his eyes. 'Ah, I will be sad to see you go.'

Go? Go where?

The back door opened and Doreen Wilkes, a tall lean woman

of two-and-forty years, whipped into the passage and stabbed her husband's shoulder with her finger. 'Where the fuck is Edmund? He's meant to be watching the alley.'

Wilkes paled and let go of Nell's hair, but quickly regained his swagger. 'Quit squawking. Nellie's still here.'

Doreen glanced over Wilkes's shoulder at the bar door, then lowered her voice. 'We can't afford to cock up this arrangement.'

Nell was surprised to hear something that sounded like trepidation in her mistress's voice. She dreaded to imagine the punishment Wilkes had in mind for her if it disturbed Doreen, who was harder than nails.

'Have you told her yet?' asked Doreen.

Wilkes smirked. 'Nay, she's yet to hear my amusing tale about an ungrateful wretch who finally gets her comeuppance.'

Doreen turned to Nell. 'It's a way for you to repay the care we've given you the last seven years.'

Care? A sneer must have crossed Nell's face for Doreen's trepidation suddenly gave way to anger. Her sharp-boned cheeks flushed and her pebble-grey eyes narrowed.

'Do you think, missy, that Lord Hammerton's letter describing your wicked deed has somehow lost its power to send you to the gallows?'

That letter ... Nell had searched the tavern for it many times, without success. Each time it was mentioned, she remembered how Lord Hammerton had prised the bone-handled knife from her hand and called her 'a child of the devil'. When Nell was younger, Doreen had frequently invoked 'the letter' as a means of bending Nell to her will. The vile woman had even taken her to a hanging at the crossroads just outside town, so Nell clearly understood what would happen to her if she stepped out of line or tried to escape.

Nell clamped her mouth shut against the hysterical laughter suddenly bubbling up in her. If Doreen knew that she feared what was hidden within herself more than that damned letter, what would

she say? Nell's secrets were uncoiling deep in her belly; barbed
tendrils that drew blood as they slithered into her heart and mind
and slowly choked her. Piggy's dagger – if she managed to get away
with it – would fund the peaceful future she craved, but unless she
could find a way to live with and perhaps make up for what she'd
done, that future would be but a dainty cloth trying to cover up the
festering wounds of self-loathing and despair.

She wondered why she'd gone ahead with her performance tonight,
even though Wilkes had been present and was likely to be angry with
her. Had she done so because it was a frighteningly subtle way of
attracting the punishment she felt she deserved? It would be more
palatable to see her weak act of rebellion as a forced incentive to flee
the tavern instead, but Nell sensed deep in her heart that she had no
love for herself and would rather escape the here and now altogether.

'I'm going to find Edmund, the witless fool, to make sure he
watches the alley tonight,' Doreen told her husband, and slammed
the door on her way out.

Wilkes put a hand on the wall either side of Nell's head and
slipped his knee between her legs. 'I've had a generous offer from
a fine fellow who's been sent here by the King to hunt down those
who've chosen to ignore their obligations to fill the royal coffers.'
He raised his knee until it pushed against her groin. Nell held her
breath, averted her eyes from his crooked teeth and shifted her
stance slightly so he'd not feel the dagger resting against her inner
thigh. 'He requires a companion to warm his bed for a few months
while he journeys around our fair Isle of Squinte. You delighted
him this evening, sweet Nellie, and he's paying handsomely for the
privilege of being first to breach your maidenhead.'

Tears burned the back of Nell's eyes. She gritted her teeth, not
wanting to give Wilkes the satisfaction of seeing how afraid she was.
He jerked his knee up hard into her groin and she screamed and bit
her tongue. He stepped back, grinning, and crossed his arms over
his chest, apparently satisfied.

Nell curled over her knees in an attempt to stop the pain spreading through her belly. As her groin throbbed, she realised she was holding her breath, something she'd often done after her father's death when she was eight – the moment her life had soured. Back then, she'd held her breath until she saw stars, believing that if she could stop breathing, she'd die and go to a place where no one could hurt her.

Wilkes pulled Nell to her feet and over to the bar door. He opened it and pointed over the boisterous crowd to the man who was holding one of Exotic Lola's veils over her nose and mouth while the crowd counted and clapped.

'At dawn, you'll pass into the keeping of Lord Oliver Bente,' he told her. 'He's a little busy tonight.'

Bile scalded Nell's throat as she recognised the back of Piggy's ginger head. His dagger burned hot against her leg.

The crowd continued to count slowly, 'Four-and-thirty, five-and-thirty ...' while Lola clawed frantically at Piggy's hands.

Nell now understood why Doreen had been worried about her husband cocking up the deal they'd made with this man. She tried to move towards Lola to help her, but Wilkes held her back.

'Fifty!' the crowd roared.

With dramatic flair, Piggy whipped the veil off Lola's face and kissed her hard on the lips. The crowd cheered and drummed their fists on the tabletops.

Nell wanted to tear out her hair. She'd played with Piggy, and now he wanted to play with her.

When Lord Oliver Bente turned and saw her standing in the doorway, he half-closed his eyes and slowly kissed the air between them.

The hobgoblin had come to sip her sweetness until she died. She wondered if she had any sweetness left for him to drink.

It was time to grab her belongings, find a way to sneak past Edmund, and get away from the Boar's Den as fast as she could.

Chapter Three

The Hollow

Plump beads of dew sagged from the branches in the forest clearing, then dropped to the ground with a dull plop. Fallen leaves shifted in the gathering breeze – a squall was coming. Somewhere not far away a vixen screamed like a woman in pain, and a fieldmouse dropped the shrivelled cup of an old acorn and scurried to the safety of its home amid the roots of a tree.

Maye Hannigan lifted her weary head off the ground. She'd not yet the will to uncurl her frail body, so she propped herself up on an elbow and stretched her other arm towards the night sky. The full moon cast a grey, gloomy light through swirling clouds and she strained to gather even a small amount of its brightness. Only the moon's power could replenish her essence and give her the strength she needed to leave this shadow-filled hollow between her old life and the place she longed to reach – the gilded doorway she'd seen at the moment of her passing.

Once the moonlight had warmed her fingertips, she forced herself to sit up. Lying on the ground with her eyes squeezed shut like a frightened child listening for menacing footfalls in the dead of night wouldn't ease her troubles. With her back to the three graves – her own, and those of her two companions – she cupped her hands and moved them in slow circles to gather as much of the meagre light as she could. The movement reminded her of how she'd once caught spring water as it bubbled out of the ground and down a rocky hillock near her family's cottage.

The moonlight thickened in her palms and slowly transformed into a few pearls of silvery nectar, moondew, that seeped into her spectral body. As it soothed the aches and pains of her ghostly bones, she let out a long breath of musty otherworldly air. She could not yet see the glow of her aura, but even a small amount of moondew slowed the withering of her soul, temporarily stopping her from turning to dust and blowing away, like a scarecrow's tattered clothes whipping away, bit by bit, in the wind, until only a shadow of herself remained.

Rain was coming, fast. She could smell it on the wind. It was once one of her and her sister's favourite scents – nature's fragrant celebration of the moment when sky touched earth – but now it only foreshadowed a blanket of clouds across the moon, another night wasted. For four months, whenever the night sky was bright and the townsfolk's minds were as quiet as they could be in these troubled times, she'd called to them and beckoned with ethereal fingers, hoping her cries would part the veil between the realms and draw someone to find her unholy grave.

'Hester …' Her identical twin sister's name fell from her lips and disappeared. She'd not yet gathered enough moonlight to hold it in the air, let alone send her warning across the hills and into Hester's mind and dreams.

She called again, but her voice was fainter and heavy with regret. Why had she not accepted Hester's apology and spoken words of forgiveness? Why had she pursed her lips and turned away from her beloved sister so many times during their last few weeks together?

Drops of rain fell. Thrusting her arms skywards, Maye stretched and twisted towards the thin shafts of light that disappeared whenever the wild wind thrashed the branches of the trees that bordered the small clearing. She'd vowed to stay in this place until Hester was safe, even though she ached to soar heavenward, to hear again the celestial voice that had sung to her immediately after she died, while she hovered in shock over her crumpled body. But as each night passed, her ability to hold the light weakened, and she sometimes wished she'd never seen the gilded doorway beyond the moon if she was destined to fade into shadow like the withered souls that dwelt in the forest at the clearing's edge.

A shiver of foreboding chilled Maye's thoughts. Would Hester be safer if she held her tongue? Was she leading her, or whomever responded to her call, into danger?

Maye had asked herself these questions many times, and the answer was always the same. If the man who had killed her, who hid his madness behind an ordinary face, killed again and she had done nothing to prevent it, she would never rest peacefully wherever she ended up.

Chapter Four

Maureen

At the top of the rickety staircase that led to her bedchamber, Nell wrapped her arms around herself and doubled over. Panic caught her breath. What had she just done? She could not have conjured a better punishment for herself if she'd tried.

Straightening her back, she gouged the chunks of oatmeal from her face then scrubbed her cheeks roughly with the hem of her skirt while she considered her choices.

Outwit Edmund and run far from here. Or find a way to return the dagger and become Piggy's companion.

Nell stifled a cry with her hand. She couldn't bear the thought of him touching her … forcing himself on her. If he found pleasure in suffocating Lola, what else was he capable of? He made her blood run cold.

Time was racing by. She needed to leave post-haste.

To give herself courage to grab her belongings and to flee into the unknown, she pictured herself living in her own cottage on the cliff high above Longport, a town she'd once visited with her parents. There, if she let them, the emerald waters might wash away the stains on her conscience and the briny wind clear her mind of the past. She could sleep peacefully each night, and awaken refreshed and redeemed in a safe home, which was something she hadn't experienced since her father's death.

Trembling with the sad certainty that achieving peace of mind and heart was nigh on impossible in the real world, Nell twisted the rusted door ring and stepped into the bedchamber she shared with Maureen and Maureen's son, Eben. The odour of sickness was overpowering, and didn't mix well with the more familiar smells of horse manure from the stables beneath the room and mildew from the rotting floorboards. She tiptoed across the tiny room and opened the shutter of a narrow window, but the rushlight on the washstand barely flickered in the feeble waft of fresh air.

Eben, a two-and-a-half year old who'd recently discovered the merits of screaming and throwing himself on the ground when he didn't get his way, was sleeping peacefully in his mother's crooked arm on one of the two narrow beds that had once served as storage shelves. Maureen was wheezing and gasping for breath as she slept.

Nell decided not to wake them. She didn't have time to explain her sudden departure to Maureen or to indulge in a long and painful farewell. It was better for everyone if she just grabbed her things and ran before Piggy realised his dagger was missing.

Moving swiftly and quietly, she stuffed the least shabby of her undershirts, her writing implements and her father's old leather water flask into a bag, and slung it across her chest. She'd have to make do with the two coins Piggy had poked down her cleavage until she could sell his dagger because Edmund was guarding the alley, which was where she'd buried her savings. Clenching her jaw, she quickly knotted her remaining clothes and some thin blankets end to end to form a flimsy rope. She tied one end to the leg of the washstand and flung the rest of it out the window, which overlooked the back of the inn's stables. She had no idea if the rope would hold her weight, and it was too dark to see how far above the cobblestones its end dangled. She'd not get far out of Stonhard with a twisted ankle, but she'd have to take her chances.

She poked her toes into her worn boots, and retrieved from under her pillow the necklace her parents had given her on her seventh birthday. She looped the thin leather lace around her neck and tucked the polished pearl shell beneath the bodice of her dress for safekeeping. It was time to go.

She hoisted herself onto the windowsill. It was harder than she'd thought to get through the window as it was a tight fit and her legs kept tangling in her skirt. She managed to get her left leg out so she was straddling the sill, then drew her right knee up to her chest and pushed her foot through the opening. Now her dangling legs were crossed at an awkward angle. Turning her torso towards the bedchamber, she curled her waist over the sill and unhooked her legs. She grabbed hold of the rope, dreading the moment it took her full weight, and prepared to wriggle backwards.

'Nell?' Maureen's voice crackled like dry leaves. Nell held her breath, hoping she would fall back to sleep. 'Take Eben with you.'

'I'm sorry, Maurs, but they're after me. I'd only put him in danger.'

'Please! I'm dying.'

Nell pulled herself back over the windowsill and fell onto the floor, then picked herself up and hurried over to Maureen. Her dark blonde hair was soaked with sweat, and her breath was shallow and laboured. Nell grabbed the pillow off her own bed and slipped it under Maureen's head, then dribbled water from a cup into her parched mouth. Eben's thumb slipped out of his mouth but he didn't stir.

At the washstand, Nell wet a cloth and returned to gently wipe Maureen's fevered brow. She'd developed a persistent cough not long after Eben was born, and had been hacking up blood for the last six months. The apothecary who supplied her tonic had told Nell that it was only a matter of time before she succumbed to the illness.

'I've left it too long to make things right for Eben,' said Maureen, every word a desperate gasp for air. 'I really thought Jack would come when he heard he has a son.'

'He mightn't have received the two letters we sent him,' said

Nell. 'The messengers might not have made it to Bellayne for any number of reasons.'

She was damn sure that Eben's father hadn't received any of the messages Doreen Wilkes had promised to send on Maureen's behalf. Doreen made a bucketload auctioning the wenches' unwanted babies at the sly-market and would be eager to get her hands on Eben once Maureen died. Maureen had been one of the few young women at the tavern who had chosen to keep her child, even though the Wilkeses made her work extra hours for the privilege.

'Nay, Jack despises me and I do not blame him.' Maureen began to cry, exacerbating the bubbling in her chest.

She'd told Nell how she'd discovered she was with child two weeks after leaving Jack, her betrothed, for a man who'd promised her riches and travel. The bastard had dumped her in Stonhard when she was seven months gone. Maureen had been unsure which man had fathered Eben, until he was about eighteen months old and his hair darkened and his eyes changed from blue to green – just like Jack Lea, and nothing like the blond man who'd deserted her.

'For Eben's sake, I should've put aside my shame and my fear of the Wilkeses and taken him there myself before I got sicker, but –' She stopped to retch into a cloth that was already stained with blood. 'But I'm a coward, plain and simple. And now I'm leaving my boy all alone in the world! There could be no greater punishment for my sins. I know I've no right to burden you, Nell, but please will you take him to his father? I want to die knowing he'll be safe.'

Nell was lost for words. She should've been a long way from the Boar's Den by now, and how was she going to outrun Lord Bente and the Wilkeses with a small boy in tow?

Holding the child against her body with one arm, Maureen lunged forward, grabbed Nell's hand and placed it on Eben's head. He stirred and yawned, peaceful in a dreamworld where his mother's distress couldn't touch him.

'Look at him, Nell. I'm begging you. You're the only one I can trust to keep him safe.'

Eben's cheeks were rosy against his fair skin, and his black hair flopped, as usual, across one eye. Nell could still hear his first feeble cries on the day he was born, and feel the way his tiny hand had curled around her finger when she'd wrapped him in a blanket and held him close.

'I'm begging you, Nell. Please, please …'

Nell clasped Maureen's hand between hers. 'I promise to take Eben to his father.'

Maureen held tight to her child and rocked back and forth, whispering her thanks over and over until Nell couldn't bear to hear the grief and hope in her voice a moment longer. She wrapped her arms around Maureen and Eben both and whispered a poem about angels lighting the way for lost children.

A short while later, Nell finished writing the two letters that Maureen had asked her to write – one for Jack Lea and another for Eben to read when he was old enough to understand his mother's heartfelt words – then kneeled beside Maureen's bed and squeezed her hand. Maureen was humming one of Eben's favourite songs.

'Your lullabies for Eben oft helped me towards sleep,' she told Maureen, wanting to give her a little more time with her son before Nell took him away from the Boar's Den.

'Jack once told me that even the larks and the bullfrogs fell silent so they could hear me sing. A bullfrog!' Maureen laughed softly as she stroked Eben's back. She burrowed deeper next to him and closed her eyes. 'Jack said my smile touched his heart. Oh Nell, I wish I'd believed …' She fell into silence.

'Maurs?' Nell said, hoping to feel the rise and fall of her friend's chest beneath her shaking hand. Nothing. Maureen was gone. Eben had lost his mother.

Feeling numb with shock, Nell eventually forced herself to move. She draped around her shoulders the shawl Maureen had given her for Eben; it had a blue and yellow fringe and a slightly crooked angel that Maureen had stitched onto a corner with brown thread. She put into her bag the letters she'd just written and also grabbed some spare clothes for Eben and his favourite wooden cup.

She turned to look at him. They needed to leave now but she didn't have the heart to lift the child out of Maureen's arms.

Someone shouted in the alley below. Nell's heart pounded and her mouth went dry. They were coming for her. She'd left her run too late. She eyed the door and the window, desperately seeking inspiration. She didn't have enough time to secure Eben to her body, even if it were possible for both of them to squeeze through the narrow window. Perhaps she could toss Piggy's dagger out the window to pick up later, and pretend to be asleep. Or …

More shouting. William Wilkes was cursing her name at the bottom of the stairs.

With her heart in her mouth, Nell lifted Eben from his mother's lifeless embrace and squeezed under the bed. He wriggled in her arms as she huddled against the wall, trying desperately to slow and quiet her panic-stricken breaths.

The door slammed open. Lantern light splashed erratically around the room. Nell stuck her thumb into Eben's mouth when he whimpered.

'She's gone … out the window,' said Wilkes.

She heard a thump and a scuffle, then Piggy said, 'I told you that whore stole my knife! You'd best get her back or I'll burn your fucking tavern to the ground with you both tied to your bed.'

'Gather as many men as you can to search the streets while Edmund hastens to the harbour,' Doreen yelled at her husband. 'Tell him to stay there until all the ships have sailed.'

Another thump. A grunt. A slap and a cry of pain – Doreen's, Nell thought.

'Wake this other wench,' Bente said, 'and find out how much of a head start the girl has.'

Blood pounded in Nell's head as Doreen walked between the beds. 'She's dead ... and Nell has stolen the boy.'

'You're coming with me,' said Bente, presumably to Doreen, his voice shaking with anger. 'We'll ride out to the crossroads. She can't have gotten far.'

Nell heard Doreen pleading with Bente not to burn down the Boar's Den as all three left the bedchamber and ran down the stairs.

Eben started crying. Holding him close, Nell crawled out from under the bed. The hobgoblin was coming after her. She felt sick with fear.

How was she going to keep her promise to Maureen? And what would she do with Eben if Jack Lea was no longer in Bellayne?

Nell wrapped Maureen's uneaten supper of bread and cheese in a cloth, pushed it into her bag, then tiptoed to the door and peeked down the stairs. The alley was deserted now that her foes were preparing to hunt her.

Carrying Eben on her hip, she slunk down the stairs and headed towards the alley behind the stables. She hurried through the dilapidated gate, but stopped suddenly when she heard whimpering. Emily was huddled on the ground in a splash of moonlight beneath her bedchamber window.

'What are you doing here?' Nell asked.

'Go while you can,' said Emily, who must have heard the commotion. 'Before they find you.'

'Come with me,' Nell said.

Emily shook her head, her scarred face streaked with tears. 'It's too late for me.'

Nell knew she was partly to blame for Emily's present circumstances, and wished for the umpteenth time that she'd warned her when Wilkes tracked her down to the wool merchant's home where she was working as a servant. Nell would never forgive herself for not acting to save the girl – just one among her many sins. She grabbed Emily's arm and tried to pull her up, but Emily curled in on herself and resisted.

Lantern light flickered through a crack in the stables' back wall and someone shouted, 'Head to Coastway Road.'

Nell cursed. Doreen had already sent Edmund to the harbour, and now someone else was watching the main road to the north. There was only one other way to reach Bellayne and it would add at least a week to a journey that was already likely to take her two.

'Save the boy,' said Emily, pulling her hood over her head. 'I'll lead them away from you.'

She leaped to her feet and ran back towards the inn before Nell could stop her, or tell her she could have the savings she'd buried behind the privy.

A horse whinnied and hooves clattered on the cobblestones in front of the stables. 'There she is!' someone shouted. 'Get after her.'

Taking advantage of the head start Emily had generously given her, Nell ran down the alley towards the maze of streets that would eventually lead her and Eben to Flegg Road, the long and winding way through woods and over hills to Bellayne and Jack Lea.

Chapter Five

In the Woods

At the end of a lane on the outskirts of Stonhard, Nell crouched
behind a fence and watched the beginning of Flegg Road for any
sign of Lord Bente or his men. Nothing seemed to be moving but
she was reluctant to break cover and head into the woods.

Eben was sobbing against her shoulder and calling for the
mother he'd never see again. How was she going to explain that to a
two-and-a-half year old who had no concept of death?

Both her own parents had been gone by the time she was ten,
which was old enough to understand that death was final and they
were gone for good, except for the memories that haunted her still.
Now that she was away from the chaos of the Boar's Den, there
would be nothing to distract her from those dark flashes of that
terrible day her mother had left her, and no way to stop the pall of
despair thickening around her.

Something behind her made a brief scuffing sound. She spun
around on her haunches and peered into the darkness. Who or
whatever had made the noise was keeping to the shadows.

A crow walked into a patch of moonlight – surely an oddity at
this time of night. It appeared to be studying her, its head cocked
to one side. Nell thought about her eerie encounter with the three

crow-like men at the tavern, and remembered one of her mother's sayings about crows appearing to those who were soon to die. Was her journey to Bellayne, and then to the mainland of Lanbricke, ill-fated before it'd even begun?

The crow flapped its wings and Eben started to wail. Nell ran into the hush of the woods with him in her arms.

Nell woke at first light with a fiery crick in her neck, and saw that the ditch she and Eben had stumbled into in the dark was crawling with bugs. Grey clouds swirled slowly in the pale moody sky, no doubt heralding a run of drizzly days. Eben must have awoken some time ago because he was covered in mud and swishing his hands through one of the many rank-smelling puddles. He was talking to himself earnestly and she wondered what was going on in his mind. Was he talking to his mother, wondering why she wasn't with him? They'd never spent a day apart.

Nell rolled onto her back, closed her eyes and let tears of sadness run down her cheeks, over her ears and into the dirt. She'd stayed awake last night for as long as possible, guarding Eben, and when she did sleep it was turbulent with memories of her life before the Boar's Den. She was exhausted before she'd even sat up.

When Lord Bente and the Wilkeses didn't find any trace of her at the harbour or on Coastway Road, they'd scour the isle for her. She and Eben would need to move as fast and as stealthily as possible through the hills of the midlands, which meant keeping an ear out for other travellers and hiding in the woods until they'd passed. She dreaded to think what Bente would do to her, and maybe Eben too, if they were caught. The image of him suffocating Exotic Lola with one of her veils was fresh in her mind.

She'd have felt braver if Emily had come with her instead of acting as a decoy. Nell hoped she'd kept on running too, but suspected she'd have doubled back to her bed at the tavern, if she'd not been caught. Emily had told Nell often enough that she'd given up all hope of ever escaping the Wilkeses.

'Where Ma, Nellie?'

Nell swallowed her tears and opened her eyes. How was she going to tell Eben that his mother was dead and he'd never see her again? Was now even the right time to tell him? She could hardly spring the sad tidings upon him and then expect him to let her change his filthy clothes and get moving. And what were they going to eat? She still had the last of the bread and cheese from Maureen's uneaten supper in her bag, but it wouldn't last long. And if she did find food, how was she going to cook it without a fire? How would she dry Eben's clothes and shelter him when the rain came?

She pulled him closer so they were nose to nose and she was looking straight into his apple-green eyes, one of which had sleep in its corner. She twitched her nose against his and said gently, 'Your ma's sick today.'

'Sick, cough, cough,' he said, and mimed retching into both hands.

She pressed her lips together and nodded. Lying to him felt wrong but she needed time to work out what she was going to say. She just hoped he would remember the many ways Maureen had shown her love for him.

She ruffled his hair, which was thick, black and dangled just past the bottom of his chin. Maureen could never get him to sit still long enough for her to cut it, so she'd taken to slicing off bits and pieces with a knife while he slept. The result was messy but it suited him.

'Come on, scruff, let's get you clean and dry,' said Nell, lifting the wet tunic over his head. She'd need to scrub it in the first stream they came across and then tie it to the outside of her bag to dry.

She dampened a cloth with water from her father's leather flask and wiped his face and hands.

Eben rubbed his eyes and plonked down on his bottom. 'Ma better now,' he said, sticking his thumb in his mouth.

Nell usually told Eben a story in the morning while Maureen summoned the strength to get out of bed. His favourite featured a mischievous troll named Hokey, who got into many a scrape and often lost his breeches. Eben had loved searching their shared bedchamber for the small pair of patchwork breeches Maureen had made for the imaginary troll. Nell mentally kicked herself for forgetting to bring them.

'Remember how Hokey loves going on adventures?' she said.

Eben stuck his thumbs in his ears, waggled his fingers and wriggled his bottom – one of Hokey's favourite moves. 'Hokey naughty,' he giggled, flicking his tongue in and out of his mouth.

'Well, your ma wants me to take you on an adventure to meet your father,' Nell continued, before concern twinged her mind. What would happen to Eben if Maureen was wrong about Jack Lea being Eben's father, or if Jack didn't believe it to be true?

Eben cocked his head and his hair flopped over his right eye. 'Ma hide in trees,' he said, pointing over Nell's shoulder. 'Ah, boo.'

'Nay, your ma's too sick to play today. She wants me to look after you.'

He sucked his lips inward and shook his head slowly, a familiar sign that his mood was about to change for the worse. 'Nah-uh, Ma hiding.'

She persuaded him put on the dry tunic and hose, then to let her take his leg in her lap so she could put on his boots. But he pulled his foot from her hands and looked close to tears. He was obviously confused by their whereabouts, whether or not he sensed something more was wrong.

'Remember Brown Boy?' Nell said, referring to Eben's favourite hound back at the tavern. He nodded. 'Well, he's the *father* and Girlie is the mother of the puppies you love to tickle. And we're going to meet *your* father.'

'Where Brown Boy, Wee?'

Eben always pronounced Nellie with 'wee' at the end instead of 'lee', and often shortened it to Wee.

Picking up a stick, Nell drew a circle in the dirt, then a windy path with another circle at the end of it. 'This is where Brown Boy lives. And this is where Wee and Eben have to walk, walk, walk to meet your father.'

'No walk, walk. Where Ma?'

'She's asleep.'

'Wake up! Wake up!' shouted Eben, his face flushed with distress.

He'd gleefully shouted those words many times as he jumped from one bed to the other in the mornings to rouse Maureen and Nell. There was no bouncing or laughter today. He'd had enough of her bullshit.

The following morning, Nell came across a large group of Travellers, some of whom smiled and greeted her as she fell in with them near a small village and its market. If Lord Bente or his men had offered a reward for tidings of Nell's whereabouts, she and Eben would be less conspicuous in a crowd. As an added precaution she'd wrapped scarves around their heads, to hide her mass of chestnut hair and to give the impression Eben was a girl.

Eben's stomach grumbled loudly as Nell picked him up and perched him on her left hip. His legs dangled lethargically against her thighs instead of wrapping around her. A faint smell of urine wafted from his hose; he must have dribbled in them again. She couldn't do much about that until his spare pair dried, but felt guilty that he wasn't as clean as Maureen had kept him. Nell smelled somewhat ripe herself and longed to scrub her armpits and hair in a warm bath.

One of the Travellers, a robust woman with stringy hair carrying a bairn in a sling around her neck, stopped at a stall selling dried strips of mutton. Nell stood beside her and bought two handfuls of the strips using part of one of the coins Bente had poked down her cleavage at the Boar's Den. At other stalls she bought two pickled eggs to munch on immediately, some bread and cheese, and pieces of dried apple – enough to last them both a few days.

Eben shoved a hunk of bread into his mouth, and licked the apple.

Then he grabbed another hunk of bread and, before she could stop him, threw it to a skinny dog. 'Num, num,' he said, aiming a crumb-speckled smile at the grateful dog. One less piece of bread for them, but Nell thought that a small price to pay to see Eben's face light up.

Eager to leave the market, she ducked behind a fishmonger's stall and headed to the road. And stopped in her tracks when she saw three men dressed in black robes sitting on a log. It was them, the men who'd bewitched her in the Boar's Den. Had they followed her from Stonhard? Were they Lord Bente's men, sent to keep an eye out for her until he and Doreen Wilkes caught up to them?

She and Eben were out in the open and any sudden movement would alert the men to her presence if they'd not already been following her. Nell lowered Eben to the ground and pulled down his hose as if he'd asked to pee to give her time to look for an escape route. She'd have to cross another open field to reach the woods, so decided to go back to the market, change herself and Eben into their damp spare clothes, and wait for the Travellers to leave so they could walk out with them.

Eben flapped his doodle but nothing came out. She pulled up his hose and glanced back at the men. They were gone. Instead three crows were perched on the log in their place.

She shook her head, relieved. Lack of food and sleep were making her barmy.

It was two nights later, sitting beneath the soft light of the waning moon, that Nell decided it was time to answer Eben's persistent questions about his mother. She leaned against a tree and sat Eben on her lap so he was facing her and straddling her waist.

'No ride horsey,' he said with his thumb in his mouth. He was worn out, melancholic and hungry. The eggs she'd pinched from a farmyard henhouse hadn't filled him up; he'd hated the taste and feel of their rawness in his mouth.

'Nay, no horsey tonight,' Nell replied, still not sure how to talk to him about Maureen in a way he'd understand. She put his hand on his chest. 'Can you feel your chest going in and out each time you breathe into your nose?'

He nodded gravely, perhaps frightened by her serious tone.

She gently put her hand behind his head and pulled him forward. 'And if you put your ear against my chest and listen, you'll hear something that sounds like a little drum. It's called your heartbeat.' She wrapped her arms around him and tapped his back with her fingers in time with her heart as he snuggled against her. 'Sometimes when we get really, really sick, like your ma, our breath and heartbeat stop and don't start again. That means our body's died and we can't live any more with the folk we love. I'm sorry, Eben,' she said, choking on her tears, 'but your ma got too sick and she stopped breathing. She didn't want to leave you … never, ever … but she had to and –'

Nell pressed a hand over her mouth. She'd wanted to stay strong for Eben's sake but couldn't help herself. He leaned back against her bent knees, his lips beginning to tremble.

'When someone dies,' she said after catching her breath, 'they go to a beautiful place called heaven, which is up there behind the sky.'

She'd no idea where heaven was or if it even existed, but she had to comfort him with something.

'Ma not birdie,' he said seriously.

'No, but she had special wings that we couldn't see to help her fly up there.'

'She come back?'

Nell shook her head, unsure if he'd asked a question or made a statement. He gripped Maureen's shawl and thrust his thumb into his mouth.

'Heaven has lots of angels and puppies to look after your ma, and a rainbow that always stays in the sky. And she can look down and see you.'

He looked up at the sky. 'We go heaven, Wee?'

'One day.'

Chapter Six

Hear Thee

In the hollow, beneath a glorious giving moon, Maye Hannigan joined hands with her companions and all three floated above the bluebells to form a ring – which Irma persisted in calling a 'garland of ghosts', much to Maye's and Gracie's annoyance. After four cloudy nights in a row, they were desperate to call to their loved ones – or to anyone willing to follow their song along the overgrown and often boggy path to the wildest patch of old forest where their graves lay.

Maye sighed deeply as moondew, warm and silvery, swelled within her bosom and cascaded through her whole body, lighting her aura and allowing her soul's song to fly free for a while. The three of them hummed and danced slowly in a circle until an orb of creamy light appeared in its centre.

Gracie Alcorn, once a carefree child of eleven with joy-blushed cheeks and glossy brown plaits, lifted her chin and sang sweetly about one of her favourite nights with her family.

'At dusk by the fireside, while we mend a tangle of torn tunics and hose, my mother and I are talking about my wish to become a maker of beautiful gowns one day. My father and my five older brothers, a rowdy mob of farmers and hunters, burst through the door and carry us out to a meadow, where they have laid out a feast upon a blanket. Oh my, there are candles, jars of wildflowers, plump cushions, and my father has made an enormous cake, his first ever. He takes my mother in his arms and they dance while my brothers tap their ale mugs with sticks and sing a ballad in loud tuneless voices.'

Though Gracie's voice was clear and strong, Maye felt the girl's hand trembling in hers. Her face was wan now, and her waist-length plaits, tied with the yellow ribbons she'd often worn in her old life, were dusty and dull. The hollow was no place for a child.

Irma Linke, a willowy young woman of seventeen, who'd once danced through life on lightsome toes devising many a mischievous deed, increased the pace of the circle until their hair streamed out behind them, and lime-green and orange sparks flew from their dancing feet. The orb of light grew around them until they were floating inside what looked like a shimmering transparent egg.

Maye glanced at the Shadowfolk who crept from among wood anemones and ferns and into the clearing to sit beneath the orb of light. They were wispy dove-grey shapes made of a pallid haze finer than smoke or mist, and made a faint rustling sound as they moved, like the pitter-patter of mousy feet, like shivers upon the wind. She assumed they came to bask in the light that emanated from the orb because they were no longer able to gather and transform moonlight into moondew for themselves. Or perhaps it simply comforted them, or gave them hope. Maye didn't want to think about how long the Shadowfolk had dwelled in the hollow, for her own soul was fading day by day and she feared she'd soon be joining them, doomed to flutter for eternity like a desiccated leaf on gusts of stale air.

In a husky voice, Irma sang about the time her dear friend, Sister Winifred, had tripped on the towpath and accidentally dropped her favourite laying hen into the fast-moving waters of the Eel. Although the nun couldn't swim, she'd thrown herself into the water, grabbed a floating branch and followed the bobbing chicken down the river, while Irma ran along the bank shouting for help. By the time an angler fished the hen and the bedraggled nun out of the water and onto his boat, the might of the river had forced Sister Winifred's habit halfway up her back, revealing her moon-white legs and part of her saggy bottom.

'After that,' sang Irma, her short blonde curls bouncing around her sharp elven features, 'Sister Winnie and me nearly wet ourselves laughing each time we cracked the top off a boiled egg at breakfast.'

Gracie giggled. It was good to hear her laugh, Maye thought. There wasn't much merriment in the hollow. And it was good to see Irma behaving more like her old playful self. Of late, a scowl had warped her bright-eyed countenance and her wit had soured, leaving a bad taste in all their mouths.

Empowered by their love and good intentions, the orb of light bloomed into a magical starburst of silver swirls and iridescent sparks, and carried their call over hill and dale to Bellayne, to the hearths of their old homes.

Seeing the hollow aglow always broke Maye's heart for it was both beautiful and terrible to behold. With its crooked trees, moss-covered rocks and carpet of bluebells it looked like the perfect setting for lovers and faeries, not hidden graves and a broken child. And Maye had only to look at the Shadowfolk to know that things didn't always turn out for the best as they did in faerie tales.

She thought about Hester, who had shared their mother's womb with her, and all her dreams and secrets. She wanted to keep the light-hearted mood so decided to sing about one of the last happy moments she'd shared with her sister, just two days before Hester had embarrassed her so deeply and betrayed their special twin bond. Hester, her sapphire-blue eyes watery with spiteful mirth, had been telling Maye about Posey Browne's latest shenanigans with a young knave in Maiden's Well woods. Maye wasn't interested in tittle-tattle, but Hester had told the story with such animation that Maye, a crimson blush upon her cheeks, had laughed in spite of herself.

But just as Maye shyly opened her mouth to sing, she saw a look on Irma's face that frightened her into silence. Had Irma touched the mind of the man who'd wrapped a cord around each of their throats? Had he killed again? Was he creeping closer to Hester?

Irma caught Maye watching her and turned her face away. Then, as if to reassure Maye, or perhaps to deceive her into thinking nothing was amiss, Irma nudged Gracie to get her attention, then bent her arms into wings and clucked like a hen.

Instead of laughing, however, Gracie wrapped her arms around herself and cried, 'My father's anger is louder than my whispers.'

As soon as the circle was broken, the orb of light shrank and disappeared.

Maye rushed to comfort Gracie. When Irma didn't join them, she glanced back at her and froze. Irma, her jaw clenched, her gaze intense, was facing Bellayne and muttering to herself. Had she forgotten how careful they had to be with their thoughts? How their bitter calls for vengeance had led to Gracie's death?

Anger, sharp and acrid, bit into what was left of Maye's kind-heartedness. Irma was planning something; Maye could feel it. But she wouldn't let Irma put Hester, or anyone else, in danger, not this time.

Just after dawn, Sister Winifred came back from checking the henhouse to find a piece of parchment nailed to the wooden door leading into St Clements's kitchen garden. She put her basket of eggs on the dewy ground, then tugged the parchment free and uncurled it. Her stomach curdled as she studied the drawing of a monk pushing a girl's head beneath the lifted hem of his robes. She slumped against the garden wall as she contemplated the warped messenger's latest offering and the thrill he or she was obviously getting out of spreading such suspicion and malice.

The garden door swung open and Sister Winifred cried out and dropped the piece of parchment.

Jack Lea appeared carrying a hunk of bread and a boiled egg. After his night shift emptying the privies all through the town, he often stopped at the refectory to break his fast before heading home to the farm he and his ageing father tended.

'Sorry, Sister,' he said. 'Did not mean to startle you.'

Sister Winifred pressed a hand over her mouth to stifle a sob. Her role was to comfort folk, not fall apart in front of them.

'Oh God, is it Irma? Are there tidings of her?' asked Jack, shutting the door and hastily stuffing the bread and egg into his pocket.

Shaking her head, Sister Winifred ignored the screeching of her old knees as she bent to pick up the parchment. She handed it to him.

'For Christ's sake,' he said, and crumpled it in his hand. 'As if we did not have enough to cope with.'

'Is it aimed at one of the brethren?' asked Sister Winifred, stepping closer when she saw two Greenfriars in their olive robes hurrying across Holy Apple Row to the chapel. 'Did one of them take the girls?'

She never said the word 'killed' aloud but it haunted her dreams and now her waking hours too. Like most of the townsfolk, she'd lost faith over the last four months that Irma, Maye and Gracie would come home. To make matters worse, Gracie had disappeared during a bout of heavy rain that had flooded the roads and isolated Bellayne for two weeks. The sheriff's men had accounted for the movements of any travellers lodged in the town, thus quashing the long-held theory that a stranger had taken her. The townsfolk had been shocked to realise that a fiend – most likely a murderer – walked among them.

Jack shook his head, straightened his floppy hat that had seen better days, and scuffed his boots on the grass, obviously trying to hold in his grief for Irma. Their friendship had deepened in the months before her disappearance, and Sister Winifred had often seen the special look that passed between them – that moment when two folk suddenly saw each other in a different light but were shy about exploring it in case their feelings weren't returned.

Sister Winifred had watched Jack grow from an awkward boy

into a young man of four-and-twenty who was comfortable in his skin, so it was troubling to see the stoop return to his tall lean frame, and to notice the way he hesitated before speaking as if doubting that anyone would be interested in what a nightsoil-collector had to say.

'I want to know what happened to them, but then I also do not,' she said, feeling frail for the first time in all of her one-and-seventy years.

'But we need to know,' said Jack. 'To stop it happening again.'

'And why Gracie?' Sister Winifred continued. 'She's so much younger than Maye and Irma. It doesn't make sense to me. But then none of it does.'

She clenched her fists as she imagined the fear that would have gripped Gracie Alcorn six weeks ago as she was abducted on her way home to her family. They needed to stop this unknown fiend. But how?

'I fear it never will,' said Jack, putting an arm around her shoulders and leading her towards the garden door. 'Let's get you and these eggs inside.'

Sister Winifred took the parchment back from him and squeezed it hard in her hand. She vowed to keep her eyes open everywhere, even within St Clement's, and look at people and in places she didn't wish to.

Chapter Seven

A Dark Night

Nell looked frantically up and down the bank of the narrow fast-flowing stream. 'Eben! For God's sake, where are you?'

He'd been standing beside her only moments ago when she kneeled down to wash her face in the frigid water. She headed upstream a few paces, checking behind rocks and bushes, and then ran downstream. He couldn't have gone far during the short time she was distracted.

'Eben, please call out to Wee! Oh, God … if you can.'

She jumped onto a rock, her eyes raking the water, praying she didn't see his little body floating there, his dark hair fanned out, his face blue and cold …

'Eben!'

She slipped off the rock and cracked her knee on another smaller, sharper one. She let out a roar, and limped downstream until she could see where the stream widened and slowed into a pool of still, shadowed water. A willow's leafless branches and dangling catkins hung low over the pool, creating a hideaway, a feathery cave, a sheltered grave …

'Eben!'

She plunged into the pool, not quite thigh deep at its centre, swiping branchlets out of her way, and searched for him with her hands and feet until she was certain he'd not sunk to its bottom. As she waded back to the bank, dripping wet, a flock of birds burst up from the woods not far away. She ran in that direction, hoping it was Eben who'd disturbed them.

And then she saw him, crouched on the mulchy ground and rocking on his haunches, his face in his hands. His head and narrow shoulders slumped as he stood and brushed his hands, then he shuffled over to where the lower end of a mossy log was touching the ground. He clambered onto it and inched along, looking like a frog as he poked his bottom out then tucked it back in. When he reached the end of the log, which was wedged between two boulders and less than two feet off the ground, he looked up and said with a tinge of desperation, 'Look Ma-ma. Me fwy heaven.' He bent his elbows, flapped his hands fast and jumped, never once taking his eyes off the patch of sky visible through the treetops.

Nell looked up at the sky, to where some folk believed heaven was, and whispered, 'If you are real, then please help him.'

Later that evening, as the cold rain bucketed down, Nell huddled under the shelter of small branches and ferns she'd made and listened to Eben crying for his mother. His repeated 'Maa, maa …' made him sound like a lost lamb, but he flinched away from her every attempt to stroke his back or hold him close and rock him to sleep.

Water trickled through the thatch of ferns and dripped down her back. She shivered, and blew tepid air into her cupped hands in the hope of thawing her frozen fingers. She'd covered Eben with her cloak to keep him dry and warm. Every part of her body was crying out for rest but she couldn't lie down and curl herself around him until he was asleep and oblivious. She wished that someone powerful enough to ward off danger and nightmares would enfold her in strong arms, so she wasn't exposing her back to the pitch-black woods and whatever was stirring in the night, or to Lord Bente's wrathful approach.

She'd been eight the last time her mother – or anyone for that matter – had comforted her to sleep, and she still remembered the warmth and peace that embraced her as her mother filled the room with sighing, lilting, soothing songs. But not long after Nell's father died, her beautiful, sorrowful mother had climbed into the bed of her elderly employer, Master Elmer Long, and left Nell alone to face the shadows that danced wickedly on the walls of her bedchamber.

Nell vividly remembered the day that Elmer Long had beckoned her into his library, closed the door and settled into his cushioned chair. He'd patted his knee, calling Nell over to him and promising to read her the book that he'd given her yesterday, for her tenth birthday. For her mother's sake, Nell had pushed aside her reluctance to be near him and climbed onto his lap and turned her head so that he could see her smile. He liked it when she did that.

He'd swept her hair over one shoulder, fiddled with her earlobe for a moment, then reached around her waist and laid the gilt-edged book in her lap. His stomach pressed into the small of her back. She wished that her mother would come in from the garden.

Elmer stroked the book's leather cover with very clean fingers, before easing it open. Nell gasped; she'd never seen such a beautiful picture before. Two golden-haired girls with angelic smiles were standing beneath a crescent moon in a meadow of wildflowers. One of the girls held a sleepy black kitten in the crook of her arm.

In a low murmur, Elmer began to read. Nell gazed at the picture as he held her hand. He moved his other arm to sit under the slight curve of her tiny breasts. She tensed and arched forward, but the weight of his arm held her in place and, seemingly unaware of her discomfort, he continued with the story. His voice droned on and on, reminding her of lazy bees, and she longed to run outside to the garden. His breath was warm and moist on the back of her neck, and she itched to scrub the spot clean.

Suddenly he was moving beneath her. "You have the prettiest amber eyes I've ever seen,' he panted. 'And your little pot belly makes me ...' He gripped her hand and shuddered. The book fell to the floor.

The library door opened and Nell's mother stood there, proffering a posy of roses. Nell remembered white petals fluttering through the air as she walked over to Pearl, keeping her back straight and taking slow steps as all good girls should.

'My sweet, sweet girl,' Pearl said, leading her from the room.

In the kitchen, Nell waited nervously for her mother to say something about what had just occurred. But Pearl continued to mull wine and place goblets and roasted meat onto a tray for the midday meal as if nothing was amiss. Pearl had frequently turned away when Nell needed her the most, hating to see the haunted look on her daughter's face.

Nell had learned to cry on the inside. Every night, curled into a ball, her head hidden beneath the blankets, she had prayed for help from Above, for a sign she wasn't alone. No help had come. Not then, not now, and probably not ever.

That hadn't stopped her feeling a hollow place in her heart that ached to know that life – her life – had meaning. She yearned for a deep sense of belonging – but with whom or what she couldn't yet define. In that calm space between sleep and waking, the only time her mind was still, she'd occasionally sensed that a part of her already knew the answers to at least some of life's mysteries. If she could only stay in that space long enough to grasp and hold that fleeting, amorphous idea, she believed she'd understand the secret to living fully, with faith and courage, instead of merely surviving.

She'd spent so many moments dreaming about the life she'd have once she reached Longport. She'd live on the beautiful green cliffs overlooking the bustling town and glittering sea, and would put to good use the reading and writing skills Elmer Long had taught her. She would teach the daughters of wealthy merchants for money, and in her spare time she would teach the same skills to poor children for free. Not only would it help to atone for her many sins – well, that wasn't entirely true – but it was a way to share her only worthwhile value: the gift of story-telling. Guilt and shame, however, always jolted her from those reveries the instant she awoke properly and remembered who she was and what …

Eben suddenly sat up and let out a wail that bounced off the trees and echoed back to Nell's heart. She reached for him, but he thrashed his arms and screamed as if she were trying to hurt him. Even though his face wasn't visible in the dark, she could see in her mind his wide frightened eyes and his thumb poked into his trembling mouth.

'Heaven nasty,' he cried through pitiful sips of air.

Nell cried too, silently, so she didn't distress him further. How could she continue to comfort him with stories about his mother being in heaven when she herself didn't believe it was true?

Nell's mother had believed in angels and faeries – or said she did, when all was rosy – but Nell had taken after her father: an amiable, practical man who thought that people made their own heaven by offering kindness and a helping hand to others. He'd often told his wife that she lived with her head in the clouds and missed what was going on around her, especially when trouble knocked at the door. On those occasions, Pearl retreated to her magical world and let other folk, usually Nell's father, get on with what needed doing. Once the trouble had passed, she'd open her arms, smile beautifully and say, "There, that wasn't so hard, was it?"

Even as a child, Nell had understood why her mother had taken up with their master before her marriage bed was even cold. She'd wanted Elmer Long to take care of her while she continued to live her dreams in her imagination.

Water seeped beneath the cushion of fern fronds Nell and Eben were sitting on, wetting her dress and bottom. A cold, dull ache spread through her lower back. Once Eben was asleep, she'd lift him onto her lap or he'd be soaked through by morning.

She began to hum, slowly and deeply, and straightened one leg and shifted it sideways so she was barely touching him with her calf. She hoped he'd sense her willingness to look after him, and know that she'd gladly put aside her own dreams of achieving freedom on the mainland until he was safe in his father's arms.

Doubt poked Nell sharply in the gut. Whom was she fooling? She was fumbling in the dark, unravelling on the inside, and nearly as frightened as Eben was. Maureen should never have trusted her to get him to Bellayne.

And what right, Nell asked herself, did she have to a peaceful life? None. Not after what she'd done.

To keep her mind away from the crippling dread that often sapped her will to survive, she cast about for a story to tell Eben – to soothe him and perhaps give him a safe space to think about his mother. If she changed the story slightly each night, she could help him hold in his memory all the things he'd loved about Maureen.

> '*"Touch me with your finger," said the star to the little boy,*
> *"The one you miss is here with me,*
> *She's stroking your brow and singing her love.*
> *Whisper, whisper, whisper,*
> *Close your eyes.*
> *Her light shineth still.*
> *We'll watch over you this night and all nights to come.*
> *Whisper, whisper, whisper …"*'

Eben's eyelids fluttered for a while as he looked at the sky, then slowly closed. When she was sure he was asleep, Nell lifted him onto her lap and nestled his head against her chest. His soft breathing lulled her to sleep.

Crow wings flitted across Nell's closed eyelids. She fought to escape from the dream that was sucking her in, pulling her backwards to the day following her tenth birthday …

Heavy rain pelted the shingled roof and a stiff breeze whistled through the gaps around the closed shutters, bringing the smell of dampened dust into Elmer Long's dining hall. Nell stood a couple of paces from the table, staring at the remnants of a half-eaten meal. A fly flitted between a leg of mutton and the pool of wine that had splashed out of her master's overturned goblet. With her eyes, she followed a trail of breadcrumbs from the cut loaf of seeded bread to Elmer Long's outflung arm. The crumbs disappeared beneath the top half of his body, which was slumped sideways on the table. Only the arm of his chair kept him from toppling onto the floor.

Even unconscious, his body leaned towards her, pressing against the air until she couldn't breathe. She was afraid that he'd suddenly wake up. She didn't want to see his white-whiskered round face leering at her. She whimpered, wanting to step back, but knew that if she did, if she looked any further to her right, the sky would fall and smother her with angry clouds.

Voices drifted into the room from the front yard, startling her, making her more aware of what she was seeing. She could no longer pretend she was dreaming.

A woman's shrill laugh echoed down the passage, and Nell wondered if she should hide behind the heavy drapes bunched at the side of the window, or climb out of the window. But she couldn't find the will to move. Nothing mattered, not any more. She kept staring at the table, never allowing her eyes to flick to the right.

The fly abandoned the mutton and circled over her master's back before settling on the dark stain that seeped from a tear in his leather jerkin.

The door to the dining hall opened. A woman screamed.

Urine flowed down Nell's legs and trickled into her boots. Her knees buckled. She collapsed on the floor.

A man, dressed in a cloak with gold braid on the hem, clamped a hand around Nell's wrist and prised the cold knife from her hand.

The woman – Elmer Long's daughter, Christiana – held both

hands over her mouth and sobbed, 'God in heaven, what have you done?'

Nell couldn't answer. She closed her eyes so they couldn't flick to the right and see …

Nell jerked awake, and remembered instantly the many times she'd begged the God some folk believed in to grant her the oblivion of the long, long sleep.

Chapter Eight

Of Shadows and Guilt

Sister Winifred, her ancient ankles creaking, hurried up the path towards the porch of St Clement's where a throng of folk had gathered.

'You'd have to be fucking blind to ignore this, Sheriff,' shouted Lex Alcorn, shoving a tattered piece of parchment in Arundell Birch's face. 'It was tacked to my barn door.'

Gracie's father and his five sons, burly lads ranging in age from sixteen to twenty-four, had cornered Sheriff Birch and weren't allowing him to either leave or enter the church. Lex's wife, Meryl, a fine-boned woman with narrow sloping shoulders and a look of desperation in her eyes, was tugging on her husband's sleeve.

Sister Winifred pushed through the crowd, some of whom were trying to attend the evenfall blessing, and tapped the tallest and broadest of Lex's boys on the shoulder. He was standing on the bottom step, legs akimbo, arms crossed over his thrust-out chest, barring the sheriff's exit. He had the decency to mumble an apology as he stepped aside to allow Sister Winifred to pass.

Giving Meryl a sideways glare, Lex tensed his jaw and wrenched his sleeve from her grasp. Sister Winifred was shocked by his careless treatment of the wife he adored, and even more shocked by his appearance. A short, stocky man, he'd lost weight after Gracie's disappearance and looked as if he hadn't slept properly since. His greying hair was dishevelled and unwashed, and splotches of food marked his rumpled tunic. He'd always been an argumentative fellow but Sister Winifred had never known him to be physically aggressive before now.

Sheriff Birch, a tall, brawny man in his early forties with long flaxen hair and a short beard, took the parchment from Lex's hand and held it up to the lantern outside the porch door. He rubbed his temples and let out a sigh of exasperation.

'These drawings – this is the fourth I know of – are the creation of a disturbed mind. And they are becoming more frequent.'

The youngest Alcorn son, newly sprouted whiskers on his top lip, pushed his father forward, egging him on to greater folly.

Lex ripped the parchment from the sheriff's hand and held it aloft. 'We all know this man,' he shouted, spittle spraying from his mouth.

Gasps rippled around the crowd, although Sister Winifred wondered how many of them could actually see the drawing from where they stood. She wished that she'd not seen it, nor Meryl either.

'That's my Gracie,' cried Meryl, gazing in horror at the picture of a little girl lying upon a cart loaded with barrels. There was a knife sticking out of her chest, and one of her yellow hair ribbons had unravelled.

Meryl turned and stumbled down the stairs, weeping.

Sister Winifred, concerned that her presence was the only thing preventing the Alcorn men from attacking the sheriff, stood her ground. She'd find Meryl as soon as this situation was resolved.

'Be reasonable, Lex,' said Birch. 'These messages are spreading poison, not truth.'

'Where smoke curls, fire smoulders,' shouted one onlooker. And was no doubt pleased when a number of folk agreed loudly with his wisdom.

'This here is Jack Lea,' said Lex, pointing to the man driving the cart. 'We all know he was rejected by Irma Linke!'

The man in the drawing was wearing a bright green shoulder cape, which was indeed very similar to the one Jack sometimes wore for his own amusement when collecting nightsoil from the privies in town. His cape had small bells sewn onto the waist-length liripipe hanging from its hood.

Sister Winifred stepped closer to Lex and gently took his hand. 'Lex, you know Jack would never harm your dear Gracie.'

Lex completely ignored her, as if unaware of her holding his hand. 'Why is Sheriff Birch allowing this fiend to take our girls?' he shouted to the crowd.

'For God's sake, man,' said Birch. 'I've four daughters of my own and want to catch this beast as much as you do.'

'Nay, not as much as I do, Sheriff.' A sob broke from Lex's mouth. 'And me and my boys will see justice done.'

Sister Winifred's gut churned. Lex Alcorn was coming undone. She had to warn Jack as soon as possible.

Wanting to experiment with her newfound weapon, Irma Linke delved into the store of moondew within her heart and forced some of it back down her arms to her hands, where she cupped it as if holding a frail baby bird. Into that precious nectar, she poured all the anger and guilt that was festering in her soul.

To summon that anger, she'd only to think of how the angel with the mesmerising voice had beguiled the three of them into believing – falsely, as it turned out – that celestial help would be forthcoming if they chose to stay in the hollow until their kith and kin were safe. They'd been tricked; abandoned and forgotten. Gracie was the only one of them who could hear whispers from the heavens now. And those rare messages were aimed at comforting them, rather than giving an idea of what they were supposed to do to leave the hollow and find their way to that gilded door. Irma couldn't understand why the angels no longer spoke to her or Maye. Gracie was only eleven years old, for pity's sake.

Moondew and anger churned within her hands to form a wicked ball of otherworldly fire, no bigger than a pea. Once it began to crackle and spark, she crouched in the fork of the sprawling, centuries-old oak, her sanctuary, and peered down through its branches at Maye, who had been watching her ever since she'd caught her directing further muttered curses at Bellayne.

After Irma's death three months ago, she and Maye — at Irma's insistence — had invaded their killer's dreams night after night and pushed themselves into his first waking thoughts. But their onslaught had not turned out as planned. Instead of stirring his madness so it became obvious to the townsfolk, instead of urging him to loop a noose around his own neck, it had caused him to lash out and strangle Gracie on her way home from buying eggs for her mother. During the long nights since they'd become three, Irma and Maye had often wondered whether he'd have killed again if they'd not interfered with his mind.

Irma sensed that he was stewing in his own madness, failing to contain the poison that was eating away his reason. She could not hear his thoughts, but she imagined he was desperately thinking of ways to keep hidden what he'd done to them.

Even if someone did find their graves, she wondered what that would achieve. Their loved ones would know they were dead, but that would bring no answers or justice, or relief from fear.

Maye, seated on a mound of grey weathered rocks, was singing a cradlesong about sprites while she combed Gracie's crinkled brown hair with her fingers. Behind them, Irma could see her own foot poking through the weeds growing on her shallow grave. Scavengers had gnawed and pecked their way through the leather boot and flesh to expose the bones of her ankle and toes. She and Maye kept Gracie's attention away from that gruesome sight as much as they were able to by occupying her with games and songs.

Gracie's head lolled towards her chest as Maye's singing soothed her. The child was growing more withered by the day. Her ghostly form had lost its little-girl plumpness, and her once inquisitive light brown eyes no longer sparkled. She needed a hearty supper, a rich milky pudding, and her mother's loving arms around her.

Irma couldn't bear to hear Gracie crying for her family, nor the thought that the girl might be left alone to wander the hollow. She'd been the last of the three of them to die, so it seemed likely to Irma that she would also be the last to fade into shadow. Irma and Maye had tried many times to convince her to soar heavenward, but Gracie refused to leave until her mother found peace. Irma wasn't sure if that day would ever come.

They needed to stop or unmask their killer now, before it was too late to save Gracie – or, God forbid, his next victim.

Irma straddled a solid bough and hurled her fireball at the Shadowfolk who were gathered at the foot of her oak. Over the last two weeks, she'd noticed their tendency to congregate near her. Maye said it was her imagination running amok, but Irma wasn't so sure. The Shadowfolk were becoming more distinct to her, more than fleeting glimpses of faded faces. She'd discovered otherworldly fire by accident when she'd flailed her arms to scare them away.

The ball broke open with a muted *pfff* when it hit the ground, and gave off a weak shower of sparks. The Shadowfolk scattered in panicked grey swirls, giving her no time to see if she'd marked or harmed them in any way.

She slumped back against the oak's sturdy trunk, feeling sick about misusing the moondew's power, warping something so beautiful into a treacherous weapon. Her dear Jack would be horrified if he could see what she'd become: a dark-hearted wraith who longed to run a sword across the throat of the killer who had sentenced them all to this misery.

Three months prior to that terrible day when Gracie was killed, Irma had witnessed – though she wasn't aware of it at the time –

their killer's ability to lead the townsfolk astray. During the search for Maye, he'd been among the first to suggest that a stranger had taken her, so the search had been concentrated in the forests bordering the main road to the west of Bellayne. Conveniently, he'd then 'stumbled' upon the book and bag Maye had been carrying at the time of her disappearance, and succeeded in steering the townsfolk away from the real burial ground to the southeast of the town.

When he'd appeared on the towpath in front of Irma a month later, she hadn't the slightest inkling that her life was about to end. Once he'd caught his breath, he'd pointed at the path leading to Maiden's Well and croaked Maye's name. Irma hadn't hesitated before following him into the woods. She remembered still the kick to the back of her knees that had floored her, and how her gasp of shock had been the last earthly breath she'd taken.

Another ball of fire, half the size of the first, formed within her hands without much effort on her part. Although her store of moondew was diminishing quickly, it was getting easier to harness malice; a sad thought.

Irma threw the second fireball at the large bough she was sitting on, to see if it could harm something rooted in the mortal realm. If she squinted, she could almost conjure a wisp of smoke and a faint burn mark on the bark.

'What are you doing?' asked Maye, as she made a featherlight landing on a bough slightly above and to the right of Irma. She had never entered Irma's sanctuary before.

'Nothing,' answered Irma, scooting forward to cover the burn mark with her foot, just in case it was real. With a start, she felt warmth beneath her bare sole.

'I don't believe you. Have you forgotten that Gracie is here because of you?'

Irma hung her head. 'Nay.'

'I will not let you put my Hester in danger,' Maye said, swiping long waves of her raven hair from her face. Her jewel-blue eyes glittered with anger. 'I want you to leave the hollow now, while you still have the energy to fly.'

'What?' Sadness quivered in Irma's throat. 'Nay, I'll not abandon you.'

'Promise me upon Hester's life then, Irma. Promise me you'll leave him alone.'

Irma hardened her heart, thinking of the greater good for Gracie, and broke the promise she'd made to Maye about never speaking of their killer in front of the girl. 'He is restless, Maye. I can feel him, no matter what I do to stop it, and I'm afraid he will –'

'Shut up!' Maye, who rarely raised her voice in anger, spoke through clenched teeth. She flew back down to Gracie and pulled her close, tears streaming down her beautiful oval face.

Irma knew those strong words would have cost Maye dearly. Not long before she died, Maye had decided to join the convent at St Clement's and dedicate her life to God and to helping the children at the orphanage. Irma thought that if Maye had had the chance, she'd have been a sweet, caring nun with her grace of body and spirit.

She examined the bough to see if her ball of otherworldly fire had burned the bark. It hadn't entered the mortal realm in the way she'd hoped, but it had melted a small part of the tree's shimmering green aura, and the area surrounding the hole was now a sickly shade of grey. She'd have to do better than that if she wanted to stop their killer killing again.

A scream from Gracie caused her to spin around.

'I'm going home,' the girl called out.

Irma looked desperately for the gilded doorway, but there was no sign of it. Instead, Gracie soared into the air and hurtled towards Bellayne before Maye and Irma could stop her.

Maye and Irma arrived in Bellayne to see Meryl Alcorn leaning over the waist-high parapet of Monk's Mill Bridge, the dark waters of the Eel roiling beneath her. She was hunched like an old woman who had tired of all the sadness in the world, and her once lustrous coppery hair hung in limp strands about her face. Her barely there aura was a murky grey.

When Maye and Irma caught up with Gracie, she turned to them and said, 'My mother has no light.'

Knowing that someone in the town had taken her daughter must be an unbearable burden, thought Irma.

Maye touched Irma's arm. 'What is Goodwife Alcorn doing?'

Meryl looked around as if to make sure she was alone, then climbed up on top of the parapet. She plucked a cross made of twigs from her bodice and pressed it to her lips.

'I made that for you,' Gracie to her mother.

Meryl lay down on the stone capping and curled on her side. Gracie flew up to the bridge to try to push her back from the edge.

Irma didn't think the fall from the bridge would kill Meryl as it wasn't high enough, but the deep ice-cold water might, if she was in it long enough.

'My mother cannot swim,' Gracie cried.

Maye went to Gracie and pulled her close. 'Hush, child, there is nothing you can do.'

Meryl slowly rolled forward until one leg dangled over the river and then closed her eyes. The gentle soughing of what might be her last breath shivered through the air. She stretched out an arm.

Gracie screamed, wrenched herself from Maye's embrace and flew at her mother. 'Noooo!'

Meryl's eyes fluttered open. She held up her hand and touched the air. 'Gracie?'

Chapter Nine

Sylvan Jimm

Nine days after leaving Stonhard, Nell pulled Bente's dagger from her pocket and put it on the ground, then tucked her skirts up around her waist and squatted over a pile of leaves. Her thighs quivered as she strained to unclog her back passage while keeping her balance. Beside her, Eben twisted from side to side, trying to yank his wrist from her grasp.

'Eben, please, hold still.'

She couldn't let him go because he'd scamper off into the woods looking for Maureen – a heartbreaking venture for them both. Sometimes it seemed as though they were travelling backwards, not forwards to Bellayne.

Eben dropped to his haunches and leaned back, a move she hadn't expected. She tilted left and piddle ran down her ankle, seeped into her boot and stung the blisters on her heel.

'Shit! Please, I'll not be long, Eben.'

He scowled at her through his tangled hair, his face streaked with mud and tears, his light-green eyes red-rimmed from crying. He looked like an urchin in his dirty tunic and torn hose.

As she tightened her grip on his wrist, he snarled – perhaps imitating Brown Boy – then sank his teeth into her forearm. She lost her balance and toppled forward. Her hands landed in the piddle-soaked leaves.

Eben ran onto the muddy road, stood in one of the countless puddles and started to bawl. 'Hate heaven. Hate Nellie.'

He'd learned the word 'hate' at the Boar's Den – something the wenches shouted often. She wondered if he knew what it meant, and whether other children his age – children growing up in comfortable homes – said it too.

She crawled over to a dying tree and slumped against it. *I hate me too*, she thought. She was doing her best to keep Eben safe and show him she loved him, but she felt as if a briar patch had sprung up between them. Nothing she said gave him comfort; it only seemed to make his sadness worse. Only this morning she'd tried telling him a Hokey story to cheer him a little, but he'd kicked her hard on the shin and said, 'Hokey yukky. Lost, lost, lost.'

Nell was sure he blamed her for his mother's sudden disappearance. She could not deny that his heated words hurt, a lot, but he needed to express his grief and frustration, so she was just going to have to suck it up. Maybe one day he'd remember their friendship, the many hours they'd laughed and played together, before she'd have to say goodbye and leave him with his father in Bellayne.

'Allow me to sprinkle a little sunshine over your gloomy day,' called a cheery voice from somewhere behind her.

Without stopping to think about drawing attention to her only valuable possession, Nell lunged for the dagger and shoved it into her pocket. Her heartbeat and breath collided. Who was it? One of the crow-like men?

'Sylvan Jimm, at your service,' continued the voice from behind a large beech. 'But my friends call me Jimm.'

Nell straightened her skirt and turned to face the stranger. How long had he been watching her? Had he seen her panicked scramble for the dagger, the item that would fund in one swoop a one-roomed cottage on the mainland and some new attire, and give her some time to settle before she needed to find work? And if Jack Lea was no longer in Bellayne, or not interested in his son, she would need the proceeds from the dagger to support Eben too.

A lean man in his middle twenties leaped from behind the tree and grinned at her. The afternoon sun flickered through the leaves, lighting the dark brown coils of hair that snaked wildly about his shoulders. He winked, then juggled five brightly coloured balls, throwing the balls high, back-flipping, twirling, and catching them all again with lightning-fast sweeps of his arms.

Laughing and clapping, Eben left the muddy puddle and trotted over to him.

'Where did you come from?' demanded Nell, upset by how easily he'd placated Eben.

'Why, from this path through the forest,' he said, as if it should have been obvious to even the dimmest of folk.

Nell hadn't noticed it earlier, but now saw a narrow, well-worn path through the dense oak, ash, hazel and beech trees.

He moved closer to her, leaving Eben rolling the balls in the mud, and said, 'I bring you a warning.'

She stepped back. 'A warning?'

'Two days ago in Appleford, I overheard a disturbing conversation. A woman of some forty years was desperately searching for her grandchild who'd been snatched from his bed by a servant who worked in her tavern. When she didn't find any sign of them on Coastway Road, she headed east to Appleford and waited at the crossroads in case the servant had taken the Flegg Road. The short, ugly lord travelling with her is offering a large reward for tidings of your whereabouts … Nell.'

Nell spun away from him and scanned the woods for signs of an ambush. She slipped her hand into her pocket and wrapped it around the hilt of the dagger, wondering if she had the strength to overcome Jimm in a fight. Though he wasn't much taller than she was and moved lightly, she'd seen well-defined thigh muscles beneath the leaf-green material of his leggings. Still, she'd rather die than let Lord Bente capture and defile her.

Jimm raised his arms and turned his open palms to her. 'Fear not the messenger. I've been watching for you in order to help you.'

'Why? That makes no sense. I'm a stranger with nothing to give you.'

Did his eyes flick towards the pocket where her knife was hidden? Had he overheard Piggy lamenting the loss of his jewel-handled weapon?

'Lord Bente was rough with one of my friends,' Jimm said. 'A bonny lass just doing her best to please him.'

More likely he was herding her into an ambush. She was also wary of the sneaky way he'd separated her from Eben. He could snatch the boy off the ground and dash into the woods before she could stop him. She needed to offer him something greater than Piggy's reward, without giving up the prize of the dagger. Perhaps she could exaggerate Jack Lea's wealth and circumstances.

'I do not believe you ... but perhaps we could be of mutual benefit to one another.'

Jimm raised one eyebrow, a smug expression on his face. His eyes were bark-brown and cunning.

'I did not steal the boy,' Nell continued, 'and he's no kin to the woman you came across in Appleford. His mother died, and I promised to take him to his father in –' she caught her tongue before it said Bellayne – 'in Carrileck.' She looked Jimm in the eye, licked her lips and hoped she sounded sincere. 'Lord Lea will pay handsomely for the boy's safe return.'

She'd be heading to the port of Carrileck herself after Bellayne, with or without Eben, to sell Bente's dagger and buy passage on a ship to the mainland.

'If the boy's father's so wealthy, why did he not send an escort to Stonhard?' Jimm asked.

'He planned to, but fate intervened and Maureen died before he arrived. Our mistress would have sold the boy on the sly-market, so I took him and ran.'

'Ma-ma gone,' said Eben, hearing his mother's name. He was rocking one of Jimm's balls in the crook of his arm. 'Nellie hide her.'

'Why would this lord pay for a servant's bastard child?' asked Jimm. 'Methinks your story has little merit.'

Nell delved into her imagination for a plausible explanation. She wouldn't let this sly forest-dweller outwit her. 'Ah, it's the same age-weary tale. Lady Lea banished her younger sister, Maureen, from her hearth when she caught her frolicking in the barn with Lord Lea. Since then, Lord Lea's wife has borne him only a gaggle of daughters. He'll pay well for the boy ... his heir.'

'Mmm.' Jimm lowered his gaze while he considered her story. Even though he seemed absorbed in drawing circles in the dirt with his toe, she could feel him studying her for any hint of deception.

She shaded her face with her hand, as if blocking out the sun, and pretended to watch Eben, who'd cast aside the ball and was staring at the ground. Even though he was a sturdy little fellow, he looked shrunken, as if part of him had died along with Maureen. The fight had gone out of him.

The smell of old campfires wafted up Nell's nose. She gasped. Jimm had moved closer without her noticing.

'What guarantee do we have that Lord Lea will pay for the boy once we arrive in Carrileck?' he asked.

Nell straightened her back and stepped forward until she was close enough to get a whiff of dampness beneath the stale smoke on his clothes. 'My plan is to deliver the boy only after I've received payment for my trouble. And methinks that plan will work better now you're here. I could wait in the woods at the edge of town with the boy, while you negotiate a fair price for our services. And I'll give you a third if you lead us away from Lord Bente and help us to get to Carrileck.' She would find a way to lose Jimm once they neared Bellayne, which was on the road to Carrileck. 'What say you?'

Jimm caught hold of her hand and pressed it to his lips. 'I'm at your service. The prospect of a lordly ransom far outweighs the reward offered by the pair seeking you.'

Nell smiled, glad that she'd averted danger and now had someone to help her with Eben.

'Though we'll have to consider a larger cut for me – half seems fair,' he added. 'From what I've seen, you'd be sorely challenged reaching Carrileck on those pretty plump legs.'

Plump legs? Nell's smile puckered. How much had he seen while her skirts had been up around her waist? He was acting congenial, but still watching her like a hawk. She'd have to watch her back and sleep with one eye open.

At twilight on their fourth night of travelling with Sylvan Jimm, Nell sighed contentedly as she sat beside the fire and rubbed her belly, which was full of rabbit and cabbage, food that Jimm had stolen from God-knows-where. She and Eben were warm, dry and well-fed. And Jimm had led them around the ambush awaiting her in Appleford, as promised, and along narrow forest paths that smelled of mushrooms and moss and kept them away from other travellers. Thanks to his woodsmanship, they were many miles closer to Bellayne. She tucked Maureen's shawl around Eben, who'd fallen asleep with a milky smear on his top lip from the sweet posset that Jimm had made him from pilfered milk and honey.

Jimm stirred spices into the warm milk and handed her a cupful. She sipped it, luxuriating in the creaminess upon her tongue.

He crouched in front of her and smiled. 'How much silver will we demand from Lord Lea? Two bags perhaps?'

Two bags of manure more like, thought Nell, choking on some milk. She didn't like to think what Jimm might do if he discovered that Jack Lea was a humble farmer and nightsoil-collector, not a lord. If she had to, she'd appease his anger with a share of Bente's dagger when she sold it in Carrileck.

'And then across the sea we'll sail,' she sang, feeling suddenly light-headed and dreamy. Jimm's delicious spices were sending her to a happy, happy place.

'You forgot to tell me something,' he said.

'Mmmm?'

'What's Lady Lea's name?'

He was speaking of Maureen's fictional sister, but Nell couldn't summon a name to her numb lips. She was too busy floating, dancing with clouds.

And then she crashed into a black, crow-shaped cloud and plummeted down, down ... to Elmer Long's dining hall.

Christiana Long looked at her dead father, then down at Nell. 'God in heaven, what have you done?' she cried.

Nell couldn't answer, not now that she'd glimpsed the crumpled figure lying on the floor to her right. She crawled towards it, wishing that she could go back to yesterday and be a good girl again, and trying not to notice the way the blood on her hands stuck to the floor each time she moved.

When she was close enough to the figure to see that its eyelashes and chest were still, a strange mewling sound rose from her constricted throat and her thoughts fragmented. Her mother. Grey. Still. Dead.

The back of one of Pearl's hands, and her bottom lip and chin, were smeared with vomit – the purged remains of her last meal. Her fingers were curled inwards slightly, as though beckoning to her daughter.

The man with gold braid on his cloak tossed the knife he'd taken from Nell's hand onto the floor, then hoisted her over his shoulder so that her head hung down his back. Christiana stepped aside and let him carry Nell past her into the passage.

'Jealousy must have turned the poor girl's mind,' she cried. 'Oh, Lord Hammerton, what will become of one so young?'

Nell woke, and struggled to dislodge the heavy weight of despair from her chest so she could breathe. The memories that she'd buried deep for seven years had festered and grown in the darkness and were now dragging her down to the bottom of a frightening pit from which she feared she would never escape.

Thunder rumbled and lightning forked across the sky. She huddled in her cloak and noticed that the fire had gone out; Jimm must have forgotten to stoke it. She tucked her skirt tight around her legs to keep warm and realised that her pocket was empty, weightless. Bente's dagger was gone.

She crawled in the dark to where Jimm and Eben had been lying and patted the ground. No sign of the dagger. Eben, who was cuddling one of Jimm's juggling balls, muttered in his sleep as she touched his head and thanked goodness that he was still there. But Jimm was gone. And he'd stolen her future.

She stood and stumbled away from Eben. Rage surged through her body, and she fisted her hands over her thighs, tilted her head back and screamed at the sky. Bellow after bellow that echoed the thunder. Her throat ached and burned but she couldn't stop. Without the dagger, she couldn't get off this isle. Which meant it was only a matter of time before Bente found her. She may have escaped the Boar's Den, but she'd never escape her fate, her punishment for all that she'd done.

Her screams turned into a long continuous moan that bored through her heart.

'Stop, Nellie! Stop, stop!' Eben sounded terrified.

'I'm sorry,' Nell gasped. 'It was just a bad dream.'

'Wee scare me,' he cried, his voice small and shaky.

'Oh God, I'm so sorry,' she said.

She needed to get him to safety before she fell apart completely. She was as broken in spirit as Emily. Beyond help; beyond redemption.

An hour past midnight, after emptying the privies of the cottages on the other side of the Eel from the main town, Jack Lea eased his horse and cart to a stop just shy of Monk's Mill Bridge. It was a place both man and beast knew well and looked forward to. Alighting from the cart, Jack climbed down the riverbank's moderately steep slope in the dark, parted the reeds at the water's edge, and washed his hands. Then he reclined against a grassy mound and unwrapped the meal his father had packed earlier. This involved unravelling several layers of cloth and string, with no cheating – in the form of sniffing and feeling – in the game they'd been playing together for years.

'Bugger,' Jack said to himself, having guessed wrong again. It was kippers and sweet roasted onions within the thick slices of buttered bread, not ham, cheese and eggs. Cerdic, his father, was now seven points ahead.

After the first satisfying bite, Jack closed his eyes and listened to the song the Eel was singing, which varied depending on the amount of rain, and his own mood and willingness to hear it. In these troubled times, he'd noticed that he often concentrated more on the sound of his chewing, rhythmic and predictable, so as not to drift towards thoughts that saddened his heart, and happenings he couldn't change or fix.

To test his own fortitude, he swallowed and unclenched his jaw, preparing to be swamped by memories, if only for a moment.

Steady lapping, pulling him closer, deeper. Sweeping currents, carried away, away. Irma, where are you? Nothing to hang on to in the deep, no foothold. Come home.

> *'I remember your arms,*
> *A delicate beckoning*
> *as you danced for me …'*

Jack almost tumbled headfirst into the water, uncertain for a moment whether the river was actually echoing the sentiments running through his mind.

Then he realised, a tad embarrassed, that someone was singing a well-known ballad about lost love, and it sounded as if it was coming from the direction of Maiden's Well, a hundred yards or so up the towpath.

As he listened closer, he recognised Brother Caddock's soaring baritone – he'd heard it often enough inside St Clement's – although the sorrowful, heartfelt tone had thrown him for a moment. Caddock sounded so lost in his own pain that Jack wondered if he should go and sit with him. Sometimes people needed to know they weren't alone.

> '... *your waist curving,*
> *Moving just out of reach.*
> *Your last words*
> *Lost in the air*
> *As you danced*
> *Away from me ...*'

Jack had never been sure if the girl in the song had died or chosen to leave her lover, but he knew damn well that Irma would have fought like a wildcat to stay. She'd loved her life, especially the moments she spent dancing freely in nature.

Suddenly not hungry, he rewrapped his meal and stood. He stomped his feet to get his blood flowing and bring himself back to the present, and then he ran up the bank, wanting to leave behind the empty space that Irma had once filled with laughter and crazy plans such as hill-racing and raft-making.

As Jack patted his horse's rump and climbed aboard the cart, he wondered why Brother Caddock, who had entered the abbey at such a young age, was singing about a lost lover. And why was he singing such a song in the middle of the night right by the spot where his sister's body had been found floating many years ago?

Just before dawn, Jack arrived home, then stabled his horse and loped up the hill to Lea Cottage. As he approached the stairs to the porch he smelled pipe smoke and called out to his father who often sat there when pain kept him from sleep. 'Dad, are you unwell?'

His father said, 'We had a visitor during the night, more than one I'd say, going by the sound of their footsteps on the floorboards. They tried the door, but I'd barred it. By the time I came out here, they were gone.'

Recalling Sister Winifred's warning about Lex Alcorn and his sons suspecting him of having had something to do with Gracie's disappearance, Jack opened the cottage door, grabbed a lantern and lit it with embers from the kitchen fireplace. He inspected the door and shuttered window for signs of tampering and found none.

Cerdic Lea groaned as he struggled out of the chair and massaged his dicky hip when he was on his feet again. He picked up the fire poker that was propped against a low table and limped inside. 'Time to break our fast, lad.'

Noting the grim set to his father's bearded jaw, Jack chose not to comment on the fact that Cerdic was too old and unstable to wield a poker as a weapon. 'Maybe we should move to the castle. Birch will put us up until Lex sees sense.'

'I will not be scared from our home.'

'Just for a few days, and especially on the nights I'm away collecting nightsoil.'

Cerdic turned away and stoked the fire with the poker. 'How many eggs do you want?' he asked, marking an end to the conversation.

Chapter Ten

Out of the Fat

Nell staggered up a windy, hilly, mud-slicked path, hoping to find a dry resting spot for the night. She and Eben had been lost in the forest for the last four days since Jimm had deserted them, and had walked into one dead-end after another. Even the most promising paths had soon narrowed, ending in briar walls, or swamps of smelly water and swarms of biting gnats; and each wrong turn seemed to lead them deeper into the forest. She'd heard no voices during that time, not even the lowing of a cow, and had given up all hope of reaching even the smallest of dwellings.

Eben whimpered against her neck. They were both sick – most likely, Nell suspected, from drinking stagnant water, as she'd been unable to find a stream. Fever ravaged his sweet body, and he hovered in a frightening state somewhere between life and death. She didn't have the strength to carry him unaided, so had wrapped Maureen's shawl between his legs and around his waist, then knotted its ends around her neck. He was hanging limply in front of her, with one of her hands cupping his bottom and the other holding tight to one of his. He needed help, and she cursed Jimm for not abandoning them near a village.

When her energy flagged, she dropped to her knees, still

supporting Eben with one arm, and crawled to the top of the hill. She imagined she must look something like a drunken, three-legged hound.

On the other side of the hill was a road, and she could see signs of recent use – hoofprints and fresh horse droppings. But she had no idea which way led to Bellayne.

The swishing sound of a fast-flowing stream filtered through the trees on the other side of the road. She longed to flood her mouth with fresh, sweet water, and to dribble some into Eben's in the hope of reviving him. She squinted into the gloom again to make sure it was safe to cross, and saw a light flickering through the trees further down the hill.

She crept down the road, keeping to its edge, until she could see that the light came from a campfire, not a cottage. After shuffling forward a few feet, she could see someone squatting beside the fire, but was reluctant to call out and ask for help until she had a better idea who they were.

A twig snapped, just behind her. Before she could turn around, someone wrapped an arm around her throat, pressed up against her back and said, 'Blessings be! My wandering maiden has found her way back to me.'

Nell couldn't speak. *Piggy?*

'I shall relish our reunion,' said Lord Oliver Bente. 'But first you must beg forgiveness for your disobedience.'

He pushed her towards the fire, where the figure turned out to be an uncharacteristically dishevelled Doreen Wilkes, stirring the contents of a pot. She looked relieved to see Nell, which wasn't surprising considering Bente had threatened to burn down the Boar's Den if they didn't find her.

Bente grabbed Eben under the armpits and tried to pull him out of the sling. Eben moaned, but didn't open his eyes. Nell hung onto him, until Bente gripped her shoulder and dug his thumb into the tender hollow just above her collarbone at the right of her neck. Pain bloomed in her head and chest and her hold on Eben weakened, but still she clung on. She would protect him until it was no longer possible; 'to the death' as knights in tales were fond of saying.

Bente's sparse gingery hair was wet and sticking up, as if he'd just washed in the stream, and his small black eyes glinted with malevolence as he pressed his other hand over Eben's nose and mouth, threatening to suffocate the child.

'One, two,' he counted.

Nell dropped her arms, defeated.

Bente unknotted Maureen's shawl, grabbed Eben by the back of his tunic and dangled him in the air. His little body was as limp as a ragdoll. Nell had never imagined feeling so sick in her heart or so helpless.

'Where's my dagger?' demanded Bente, his misshapen nose glowing an ugly red.

Nell shook her head, confused. Since Eben had become ill, she'd forgotten all about the fucking dagger. It was hard to comprehend how she'd cried and raged for the loss of an inanimate and ultimately worthless thing.

Bente shook his finger at her, angered by her response, and dropped Eben on the ground. He landed with a soft thud, partially on his side, his right arm caught under his body, his left hip aimed at the sky. Half of his face was pressed into the dirt, but thankfully his mouth and nose were clear.

Nell screamed and lunged towards him, but Bente pulled her back and hung on to her cloak.

'How will I punish thee?' he panted, wrapping an arm around her chest from behind and grinding his pelvis against her buttocks. 'Let me count the ways.' Then he pushed her away suddenly. 'You stink. And you look worse than a drain-soiled rat.'

He turned to Doreen, who was over by a large tree feeding his horse. 'Clean her up,' he shouted, 'while I eat my supper. I'll need my strength for a looong satisfying night.'

Fear coursed through Nell's body. Was she to lose her maidenhead this night? Once Bente was fed and watered, he'd claim his piece of flesh – and if she wanted Eben to live, she'd have to give him whatever he demanded. *Oh, God ...*

Eben's eyes opened, but they were unfocused and wavering in all directions. His limbs twitched every now and again as if trying to hold on to life.

Nell crawled over to him. 'Please, he needs help.'

Bente finished ladling stew into a bowl. 'Move away from the brat or I'll put him out of his misery for good.'

'He's just a little boy. Please, I beg of you, do not punish him.'

'I'm punishing *you*,' Bente said. 'I'll make you wish you'd never fluttered your eyelashes at me. No one makes a fool of me. Get away from him – now!'

Nell scuttled backwards, wondering if she could convince Bente to let Doreen take Eben to someone who could help him.

Doreen returned, lifted the pot off the fire using a sturdy stick, and threw two short logs onto the dwindling flames. She placed a cushion on a low tree stump in front of the fire for Bente to sit on, and asked if he required anything else.

Nell was surprised by the change in Doreen; not just her appearance, which was frazzled, tense and ungroomed, but her demeanour too. She was obsequious, no longer in charge, at the mercy of this cruel man. Nell could see that Doreen would do anything to protect herself and was unlikely to help Eben.

Bente sat on the cushioned stump and wriggled his shoulders, as if grateful for the warmth of the fire at his back, then he dipped a hunk of bread into the bowl of stew and slurped it into his mouth. The sound curdled Nell's already raw stomach. It reminded her of the time she'd seen a fox lapping at the bloodied throat of a lamb.

Noticing a pail of fresh water by the fireside, Nell licked her dry, blistered lips and appealed to Doreen. 'Eben needs water. Please, wet a clean cloth and dribble some into his mouth.'

The look Doreen gave her would have sent sparks flying off flint. 'You've no one to blame but yourself, missy. I wouldn't piss on you if –'

Nell leaped to her feet and ran to the pail, not caring if Bente hurt her. Eben needed a drink. She cupped her hand and filled it with water.

But as she turned to run to Eben, Doreen stepped into her path and backhanded her. Nell reeled sideways, but stayed on her feet.

Bente clapped, apparently enjoying the entertainment as he ate.

Doreen grabbed Nell's hair and reeled her in until their breasts were almost touching. 'When Lord Bente returns to Lanbricke three months hence, you, my girl, will face the hangman for the murder of your mother and your master. I've passed the letter – Lord Hammerton's witness declaration – into Lord Bente's keeping.'

Nell moaned, and her stomach churned and cramped. She'd failed Maureen. Even if Eben survived, he'd never meet his father now. And perhaps it'd be better if the beautiful boy didn't survive, not now that Bente controlled what would happen to him.

'In the meantime, you'll travel as Lord Bente's slave,' said Doreen. 'When he wearies of your charms, he'll rent you out to every Tom, Dick and Henry until he recoups his losses.'

A stream of vomit suddenly spewed from Nell's mouth and splattered over Doreen's flat chest.

'You dirty wretch!' Doreen lurched backwards and bumped into Bente, who cursed and flung his arms into the air, vainly trying to keep his balance on the stump. The bowl of stew tumbled to the ground.

Bente grabbed the hood of Doreen's cloak with one hand as he toppled backwards into the blazing fire. His other hand disappeared into the coals. Flames licked his back and breeches. Still clutching Doreen's hood, he frantically tried to pull himself upright, but only succeeded in dragging her off balance. She fell between his splayed legs and landed on his stomach. His head jerked backwards and what was left of his hair caught alight.

Bente's bellows of agony might have distressed even the hardest heart, but Nell couldn't summon a thimbleful of compassion as she scrambled forward and grabbed Doreen's outstretched hand.

When Bente held on tight to Doreen's hood, Nell picked up the sturdy stick that Doreen had used to lift the pot from the fire and whacked his arm until he let go. As soon as she was free, Doreen crawled over to a patch of long, damp grass and rolled in it to extinguish the flames.

Bente lurched from the fire, tore off his burning cloak and stumbled towards the stream, slapping at the flames on his scalp and screaming.

Nell tipped most of the water in the pail onto Doreen's legs, then doused the smouldering hem of her own skirt and kneeled beside Eben, who was shivering and twitching still. She lifted him onto her lap. His breaths were shallow, mere puffs, and in the firelight his lips appeared to have a bluish tint. She touched his brow with the back of her hand. It was cold, frighteningly so. She wet her fingers in the pail and slipped them into Eben's mouth.

'Help me,' cried Doreen. Always a thin woman, she now looked old and brittle, like a piece of dry straw about to snap in the middle. She waved her hands uselessly over her burnt legs. Strips of something hung from them; Nell couldn't tell whether they were remnants of her skirt or flaps of charred skin.

'If I leave Eben to help you, he will die.'

Doreen stretched her arms towards Nell. 'Noooo! Please, don't leave me. I cannot walk.'

Nell felt something harden within herself as she stopped listening to the woman's pleas. It wasn't that she was punishing Doreen for all she'd done – well, perhaps a part of her was glad to see her power stripped away. Rather, she was making a choice to try to save Eben's life. Helping Doreen would waste precious time and she wasn't sure how much longer he had.

Tucking him inside her cloak, she grabbed her bag and eyed

Bente's horse – a powerful-looking beast. She'd never ridden one, but would have to try. They needed to get far away from Lord Oliver Bente as quickly as possible.

Nell put a blanket and the pail, which had enough water left for two good drinks, within Doreen's reach, and hurried over to the horse, ignoring Doreen's cry of 'Don't you dare leave me here.'

Bente was a short man, so he'd tethered the horse next to a log to make it easier for him to mount. It was a blessing for Nell too. She wrapped Maureen's shawl around her chest and waist to secure Eben, then untethered the horse and stood on the log.

'Take me with you,' pleaded Doreen. 'I can direct you to a healer who lives in the woods this side of Orcke. Bente went to her for his piles. She'll be able to help Eben.'

'Which way is Orcke?' asked Nell.

'Take me with you and I'll tell you.'

'Nay, but if I find her, I'll send her to you.'

Doreen scoffed. 'I do not believe you.'

'I give you my word,' said Nell, meaning it. 'Where does the woman live?'

Doreen turned her head sharply away. 'If I'm to die, so can Eben.'

Nell's first attempt to mount the horse failed, and she had to hold the reins tightly to stop it rearing up on its hind legs. She tried again, mindful of not crushing Eben, and used all her remaining strength to hoist herself onto its back, and grabbed hold of its muscular neck before it bucked her off. It snorted and shied sideways, but she gripped its sides with her feet and legs and kept her seat. She looked at the road, trying to decide which way to go.

'You won't find the healer without my help,' Doreen said.

Nell remembered that Doreen had looked to the left when speaking about Orcke, and that was the same direction as Bellayne. She pulled on the reins to turn the horse's head left.

'He was still breathing,' said Doreen.

Something in her tone chilled Nell. She turned the horse around to face Doreen, who was shivering as she draped the blanket over her burnt legs. 'What?'

'My cousin's father was still breathing when she arrived at his home the *first* time, a half hour before you discovered him.'

'What are you saying?'

Nell shook her foggy head to dislodge the memory of Lord Hammerton prising the knife from her hand, and Christiana Long's words: *Jealousy must have turned the poor girl's mind.* How could Doreen know that Christiana had arrived in the dining room before Nell? And what did she mean that Elmer Long was still breathing then?

'Take me with you, or leave Eben here until you return with the healer, and I'll tell you the rest,' Doreen said.

Eben whimpered, reminding Nell that she was wasting time. Even though she was desperate to hear what Doreen had to say, she pointed the horse left along the road and dug her heels into its flanks as she'd seen other riders do.

The horse took off, faster than she'd expected. She could feel the blanket across its back slipping sideways under her.

'Eben will die,' screamed Doreen, 'and it will be your fault.'

Nell made it as far as the bridge over the river – perhaps two miles from Doreen and Bente – before the horse slowed to a halt. She clacked her tongue and jabbed it with her heels without success. It refused to go any further.

She whacked its rump with her hand – just as something, most likely a branch, crashed to the forest floor. Startled, the horse tossed its head, then reared and threw them off.

Nell wrapped her arms around Eben and took the full impact of their landing with her back and head. Her mind faded to nothing.

A noose dropped down before her, suspended against the black of her unconsciousness. This was her fate now. Bente's men would hunt her down, and Bente would drag her to the gallows himself.

In the past, she'd often wished herself dead, to escape the crippling weight of guilt and the fear that she'd murder again, but Doreen's sly, cryptic comment about her cousin, Christiana, had given Nell a glimmer of hope. Was there more to discover about the day her mother died, other than what she remembered or had been told?

She looked through the noose, deep into the past and Elmer Long's dining hall. She could see herself – a fragile girl of ten years – standing near Long's body, which was slumped on the table amid his midday meal.

She looked at the knife in young Nell's pale, delicate hand and tried to remember the rage she must have felt when she plunged it into his back. She'd hated him, it was true, and had wished him dead, but had never been able to recall the actual moment of murder, despite Christiana and then Doreen telling her for years that she'd killed both Long and her own mother.

Nell wriggled her dreaming fingers, trying to feel the moment when she'd picked up the knife – but she'd only become aware she was holding it when Lord Hammerton had wrenched it from her grasp.

Something niggled then, a whisper of something important, but it faded, as did the noose and the dining hall … and suddenly she was in another dreamscape – a homely bedchamber.

The three birdlike men, the Crows, were sitting side by side on the windowsill, staring at her with slanting eyes. They were talking to her, serious looks upon their golden faces, but their voices were muffled.

She strained her ears until their words became clearer.

'The end is not the end,' they said in unison. 'You must look beyond.'

She tried to say, *Tell me about the knife*, but her sleepy lips wouldn't move.

'Between your heartbeats, silence whispers,' they said.

~

Nell awoke in a soft bed, her heart banging wildly, and saw three crows perched on a windowsill to her right. She cried out in fright, and the birds turned, their sharp feet tapping on the wood, and flew away.

The Crows in her dream had been sitting on that very windowsill, in this very bedchamber. What was going on in her mind? And where was she?

The one thing she knew for sure was that men couldn't turn into crows.

Or could they?

Chapter Eleven

Larke-upon-Eel

'Ma,' yelled a voice right next to Nell's left ear, 'she's awake.'

She turned her head to see a boy who was about ten, with a thick thatch of carroty hair and twice God's allocation of freckles, and two little girls with similar colouring sitting cross-legged on the floor.

'Where's Eben?' she asked.

'See, I told you she wasn't a stinky corpse,' the boy added, and the girls, who were wearing dresses made from patches of mismatched cloth, squealed and ran from the room. The boy grinned at Nell and rolled his eyes as if to say 'Girls!'

Another voice came through the sackcloth curtaining the doorway. 'You lot could wake the dead, but Lord help you if you wake the babes. Get outside before I make sausage from your tongues.'

The boy ignored the woman's threat. He kneeled on the straw mattress and whispered to Nell, 'While you were snoring, your mouth was hanging open and some flies –'

'Rusty, out now!' A sturdy woman wearing a floppy straw hat decorated with what looked to Nell like a dead chicken pushed aside the sackcloth. 'Go and help your pa in the fields. I'm in just the mood for a good fry-up and eternal silence.'

Rusty sprang to his feet, but managed to get the last word as he disappeared through the doorway. 'I swatted *most* of the flies before they landed, but one or two tickled your tongue.'

As the woman moved closer to the bed, Nell could see that the chicken on her hat was made from a pair of stuffed hose with real feathers attached and pebbles for eyes.

'Firstly,' said the woman, who was about five-and-thirty and had the same ginger lashes and hazel eyes as her son, but only a smattering of freckles on her weather-reddened nose and cheeks, 'please excuse my hat. My children insist that I wear their creations for one week per month. And secondly, your boy is safe and well. Poppy, our eldest, works with the village midwife and has treated you both with all sorts of potions.'

Nell burst into tears as a wave of relief surged through her. She hadn't killed Eben. *Thank God!*

The woman patted Nell's arm, introduced herself – 'I'm Flannery Goodfield' – and explained how her husband, Rhod, had found Nell and Eben lying unconscious on the road two nights ago. 'You've been drifting in and out of sleep ever since and not making much sense. How came you there, lass?'

Nell gingerly prodded the lump on the back of her head, remembering how Bente's horse had thrown her and Eben off its back. Was Bente still hunting them, she wondered; and had anyone found Doreen Wilkes?

'I know not,' she muttered, unhappy about lying to folk who'd generously taken her and Eben into their home and saved Eben's life.

'Well, Nellie,' said Flannery, 'thank goodness you're both safe here, for there's been much strangeness afoot in our shire.'

'Oh?' said Nell, feeling giddy and nauseous, and concerned that Eben had apparently told Flannery her name.

'A man and a woman, both with terrible burns, were found yesterday morning on the banks of the Eel near the village of Orcke. From the woman's delirious ramblings, it seems they were set upon, but by whom we've yet to learn. Orcke is almost five miles from Larke-upon-Eel, but still such happenings are too close to home.'

'How do they fare?' Nell asked, and held her breath as she awaited Flannery's response.

'The woman's legs are badly burned, and she did more damage to them when she crawled to the river. She slips in and out of consciousness apparently. The man hovers near death and has not woken at all.'

Nell shrivelled on the inside. Once Doreen regained her senses, she'd tell the closest sheriff that Lord Bente was an agent of the King and give him Nell's description. Soon there'd be nowhere to hide.

She looked around the cramped but neat room, avoiding Flannery's eye. Spare clothes were stacked on a waist-high shelf alongside a washbowl, which was decorated with smiley flower-faces – most likely painted by the same children who'd created the stuffed chicken, thought Nell, going by the smudges, drips and general wonkiness. Suddenly she noticed her freshly laundered dress hanging on one of the pegs near the doorway. Someone, most likely Flannery, she assumed, had sewn patches over the parts that had been singed when she'd pulled Doreen out of the fire.

Two days later, Nell sat with the Goodfields at their table after eating a hearty supper of cock-a-doodle stew made from one of the old roosters, and bread pudding with cream. Eben was sitting on Rhod's lap, and turned to wipe his fingers on the man's wiry orange beard. Rhod growled and pretended to eat Eben's hand, and Eben squealed with delight. Nell watched smoke from the fire in the centre of the room drift up to the hole in the well-tended thatched roof while she struggled not to cry. Eben had barely looked her way since they'd both recovered.

Flannery wiped three-year-old Scarlet's face, then leaned towards Nell and said softly, 'Seeing you lying near death frightened him, lass.

Don't lose heart. He'll come round in a day or two and be climbing all over you.'

'I hope you're right,' Nell said.

She had decided to ask Flannery and Rhod if Eben could stay with them while she travelled to Bellayne to find Jack Lea. It was well over three years since Maureen had left Bellayne, so there was a chance Eben's father might not even live there any more. Also, if the shire's sheriff was now on the lookout for her, and caught her along the way, at least Eben would be safe. She was sure the Goodfields would do all they could for him in her stead, but the thought of leaving him behind brought little joy. She wondered if he would even let her hug him goodbye.

'Pa,' piped up Rusty as he dried the utensils that Cherry and Rose were washing in a tub of water at one end of the table, 'is Nell your mistress? My friend Pete says his mother —'

Flannery half-rose from the bench seat and cuffed Rusty lightly over the ears. Nell stifled an embarrassed titter.

Rhod said, 'Go and feed your hens, boy,' then looked at Nell. 'Sorry, lass, but our lad sometimes gets carried away.'

Rusty ran out the door chuckling, but Nell knew what he'd said wasn't funny. If the villagers were gossiping about her presence in the Goodfields' home, they were likely to repeat that gossip to any of the sheriff's men who came looking for the person who had attacked Lord Bente and Doreen Wilkes.

Nell was about to tell Flannery and Rhod about Eben's father and her plan to travel to Bellayne to find him, when Poppy, the Goodfields' eldest, stepped in from outside. The long-legged young woman with fluffy auburn hair picked up the bowl of stew that Flannery had left warming by the fire, and sat beside Nell on the bench seat, so close that their thighs were touching. Nell couldn't help feeling that the move was deliberate, as if Poppy was trying to get her attention.

Flannery studied her daughter's face. 'What troubles you, lass?'

'Tidings came from Orcke today,' said Poppy. 'The man with burns – a Lord Bente, according to some papers he was carrying – died just after noon. He was an agent of the King.'

No one spoke. Even the children, sensing the tension in the room, paused in their amusements to study the grown-ups' faces.

'Soldiers landed at Stonhard this morning and soon will be crawling all over our shire to look for his attacker,' continued Poppy. 'They've no idea who the woman is as she's still delirious with fever. Her burns are putrefying and it seems certain she'll lose the lower half of one leg, if she survives at all.'

'Grave tidings indeed,' Rhod said.

Bente dead. Shivers raced up Nell's back. Even though she'd not pushed him or Doreen into the fire, the soldiers would soon be snapping at her heels.

She prayed that the Goodfields wouldn't suffer any reprisal for having taken her and Eben into their home. She remembered how Flannery had mended her burnt dress and felt ashamed. She should have been honest with her and Rhod right from the start, especially about the danger she'd brought with her.

'I'll leave upon the morrow,' she said, unable to keep sadness from her voice.

Poppy relaxed the pressure of her leg against Nell's.

Chapter Twelve

The Well

Nell stood in a circle with the forty or so women attending the Giving of Thanks gathering held in Larke-upon-Eel each Sunday evening. She wore a borrowed white tunic, and on her loose hair sat a circlet that Cherry and Rose had braided for her from scraps of colourful cloth. The small field glowed with lantern light, and behind them a waterfall trickled down a hill, where ferns and patches of lichen flourished among the silvery-veined rocks. Nell breathed in the earthy perfume of damp herbs and rich soil and wished she didn't have to leave the Goodfields tomorrow, or say farewell to Eben.

Flannery turned to Nell. 'I'm so glad you're attending your first gathering with us. We hope to see you —'

'Aye, we hope you come back to see us another time,' said Poppy, standing on Nell's other side.

Her gold-brown gaze was steady and her brow slightly furrowed until Nell nodded that she'd received her silent message: *Take your troubles and run far away from us.*

Thimble, the scrawny, hunched village midwife and leader of the gathering, began to speak. 'When we forget where we came from, we fall into despair. Sometimes, when we feel alone and burdened, panic and fear close our hearts and we cannot see the miracles that we pray for so desperately. During these times, it helps to remember that we are also a part of something greater. If we calm our hearts, we can feel the soothing essence of life flowing through us every day. Close your eyes now, open your palms to the heavens, and give thanks for all that we receive from the unseen.'

Nell opened her hands, hoping to hear a whisper from the heavens, but the only thing she heard was her own voice urging her to remember what she'd forgotten about the knife that had killed Elmer Long.

Beside her, Poppy let out a small cry of surprise, followed by a long contented sigh. Glancing sideways, Nell saw that Poppy was moving her hips in slow circles, perhaps to a heavenly rhythm that only she could hear. She looked around the circle and saw that many other women were doing the same thing, and most had relaxed smiles upon their faces. Even the young mother who, Flannery had whispered to Nell earlier, had lost her six-month-old baby two weeks ago was swaying gently from side to side while she cradled her lower belly with her hands and looked at the crescent moon.

Why can't I feel anything? Nell wondered. Was such a connection with the heavens only available to a chosen few? Good folk, who didn't have terrible secrets in their past?

'Our hearts are the link between heaven and earth,' continued Thimble, 'and with each other. Allow your feet to sink into the earth, into the arms of our sacred mother, and give thanks for the nourishment that we and our families receive from her each day. Let her hold and support you. And once she entwines with the holy breath, share your joy and dance together.'

Thimble's words reminded Nell of what the Crows had said to her in the dream before she awoke in the Goodfields' home: *Between your heartbeats, silence whispers.* Her own heart felt as if it was shrivelling at the thought of leaving Eben, and she realised that the love she held in her heart was for him only. She could find none for herself. She had the strangest feeling that her life was slowly dissolving. Soon there would be only coldness where her shadow had once stood.

Nell gasped as she suddenly recollected what was troubling her about the day her master and mother had died. Lord Hammerton had taken the *cold* knife from her trembling hand. But if she'd used it to stab her master, and held it in her hand for so long afterwards while she stood staring at the table, wouldn't the knife have been warm?

As the women sang and danced around the fire, Nell stepped away towards the waterfall and tried to put herself back in the dining hall that terrible day. She saw the blood pooled on the floor around Elmer Long's chair – so much blood. If she had stabbed him, wouldn't there have been blood on her shoes and on her dress? It had been many hours after Lord Hammerton and Christiana Long had taken her from Long's home that Nell was finally able to scrub his blood from her hands. She remembered the few small stains on the bodice of her dress, but her shoes – new, her prized possessions – had been spotless. Which surely meant she hadn't gone anywhere near the pool of blood on the floor. But why then had she picked up the knife that was sticky with her master's blood? It was an odd thing for a shocked, frightened girl to do.

She remembered Doreen Wilkes's words by the river, the words that her cousin, Christiana Long, had apparently said to her: *He was still breathing when I arrived home.* Had Christiana stabbed her father and then blamed it on Nell? She'd made no secret of the fact that she was angry about her father's betrothal to Pearl, who was still young enough to bear Long a son who could snatch away Christiana's entitlement to her father's estate. But if Christiana had killed her father, how had Nell's own mother died? Had Christiana stabbed her too? But none of that fitted with Christiana's words to Doreen: *He was still breathing ...*

Nell sank to her knees and put her forehead on the cool, ankle-length grass. The notion that she was a killer had been drummed into her for so long that she'd never thought to question it. Had she hated herself, wished herself dead all those years, for no good reason? She knew that folk did terrible things for money, but she couldn't fathom how two women could conspire to blame two unnatural deaths on a girl of ten. Grief for herself welled in her chest and spilled over.

Poppy touched Nell's back. 'What's the matter?'

Nell sat up and shook her head, unable to answer.

Poppy picked up a goblet lying in the grass beside a natural well nearby and filled it. 'Here,' she said, handing it to Nell. 'Some say that the spring water is blessed and can heal aches of the heart and mind. And that if you look into its depths, it may reveal to you something about your life.'

Nell sipped the fresh, sweet water, wondering if she had the courage to look into the well.

'I'm sorry that you've to leave us so soon,' Poppy said, 'but the King's men do not care who they hurt. They have been known to burn down innocent folks' homes to pay for someone else's misdeeds. My mother has a generous heart and she insisted that you join us tonight, but I'm frightened that someone will tell the sheriff we have a stranger living in our home.' She lowered her head for a moment, as if finding the right words. 'You must leave tonight.'

Nell's throat trembled. 'Can Eben stay with you? They *are* looking for me, but only me. Eben is an innocent child.'

Poppy held Nell's hand but shook her head. 'Given that all my family has red hair and Eben doesn't, we cannot hope to pass him off as one of ours, even if the villagers keep quiet. And when the soldiers come to our home, they might take him. I'm sure you do not want that.'

Nell shook her head, thinking that Eben was most likely doomed either way.

'I'll pack you what food we can spare,' Poppy finished.

'I'm sorry I've brought this trouble to your home,' Nell said. She crawled over to the well to wash tears from her face, and saw tiny màuve flowers growing in the grass surrounding it.

'Just before the gathering began, I spoke with a friend of ours,' Poppy said, 'someone I'd trust with my life. She's going to send her husband to a village between here and Orcke where he has family who've no love for our King or his men. They will spread the word that you stole from a number of folk in the area and were spotted heading towards the wilds on the east coast, where many vagabonds go to hide. Hopefully that will confuse the soldiers long enough for you to get to where you're going and hide.'

Nell looked at the reflection of the moon and stars on the well's surface and wished that it really was possible to feel the holy breath upon her face. She'd never felt more alone in her life.

'I thank you for all you've done for me,' she said.

The water suddenly churned, and then stilled. Nell leaned forward, wondering if it was wise to look into something that might be bewitched but desperately hoping to see proof that she wasn't a killer.

Her reflection wavered and she sucked in a shaky breath, for within her face she'd glimpsed something of her mother – perhaps her strong, straight nose, or the subtle kink at the end of each eyebrow.

'Touch the reflection of the moon and the stars,' said Poppy, 'and you'll begin to know that we can feel heaven here on earth. We're not as far from the Light as it seems.'

Nell held her breath as a picture of herself suddenly appeared in the water. The scene was hard to make out though, because her figure filled most of the foreground. Her hair was dishevelled and there was a gash on her forehead, and she appeared to be talking to someone standing in a part of the room that she couldn't see. Candlelight cast flickering shadows on the wall behind her, where something green – a cloak, or curtain perhaps – hung.

It was peculiar for Nell to see herself as other people saw her. Being short in stature, she tended towards dumpiness, but she was more graceful than she'd imagined; her years of performing at the Boar's Den had given her a straight spine and smooth curves. She was holding clasped hands against her bosom, and the gesture reminded her of Pearl when she was imploring folk to see things her way.

After a fleeting glance behind her, the Nell in the picture opened her mouth wide, as if shouting or screaming, and lunged across the room. An unseen person grabbed a handful of her hair, wrenched her head backwards, and wrapped his or her hands around her throat. Nell fell to her knees.

Nell cried out. She was lost, suspended between the depths of the well and the here and now.

A firm hand grasped her shoulder and pulled her away from the pool.

'Sometimes,' Poppy told her, 'the water warns us of danger.'

Nell clutched at her throat. 'It was more than a warning … it showed my fate, my death.'

Chapter Thirteen

The Scarf

The following Sunday, Irma Linke diminished her aura and peered into the candlelit church of St Clement's. She was looking for the man who had strangled Gracie Alcorn's innocence. If he wasn't here at the vigil held every Sunday night for the missing girls, which most of the townsfolk attended, Irma would use some stored moondew to sense him out. It was time to strike him down. She didn't know how long she would have the strength to summon the otherworldly fire, or to fly.

Maye and Gracie were already inside the church, sitting on the floor at the front. Both had wanted to see how Gracie's mother was faring. And all three of them were desperate to know if the bond between mother and daughter might penetrate the veil between the realms again, as had happened when Gracie had stopped her mother throwing herself off Monk's Mill Bridge.

Hester Hannigan, Maye's identical twin sister, entered the porch and stood close to Irma as she looked over the congregation, most of whom were already seated. Hester, a seamstress well-known for the eye-catching jewel-coloured aprons she created out of cast-off material from her wealthy employers, was wearing a brown shabby tunic over her shift. Her raven tresses, usually clean, glossy and artfully wild, were unkempt and tied back with what looked to Irma like a grey rag. She was kneading her throat with one hand and roughly scratching her head with the other as if trying to dislodge a splinter.

After taking a shaky breath, Hester entered the church, keeping her eyes on the floor and hugging the back wall as if trying not to draw attention to herself. Besides the obvious, Irma wondered what was troubling her.

But all thoughts of Hester Hannigan fled when Irma spotted the killer. He was there, inside the church.

Sister Winifred stood in the side aisle because she was too unsettled to sit. She imagined the foundations of St Clement's, of all Bellayne, shaking beneath her feet, threatening to knock them all to the ground, where they'd grovel and beg forgiveness for allowing evil to thrive among them. She barely heard Father Emlyn as he read aloud the names of the missing girls, which were inscribed upon a delicate sheet of vellum, lovingly illuminated and kept inside the mahogany and gilt blessing box. Each week, Maye's and Gracie's families added a new story about their daughters to the box, and Sister Winifred did the same for Irma Linke, who had grown up in St Clement's orphanage.

Her offering for the blessing box tonight was a story about how her beloved Irma had chosen to stay on at St Clement's and teach in the church's school, which was open to all children, including those of low birth, so she could show her gratitude for the years of care she'd received. The school had been running now for ten years, and was one of Father Emlyn's finest and most hard-won accomplishments. Some of the Greenfriars, and many of the town's wealthy elders, had opposed the schooling of peasants and of girls especially. Irma had been a quick-witted and enthusiastic teacher, who'd believed that learning was best done with a dash of humour. She'd encouraged her pupils, all girls, to look for the best within themselves, and they were heartbroken and inconsolable still over her disappearance.

Sister Winifred noticed Hester Hannigan enter the church; she was barely recognisable in a drab outfit. Despite that, many heads turned to look at her – not just because she was a living reminder of the girls they'd lost, Sister Winifred guessed, but because of her extraordinary beauty. The nun gave a name then to the restlessness that was eroding her faith daily: it was fear. In a small town of only thirty-five young women, the odds of attracting the attention of the killer were high. And Hester, in particular, stood out, even when dressed as a raggedy waif.

Julian Simms, resplendent in a peacock-blue cape that he swished dramatically and often, was stacking paint pots and other implements of his craft against the wall beneath the mural he was currently working on. He stepped into Hester's path and spoke to her. She shook her head and held up a don't-come-near-me hand, barely breaking her stride as she continued along the side aisle. Sister Winifred imagined a collective sigh of disappointment when Hester turned away from them all to enter the private alcove of the Lady Chapel instead of joining her mother in the front pew.

Necks suddenly craned in a different direction when Goodwife Browne, a fair lump of a woman not shy about expressing her opinions, marched up the nave with her three daughters in tow. She stopped beside Sheriff Birch, who was sitting with his own daughters and elegantly dressed wife, and demanded a hearing.

Before Birch could draw breath, Goodwife Browne clapped her hands loudly three times. Some young women and their mothers, about twenty altogether, obeyed her command, quickly gathering behind her like anxious goslings scurrying to keep up with a demanding goose.

'We want you, Sheriff, to put our girls under constant guard until you have caught this godless creature,' said Goodwife Browne. 'Either at the castle with your own fortunate daughters, or here at St Clement's.'

'We've no room,' interrupted Brother Caddock, striding down the aisle towards the group. He was a beefy man not given to smiling.

With his usual unhurried grace and calm, Father Emlyn caught up to Brother Caddock and put a pacifying hand on his shoulder. 'We'll gladly offer you all a safe bed for the night,' he began, before Goodwife Browne interrupted and continued her tirade.

Sister Winifred noticed that the only person inside the church not watching Goodwife Browne's performance was Brother Idris, an energetic monk of thirty years and Brother Caddock's rival for the abbotship now that Father Emlyn was planning to step down due to ill health. Idris strolled over to a side table near Julian Simms's mural and picked up a large book. Cradling it in one arm, he opened its cover and, apparently reading, meandered in an absent-minded manner towards the Lady Chapel where Hester Hannigan was praying by herself. Sister Winifred couldn't fathom why Idris seemed oblivious to what was going on in front of him; he was usually the first to rush to Father Emlyn's assistance.

'It's all right for some,' shouted Goodwife Browne, calling Sister Winifred's attention back to the nave. 'Your good lady and daughters sit safe within the castle walls, Sheriff. It's your duty to protect us all, including those not noble born.'

'Hear, hear!' someone shouted.

'Save our girls,' someone else cried, and the chant was taken up. 'Save our girls!

Maye had followed her sister into the Lady Chapel with its handful of cushioned seats and its smell of incense and lingering perfumes. She gasped in shock as Hester unwound the tattered grey scarf holding back her sable hair and roughly probed the weeping edges of a bald patch on the crown of her head. The bare skin, about three thumbnails in size, was raw and inflamed, and Maye guessed that her sister had worried the spot so often that it couldn't heal. Why was Hester hurting herself? Was it because Maye had once called her a strumpet? Maye felt sick with shame at the way she'd refused to forgive her sister, preferring instead to watch her suffer.

Hester had been a mischief-maker from when she was a wee girl, and had impersonated Maye many times over the years. The last time was just a short while before they were separated in the most tragic of ways. Maye was unwell, and so Hester had gone in her place to assist Brother Idris with the orphans' rehearsal of *Noah's Ark*. Pretending to be Maye, Hester had cornered him at the end of the day and suggested a tryst at Maiden's Well. When Maye found out about her sister's trickery, she was mortified and had responded with a torrent of bitter words. Afterwards, she had allowed a rift to widen between them. Given time, she'd have calmed and built a bridge over the rift, but her killer had taken that time from her.

Hester kneeled before the altar of the Blessed Virgin and lit a candle. Maye stroked her sister's face and whispered an apology in her ear. Tears welled in Hester's vibrant blue eyes but she gave no sign that she was aware of Maye's presence.

Hester glanced over her shoulder as if making sure no one was watching her, then wrenched several strands of hair from her scalp, stifling a cry of pain with her other hand. Blood oozed from the wound. She held the hair over the candle flame, and a few moments later all that remained was a fleeting smell of singed hair and a dusting of ash on the altar cloth – the same cloth their mother had embroidered sixteen years earlier as an offering of thanks for the safe delivery of her twin girls.

Maye doubled over as grief and helplessness tore through her. She couldn't touch her sister with a comforting hand, or warn her against the killer, no matter how hard she willed it. And Hester's actions frightened her, because she sensed a deeper emotion than grief was motivating her sister's self-punishment. Maye had inkling of what that might be, for it troubled her too: the fear that her killer had mistaken her for Hester.

Irma believed their killer had chosen his victims at random, but when Maye considered the timing and place of his attack on her, she was almost certain that he'd specifically targeted Hester or herself.

She hoped that her suspicions were groundless, but she knew folk often had trouble telling her and Hester apart, especially when they were dressed in identical uniforms of dung-brown kirtle, white apron and coif.

The killer had been waiting for her within a copse of trees along a short cut that both she and Hester took on their way home from work at Lambley Manor. Their mother had forbidden them to use the treacherous path because it involved crossing a derelict footbridge, but each girl had ignored her for different reasons. Usually Hester would travel the path first, keen to meet with her friends as soon as it was time to put down needle and thread. Maye preferred to spend an hour reading in her master's library. On the day Maye died, however, Hester had been required to help dress the lady of the house for an important occasion. And Maye had rushed home to look after their mother, who had recently broken her arm.

When Maye remembered the words the killer had uttered as he tightened the rope around her throat, she couldn't dispel the thought that the attack was personal: *Begone! Begone from my life*. But she couldn't fathom how those words related to her, considering their contact hadn't extended much beyond polite greetings and general comments about village life. Nor could she understand how she had upset him to such a degree that he wanted to kill her. The only explanation she could think of was that he'd intended to kill Hester.

Maye feared that her bright but thoughtless twin might never see her seventeenth summer.

Bitterness and hatred – the essential ingredients for churning moondew into otherworldly fire – stung like needle-pricks as they surged into Irma's hands. She was hiding up in the rafters, with the dust motes that had collected in their crannies for more than two hundred years. She looked down on the man who had killed and then buried Gracie Alcorn while she and Maye had looked on in horror. She hated seeing him in the church, the only home she'd ever known, and standing close to the spot where she'd taken her first steps, finally brave enough to let go of Sister Winifred's hand.

His aura was scarred with dark slashes, but none of that was obvious to mortal eyes; just as his reason for killing herself and Maye – if he had one – wasn't apparent. But Irma had followed him many times, and had caught him looking at certain items that, if discovered in his possession, would prove he'd been involved in their murders. Unfortunately, she hadn't yet found a way to break through the veil between realms to draw others' attention to those items.

Meryl Alcorn, who had remained on her knees praying while Goodwife Browne needled the sheriff's conscience, suddenly stood and turned to face the congregation.

'Have you all forgotten that we're here to honour our lost girls and to call them home?' she shouted over the din. Then she pressed a pale green shift of Gracie's against her mouth and ran from the church.

Gracie slumped on the floor, crying.

Burning hatred for the man who had caused all this grief ripped through Irma. A fireball the size of a baby's head instantly appeared in her hands.

Goodwife Browne, perhaps feeling guilty for upsetting Meryl Alcorn, dabbed her eyes with a cornflower-blue scarf and said, 'I do not want to feel the way Meryl does now. No mother does.' The scarf slipped from her hands onto the floor.

Irma lifted the fireball above her head and moved slightly so she had a clear view of her killer. She saw that Maye was still with Hester in the Lady Chapel, and hesitated. If she failed to stop him and he lashed out in retaliation and killed another, Maye would never forgive her. Especially if his victim was Hester.

Sister Winifred – who Irma had once seen scaring off two vagabonds with a garden stake when they'd tried to steal a purse from one of the sheriff's daughters – pushed through the crowd and kneeled on the floor next to Goodwife Browne and the group of women. She held a small silver dish containing a lighted candle in her palms, and gazed up at the polished wooden cross that hung behind the altar.

The other nuns followed her example, and within a few heartbeats silence filled the church.

Despite the reverent hush, Goodwife Browne couldn't restrain her tongue. 'Has anyone thought to question you, Sheriff Arundell Birch?'

Trying to hush the ensuing hubbub, Sister Winifred stood and sang a hymn about courage and faith.

Hester walked out of the Lady Chapel to stand beside the nun, then picked up Goodwife Browne's discarded cornflower-blue scarf and shook it free of dust.

Irma tilted her wrists outwards and summoned her remaining strength. It was now or never. If she behaved like a frightened hen hiding from a fox in the nesting box, she'd never forgive herself.

Maye appeared from the Lady Chapel just as Irma held the fireball above her head, ready to throw. Her face twisted in anguish when she saw Irma lit up like a bonfire, and she screamed and soared into the air towards her.

Praying that her aim was true, Irma hurled the fireball at the killer before Maye could stop her. It arced through the air, sizzling and glowing blood red with vengeance and judgement, heading directly for his chest.

Maye tried to grab its tail, but her movement buffeted the air and only succeeded in knocking it off course. The fireball's searing aura passed within an inch of Sister Winifred, who fumbled and dropped the candle she was holding – then through the scarf Hester was holding – before it hit the floor, erupted in a shower of sparks and sputtered out.

Except for Sister Winifred's gasp, Hester's startled cry and Goodwife Browne's irritated *tut-tut-tut*, no one screamed or fainted

with shock. Irma assumed that none of the townsfolk had seen her
fireball, and were blaming the incident on a clumsy old nun who'd
dropped a candle.

The killer snatched the smouldering scarf from Hester's hands,
stomped out the embers, then wrapped her scorched fingers in a
clean cloth pulled from his pocket. It seemed to Irma that he held
on to her hand longer than was necessary.

Nell curled onto her side in the pile of leaves and looked at the
tears running down Eben's face, which was softly lit by the almost
full moon. Leaving the Goodfields had sent him into shock. He'd
lost his mother and now them, all in less than a month, and sadness
was slowly stealing his vitality. He'd lost his feistiness – something
Nell had never thought she'd miss – and had plodded obediently in
her wake for the last seven days without throwing a single tantrum
and barely uttering a word. He'd not eaten much either, not since
Flannery's honey cakes had run out, and she was worried that he was
losing weight, something he couldn't afford to do.

Nell knew that her own mood was contributing to his despair,
but she couldn't shake off what she'd seen in the well. If that fate
came to pass and someone did strangle her, she knew it'd be in the
not-too-distant future because in the picture she'd been wearing the
same clothes she was wearing now.

It was ironic that only moments before she'd seen the vision,
she'd begun to hope that she mightn't be a killer after all. That
maybe, just maybe, she was worthy of a better life. Of any life at all.

Eben's eyes fluttered open. He wiped his nose on his sleeve and
looked at the sky. It might be too late for her to be part of a loving
family, but it wasn't too late for Eben. She needed to get him to his
father in Bellayne, which would be maybe tomorrow or the next day
going by what a farmer had told her a couple of days ago.

Nell began to sing the song she'd written for Eben, the one she
added to each time to help him keep his mother in his memory.

' *"Touch me with your finger," said the mother to her little boy,*
"Upon this star I sit,
Sending you kisses from afar.
I still hold your hand
And rub your back,
My beautiful green-eyed boy.
Whisper, whisper, whisper,
Close your eyes.
My light shineth still
In you, Eben,
For you.
I'll watch over you this night and all nights to come.
Whisper, whisper, whisper …" '

Tears trickled from Nell's eyes as she watched Eben reach up to touch the sky with his finger. He murmured something she couldn't hear.

'You're almost home,' Nell whispered, desperately hoping that was true.

Chapter Fourteen

An Unearthly Breeze

'Someone's coming,' said Gracie, on Monday morning.

She'd been standing with her head tilted back for more than an hour, staring into the sky and waiting, forever waiting, to receive a message from the heavens.

Irma's heart sank. 'Oh God, please tell me he's not bringing another girl here.' She remembered the way the killer had taken the burning scarf from Hester's hand.

Maye, her gentle face twisted with uncharacteristic hatred, turned on Irma and screamed, 'It'll be your fault if he is – and especially if it's my sister!'

Irma stumbled backwards, shaken by Maye's outburst. Her fragile fellowship with Maye had shattered, as if she'd repeatedly whacked it with an axe. But part of her was unrepentant. She didn't regret attacking their killer, only failing to stop him.

Gracie, looking washed out and neglected in her fraying dress, shook her head. 'Nay, it's someone else ... someone who might stumble and disappear into the mist before they reach us.'

A sudden squall whipped through the hollow, swirling leaf litter and shrivelled acorns in the air and bringing a terrible coldness that turned the fog to ice. The otherworldly cloud that had been hanging over Bellayne since their deaths, made up of the fear and suspicion seeped from the hearts and minds of the townsfolk, was as filthy as the sludge that oozed down the street after heavy rain, and the stench billowing from it reminded Irma of rotten potatoes. Even the Shadowfolk, who were accustomed to the hollow's changeable temperament, buried their faded faces in the dirt.

'Something foul comes our way,' said Irma.

She didn't believe that anyone would find their graves before it was too late, before the killer killed again, no matter what the angels had promised Gracie.

The bell of St Clement's tolled, startling Sister Winifred, who banged her head on the sloping henhouse roof. She rubbed her brow, disturbing her wimple and freeing cobwebs of white hair to flutter about her face. She'd arisen early to collect the eggs before the dayspring blessing, or the Blessing of Sparrow's Fart as she secretly called it. As she scattered feed and chatted to her clucking girls, a squall suddenly swept over the hills and lashed the valley with icy rain. A strange smell tainted the air and she wondered if there was a rats' nest nearby.

Eager to get out of the frigid wind, she lifted the lids of the nesting boxes and poked around in the straw, feeling for the three dozen or so eggs she usually collected each morning. There was none.

Puzzled, wondering if someone had filched them, she unlatched the henhouse gate and prepared to run back to the warmth of the convent's kitchen. As she stepped outside, she saw an egg nestled against the gatepost, but when she picked it up, it was cracked and empty.

Hidden in the straw below it were two more eggs, not a skerrick of yolk left in either of them.

Sister Winifred struggled to catch her breath. For some foolish reason, the three empty shells made her think of the three missing girls. She'd lost all hope of them coming home. She had a terrible feeling that their spirits had long ago left their bodies.

'Where are you, Irma, my dear, dear girl?' she cried.

Pulling herself together, she wiped her eyes and noticed another egg balanced precariously on the horizontal beam above the gate. How it had got up there she couldn't fathom. Standing on tiptoes, she wrapped her hand around it and was relieved to discover that this one was full. Sometimes, she thought, she was a silly old chook herself.

She wiped the egg on her apron, then clasped it to her bosom. There was a hairline crack along the shell's bottom. Cold fingers of foreboding crept up her spine and chilled her aching bones. She couldn't even summon a prayer to her parched lips. She suddenly felt old and very alone.

In the kitchen of the Merry Monkey inn, the cook, Leticia Simms, slapped dough onto a floured wooden table in the centre of the room and wondered if she should have drowned all her children at birth. Her jowls flapped like wet piecrust over the edge of a dish as she rocked back and forth, kneading the dough with beefy forearms.

'Eight of our ungrateful brats have deserted us, and now the ninth, our youngest and dearest, is up to something. And you know best of all, Albert, that I'm never wrong.'

Behind her, something sizzled. Cook wiped her hands on a crisp white apron and turned to the fireplace. Bending forward, she stirred a steaming pot of oatmeal, then set the pot on a trivet at the edge of the hearth.

'Our boy is a ninny, Albert. Less sense than a lump of dough. And I'm sick to my teeth of getting him out of one scrape after another. Julian owes me more than he can ever repay.'

A sharp pain gripped her left hip. Groaning, she straightened and leaned against the table to catch her breath, then slurped the dregs of ale from a mug.

'Whatever his plans, he's sure to cock them up. And I ...' She struggled to swallow a gristle-like lump of anger. 'I will be left penniless in my dotage.' She pummelled the dough until it was flat and sticky and mashed into the grain of the wood, then jabbed the air with a stumpy finger. 'I blame you, Albert. If you'd not filled his head with foolish dreams of painting nymphs and unicorns on the King's great hall wall, he'd have been content to smother his urges until his father-in-law was dead. Instead, his gallivanting and flattering has raised too many eyebrows. If he's not careful, Old Ham will cut him adrift without a penny.' She slammed her palms down onto the table. 'I will not have it.'

The door to the passage opened and Alice, the scullery maid, tripped into the kitchen. She thrust a wooden bowl under Cook's nose, then put it on the floor near the back door. 'Miss Phoebe, the dirty cow, retched into her bowl of porridge and left me to clean it up.' Alice turned her long, narrow head towards the empty chair by the hearth and sneered when she spotted the full mug of ale resting on its arm. 'I see Albert's copped an earful this morning. Poor man – six months in the grave and he can't find no rest.'

Cook gouged a hunk of dough from the table and threw it at Alice. 'Get out, you snivelling rodent, before I cut the tongue from your mouth.'

Alice dodged the dough and scurried back into the service passage. Cook hurled a rolling pin after her. It hit the door lintel just as Arnod Butterball, the innkeeper, stepped into the kitchen, then glanced off his shoulder and clattered to the floor.

He picked it up and tapped it against his thigh, raising his eyebrows when he noticed the mashed bread dough. 'Is there a problem, Leticia?'

Cook shook her head. Her master's presence often rendered her speechless. Even at five-and-forty years, he retained a rugged charm that quickened the breath of many a woman, and had the most expressive face she'd ever come across, with beautiful ash-grey eyes. She'd not yet forgiven him, though, for lopping off his long dark hair. On the morning he'd come into the kitchen to show off his shortened locks and beard, she'd threatened to put him across her knee and spank him. The haircut had spoiled her fantasies for a night or two, until he slipped back into her dreams and set her bearded clam throbbing once more.

'Our guests are eager to break their fast,' he said, poking the dough with the end of the rolling pin. His face was creased with irritation.

Cook's desire cooled, and she wiped her clammy hands on her apron. She couldn't afford to lose her place at the Merry Monkey. She dabbed her eyes with a corner of her apron while she cast about for a plausible excuse for her tantrum.

'Forgive me, I'm not myself this morning. Alice mocked the memory of my beloved Albert.'

She covered her face and pretended to sob into her apron. Men often regretted their complaints, Cook knew well, when confronted with tears.

'I … I'll speak with Alice,' Arnod stuttered, backing out of the kitchen looking suitably humbled.

Cook lowered her apron and her eyes caught on the bowl of porridge that Alice had dumped on the floor near the back door. Miss Phoebe had purged her oats at least twice over the last few days. Cook's heart almost stopped beating. Was Phoebe with child?

Phoebe Butterball folded her arms over her chest and glared at her Aunt Mary. 'Why are you always finding fault with me?'

Mary put a guest's chamberpot on the floor and wiped her callused hands on her apron. She eyed the rumpled blankets on the four beds Phoebe had supposedly already made, then pointed to the washstand. 'I'm not *always* finding fault, but when I passed the doorway I saw you pouring the slops from the wash bowl back into the ewer, instead of filling it with fresh water.'

Phoebe shrugged and stared at the floor.

Ignoring the dull ache behind her eyes, Mary sought to lighten the mood before it turned into an argument – a frequent occurrence of late. She imitated the high-pitched voice of a guest who had the unfortunate habit of picking at a trio of warts on her chin: 'Would you want to wash your face in old Widow Winter's slops?'

Without even the hint of a smile, Phoebe turned her back and stuck her head out the window. Her shoulders were tense, hunched in on her slight frame. Something serious was troubling the girl, Mary had no doubt. She'd asked her what was wrong a number of times over the last month, but Phoebe always insisted it wasn't anything to worry about, just a disagreement with a friend. Mary didn't believe her.

She crossed the room to wipe some long strands of grey hair from the washstand, then stood behind her niece and looked out at the scudding clouds that greyed the morning. There was a whiff of something foul on the wind, a faint hint of decay. Mary felt drained and would have preferred to close the shutters and crawl back into bed instead of attending to the guests' needs. After no sign of her monthly flow for almost a year, it had made a sudden reappearance and persisted, so far, for two long weeks. Their chambermaid, Beatrice, couldn't have picked a worse time to break her leg.

'Phoebe love,' she said, 'if we work together, our chores will soon be done. And this afternoon we could take a blanket and a cake down to the river and add some roses to your gown. I cannot believe it's a week since we touched needle and thread.'

'I've other plans,' Phoebe said, and prodded a knot in the floor with the toe of her slipper. 'Besides, needlework is a tedious pastime. Perhaps you should finish decorating the hem yourself.'

Mary felt like she'd been slapped. She'd spent weeks making a fashionable gown for Phoebe's birthday gift out of the softest cloth that she and Arnod could afford. She'd left the emerald dress unadorned so she and her niece could bead and embroider the bodice and cuffs together. She couldn't fathom Phoebe's sudden nastiness;

it was so out of character for the usually vibrant and loquacious girl that Mary felt a twinge of fear. What was going on in Phoebe's life? Had someone harmed her? Her heartbeat quickened as she wondered if the missing girls had lost their appetites and become unnaturally taciturn in the weeks before they disappeared.

'Is it me, Phoebe? Have I done —'

'I fear that my mother is dead,' Phoebe cut in. Tears glistened on her pale lashes. 'Why else would she stay away so long?'

Why else indeed? thought Mary. Ever since she was a girl, Medwelyn, her much younger sister, had followed her own whims and fancies without regard for anyone else. Mary was weary of making excuses for her absence from Phoebe's life.

Nevertheless, she quashed her uncharitable thoughts, brushed the tears from Phoebe's cheeks and placed a hand on her shoulder. 'Be at ease, my girl. I'm sure your mother is alive and well and will appear when we least expect it. I'm sorry she missed your birthday.'

With hazel eyes flashing, Phoebe pushed Mary's hand away. 'Nay, that cannot be true. We've had no word for almost two years. Something's happened to her.'

Mary gritted her teeth. Her head was now throbbing so much that she just wanted to lie in a darkened room with a wet flannel over her eyes. How dare Medwelyn cause her daughter so much distress? Mary and Arnod had vowed never to criticise Medwelyn in Phoebe's presence, but they couldn't continue to let her fret needlessly.

She softened her voice and carefully chose her words. 'I know this will hurt you to hear it, but your mother has little understanding of time or distance. This is not the first time she's stayed away for so long. She left you in our care when you were a few months old, and didn't return until your fifth birthday.'

Phoebe, her lips drawn tightly together, flicked the end of her butter-blonde plait back and forth, as if swatting away unwanted truths. 'But you said she never missed a single birthday when I was a child.'

'You always hungered for stories about the times Medwelyn journeyed to be with you, so Arnod and I lied to please you.'

Mary reached for Phoebe's hand, but she pulled it away and shook her head. 'I do not believe you.'

'Phoebe, please –'

'And you … you were *glad* that she stayed away.'

'That's not true,' Mary said. 'Although I often wished she'd either come home or stay away for good. You fretted so during her absences, and when she was home, it was hard watching you trying desperately to please her so that she'd stay. She was careless with your affections –'

'Stop it! Stop it!' Phoebe lashed the space between them with her hands. 'You forced her to leave me with you because you wanted me all to yourself.'

'Your mother left you in your cradle and stole away into the night to follow her latest lover to the mainland. My sister is wilful and selfish, and, I'm sorry to say, she'll only return when she wants something.'

Phoebe covered her mouth and nose with her hands and shook her head.

Mary rushed forward and placed her own hands either side of the girl's face. 'I'm sorry. I should not have spoken so harshly of her.'

Phoebe wiped her nose on her sleeve. 'If my mother had not shared me with you, you would've had nothing.'

'You have been a blessed gift to Arnod and me. We –'

'My mother told me that you hate her coming here. That you're jealous of her because your own womb is barren.'

With an anguished cry, Mary swung her arm and slapped Phoebe's face. The girl stumbled sideways, hitting her hip against the washstand, and the ewer of dirty water tumbled and broke upon the floor, scattering earthenware shards at their feet. With both hands pressed against her cheeks, Phoebe began to cry. She looked devastated, her anger gone.

Mary sank to her knees. 'God help me,' she cried. 'I did not mean to hurt you.'

The puddle of water seeped beneath her knees and a frightening ache grew in her heart. Phoebe had spoken true: her beautiful, sometimes prickly niece was the light of Mary's life. If she lost her now …

'Inside my womb you did not grow, but within my heart I hold you.'

Stifling a sob with her hand, Phoebe ran from the room.

Mary looked up and saw her husband standing in the doorway, his expression concerned and puzzled. She didn't know how much of the argument he'd heard.

'What's going on?' he asked.

The bank of clouds outside gathered and darkened, dimming the light in the room considerably.

'I slapped her,' said Mary. 'Across the face.'

'What? Why?' Arnod shut the door, and sat on a three-legged stool near the washstand. It creaked under his weight. 'For God's sake, Mary, what's going on? What were you thinking?'

Mary shook her head as she picked up shards of the broken ewer and put them in her lap. She tucked her straight brown hair behind her ears with shaking hands, and turned her tear-streaked face to her husband. 'I cannot say.'

Phoebe's words had opened an old wound and Mary didn't know if she could seal it shut again. Over the years, Arnod had often reassured her that raising Phoebe was enough for him, but Mary feared that he secretly regretted their childless union. Phoebe's heated words only echoed the thoughts that had been running through her own mind since she'd reached one-and-forty years back in December. She was sure that the bitterness in her barren womb was draining her zest for life and causing more lines on her already tired face.

She longed to rest her aching head against Arnod's chest. She wished she'd stayed in bed with him this morning, snuggled into his arms, and not hurried the gentle kiss they'd shared every morning for twenty years. Her day mightn't have gone from bad to worse. Her eyes drifted from his fine-hewn jaw to the grey and brown hairs poking through the top of his unlaced shirt. She never tired of looking at him. Some of her friends, and many of the guests at the inn, often complained about their husbands, but she loved Arnod more with each passing day and could honestly say that not one of his quirks annoyed her, even his insistence on leaving their bedchamber window partially open in the middle of winter. She just smiled and burrowed under the bedcovers, content to have a reason to get as close to him as possible.

Arnod sighed and gazed at the floor. Could he not bear to look at her?

He stood, and moved towards the doorway without holding out a hand to help her up from the floor. 'I've got to go. I promised to call upon my father before I head over to Stout for the guild meeting this afternoon. The ulcer on his leg has not yet healed. It'll be dark before I'm home.'

As his footsteps echoed down the passage, Mary lifted her apron, sending the earthenware shards falling to the floor. She curled over her knees and wept.

On his way to mend a fence around the field closest to the front gate of Lea Farm, Jack Lea paused and looked over the freshly sown crop of corn seedlings. Something was wrong. A moment later, he realised that the two scarecrows protecting the crop were missing, and as he approached the place where they usually stood, he saw that the soil was trampled with hoof and footprints. He glanced around, looking for the culprit, when a flutter of red, just beyond the fence, caught his attention. One of the scarecrows had been wearing a red scarf. He ran over to and hurdled the fence. The two scarecrows, now headless and looking the worse for wear, were propped there.

'For fuck's sake,' he muttered. He wanted to believe that it was just a harmless prank involving a couple of the local mischief-makers, but the churning in his gut told him otherwise. The Alcorns, he felt sure, had just issued a warning, one that Jack's father was likely to ignore. If anything, it'd make Cerdic dig his heels in harder and refuse to budge from the cottage. Jack resolved to speak with Birch. Maybe he could make the old man see sense.

Chapter Fifteen

Maiden's Well

Sister Winifred took a breath of fresh air as she left the convent and made her way down the path towards the river. She hadn't gone very far when she heard her name called. A young nun ran up to her and thrust a piece of parchment into her hand. 'I found it in …' she said, gulping back a sob. Her usually pale, freckled face flushed a deep red. 'In the Lady Chapel.' She ran off before Sister Winifred could question her further.

Unrolling the parchment, Sister Winifred saw a drawing of two Greenfriars burying the body of a young woman in the woods. Her hands turned to ice as the messenger's malice touched her. Did the culprit know what had happened to the missing girls and, if so, why didn't he or she come forward? Sister Winifred walked briskly down the path, intent on finding Sheriff Birch.

An hour later, near Monk's Mill bridge, Birch stuffed the obscene message into his bag. He was well-dressed as usual, in an indigo shirt and black leather jerkin and breeches, but Sister Winifred noted he looked haunted and run down. His eyes were bloodshot, and his short fair moustache and beard needed a trim.

'They're not all aimed at St Clement's, you know. I've had one myself.' He looked at the ground, as if reluctant to say more. 'But some folk are saying that Father Emlyn's protecting one of his own.'

'You should be ashamed!' she snapped, then immediately regretted it.

'Oh, I confess to great shame, Sister. Three girls are lost and I know not how. I'm duty-bound to consider all possibilities, no matter how difficult. Many of the towns' elders think that Father Emlyn is well past his prime, and it's time for Brother Caddock to step up and crush the evil in our town with a severe hand.'

Sister Winifred gripped Sheriff Birch's forearm a tad harder than she'd intended, but she'd been feeling overwrought since finding the empty and cracked eggshells that morning. She couldn't contain her superstitious fear that another young woman was about to vanish.

'If I had the slightest suspicion that a Greenfriar was responsible for the disappearances, I'd demand that Father Emlyn whipped him till he bled,' she said.

'And I'd give you the whip.' Birch gently touched her shoulder. 'Now, I must leave you. Apparently, Lex Alcorn, his sons and their growing band of henchmen have started patrolling the town with scythes and hoes in hand. I must go and persuade them to return to their homes.' He mounted his horse and cantered across the bridge, passing Julian Simms and his small daughter who were heading in the same direction. Julian's usual satchel of painting implements was bouncing vigorously against his thigh and he was piggybacking Fleur.

Still feeling disturbed, Sister Winifred decided to take her prayer book to her favourite spot inside the Tranquillity Garden, overlooking the river. She'd just sat down when Brother Idris appeared with a mob of boys in tow, some of them carrying fishing poles. Idris called out a cheery greeting as they passed her and made their way down the bank.

Hearing giggling, Sister Winifred looked towards the bridge and saw two girls skipping down the riverbank towards Idris and the boys. It was Posey Browne, a floozy and bully if ever there was one, and her friend, a girl called Katherine. They were whispering conspiratorially, which set bells ringing in Sister Winifred's head. She was ashamed to admit it, but Posey set her teeth on edge. The girl always seemed to be planning mischief, usually something spiteful.

Sister Winifred was disappointed to see Hester Hannigan trailing behind the other two. Hester was gazing at the ground and seemed oblivious to what was going on around her. Since her twin's disappearance, Hester's high spirits had taken a reckless turn and her mother had shared with Sister Winifred her concerns about the way Hester had taken to staying out late at night – 'doing what with God knows who' – and seemed unconcerned about her own safety.

When the sweaty, spotty boys spotted the lasses, they abandoned their fishing poles, puffed out their chests and whistled, but they were wasting their breath. With chins held high, Posey and Katherine strutted past them, making straight for Idris, who was helping a smaller lad to cast his line into the water.

Sensing trouble, Sister Winifred stood, intending to head down the bank as soon as the stiffness in her knees passed, but she was too late. When Posey was a foot or so from Idris, she clutched her bosom, swayed dramatically for a moment, then fainted. With lightning speed, Idris dropped to his haunches and caught her before her head struck the ground.

He was helping her to sit up when she flopped back into his arms and nestled her cheek against his chest. 'Thank you, Brother,' she said, loudly. 'Your holy touch has restored me to the pinkness of health.'

Idris flinched and tried to disentangle himself from her grasp, but her persistent fingers gripped his robes while she purred and cooed and curled around him. Katherine laughed uproariously, sounding more like a donkey than a young woman, in Sister Winifred's opinion, while Hester peered around quizzically, as if she'd just awoken and wasn't quite sure how she'd come to be standing where she was. Some of the boys cheered and made kissing sounds.

Brother Caddock lumbered past Sister Winifred and shouted, 'What is this foolishness?'

The boys shuffled backwards and studied their muddy toes. Katherine shut her mouth.

'Brother Idris, what say you?' Caddock demanded.

Idris stood. His dark, hooded eyes ranged from Posey to Katherine and then settled on Hester. He seemed confused rather than angry, but Sister Winifred was never entirely sure what he was feeling or thinking. Some people thought him taciturn, but she knew that he spoke only when he'd something useful to say. The only time he looked truly relaxed was when he was teaching or playing with the boys.

As Sister Winifred barged through the lads, she felt a stirring of uneasiness. Why was Idris staring at Hester? Only a few moments had passed, but to Sister Winifred, it was one moment too long. Was he recalling the day that Hester had suggested a tryst at Maiden's Well, and wondering why she seemed intent on humiliating him? Or was he staring at her because she reminded him of Maye?

Not long after Maye disappeared, Irma had shared with Sister Winifred her concerns for Idris' wellbeing after she found him crying in the Lady Chapel. A man crying wasn't unusual in itself but he'd been holding against his chest the altar cloth that Goodwife Hannigan had embroidered to celebrate the birth of her twin daughters. At first, Irma had thought to slip away unnoticed but when his sorrow didn't ease, she'd entered the chapel and touched his shoulder. He'd grasped her hand and turned, but when he'd seen Irma standing behind him, he'd looked crestfallen, and she'd the impression that his prayers had not been answered. He'd then draped the cloth back over the altar and muttered something about dead moths.

Brother Caddock's voice rose in pitch. 'I will have an answer, Idris.'

Sister Winifred glared at Posey and said, 'Idris kindly assisted the lass when she fainted.'

Caddock fixed his vivid blue eyes upon her, as if daring her to utter one more word. Beads of sweat slid across his pink spotted scalp and dampened his ring of sandy hair. She could almost hear his pate sizzling in the sun.

Undeterred by his wrath, she added, 'Katherine will escort Miss Browne to the infirmary. After a dose of Brother Godric's bitter tonic and a large measure of fish liver oil, I'm sure she'll regain her senses.'

Caddock clapped his hands. 'Begone, the lot of you, before I cancel the midday meal.' When the children had all disappeared, he turned on Sister Winifred again. 'I'm not a fool. I saw the girl stroke Idris's cheek.'

'Then you'll have also seen that he was innocent of any impropriety.'

'I'll take this matter further, be assured of that.'

Sister Winifred didn't doubt it. She knew that Caddock would draw another black mark against Idris's name and hold the already lengthy list under the elders' noses. Sometimes, in her more bitter moments, she wondered if Caddock secretly rejoiced in the terrible happenings of the last few months. They had turned the tide in his favour when it came to choosing Father Emlyn's successor as abbot. She felt sad that Emlyn probably would not realise his long-held dream for Idris to take over in his stead. Given the troubled times, many thought him too young and too lenient.

Idris stepped between them. 'It's all right, Sister. Brother Caddock and I will sort things out. You look in need of some food and a rest.'

Sister Winifred felt heavy of heart as she struggled back up the bank. It wasn't the first time a young woman had thrown herself at Idris's feet, and it wouldn't be the last. He was a good-looking man who stirred feminine passions, no matter how hard he worked to smother his potency. He often toiled for hours in the abbey gardens until sweat soaked his robes and he couldn't push the spade into the earth one more time.

Birch's comment about Father Emlyn protecting one of the Greenfriars whirled around her mind. It was highly unlikely Emlyn would do such a thing, but if he did, Idris was the most likely candidate. Emlyn had loved him like a son for thirty years, ever since he'd found him wrapped in a blanket on the church steps.

Sister Winifred loved Idris too; she'd watched him grow from a boy with an insatiable quest to know the ins and outs of everything, to a teacher with an enthusiastic need to share that knowledge with the many children who passed through St Clement's doors. But she wouldn't turn a blind eye if Idris was the cause of so much grief. Any truth was preferable to never knowing who had taken Bellayne's beloved daughters.

Hester Hannigan ran up behind Sister Winifred. 'I'm sorry, sister.'

'Sorry? Do you think that'll stop Brother Caddock from making trouble for Idris?'

Hester hung her head in answer. Nothing could take away from her extraordinary beauty but grief and lack of sleep were evident in the dark shadows beneath her eyes and the gauntness of her delicate features. Her slender figure was bordering on too thin. 'Do you not think,' said Sister Winifred, 'that your mother has enough to worry about without enduring Brother Caddock's wrath? She mourns the loss of one daughter –.'

'I did not know what Posey –.'

'To play so carelessly with another's feelings, especially a man who's forsaken the touch of a woman … tut.' Sister Winifred clacked her tongue. 'And it's not the first time you've tormented him.'

'That'll haunt me 'til the end of my days,' cried Hester.

When Sister Winifred reached the garden seat for the second time, she realised that while she needed to rest, if only for a moment, she'd given up all hope of finding any peace in a day that had obviously been sent to try her. She dismissed Hester, who'd begun to cry. 'Leave me now,' she said, 'and get home to your mother. She needs to know that you're keeping yourself safe.' Hester ran across the road and into the orchard. Feeling ashamed at the overly harsh way she'd spoken to her, Sister Winifred prayed for forgiveness and fortitude. The pitter-patter of brisk footsteps pulled her out of her contemplation. Phoebe Butterball, flushed and out of breath, was almost level with her and seemingly uninterested in passing the time of day.

When Sister Winifred greeted her, Phoebe almost jumped out of her skin. 'Oh, I didn't see you there,' she said.

'Finished your chores already?'

The girl nodded, looking slightly guilty. 'I'm on my way to meet a friend and I'm running late.'

She bade Sister Winifred a hasty farewell, headed across the bridge and turned right, in the direction of Maiden's Well.

Sister Winifred remembered the cracked egg and longed to call both Phoebe and Hester back.

Nell spun around and around, peering wildly into the darkling woods. The full moon, still low in the sky, cast an eerie glow through fishbone clouds coloured charcoal. Beyond the patchy moonlight, the woods were shadowed and sly, keeping their secrets, stealing hers. He could be hiding within a few yards of her and she'd never see him, not until he'd moved into the open, which was nothing more than a treeless track. She strained her ears, listening for his footfalls, his breathing, the snap of a twig, but couldn't hear much over her own panting and the thrum of blood in her head.

Forcing herself to stand still, she held her hands up and outwards, as if to sense on the air the ripples of any movements he made. Her fingers trembled as they touched the dampness settling around her. Nothing.

A sound. Muffled. Indistinct. Had he called her name?

Unsure of where the sound had come from, but knowing that she needed to move fast, she ran towards a narrow break in the thicket, and then along an overgrown path where tree roots snaked out to trip her and dangling branches snatched at her hair. Her threadbare cloak snagged on vicious thorns, bringing her to an unexpected and jerky standstill. Unable to free the cloth without shredding her hands, she leaned back and tugged until it tore free.

The sound came again, from somewhere just ahead, and she realised it was the caw of a crow. Had the Crows lured Eben away while she'd been gathering fern fronds to make a bed? How cruel it would be if she lost him so close to their destination.

'Eben!' she screamed. 'Where are you?'

She stumbled over a hefty two-foot-long branch, about as thick as her wrist. She picked it up and, wielding it like a sword, crept towards an enormous old oak and what looked like an opening in the dense forest.

She peered around the oak into a clearing. Eben was standing on its far side, with his back to her, amid a carpet of bluebells.

Without turning to look at her, he pointed at the ground. 'Foot.'

Nell's mouth went dry. Had he hurt himself? She ran to him, and looked down to where he was pointing. Her mind numbed as she struggled to take in what she was seeing.

A foot, partly decomposed, poking out of the ground. And what looked very much like three grave mounds, one of which had not been there long going by the lack of weeds growing on its surface. She wondered why there were no crosses or flowers to mark the graves; and why the one in the middle hadn't been dug deep enough to cover the body properly.

Her head spun and her breath quickened. She dropped to her haunches and grabbed hold of Eben, who for once made little protest about being gathered into her arms. Nell took off along the overgrown path. From behind her came the fluttering of wings. She didn't look back.

She was going to run to Bellayne, even if it took her the rest of the night.

Chapter Sixteen

The Merry Monkey

Half an hour later, and exactly one moon cycle since they'd set out from Stonhard, Nell and Eben rode into Bellayne on the back of the cart belonging to a married couple who'd stopped for them on the main road. Along the way, the woman had given Nell a well-meaning but long-winded lecture on the folly of walking alone on the road at night – 'especially when three girls have disappeared from the town over the last few months,' she'd exclaimed with eyes agog.

Nell, dread rippling over her skin, had almost fainted when she heard those tidings. She wondered if Eben had stumbled across the graves by chance, or had he been led there by the Crows, or the beckoning hand of fate?

Nell had never contemplated the existence of fate before; not until she'd seen the picture of her own death in the well at Larke-upon-Eel. If it turned out that the three missing girls had been strangled, she was getting out of Bellayne as soon as she'd handed Eben into his father's care.

'Here we are, girl,' said the woman, as the cart stopped outside an inn with ivy clambering over its stone walls and candles flickering in its front windows. 'If you've no money for a bed, you can sleep quite comfortably in the cart.'

'Eliza, a storm's coming,' said her husband. 'Surely we can —'

'Thank you,' said Nell, jumping to the ground, and lifting Eben, drowsy and shivering, from the cart. 'We'll be all right from here.'

The man shrugged, wiped a hand over his tired face, and followed his wife into the Merry Monkey.

What now? wondered Nell, wrapping her cloak around Eben. *Whom do I tell about those poor girls?*

The road was deserted as far as she could see, and quiet, except for the first drops of rain pattering the already damp dirt. The inn's sign swayed and creaked in the gathering wind. Beyond a field on the opposite side of the road, the outline of a church was visible against the twilight sky. Going there for help was the most obvious thing to do, but she couldn't face another walk through the dark, especially not now she knew that someone in this town was making girls disappear.

She walked to one of the inn's corners instead, and came face to face with a slight lad of about sixteen who was gnawing on a meaty bone. They both shrieked, and Nell stepped back, wary.

'Sorry, miss, I've just come to take the horse and cart to the stables,' he said. 'Didn't mean to frighten you.'

'Your master … or father, is he here?'

'The master's out, due back soon. The mistress be in the kitchen, just down there, if that's any good to you.'

Nell thanked him and hurried towards the back of the inn.

Three women and a girl of about Nell's own age, all red-faced and sweating as they scraped pots and stacked dirty dishes onto a long wooden table, looked at Nell with surprise as she shut the kitchen door behind her.

She leaned her back against it, worn out and relieved to be somewhere warm and safe. 'Help me, please,' she said. 'In the woods…I saw…'

After a short silence, the tallest woman put down the tray she was carrying, wiped her hands on her apron and hurried across the stone floor to place a hand on Nell's arm. 'Has someone hurt you?'

'Nay, it's something else. On my way here I ...' Nell's dry lips stuck together as she struggled to put what she'd seen into words. She hoped that none of these women had been close to the missing girls. 'Oh, God, I'm sorry,' she cried, as piddle ran down Eben's leg and onto the floor.

Eben lifted his head off her shoulder, befuddled and a little frightened to see so many new faces peering at him. 'Wet pants, Nellie,' he said, his bottom lip trembling.

Too late now for her to give the strangers a false name. She hoped she would be gone before the King's men came looking for her here.

'Never mind, no harm done,' said the woman, and introduced herself as Mary Butterball. She turned to the lass, a petite miss with glossy hair and an I'd-rather-be-doing-something-else look upon her face. 'Phoebe, love, please take this little man upstairs and clean him up. Alice will bring him some bread and milk shortly. And then, if that's all right with you,' she looked at Nell for confirmation, 'you can tuck him into bed.'

Nell nodded, relieved that someone else was taking control. Eben curled into Phoebe's arms with barely a murmur and didn't look back at Nell on his way out of the kitchen.

Mary, fortyish and regally tall with strong, well-balanced features, looked expectantly at Nell. The other two women edged closer, obviously aware that something was amiss.

Feeling overheated and crowded, Nell muttered an apology and rushed back out into the yard. Mary followed her, shutting the door firmly in the faces of the other women.

'I can take you across to the convent at St Clement's if you like,' she said. 'Perhaps you'd rather –'

'I found three graves,' Nell blurted out. 'In the forest to the south of here. Unmarked. One more recent than the others.'

'Oh, God.' Mary groped for the wall to steady herself and bowed her head. 'Nay, it does not mean ... it must not ...'

'I heard about the missing girls on my way here,' Nell went on. 'And there was something unsettling about the graves being hidden. There were no flowers, except for the bluebells growing in the clearing.' She stopped, not wanting to upset Mary any further.

'Forgive me, it's a shock.' Looking up at the stars, Mary crossed her chest, then wiped tears from her cheeks. 'I pray you're wrong, but if it is our girls, we need to bring them home. I'll send Ned, our stableboy, to St Clement's to fetch Father Emlyn, and then on to the Pickled Eel where the sheriff's serjeant will be drinking at this hour.'

Thunder rumbled in the distance as Nell mopped up the last of the gravy on her plate with a piece of piecrust. Before she could put in her mouth, Serjeant Oswald asked her another question about the location of the graves. The others in the kitchen – a monk, a nun, Mary Butterball and her cook – all leaned towards her as she answered.

'Just before I came to the spot where I'd decided to camp for the night, I crossed a rickety bridge. I stopped beside the stream to fill my flask. The path that led to the clearing was on the eastern side of the Flegg Road.'

With a sigh of disgust, Serjeant Oswald pushed away the mug of milk Cook Simms had slyly offered him. 'Sounds as if she's talking about Shymer Forest,' he said, flicking his damp, stringy hair back from his haggard face.

He reeked of ale and cheap perfume and was obviously peeved about having his night at the Pickled Eel interrupted. Nell had heard him mutter under his breath upon arriving at the Merry Monkey that the meeting could have waited until morning.

'No one goes there,' said the cook, staring at Nell with grey calculating eyes. Her scrutiny was unsettling, almost as if the woman was undressing her. 'It's haunted.'

The nun tutted loudly and gripped the mug she was holding more firmly, as if to stop herself hurling it across the table at the cook. 'Ghosts exist in faerie tales and the minds of those addled by drink. Though I admit the existence of graves in Shymer Forest is distressing. I know of no reason why they'd be there. Does anyone else?'

A thoughtful silence followed, each lowering their eyes to stare futilely at the table or their laps.

'We prayed they'd come home safely,' the nun told Nell, breaking the silence.

If it wasn't for the families of the missing girls, no doubt desperate to know what had become of their daughters, Nell wished she'd never found the graves. Or that she'd kept her mouth shut, delivered Eben to his father, and gone on her way.

'That was not likely, Sister Winifred, not after all this time,' said the monk, who'd come in place of Father Emlyn who'd suffered a fit during the afternoon.

Sister Winifred glared at him, probably annoyed by his tactlessness and lack of compassion, Nell thought.

The nun turned to Serjeant Oswald, who was now raking his chewed fingernails through his wispy beard. 'I presume you'll be sending someone to guard the graves during the night.'

'Whoever they are, they're not going anywhere,' he said. Another man without any tact. 'And there's a storm on the way.'

'Gracie Alcorn was only eleven years old,' cried Mary, twisting her apron around one hand. Her cap was askew, and thick strands of brown hair were stuck to her long neck. The kitchen was still uncomfortably warm, even though the cook had allowed the fire to die down.

'We'll best serve the dead by getting a good night's sleep and readying ourselves to leave at first light. It's going to be a long day tomorrow,' said the serjeant, pushing back his chair and standing. 'We could be traipsing all over the forest trying to find those graves in the dark and the rain, especially if this lass can't find her way again. In my experience, women have trouble knowing up from down.'

Nell smothered a gasp. She'd not contemplated for one moment that they would expect her to return to the forest clearing.

'Enough,' said Sister Winifred, standing too. 'Sheriff Birch will hear from me about your distasteful attitude, Oswald, as soon as he returns.'

'Well, don't hold your breath, Sister. He said he'd be back by suppertime, but he's not. And I'm in charge until he does reappear. What more do you expect me to do? I'm assuming we all agree that this needs to be kept as quiet as possible until we know what we're dealing with.'

'In that case, I strongly suggest you go home to your wife rather than returning to the Pickled Eel,' Sister Winifred said.

The serjeant ignored her, turning instead on slightly unsteady feet to Mary. 'Will Arnod come with us in the morning? We'll need more help.'

She nodded. 'I'll let him know as soon as he returns. He can't be too far away now. I sent our stableboy home after he'd fetched you and Brother Caddock, so Arnod can prepare our cart in private. You'll most likely need it to bring the remains back, whoever's they are.'

'Tell him to pack an extra shovel and buckets and whatever else he thinks we'll need,' Oswald said. 'Blankets to cover them maybe. Never done this kind of thing before.'

Brother Caddock stood too, and patted sweat from his pink, ham-like brow with a folded cloth. 'I'll make the necessary arrangements with Brother Godric for the disinterment.'

When they'd all gone, Mary put an arm around Nell's shoulders and walked her up a set of stairs to a guest room. Eben was tucked up in one of the two beds in the chamber, with Phoebe sitting beside him. During the hour or so that Phoebe had been tending Eben, she'd found the time, Nell noticed, to create a web of fine braids of her gleaming blonde hair, and to discard her dirty apron and put on a clean pale blue tunic.

'You must be exhausted, lass,' Mary said. 'Mine and Arnod's room is the last on the right if you need anything. Let's hope we all get some rest, but I doubt it.' She left quickly as she began to cry.

Phoebe stood. 'Well, if you do not need anything else, I'll bid you good night,' she said to Nell.

Not wanting to be left alone, fearing the dreams she was likely to have once she closed her eyes, Nell walked with her to the door. 'Did you know any of the missing girls?'

'All of them, but not well,' Phoebe whispered, so as not to wake Eben. 'I'm friends with Hester Hannigan though, whose twin was the first to disappear last December.'

'And no one has any idea what happened to them?'

'None.' Phoebe yawned, patting her mouth with one hand. Nell got the impression that the yawn was faked.

'Your friend must be in great distress to lose her sister in such mysterious circumstances.' Nell was aware that she was rambling but couldn't bring herself to say good night.

Phoebe did it for her. 'Well, I must get to bed, and so should you. Our chambermaid broke her leg so I must be up early to tend her chores.' And she was out the door before Nell could thank her for looking after Eben.

Nell went to the washstand and wiped the dirt from her face and neck with a warm flannel, grimly aware of how badly her hands and legs were trembling. She didn't want to go back to Shymer Forest, and wished the coming of dawn to be far, far away.

Quickly abandoning any notion of sleeping alone, she climbed in next to Eben, not caring if he awoke to find her snuggled against him. She needed to breathe in his innocence and feel the rise and fall of his chest beneath her hand.

Rain lashed against the window, making Nell glad that she was sleeping indoors for the night. And the mattress and pillow were wonderfully soft.

As she struggled to keep her eyes open, she pondered Phoebe's manner – it had seemed slightly off. Given that her friend's sister could be buried in one of the graves, Nell would have expected her to be subdued or distressed. But the girl was brimming with some other emotion – not excitement or elation, but something close. And unlike her aunt, her eyes were clear, as if she hadn't yet shed a tear.

Chapter Seventeen

A Bleak Morning

Alice clattered up the cellar stairs and dumped a wedge of cheese and a cooked leg of mutton on the kitchen table.

'I barely slept a wink last night,' she whined. 'I cannot bear to think of those poor girls lying dead in their graves … and so close to home.'

Leticia Simms wrapped the meat and cheese in clean cloths and put them into a basket. 'Then stop thinking about them and serve up the porridge. Master Arnod's outside with the sheriff hitching the cart. They'll need to fill their bellies before they head off to Shymer Forest.'

Alice sniffed loudly. 'I won't have a good night's rest until the killer is caught. I could be his next victim.'

Cook sniggered and rolled her eyes. Her teeth were on edge, and she was still cheesed off with her mistress for painstakingly reading out every item on the list of food she wanted prepared, as if speaking to an imbecile who didn't have Master Arnod's best interests at heart.

Alice slammed a porridge bowl onto the table. 'My fear is not cause for mirth.'

'Your fears are fanciful. The killer's victims were young and beautiful.'

'I'm only two years older than Irma Linke was.' Alice ladled porridge into another bowl, missed it and splattered oats over the table. 'And you cannot know what goes on in a madman's mind.'

Cook flung a cloth at Alice. 'Clean that up. And I know more about what goes on in the town than you do.' She tapped the side of her nose.

Alice's small watery eyes glittered with anticipation, and Cook knew that whatever she said next would travel around Bellayne faster than she could crack an egg. *Ah, eggs.* She'd forgotten to hard-boil the eggs on Mary's list.

'Not all are holy at St Clement's. I'd watch your back next time you're kneeling to say your prayers,' she said.

Alice crossed herself three times. 'That's a wicked thing to say.'

Cook spooned cream onto the porridge and arranged the bowls in neat rows at the end of the table. 'The Greenfriars ended my Albert's life because of what he saw.'

'Oh, not that again. You're mad,' Alice snapped. 'Albert's mind had turned to mush – he barely knew what day it was. I've a good mind to tell Brother Caddock about your wicked rumour-mongering.'

Turning her back on Alice, Cook carefully lowered a dozen eggs into a pot of boiling water, and stoked the fire. The remark about Albert's mind would keep until she thought of a suitable punishment.

'I'm not the only one who thinks that something at St Clement's stinks more than the midden. There's truth in those anonymous drawings that are popping up all over town.'

'Poison messages you mean!' Alice beat the side of the porridge pot with a spoon. 'Methinks they're the work of the devil.'

'No one cares what you think.'

'Well, perhaps they should.' Alice placed the spoon on the table and neatened her apron with exaggerated care. 'I find it curious that your dear son painted pictures of both Irma and Maye shortly before they disappeared.'

Cook's heart hammered against her ribs. She tightened her grip on the poker and swivelled around.

Alice's long, angular face was alight with spite. "Tis also strange that Julian spent weeks capturing Miss Phoebe's alleged beauty for his painting of Eve in the church. And now, from her frequent morning retching, she seems to be with child.'

Mary Butterball shook Nell awake. 'Come down when you're ready for a bowl of hot oats,' she said.

Nell lifted her hand from Eben's warm belly and slipped out of the bed. She donned her tunic without bothering to wash her face, which must be shadowed after the terrible night's sleep she'd had, or brush her knotted hair, and picked up her cloak. It was torn and stained after her travels, and looked like something the cat had dragged in.

The smell of porridge and cabbage hung heavily in the service passage, turning her stomach as she made her way to the kitchen. When she entered, Mary put down the knife she was using to slice a fruit loaf and introduced Nell to her husband, Arnod, and to Sheriff Birch.

Both men looked dishevelled and bleary-eyed. They barely acknowledged Nell before returning to shovelling porridge into their mouths and discussing plans for the disinterment of the bodies.

'Do you really think it's them?' Arnod asked Birch.

'I think there's little doubt.'

Arnod dropped his spoon into his bowl and pushed it away. 'God rest their souls. And ours.'

The full force of what Nell had to do today suddenly gripped her. She grabbed the door's iron handle to stop herself fainting and a small cry fell unbidden from her mouth.

Mary immediately walked across the room to embrace her. All the tears Nell hadn't cried over the last month spilled from her eyes.

'We thank you, lass,' said Mary, 'for having the courage to do this terrible thing we ask of you. God bless you. And Eben will be safe here with me until you return.' She turned to the scullery maid. 'Alice, please ask Phoebe to sit with Eben till he wakes. He'll be frightened if he finds himself alone in a strange room.'

'Right,' said Birch, 'it's time we were on the road before the whole town wakes and follows us.'

'I'm ready,' said Nell.

She followed Mary outside to the cart, and climbed up onto its tray. Mary handed her a basket of food to hold while she added a pile of blankets and some other items to the load.

'Oswald will have collected the others from St Clement's by now,' the sheriff said to Arnod. 'We've arranged to meet them at the end of Hitchhorse Road.'

Mary kissed her husband's cheek, and was about to drape his cloak around his shoulders when Alice, her narrow face flushed, ran out of the kitchen.

'Miss Phoebe's not in her room or anywhere in the inn,' she said.

'She must be here somewhere,' said Mary, a touch shortly.

'And her bed hasn't been slept in,' Alice added.

'How can you be –'

Alice hadn't finished. 'And her coat's not on its peg.'

Arnod gazed around the yard with the confused look of a sleepwalker who had no idea of how he came to be there. 'Nay,' he said, shaking his head. 'Not my girl too.'

Nell felt nauseous as she huddled on a pile of blankets in the back of the cart, which Sheriff Birch was driving, and which was rattling and swaying jerkily along the road to Shymer Forest. She swallowed bitter-tasting bile and pressed her hands over her stomach to try and settle it. Arnod Butterball had stayed behind at the Merry Monkey to search for Phoebe.

Nell prayed that Phoebe had returned safely by now from wherever she'd run off to last night. She remembered the excitement in the girl's manner, and her braided hair and fresh clothes, and wondered if she'd gone to meet a beau.

The cart slowed and Birch asked her if this was the track where she'd set up camp the night before. Turning around, Nell recognised the dead tree on the corner of the road and nodded. Birch waited for the cart Serjeant Oswald was driving to catch up to them, then continued on through the woods. Only the hooded heads of the two monks travelling with Oswald were visible to Nell. No one was talking.

Nell draped one of the blankets around her shoulders, hunched her back, tucked her hands between her knees to warm them, and turned her thoughts away from what she was about to face in the clearing just ahead. She wondered how long she would have to stay in Bellayne – how long she *could* stay before the King's soldiers caught up with her. And then there was the terrifying vision she'd seen in the well at Larke-upon-Eel. Was she to be the killer's next victim?

She pulled out from between her breasts the heart-shaped necklace her father had made her from polished pearl shell and held it against her throat. If her father were here, he'd comfort and protect her. He'd make her a warm drink and tell her stories about his childhood – he was the son of a trader and had lived his early years sailing the seas. But he hadn't been around to protect her for a long time now.

Her mother's love had never been strong and constant like her father's, often depending on how well Nell had pleased her. Even when Nell's father was alive and they were a happy family, Pearl had many melancholic days, usually coinciding with the times her husband was overburdened with work on the estate and she had to lift more than a little finger. She'd been created to dream and play, she often told Nell, not to toil her life away. But Pearl, a slender and curvaceous woman with rich brown tresses, had worked hard after Nell's father's death to encourage Master Long to ask for her hand in marriage. Better to be a half-hearted wife than a man's housekeeper, she'd told Nell.

Nell wondered what her own future held. Without Bente's dagger, her hopes of escaping the isle of Squinte had been dashed. She knew in her heart she'd never get another chance to live a life in which she greeted each dawn with joy and a sense of wonder about how the day might unfold. Instead of teaching children to read and to tell their own stories, or tending the wild garden she'd already planted in her imagination, she'd have to hide in some godforsaken hovel in Carrileck and work or steal enough money to pay for her passage to the mainland.

'There were only three graves here last night,' cried Nell, staring at the ground in disbelief. 'I swear it.'

She shuddered as fingers of foreboding tap-tapped their way up her spine. With Phoebe Butterball missing, this fourth grave was an ominous sign.

Sheriff Birch squatted in the mud beside the freshest grave and placed a hand on the newly turned dirt. A light mist swirled around his shoulders. 'It cannot be coincidence.'

'Maybe he killed another to punish us for finding his burial ground,' said one of the monks.

'But how could he have known?' Birch stood and confronted his serjeant. 'You should never have left these graves unguarded, Oswald. And if I find out you spread word of them in the Pickled Eel –'

Oswald cut him off. 'I went straight home – ask my wife. She was none too pleased to see me.'

Nell wondered if any of the folk in the inn's kitchen last night had told others about her discovery of the graves, even though they'd been asked to keep the tidings quiet.

While the men unloaded the carts to begin the grisly task of uncovering the bodies, Nell seated herself on a log at the entrance to the clearing. She couldn't understand how such a terrible place could look so serene. She watched a line of ants carrying off the breadcrumbs she'd dropped on the ground – anything to distract herself from the sound of spades thudding into the earth and the men's soft grunts of exertion. She wondered how Eben was coping without her, and hoped he didn't think she'd abandoned him. As soon as Mary Butterball realised that Phoebe was missing, she had sent the scullery maid to the convent to ask one of the nuns to come and look after Eben until Nell returned from Shymer Forest. Nell had agreed to this arrangement, feeling that she had little choice. She could hardly bring Eben back here to this bleak place.

As she half-heartedly followed the ants' progress, she felt someone's eyes upon her. The hairs on the back of her neck stood up and shivered. It wasn't any of the four men – they were still digging with their backs to her and seemed to have forgotten she was there. She glanced to her right and saw something flutter high up in an imposing oak tree – a flash of white, as sheer as a veil, like the reflection of a face in a cloud. And then it was gone.

Butterflies fluttered in her gut as she recalled what the inn's cook had said about Shymer Forest being haunted. She glanced back up at the treetop to make sure nothing was there watching her. It was a trick of the light, nothing more. She'd let her imagination gallop far away from rational thought.

'Is it Maye Hannigan?' Sheriff Birch's hoarse whisper echoed around the clearing. 'What is your opinion, Brother Godric?'

'Difficult to be sure … she disappeared five months ago,' said the monk. 'We'll know more once we've washed the body, but from what I can see of her clothes and hair, these are most likely the remains of Maye Hannigan. God rest her soul.'

Serjeant Oswald gagged, and stumbled towards the edge of the clearing where he vomited into the undergrowth.

Nell wondered why the men had begun with the oldest grave. Maybe they weren't ready to face the fact that they'd failed to protect another innocent maiden.

Brother Godric nodded at the other monk – a darkly handsome man with high cheekbones and broad strong shoulders – who explained to the sheriff that Maye's sister, Hester, wore a ring identical to the one they could see in the grave.

'This one is tarnished but has the same blue stone. I'd recognise it anywhere.' He bowed his head, unable to go on.

Birch picked up the ring and handed it to the handsome monk. 'Perhaps you should give the ring to Maye's mother, Brother Idris. I believe you had some affection for the girl.'

Idris snatched his hand away, and jigged up and down on his haunches, as if preparing to spring up and lope into the forest.

'I meant no offence,' Birch added. 'I know Maye helped you organise the orphans' Yuletide performances, and I thought it would mean more to her mother if you returned her daughter's ring.'

Idris nodded briefly, and accepted and pocketed the ring. Then he helped Godric secure the blanket around the girl's body with lengths of cord.

Birch wiped his hands on his tunic and strode towards Serjeant Oswald to discuss how to move the body to the carts, which by necessity had been left a little way along the narrow track.

Chapter Eighteen

Shymer Forest

It was just after the ninth hour of the morning when Brother Godric reared back from the third grave and cried out, 'Dear Lord, who could bury a child face down?' He sobbed into his hands. 'Who would want to kill Gracie Alcorn, or any child for that matter?'

No one answered him.

Serjeant Oswald and Birch stopped their work on the fourth grave and laid down their spades. With leaden steps, they joined the two monks to look down upon Gracie's remains. Nell made her way across the boggy ground and stood with them, her hands shaking as she held them over her heart.

A feathery cloud drifted in front of the sun and a lone thrush trilled as Brother Godric wiped soil from one of Gracie's rotting yellow hair ribbons. He signed the cross on her filthy forehead: 'Gracie Alcorn is with the angels now.'

As the men resumed their work and Nell returned to her log, she noticed that the heads of the graves were aligned, almost as if the killer had drawn a straight line in the dirt from each murdered lass to the next, and were evenly spaced and facing away from Bellayne.

~

'It's Phoebe Butterball.'

Brother Godric's voice startled Nell. She walked across the clearing and watched as the four men lifted Phoebe out of the knee-deep grave and placed her gently on the ground.

Sheriff Birch looked close to collapse as he planted his hands on his knees and repeatedly forced the breath out of his lungs. He had a scratch, quite a deep one, on the side of his face just in front of his left ear, Nell noticed. It looked fresh, not yet scabbed over.

Brother Godric removed the sackcloth still covering the lower half of Phoebe's body, while Brother Idris brushed dirt from her face and neck with gentle, rhythmic strokes. Her killer, noticed Nell, had placed bluebells, now wilted, in her petite hands.

'Fingermarks upon her neck,' said Idris. 'And thumbprints on her throat. Methinks her killer was facing her.'

Godric nodded in agreement.

Crouching, Sheriff Birch inspected the bruising on the girl's neck. Bowing his head, he shaded his eyes with one hand for a moment, then rose and faced his serjeant. 'You should never have left the graves unguarded.'

Oswald spat on the ground. 'You cannot lay Phoebe's death at my door. Our finding of the graves is not going to stop the killer. He'll just dump them somewhere else. And if you'd not deserted the townsfolk to protect *your* family –'

'I had no choice but to take my wife and daughters to safety,' Birch said. 'Lex Alcorn threatened to make me suffer as much as he is suffering the loss of Gracie.'

'Archstone isn't so far,' said Oswald. 'You should've been home by suppertime, and yet you didn't receive the message I left for you at the castle until two hours before dawn. What delayed you?'

Birch's voice cracked. 'I left Archstone much later than intended, then fell asleep in a barn while sheltering from the storm.'

'Phoebe was still alive then, well, just before the storm reached us,' said Nell, surprised to hear she'd spoken aloud. 'She helped

care for Eben. After everyone went to bed, she went out, I think –
perhaps to a tryst. She'd changed into pretty clothes and braided her
hair. I fell asleep and did not hear her leave … or return.'

A trembling sensation rippled out from her heart and down her
limbs as she wondered if the killer had struck again because she'd
told the serjeant and others about the graves last night. If she'd
waited until morning, would Phoebe still be alive?

Jutting his chin forward aggressively, Oswald jeered at Birch. 'So
while you slept like a babe in a barn –'

Before he could finish his accusation, Birch bellowed, sprang
forward and knocked the serjeant to the ground.

Ignoring the commotion, Brother Godric moistened his finger
and rubbed at a dark smear on Phoebe's ankle. He sniffed the sticky
black mess on his fingertips and frowned, then ordered Idris to hold
up a blanket as a screen. He lifted her sodden skirt and, after a brief
examination, tucked the skirt back around the girl's lower legs.

'There is blood staining her thighs and clots in her undergarments,'
he said. 'Too much, I think, for it to be just part of her monthly flow.
A miscarriage, perhaps. I will need to examine her more …'

'Phoebe was with child?' cried Birch. 'Jesus, no!'

'I lost my baby because I sinned,' said Phoebe. She clutched her head
and a deep, heart-wrenching moan shook her body.

She was sitting with Maye and Gracie, who were trying to
comfort her. Irma was busy watching what was going on in the
clearing.

The girl who had found their three graves, Nell, looked as worn
out and broken as Irma herself felt. Her aura was thin and clung
tightly to her body, its dull colours churning like storm clouds. Irma
had to give her credit, though, for sticking around while their bodies
were disinterred. Most young women would have turned tail and run
from the foulness, the stench, the bleak reality of what folk could
do to one another.

Nell looked up then, for the third time this morning, her tired amber eyes staring right at Irma. Her lips parted slightly and Irma could see the rise and fall of her chest quicken, as if she'd sensed someone watching her.

'Your baby is waiting for you in the heavens,' Gracie told Phoebe, but she sounded tired and unsure. 'We could give her a name, if you like.'

Phoebe shook her head. 'I cannot go up there, not after what I've done.' She began to wail.

'The boy and the young woman will answer our call for help, though neither of them knows it yet,' said Gracie in the calm, oddly mature voice she used when relaying messages from above.

Irma knew better now than to criticise the cryptic and mostly useless celestial tidings Gracie passed on to them, but she could still fume and shriek with frustration on the inside. How could a wee lad help them? He wasn't even here with Nell and the four men.

A haunting whistled tune caught Irma's attention. She turned away from the clearing and the other murdered girls, and crawled along a lichen-covered bough to the other side of her oak tree, from where she could look down at the Shadowfolk gathered below. They were no longer misty, grey apparitions – she could see a young monk with scarred wrists, a soldier with a rusted sword, a scrawny woman with seven woebegone children huddled around her. She was horrified to see so many children among the Shadowfolk; it confirmed for her that Gracie wasn't going to get a faerie-tale ending just because she was a girl of eleven years.

One of the children, a boy of about twelve, stepped forward and smiled shyly at Irma. Locks of wispy hair the colour of ashes fluttered about his head, and a tattered tunic hung from his thin, bony shoulders. He held his cupped hands against his lips and whistled again. In her mind, Irma saw the wind sighing over a desolate moor. He opened his hands. A butterfly beat its silvery-grey wings on his palms, then flew up through the branches and hovered close to Irma's face. It seemed to be whispering something important in a tiny, faint voice. She leaned closer, strangely comforted by the ephemeral creature the boy had made for her, but it turned to dust before she could fathom what it was telling her.

She looked down at her hands and discovered that they were even more transparent now that they had been that morning. They were old and worn, like parchment that had been scrubbed clean and reused too many times. She squeezed them together until they hurt. The butterfly's message was obvious now; she just hadn't wanted to hear it. The Shadowfolk were calling her. It was time for her to give up any hope of entering the heavens.

Irma flew down to the ground and held her hand out to the Shadow boy. If it was her destiny to fade away into shadow herself, she wanted it to happen as quickly and quietly as possible. It was the least she could do not to distress the others. She had failed them in many ways; she wouldn't make them endure a tearful farewell.

But the Shadow boy refused to take her hand. He shook his head and pointed into the clearing behind her. To the other girls? Or to the pool of dark, creepy water that had appeared at the base of her oak tree, which Irma feared was a doorway into the nether world?

Staring at the pool, Irma realised that she had created a poisonous barrier around the hollow with her thoughts of vengeance and hatred and her making of otherworldly fire. She could feel its denseness closing around herself and her friends. Their voices were thinner somehow, their thoughts and words more fractured and unwholesome, and it was becoming harder to transmute moonlight into moondew. If Irma left the hollow, hopefully taking that poison with her, she hoped that the celestial messages might become clearer and that her friends would have more vitality to point the townsfolk towards the man who'd killed Gracie because she'd seen something she shouldn't have.

She flew back up to her tree, stood on a branch directly over the pool of inky water, and looked within herself for the courage to end her life. As she stared into the pool, she realised that neither sun nor tree was reflected on its surface. It truly was a doorway into another realm – a dark, dark grave for outcasts and sinners.

Before her courage failed her, Irma dived headfirst from the branch and plummeted towards the water faster than an arrow. She prayed her end would be fast and painless, despite feeling unworthy of such mercy. But she couldn't stop the bloodcurdling scream that flew from her mouth – and came to an abrupt halt a mere inch from the clump of white fragrant ramson flowers growing beside the pool.

Gracie appeared beneath her. Irma looked into the girl's tear-bright eyes and crumpled on the ground, defeated in mind and spirit.

Sacrificing herself should have been easy considering the soul-destroying ache that had replaced many of her fondest memories and she didn't want that same fate to befall Gracie, but still a small part of her hoped to be rescued from this nightmare. She wanted to be safe and warm; not falling and falling through the darkness, or lying alone forever at the bottom of a pit and hearing only the mournful cries of other lost souls.

Gracie helped her to stand. Maye flew across the hollow, rage red-raw upon her face, and shoved Irma hard in the chest. Irma fell to the ground again, shocked by the drastic change in her gentle-hearted friend who had once wanted to become a nun.

'Leave the hollow right fucking now,' commanded Maye. 'Go to the heavens without us. We do not want you here.'

Ignoring Maye's curses, Irma crawled over to Gracie and held her hands. 'Please,' she begged, painfully ashamed of her own cowardice, 'leave while you can still fly.'

Gracie sighed, but didn't pull away. 'Not yet, Irma. There's something else we must do – the four of us – to point Nell and the boy in the right direction.'

Chapter Nineteen

The Mortuary Chapel

Nell sat with Sister Winifred later that day in St Clement's refectory, sipping much-needed herbal tea from delicate mugs. The nun had suggested that Nell should stay in the convent's guesthouse, and Eben was napping by the fireplace on Sister Agnes's lap. He'd taken a shine to her when she'd looked after him while Nell was at Shymer Forest and Mary Butterball was occupied with searching for her niece. Nell wondered how the Butterballs were coping with the terrible news that Phoebe had been found.

Sister Winifred was hastening to finish embroidering bluebells onto a piece of round white cloth. Three other cloths, embroidered with different flowers, lay on the table, ready to take to Brother Godric, who was laying out the bodies of the murdered girls.

'It's good of you to wait another day before introducing Eben to his father,' she said to Nell. 'I get the impression that we've disrupted your plans somewhat.'

'Do not trouble yourself, Sister; you have enough worries. My plans can wait another day.'

Nell tried not to look anxious. With the possibility of the soldiers turning up any day now, she knew it was foolhardy to hang around Bellayne, but she just couldn't bring herself to abandon Eben to strangers, even someone as kind as Sister Agnes. He'd had enough changes in his life of late, and a familiar face, even if only hers, would surely comfort him just a little. She wanted also to tell Jack Lea that Maureen had regretted not bringing Eben to him sooner, and to make sure he knew some of his son's favourite, and not so favourite, things.

Sister Winifred snapped the thread with her teeth, and leaned across the table to push the needle into a spool of thread. Her elbow knocked over her barely touched cup of tea and the yellowish liquid slopped towards the other cloths. She cried out in dismay and lurched from her chair.

Nell snatched the cloths out of the path of the spreading puddle. Collapsing back onto her seat, the nun put her elbows on the table, cradled her forehead with her hands and began to cry.

'There's no harm done,' Nell said, placed the cloths on a dry part of the table.

Dabbing her pointy nose, Sister Winifred shook her head. 'What good are those cloths to the girls now? When each disappeared, I stitched her favourite flower onto one – cowslips for Maye, wood anemones for my dear Irma, celandines for Gracie, and now bluebells for Phoebe. I hoped one day to give them to each girl in person, but my prayers did not save them. And now these useless scraps are a feeble offering to the dead.'

When Sister Winifred had recovered her equilibrium, she asked Nell to go with her to deliver the cloths to the mortuary chapel, where the bodies of the girls were being laid out.

They crossed Monk's Mill Bridge, and followed the towpath to a narrower path that took them through a copse of tall straight beeches and up to the mortuary chapel. Just inside the main door, they stepped around a wooden screen carved with angels and flowering vines, and saw Phoebe Butterball lying in an open coffin upon a bier.

When Sister Winifred stumbled on her way to the coffin, Nell grabbed her arm to steady her. The small, circular chapel was heady with frankincense and Nell was thankful that the other three biers were still unoccupied.

Phoebe's pale gold hair gleamed in the candlelight, and she was wearing an emerald gown with embroidered red and pink roses on its cuffs and bodice. A pink ribbon covered her throat, and she was holding a tiny pair of purple velvet slippers. The toes were scuffed. Had Phoebe worn them when she was a little girl, Nell wondered.

Just beyond Phoebe's head, on an altar, she saw a cloth doll with rosy red cheeks, a lopsided clay mug with embedded fingermarks on the crooked handle, and a homemade book with hand-sketched flowers bordering its wooden cover. Someone had written *Maye* across it in bright blue ink.

If the vision in the well was true and Nell was killed, who would place a keepsake on the altar for her? Except for Eben, every person she'd loved was gone.

And now, in Phoebe's presence, Nell felt ashamed of herself for the many times she'd wished her life away, and for the careless and often heartless way she'd treated other folk. She couldn't *un*-write the sadistic tales William Wilkes had forced her to pen, nor return to grieving parents the silver spoon she'd stolen from them and sold before realising it'd belonged to their dead child. But once Eben was settled, and if she managed to leave Bellayne alive, she'd return to Stonhard and try to coax Emily away from the Boar's Den before someone battered her to death.

She'd never forgiven herself for not warning Emily that Wilkes had discovered where she was hiding; and could only admit now that she'd also lied to herself about why she hadn't made the effort. She'd told herself that she'd been too ill to make the journey in the rain and cold, but she'd almost recovered from the fever and cough she'd had for three weeks. The truth was: if she had warned Emily, Wilkes would have discovered her deceit in next to no time, which meant she'd have been unable to return to the Boar's Den herself.

And she hadn't been ready to face being all alone in the world, not then. Her cowardice, which included hiding the truth from Emily, had haunted her ever since; and the guilt intensified each time she'd looked at Emily's poor scarred face.

Returning to help Emily now wouldn't be an entirely selfless act – Nell was still frightened to walk alone into the unknown – and wouldn't magically dissolve the guilt she felt, but having a heartfelt purpose lifted her spirits a little and gave meaning to a life that had felt empty and soulless ever since she'd been accused of murdering Elmer Long and her mother.

Sister Winifred nudged Nell, bringing her back to the present, and asked her to take the embroidered cloths to the Greenfriars in the mortuary, which was in the undercroft of the chapel.

'Just call to them from the stairs,' she said. 'I would like a moment alone with Phoebe.'

Voices drifted up to Nell as she walked down the wide, well-swept staircase. She stopped beneath a flaming torch in a sconce on the wall and decided to wait until they'd finished talking.

One of the voices cried out in distress: '... the little girl ... not him – a devil watching, waiting. I did not see it!'

A louder voice said, '*I* should lead the funeral tomorrow. Look at him – he can barely stand.'

Someone else said, 'For heaven's sake, Brother Caddock, where is your compassion?'

'Oh, God, is it one of us?' another voice cried.

A shadow loomed on the wall below Nell, and before she could announce her presence an old monk with two feather-white clumps of hair above his ears stumbled into view. He was muttering feverishly to himself – 'I did not see it, shame upon me!' – and gave a startled cry when he saw Nell. His foot slipped out from under him and he fell forward.

Hooking her arms around his waist, Nell helped him to stand, and picked up the olive-green rope he'd dropped. But when she held it out to him, she saw his eyes were closed and he was rubbing his temples. His face was extremely pale, almost colourless, and his left eye and cheek drooped a smidgeon towards his chin. His breath smelled old and of sickness, reminding her of Maureen not long before she died.

The Greenfriar opened his eyes, looked at the rope in her hand and said, 'That was found around the little girl's neck.' He stifled a sob. 'Sheriff Birch said we could burn it.'

Someone coughed in the mortuary, startling him. He turned away from her and shambled up the stairs.

The rope's fibres prickled Nell's palm. She flung it over her shoulder so she didn't have to touch it. How could anyone choke a little girl? And why? Gracie Alcorn was much younger than the other three victims.

Nell was dismayed to see that she'd screwed Sister Winifred's cloths into a ball. She smoothed them out and, desperate to leave this sad place, turned to call out to those remaining in the mortuary.

She froze. Standing just two steps down from her was a hooded monk, his face in shadow. Her tongue clacked uselessly against the roof of her mouth when she tried to speak.

The monk slowly turned his head in her direction and an uncomfortable silence thickened between them. After what seemed like a lifetime, his hand snaked towards her and lifted the cord from her shoulder. The back of his hand brushed her face. His fingers were cold.

Nell smothered a gasp when she noticed that the rope, though frayed and discoloured from its time in the ground, was the same as the olive rope belt around the monk's waist. Had one of the Greenfriars killed Gracie Alcorn? Was that what the old man had meant when he'd mentioned a 'devil'?

Something clattered in the undercroft and someone let out a frustrated cry. Nell stepped backwards, up onto the next stair.

The monk shrugged the hood from his head and his charcoal

gaze glittered in the torchlight. She recognised his swarthy face from the clearing earlier: Brother Idris.

He nodded his head towards the old man who had disappeared up the stairs. 'Please excuse Father Emlyn, he's unwell.'

Nell wondered again why the older man was so distressed. Had he seen something in the mortuary that pointed to the identity of the killer? And if so, why didn't he speak out? Was he protecting someone? Or was he afraid?

Chapter Twenty

This Little Piggy

The following morning, Jack Lea rammed a spade into the earth and hurled the load of soil across the field where he was digging a drain that didn't need to be dug this day. But he couldn't sit still, not with the hundreds of thoughts and pictures invading his mind. Irma dead. Murdered. Gone. A cry of rage was lodged firmly in his throat, unable to break free.

Hoof beats startled him. He swung the spade up to his shoulder and spun around, ready to defend himself. But it was Sheriff Birch, not the Alcorns, galloping down the track towards him. When Birch dismounted, they each grasped one of the other's hands and gripped each other's shoulders in a rough embrace.

'Jesus, Jack, I'm so sorry.'

Jack bowed his head. 'I can't believe she's gone.'

They stepped back and discussed the horrors that'd been uncovered in Shymer Forest and the fact that Phoebe Butterball had been strangled and buried beside the other victims the same night as the graves had been discovered.

'Did you see anyone loitering around the Merry Monkey when you made your rounds the night before last?' Birch asked.

'No one other than the Butterballs,' said Jack 'I spoke briefly to

Mary – she came out of the privy just as I arrived to empty it – and I saw Arnod coming down the road when I was leaving.'

'Phoebe had gone up to bed half an hour earlier,' said Birch, 'so it was probably too early to see her. I imagine she would have waited for everyone to be asleep before she snuck out.'

'Jesus, if only Mary had told me about the graves I might've been more vigilant,' Jack said. 'I see now why she seemed out of sorts. It was nothing to do with me arriving at an awkward moment.'

Jack changed the subject before Birch could ask another question. 'The Alcorns will be baying for blood now that Gracie's been found dead. And Dad is still refusing to come to the castle.'

'He gave more short shrift when I tried to convince him to do just that yesterday. He's as stubborn as a mule,' Birch said. 'I'm on my way to see the Alcorns now, but I doubt I'll get through to them either.'

Jack returned to digging as soon as Birch had departed, but his thrusts quickly lost their power when he realised that Irma's grave was probably being dug in the churchyard at this same moment. His shoulders and legs began to shake with grief. He roared his anguish across the field, hurled the spade down the hill, then fell to his knees, hunched over them, and cried for Irma. Eventually, he lay on his back and looked at the sky. He and Irma had liked to tell each other stories using the pictures they could see in the clouds.

Sometime later, Jack wasn't sure how long because he'd dozed off, a shadow fell across his closed eyelids. Intense pain suddenly hit the side of his body, in the soft area just above his right hip. He opened his eyes and saw Lex Alcorn's boot coming for him again. He quickly rolled to the left and scrambled to his feet, but Alcorn tackled him to the ground and wrenched one of Jack's arms behind his back.

'Tie him up,' shouted Lex to the mob of men Jack could see standing at the top of the hill.

∼

Church bells chimed the tenth hour of the morning as Nell skirted the busy marketplace. She was on her way with Eben to visit Jack Lea at his farm, from where it was possible, Sister Winifred had told her, to see Shymer Forest in the distance. Nell imagined it would take some time for Eben's father and grandsire to look upon that view with anything but horror.

Sunlight peeked over the tops of the hills surrounding Bellayne to the south and east like a lopsided horseshoe for the first time that morning, causing the dewy grass to glisten, reminding her of how her room above the stables at the Boar's Den never saw the light of day owing to its westerly outlook and the fact that the neighbouring hovel then blocked its dying rays. It was a beautiful day, one that inspired thoughts of picnics and romance. She hoped that tomorrow, the day of the dead girls' funeral, would be just as fine.

The folk huddled together in small groups on the town green looked pensive and watchful. Nell heard Phoebe Butterball's name uttered a few times as she passed, and some cast curious looks in her direction. She quickened her pace and avoided making eye contact with any of them.

The image of Phoebe being lifted from her grave – her lips a ghastly shade of grey, withered bluebell petals scattered over her lifeless fingers – would never leave her mind. How would Mary and Arnod Butterball bear the pain of losing the child they'd raised as their own? Sister Winifred had told her that the Butterballs had been unable to have children, making the current situation even sadder, if such a thing was possible.

Eben, holding Nell's hand, was completely unaware that he was about to meet his father, even though she'd tried explaining it to him. He twisted around when he heard some boys laughing and said, 'Oink, oink, piggy,' as he watched them chasing a runaway pig from the marketplace. Delighting in Eben's laughter, Nell wondered how she was going to kiss him goodbye without breaking down. Given time, he'd forget all about her, but she'd think of him often, wondering what he looked like with each passing year, what sort of lad he'd grown to be. Once she left the isle – if she ever did – they'd likely not see each other again.

She could scarce believe they were about to be parted – assuming, of course, that Jack Lea accepted that Eben was his child and agreed to keep him. Despite Sister Winifred's assurances that Jack was a good-hearted soul, Nell had known of many 'good men' who'd left their sweethearts once an unwanted bairn was on the way.

As Nell's heart fluttered with sadness, she vowed to make their farewell as short and as painless as possible for Eben's sake. And once she'd left him, she'd collect her things from the convent and get out of Bellayne immediately. Given the perfect weather, she'd make a good start to her long journey back to Stonhard and to Emily.

The runaway pig suddenly barrelled into the back of her knees, knocking her flat on her stomach. Breath exploded painfully from her lungs. The boys thundered past, one stomping carelessly on her outflung hand, which began throbbing immediately. She came to her knees, shaking her dazed head to clear it, and realised that Eben was no longer beside her. He'd joined the chase for the pig, which was now heading for a grove of trees. Even though she was still winded, she scrambled to her feet and ran after him as fast as she could manage.

A large group of men emerged from the grove and marched onto the green shouting, 'Kill the beast, kill the beast. Hang him from the tree.'

At first, Nell thought the men, all wearing identical red neckerchiefs and carrying various farm implements such as hayforks and shovels, were performing a play, but when she spotted folk calling for their children and hastily leaving the green, she wondered if something more serious was happening.

The pig ploughed through the band of men, but the boys didn't follow it. They joined in the chant, punching their fists into the air. 'Kill the beast, kill the beast. Hang him from the tree.'

Eben, lagging behind the boys, came to a standstill and burst into tears.

Nell swooped him up from the ground, making her stomped-on hand throb harder, tucked his head against her shoulder and stroked his back. 'You're safe now.'

The men stopped beneath a huge old elm less than ten paces away from her. A stocky, wild-eyed man strode forth, tugging hard on a rope. She thought he'd leashed the pig, until another man stumbled into sight with the rope pulled tight around his neck. His ankles were bound and he jumped and shuffled as he tried to keep up with his tormentor. The short man jerked the rope and the captive scrabbled at his throat and fell to his knees. Blood seeped from one puffy eye and his split top lip.

'The Red Guards are keeping our town safe,' Nell heard someone behind her say.

'The Red Guards?' someone else asked.

'Lex Alcorn and his boys called a meeting last night.'

'Then blood will be spilled before the day is done. I feel sorry for Lex, losing Gracie like that, but he's lost his marbles.'

Nell turned to leave, but there was nowhere to go. A crowd had formed around her in the blink of an eye: a seething wall of angry faces.

One of the Red Guards steered a horse and cart beneath the elm, while another shinnied up its trunk and threw a rope over an overhanging branch. Their leader – Nell assumed he was Lex Alcorn – and another man, scrawny with a puffed-out chest, hoisted their captive onto the back of the cart. They untied the leash and looped the noose around his neck.

The crowd cheered and jeered.

Alcorn raised his arms and Nell saw sweat stains on his grubby shirt. 'This beast murdered four of our girls. He choked the life from them and threw their bodies in a hole. He used and discarded them like gnawed bones.'

Alcorn whirled around and punched the captive man in the stomach. He slumped forward, struggling for air.

Alcorn spat on the man's head before continuing his accusations. 'On the night young Phoebe Butterball died, this man was seen in the town. He brazenly killed the poor lass *after* the discovery of the graves in Shymer Forest, which is only a stone's throw from his farm. This morning, the sheriff questioned him *again* and let him go – *again*.' Alcorn clutched his matted hair as he paced up and down. 'And he murdered Gracie, my sweet little girl, and buried her face down in the dirt. Now it's time for Jack Lea to pay for his sins.' He stomped his feet and shouted, 'Jack Lea, hang him from the tree!'

The crowd took up the chant. 'Jack Lea, hang him from the tree! Jack Lea …'

Blood roared in Nell's ears. She couldn't believe what she was hearing. Was Eben's father a murderer?

'Jack Lea, hang him from the tree!'

The chant pounded through Nell's head and the crowd pushed forward, closing in on her and Eben. She could feel his tears trickling down her neck; sometimes, when he was really afraid or distressed, he cried silently. She stroked his back, then stood on her toes and bobbed from side to side, looking for an avenue of escape. A scruffy woman chastised her for blocking her view of the makeshift gallows; and a gap-toothed girl sitting atop her father's shoulders kicked her in the ear. Nell retched. The body odour of the aroused mob was sickening.

Jack Lea was still on his knees, hands motionless by his sides. Although he wasn't struggling, Alcorn kept the rope taut around his neck.

What would happen to Eben if his father died?

Alcorn stooped and shouted in Lea's ear, 'Why? Why did you kill my Gracie?'

Jack didn't respond.

'On your feet!' Alcorn yelled, and he and Scrawny each grabbed a hank of their captive's shoulder-length hair and hauled him upright. 'You have but a moment to speak before I whip the horse and pull this cart out from under your arse-stinking body.'

Sweat oozed onto Nell's palms as she pushed Eben's face into her chest, shielding him from what was going on. She'd never forgotten the only hanging she'd ever seen, when she was eleven, and didn't want a similar memory etched into his mind. And his father wouldn't die easily; the drop was too short. His body would writhe and twitch while he slowly choked.

Scrawny tied Jack's hands behind his back, while Alcorn clawed his fingers into his shoulders and shook him back and forth.

'WHY? WHY? WHY?'

The crowd was silent, holding its breath.

Jack opened his eyes. 'I did not –'

Before he could finish, Alcorn punched his fist into the air and signalled to the driver of the cart.

'Five … four … three,' he chanted, and the crowd joined in.

Nell's body shook as if she were in the grip of a fever.

'HOLD!' shouted a voice, and Sheriff Birch rode into view.

Nell let out the breath she'd been holding so tightly.

Birch and three of his men shunted the mob aside with their horses. When they reached the tree, they dismounted and one of them ran to the front of the cart to steady the horse, while another pulled the driver from his seat.

Birch leaped up onto the back of the cart and unsheathed his sword. Crossing his arms over his chest, Scrawny stepped in front of Jack Lea.

Birch raised his sword and swung it in a vicious arc, and Scrawny dived from the cart, letting out a high-pitched yelp as he hit the ground. The sword sliced sideways and severed the rope about a foot above Jack's head.

Pulling a knife from the waistband of his breeches, Alcorn darted forward, wrenched Jack's head back and held its point against his throat.

'This is not justice, Lex. It's murder,' said Birch.

'He killed my Gracie. And you let him go.'

'I questioned Jack this morning to find out whether he saw anyone loitering near the Merry Monkey on the night Phoebe Butterball disappeared. You know very well that he was there collecting nightsoil. Mary was with him the whole time, and Arnod saw him leaving as he arrived home from Stout. Phoebe had just gone to bed not long before Jack arrived. He is not a suspect.'

Alcorn sneered and addressed the crowd. 'I ask you, how can the sheriff be so sure?'

Shouting their opinions, the crowd surged forward. Someone shoved Nell in the back and she stumbled closer to the tree. Eben whimpered. A stench of urine wafted around her. Had people pissed where they stood, she wondered, so they didn't miss a moment of the action?

Standing out of the sheriff's reach, Scrawny hammered the sides of the cart with a lump of wood. 'Can we trust the sheriff?' he yelled.

Birch shouted above the din: 'Jack Lea was with me when Irma Linke and Maye Hannigan disappeared. He is not the killer.' But Nell doubted many could hear him.

Alcorn rolled his bulging eyes heavenward. 'It's fortunate that the sheriff can vouch for his long-time friend. Since the time of Irma's disappearance has never been pinpointed, they must indeed be close to each other's bosom.'

Many stamped their feet. Nell felt their anger pulsing through the ground and up her legs.

Alcorn wrenched Jack's head back again and ran the tip of his knife from one side of his throat to the other. 'If he bleeds, he is guilty!'

Beads of blood oozed from the fine-scored line but Jack didn't flinch or shut his eyes.

'GUILTY!' shouted many in the crowd.

About a dozen men jostled others aside and ran towards the cart. Birch raised his sword, and told his men to strike down anyone who attempted to come closer.

A small woman wearing a black dress and shawl emerged from the crowd and stood next to the cart. The crowd quietened. Nell assumed the woman must be Goodwife Alcorn.

'I do not know if Sheriff Birch speaks true,' she said to Alcorn, 'or if Jack killed our Gracie, but if you cut his throat, you will lose me too.'

Still holding the knife, Alcorn gouged his face with his knuckles and rolled his head like a crazed, tethered bull.

'I felt her, Lex, the other night on the bridge when I wanted to die. Gracie's breath touched my face. I want to lay her to rest tomorrow with a peaceful heart.' And she turned and walked away.

Throwing his head back, Alcorn bellowed, then savagely booted Jack from the cart. With his hands still bound, Jack hit the ground shoulder first and rolled onto his side.

Alcorn flailed his arms at the onlookers and screamed, 'Begone! Begone the lot of you. Leave me be.' He lumbered into the grove of trees, looking like a wounded animal seeking a secluded place to lick its wounds.

With a small knife, Birch cut through the noose and the binding around Jack's wrists and ankles. Jack wiped blood from his throat with his shirt and nodded his thanks. Swords flashing in the sunlight, the sheriff's men formed a protective circle around him while they waited for the disgruntled and disappointed crowd to disperse.

A number of scuffles broke out around Nell, and she heard a well-dressed woman say, 'Well, that was a fucking waste of time.'

The runaway pig emerged from the trees squealing, and trotted at full speed towards the marketplace. Some of the boys resumed their chase, but this time they were brandishing sticks and hurling stones.

Eben lifted his head off Nell's shoulder and oinked; a tentative sound, as if he wasn't quite sure the ogres had gone and it was safe to come out of hiding. He was looking right into her eyes, something he hadn't done since Maureen died.

How, Nell wondered, was she ever going to leave this sweet boy? Perhaps this frightening event was a good excuse to put off their parting for one more day. She could hardly introduce Eben to his father when he was covered in blood; she didn't want their first meeting to be tainted by fear.

Rubbing his throat, Jack stood up and slowly surveyed the crowd. Was he looking for folk he'd once called 'friend'? 'Twas strange, she thought, that father and son were standing within a few feet of each other, yet neither had the slightest inkling they were kin. They both had black hair, fair skin and the same fondness for gnawing on their bottom lip.

Eben tapped Nell's leg and showed her the curly tail he'd made from the scarf he was wearing. He held it against his bottom and squealed like a pig.

She laughed, despite the lingering tension on the green, and the sound caused Jack Lea to look straight at her. Nell saw that his eyes were a deep sea-green, leaving her in no doubt that Maureen had been right about Eben's parentage.

Jack frowned, slowly shook his head and turned away. Even though he'd not spoken, his thoughts were obvious to her. *What sort of mother brings a child to watch a hanging?*

Chapter Twenty-One

The Leas

The bell of St Clement's tolled the tenth hour and the funeral procession left the mortuary chapel and moved along the towpath towards the bridge. A wave of murmurs rippled through the mourners when the sun crested the hills and bathed Holy Apple Row with soft, dappled light.

Nell stood in front of the orchard opposite the churchyard, thinking that the day was too beautiful for a funeral. It was a day for barefoot maidens to dance in a meadow of flowers.

Eben nudged her leg with his shoulder and showed her his blossom-filled hands. 'Put on head,' he said. There was a petal stuck with dribble to his chin.

She nodded, and he stood shakily on his toes and stretched his arms upwards.

When she realised that he meant *her* head, her breath caught in her throat. She kneeled and put her hands on his waist while he sprinkled pink and white petals over her. She was saddened that he'd just begun to warm to her again as she was readying herself to leave him.

As soon as the mourners had filed into the church, she was going to Lea Farm – instead of to the castle to meet with Jack Lea because the sheriff had banned all visitors until after the funeral. She wanted to see where Eben would grow up – assuming that Jack wanted to keep his son – and carry that memory with her on her lonely journey back to Stonhard.

Father Emlyn, swinging a censer, led the coffins over the bridge towards the church. He looked a lot better than when she'd encountered him on the stairs in the mortuary. He was still extremely pale, but his steps were steady and he radiated calm and strength. She could see now why the townsfolk had begged him to stay on to guide and comfort them in their time of need, even though, so Sister Winifred had told her, he'd wanted to step down three or four months ago. If Father Emlyn thought he could still make a difference to the lives of others, Sister Winifred had said, then he'd stay until he dropped from exhaustion.

Nell thought again of the words the monk had muttered, and the olive cord he'd dropped on the stairs – the same cord that had been found around Gracie Alcorn's neck. *A devil watching, waiting. I did not see it!* he'd said. What had he meant?

Just behind Father Emlyn, Nell saw Brother Idris, the exotic-looking monk who had alarmed her on the mortuary stairs. Had he told her to excuse Father Emlyn's behaviour because he was worried that the old man had said something damning?

One by one, the coffins and then the families of the dead passed in front of Nell. The church bell tolled on and on, a dirge that would ring in folks' broken hearts long after the funeral had ended.

Goosebumps prickled Nell's neck and arms as she watched the final coffin disappear through St Clement's doors. There was every chance the girls' killer was standing among the mourners.

Eben jumped over a tussock of grass and followed a blue-winged dragonfly along the stream that flowed through the meadow at the bottom of Lea Hill. 'Birdie, Wee.'

'It's a dragonfly.'

'Birdie.'

'Dragonfly.'

Eben, his brow furrowed with irritation, stopped and shook his finger at Nell. 'Birdie.'

'Watch out, or the birdie might peck off your nose.'

He squealed, held a chubby hand over his nose and resumed his chase while Nell trudged up the track to Cerdic and Jack Lea's home. She was dumbfounded but relieved by Eben's sudden desire to play with her and wondered what had changed in his mind. Perhaps the constant fear she'd felt on their journey to Bellayne had rubbed off on him, adding another worry to his grief. She was still afraid but he seemed calmer now that they were staying at the convent's guest hall.

They rounded an outcrop of boulders and Nell looked up at the Lea's cottage, which was perched on a grassy bank about halfway up an undulating hill, its weathered timber giving off a silvery sheen. A frisson of sadness constricted her throat, as she thought how her own dream of owning a cottage on the mainland was nothing more than a fantasy now and always had been. She doubted that she'd ever escape the isle now. Even if she – and Emily, if she could be persuaded – found a place to hide in the seedy part of some town, they'd be living among the wretched and those who made them so, and would always be looking over their shoulders.

'Birdie gone,' shouted Eben, sounding a little upset. Nell could hear his boots scuffing the lush grass just behind her. At the vegetable patch, not far from the porch stairs, she bent down and wiped her eyes before he caught up with her. She was glad that he'd now grow up far away from the alleys of Stonhard with a family that would love him well. Sister Winifred had assured her of that.

Minty freshness wafted from the garden. Nell plucked a few leaves from one of the plants, rubbed them between her fingers and then closed her eyes as she remembered an afternoon, not long before her mother died, when the two of them had been harvesting herbs and vegetables from Elmer Long's garden. Over the last seven years, Nell had avoided thinking about those special times because she didn't believe she had a right to those memories, not after she'd been told that she was responsible for her mother's death. But this time, the memory refused to fade.

Pearl, her wavy, chestnut hair piled messily on her head, had been wearing her favourite gardening apron, which she'd made from patches of her late husband's clothes. It had two pockets at the front to hold trowel and fork and other odds and ends. While they sat in the shade munching crisp baby carrots, Pearl had twirled Nell's hair around her fingers and asked her to guess what she had in the pocket of her apron. Nell, who'd just spent a tense morning writing poetry while her master tweaked her plaits and sat too close, wasn't in the mood for games. She pretended to sneeze, dislodging her mother's hand from her hair, then smiled and said, 'Something sweet?'

'Mmm ... yes.'

'Something you cooked?'

Pearl had clapped a hand over her mouth and laughed, a slightly hoarse but pleasing sound. 'I hope not. Close your eyes and hold out your hands.' When a rough little tongue nuzzled Nell's palm, she'd opened her eyes and kissed her new ginger kitten.

Instead of smiling or looking pleased at her daughter's joy, however, Pearl had sighed and closed her eyes as if the planning of and giving a gift to Nell had exhausted her. Nell had quickly placed the kitten into the basket of vegetables then encouraged her mother to lie upon the grass while she rubbed her feet.

Nell tossed the mint leaves back onto the Lea's garden and stood, her heart pounding, threatening to break her chest open. She'd just remembered why she'd picked up the knife that'd been used to stab her master. She'd been afraid that he'd sit up, that he'd come back to life and whisper in her ear, that he'd hurt her mother who was lying helpless on the floor. She hadn't wanted to touch the knife at first, to lift it off the chopping board, because it'd been covered in blood. Her hand had shaken as she gripped its hilt, sending icy ripples up and down her back. She'd backed away from the table then, so she could guard her mother, and had just come to a standstill when she heard voices in the passageway, which, as she'd quickly discovered, belonged to Christiana Long and a Lord Hammerton.

Instead of feeling relieved that the knife had already been covered in blood, Nell felt an emptiness, as if there was a hollow in her heart that could never be filled. Finding out the truth of what had happened that day might help her to see herself in a kinder light, but it was not going to change her life for the better in any way now. Who would believe her?

'Birdie lost,' said Eben, plopping down on the grass with a dejected air.

'You might see it again later.'

'Nuh-uh, gone.'

'I wonder what's up there,' said Nell pointing to the porch, aiming to distract him before he started crying. Walking up the well-worn path in the grass, she saw that the door into the house, flanked by two comfortable looking chairs, had been painted leaf-green, a welcoming colour. They'd almost reached the stairs when she noticed something hanging from the roof beams. It was a noose, charred and still as there was no breeze to move it. After telling Eben to stay where he was, she ran up the four steps and saw a pile of ash and some burnt straw beneath the noose. Fire had licked and blackened some of the floor planks right in front of the door. She ran down the stairs, slung Eben onto her hip and hastened down the hill.

Jack Lea heard the muffled tolling of St Clement's bell through the castle walls. He lurched off the comfortless bed and paced around the cell. He was trapped down here while the townsfolk followed Irma's coffin on its final journey to the churchyard. He wanted to be out there with her.

Birch had locked him up for his own safety, he'd told Jack, and then refused to let him out for the funeral because he was worried that Lex Alcorn and his cronies would cause trouble if they saw him near the church. Or that Jack might pay the Alcorns back for what he suspected they'd done to his father, Cerdic.

Irma, eight years old, giggling when Jack stumbled while carrying a barrel of nightsoil.

And again, several years later, pelting him with lumps of cold porridge when he refused to dress in wig and kirtle to play the Crone at a midsummer festival.

Jack gripped the cell bars until his knuckles burned and pressed his forehead hard against the cold iron. How long was Birch going to keep him locked up? Until the killer was found?

There wasn't much hope of that happening anytime soon, considering the sheriff and his men had found not one clue in five months. Lex Alcorn and his Red Guards would soon be dragging other innocent people from their beds and swinging them from the nearest tree. Fear was eating the town alive while Birch twiddled his thumbs.

He slammed the heels of his palms against the bars, and immediately regretted it. Pain shot up through his wrists and jarred his already aching shoulders.

Irma crying on his shoulder when she caught her first love – a pimply but cocksure lad – canoodling with Posey Browne at Maiden's Well.

Irma all grown-up, eating chestnuts on the porch, slipping her hand into his for the first time.

Irma ... lonely and cold in her grave.

With an anguished cry, Jack spun around and booted a small table across the cell. Bread, cheese and ale splattered on the floor and back wall.

Nell walked down the dungeon steps through a fug of musty air and stood in the narrow passage that ran along the front of two adjoining cells. Light shone through a slitted window at the top of the stairs but did little to penetrate the gloom.

The first cell was empty, but a torch burned on the wall outside the next one. Taking a deep breath, she hitched Eben high on her hip. He was about to meet his father.

The rumpled bed in the second cell was empty, but when she squinted into the darkness, past a table lying on its side, she could just make out a hunched figure sitting on the floor in the back corner.

'Jack Lea?' she asked, wanting to make sure.

He stretched out his legs and crossed his ankles. The toe of one boot flicked from side to side like a cross cat's tail.

'I saw you yesterday on the village green,' he said, his voice hoarse. 'Standing front row at the gallows, having a merry old time.'

'I wasn't having a merry old time. I was looking for you,' Nell said.

The boot toe stilled. 'For me? Why?'

'I bear a message from Maureen, your former betrothed.'

'Maureen? I've not heard from her for more than three years.'

'She sent you two letters with a messenger.'

'They never reached me.'

Nell put Eben on the ground and handed him Sylvan Jimm's red ball to play with. Eben rolled it towards the stairs and scampered after it, and Nell took Maureen's letter out of her bag.

'Here, read this,' she said, passing it through the bars.

'I thank you for bringing him home,' said Jack a few minutes later. By the hitch in his voice, Nell could tell he'd been crying.

She walked back to his cell and leaned against the wall opposite. He was sitting on a stool close to the bars now, his forearms resting on his splayed knees. His left eye was puffy and black, and there were bruises and an angry red welt across his throat. He'd washed and changed into clean breeches and a dark green undershirt since yesterday, but his shoulder-length hair was dishevelled.

'You look like someone threw you into a pit full of grumpy badgers,' she said.

'I want to see him up close – my son – but I'm afraid of scaring him.' He scratched his black-stubbled jaw and sucked in a jerky breath. 'Was Maureen sure …?'

'Not at first, but the older he got the more she could see you in him. But it's something you're going to have to judge for yourself.'

He nodded thoughtfully. 'Did she suffer?'

'Her life in Stonhard wasn't easy, but she died knowing that you and Eben would be together … if that's what you want.'

'I was angry and upset when she left me, but I never wished her ill.' He dug his fingers into his thighs and groaned. 'Ah, God, I would have helped her. Why did she not come back to Bellayne?'

'Shame. Guilt. I cannot say for sure. Perhaps she was punishing herself. On the night she died though, she was desperate to make things right.'

'Then I'm glad she had a kind and faithful friend to bring our boy home.'

Nell pressed her lips together and tried not to cry. 'I am neither kind nor good. And I needed quite a few jabs with a pointy stick along the way to fulfil the promise I made her.'

Silence stretched between them.

'And yet here you are,' he said.

Along the passage, just out of his father's line of sight, Eben kicked the ball and sang a few lines that he'd plucked from two or three songs Maureen used to sing.

Jack pressed the side of his face against the bars, trying to get a glimpse of his son. 'I want to rip these bars apart and wrap my arms around him, but Sheriff Birch is refusing to let me out.' Though he kept his voice low, probably so he didn't frighten Eben, Nell could hear both his longing and his anger. 'The Red Guards attacked my father last night. They strung up a straw man on our porch and then set it and the porch alight.'

Nell was about to confess that she'd seen that for herself, but he spoke first. 'My father was jolted awake by the smell of smoke. He grabbed a pail of water and limped to put out the flames. He has a dicky hip and usually uses a walking cane.' He bowed his head and clenched his fists. 'Once the fire was out, he decided to make sure our animals were safe in the barn. He slipped down the stairs and broke his leg.'

'Shit!' said Nell, who'd not yet heard about Cerdic Lea's injury.

'He's at the infirmary. Brother Godric said he will mend in time.'

'The Red Guards have gathered outside the castle walls. They're demanding that the sheriff avenges the dead girls. Other folk, those who aren't so sure of your guilt, are vowing to tear the town apart to find the killer. I don't think you'll be going home anytime soon,' she said.

Eben kicked the ball a little too hard and it rolled beneath the cell bars. Jack stopped it with his foot, then rolled it back into the passage. Eben shuffled over to the bars, keeping his gaze on the stranger, and picked the ball up.

'I can see he is mine,' Jack said. 'He has the Lea eyes – green as our meadows, my mother used to say. She'd have loved to meet him. We lost her last year.'

He suddenly stood and paced back and forth along the front of the cell, inadvertently frightening Eben, who darted behind Nell and hid his face in her skirts.

'Eben cannot stay here,' he said, 'even if Birch honours his promise to release me from this cell so I can sleep upstairs tonight. It's not safe. Lex Alcorn could have friends within the castle who might harm me – or my kin. We need to keep Eben's identity secret for now, just in case. It's best if he stays with you at the convent, or with Sister Winifred if you need to head back to your family.'

'I'll stay and keep Eben safe,' said Nell, horrified by the idea that someone might harm Eben to get back at his father.

She would prefer to stay longer, until Eben stopped seeing his father as a stranger, but that might not be possible. She remembered what the Crows had said to her: *The end is not the end, you must look beyond.* Were the words prophetic? Did they mean that she should stay in Bellayne until Eben was settled into his new life?

She became aware that Jack was watching her, waiting for her to speak. She knew she had an unusual way of screwing up her face when deep in thought.

'The sheriff should arrange a meeting between Lex Alcorn and yourself to discuss why he still thinks you're guilty of killing his daughter,' she said, changing the subject. 'Yesterday on the green, I heard the sheriff vouch for your whereabouts when two of the girls disappeared. Surely if –'

'He lied.'

'What?'

He gripped the bars and looked her in the eye. 'I was not with Birch when Maye and Irma disappeared.'

'Why did he lie?'

'I know not. Mayhap it was all he could think of on the spur of the moment. I'm vexed with Birch right now, but he did save my life.'

'By saving you, the sheriff has also protected himself,' Nell said thoughtfully. 'If he claims you were together when two of the girls disappeared, he cannot be accused of being somewhere else.'

'Nay.' Jack shook his head and pushed his long, slightly hooked nose between the bars. 'Birch has four daughters – and he's like kin to me. You're wrong. He has ill-used me today, but I cannot believe he's a killer.'

'But someone you know is.'

Chapter Twenty-Two

St Clement's

In the hollow, Glynn, the Shadow boy, was telling Irma the story of his life. She no longer had the strength to fly up to her sanctuary, so he sat with her on the ground beneath the huge oak. He, his mother and his six siblings had died of starvation one long harsh winter more than a hundred years ago, and had been trapped here ever since. Their mother, who'd had a fondness for ale and abusive men when she was alive, had been unable to face the fact that she had neglected her children so terribly, and had steadfastly refused to acknowledge the gilded doorway when it appeared to them. She had taught her children to hide even from the moon's gentle light, and by the time she realised her folly, it was too late. They had lost all connection to the heavens.

'But you and your friends have given us hope,' Glynn told Irma.

Gracie stood, catching Irma's attention, and stared intently at the sky. 'We must go to Bellayne,' she announced after a few minutes of listening for whispers from the heavens. 'The four of us.'

'Irma's not going anywhere near my sister,' shouted Maye. 'And besides, she's useless and can barely fly.'

'We must help her then,' Gracie said.

Irma was saddened to hear Maye speak of her with such a

contemptuous tone and wished she could find a way to mend the rift between them. She was more concerned, though, by the look on Gracie's face; the girl look troubled. What did the angels want the four of them to do?

Grateful to reach the shelter of St Clements' porch untouched by the countless sticks that were flying through the air like deadly arrows, Nell shook leaves from her hair and brushed them from hers and Eben's cloaks. While she'd been looking for Sister Winifred to ask if she could stay at the convent longer, she'd heard that Father Emlyn had decided to give an impromptu afternoon blessing, which wasn't due to start for another half hour.

Wind gusted through the doorway, chilling her, and the dim light, owing to the presence of tumultuous, grey clouds, further darkened her mood. She was upset that the Leas had become targets for the townsfolk's rage and that it was too dangerous for Eben to settle into his new home.

A willowy man in his late twenties was peering into a waist-high urn on the left side of the chapel. He almost jumped out of his skin when he caught sight of Nell, as if he'd been caught doing something he shouldn't. He scratched the back of his neck with the scroll he was holding, then with a swish of his peacock blue cape he hurried over to a row of paint pots arranged in descending height against the wall beneath an astonishing, not yet completed mural. Nell recognised its scenes as the Garden of Eden, and the birth of Jesus in the stable.

No one else appeared to be in the church, including Sister Winifred, so Nell stepped closer, drawn by the most beautiful Mother Mary she'd ever seen. She looked as if she was made of flesh and blood rather than brushstrokes and paint. There was a subtle hint of mirth in her serene countenance and Nell wondered what had amused her. She touched Mary's hands, which were cupped one inside the other, and noticed a large smudge of grime on the paintwork right where her fingers rested.

'Many touch my Mary to see if she's warm and living,' said the man in the blue cape. 'It's also said that if you gaze into her eyes, you can feel her hands cup your heart. Folk come from across the seas to see her.'

Eben *baa*-ed and kicked his legs against Nell's thighs when he saw a sheep among the many animals in the foreground. She put him down so he could look more closely.

A little girl, a year or so older than Eben, with tangled light brown hair stepped out from behind one of the pillars, next to where the man was now inspecting brushes and mixing paint. Over her dress she wore a blue tabard emblazoned with an 'S' and a pear tree, and a wooden sword in a scabbard was attached to her belt.

She took Eben's hand and pointed to some smudges of white paint along the bottom of the wall. 'Angel footsteps,' she said.

Eben's eyes lit up, though he probably had no idea what an angel was, Nell thought. He was just grateful to have another child to play with. He crouched next to the paint smudges and touched them with a finger.

The man introduced himself to Nell. 'Julian Simms and my daughter, Fleur.'

When Nell commented on his surname, he added that he was the son of Cook Simms, whom Nell had met at the Merry Monkey. Spots of blue paint speckled his nose, and while his face was clean-shaven he had a peculiar tuft of hair on his chin. It looked as if he'd plucked a piece of cloud from the sky and stuck it there. His eyes roamed unsubtly over her face and body while he preened and pointed out the exquisite detail in his nativity scene.

Tilting her head, she squinted at a camel's hindquarters, wondering if it was a trick of the light or if she could see a man's face within the hair and shading there.

Julian finally noticed that her attention had wandered, and he leaned close and tittered in her ear. 'Sometimes I amuse myself by mocking people who vex me.' He pointed to the camel's backside. 'Meet my father-in-law, Hammond Carpenter.'

Nell was thinking of a suitable response to the odd declaration, when the blood drained from Julian's face. He threw his arms into the air and shouted, 'Nay!', then ran to his daughter, who was standing by the urn he had been lurking at earlier. The girl was about to poke a scroll down the urn's narrow neck. Nell saw an open satchel on the ground nearby and a number of scrolls scattered over the floor.

Unaware of her father's panic, Fleur dropped the scroll into the urn and turned to Eben, who had three more balanced on his outstretched forearms. With a garbled cry, Julian snatched the scrolls from Eben, and slapped his daughter's hand. A look of puzzlement crossed her face before she burst into tears.

While Julian calmed his daughter, Nell picked up the scattered scrolls. When she reached for the satchel to return them to it, she saw a beautifully illuminated book cover inside. It was called *Simms's Nymphs of Wood and Sea*.

She wondered why he was so distressed about the scrolls. The children hadn't damaged them, and she was sure it would be possible to fish the lost scroll out of the urn. Using the satchel as cover, she unrolled one of the scrolls a bit – and blanched when she saw the drawing.

She quickly shoved it into the long pocket that rested against her inner thigh just as Simms turned away from his daughter, darted over and snatched the satchel from her. His sleek, beribboned fair hair was now hanging across his face, which had turned cherry-red.

'What seems to be the problem?' asked a male voice from somewhere behind Nell.

Julian tittered and tweaked the tuft of hair on his chin. 'A minor mishap, Brother Caddock, nothing more.'

With hands laced behind his back and stern jaw tilted upwards, Brother Caddock inspected the mural. Nell got the impression that he was scrutinising the extraordinary portraits of Mary and Eve for signs of irreverence.

'Mmm,' he said, turning to face Julian, 'your father-in-law has been enquiring about your progress. I told him that I'm taking a special interest in your work, not to mention your comings and goings.'

Julian's eyelashes fluttered rapidly, giving Nell the impression that he was nervous, and he couldn't hold the monk's gaze. He muttered something about getting back to work and turned away.

Nell couldn't see Sister Winifred yet, so she led Eben to a pew.

Standing at the back of the church, Nell saw Julian Simms's mother, the intimidating cook from the Merry Monkey, having a whispered conversation with none other than Lex Alcorn who'd buried his daughter this morning. He was half-facing her, his hands clamped stiffly to his hips, but then he swivelled abruptly and looked at Nell – or was it Eben he was staring at? She wasn't sure, but either way his glare made the hairs prickle on the nape of her neck.

The four ghosts hovered above their newly dug graves in St Clement's churchyard and listened to the plainsong drifting from the church.

Following Gracie's instructions, they joined hands, felt into the store of moondew within their hearts, and began moving in a slow circle. As Gracie asked Phoebe Butterball to sing, Irma thought she looked nervous and tense. After communing with the heavenly ones, Gracie was usually calmer and less afraid, but that wasn't the case now.

'Why are we here, Gracie?' asked Irma.

'We must lay a pathway of mist.'

'What for?'

'So the little boy can find something important.'

'And what else?'

'Nothing,' said Gracie, not looking any of them in the eye.

'Leave her alone, Irma,' said Maye.

Irma remembered the warning Gracie had given them some

time ago about someone stumbling and disappearing into the mist while on their way to help them. She hoped the little boy wasn't in any danger. She was carrying enough guilt already.

Phoebe butted in; no doubt keen to avoid listening to another argument. 'My mother Medwelyn sang me this song when I was a little girl. I pray that my baby Lillian can hear me sing it to her now.'

She began a cradlesong about a family of swans, her voice as breathy and haunting as the softest melodies from a flute.

As the light quickened and flowed through their hands, the four of them lay belly down upon the air. The pace of their circle increased until they looked like a spinning silver ring.

Instinctively, they released hands at the same time and stretched their arms forward until their fingertips met at the centre of the circle. Tendrils of pure-white mist poured from their fingers and snaked towards the ground.

A wren, the straggler of a flock crossing the churchyard, faltered in its flight as it passed through the ghostly ring. Irma saw its little eyes widen in astonishment before it chirp-chirped and flapped after its kin at a cracking pace. If only they could be as visible to the townsfolk, thought Irma.

The thickening mist swirled around and over wind-pitted headstones and wooden crosses, through the lychgate, along the winding path, and up the porch steps to the church.

Chapter Twenty-Three

Mist

Halfway through the blessing, Eben stamped on Nell's thighs and tried to climb over the back of the pew. She grabbed the ties of his hose and pulled him onto her lap, then kissed his hair – freshly washed and smelling of lemons – and tickled his palm, hoping to distract and calm him. It wasn't long, though, before his body stiffened again. He twisted around and dug his chin into her shoulder.

Nell half-turned to mutter an apology to whomever was behind them, and saw Julian Simms and his daughter. Fleur was fanning her linked hands above her head, perhaps mimicking the wings of a bird or a butterfly. Her fawn-coloured eyes with their long black lashes were mesmerising in her heart-shaped face.

At the altar, Father Emlyn opened a wooden chest about a foot wide and burnished a deep red. 'Inside this blessing box are four scrolls,' he said, 'one for each maiden we laid to rest this morning. Upon them are written the precious memories of their kith and kin. After discussions with their families, we have decided to frame the girls' life stories and hang them in the Lady Chapel with the Virgin Mother. If anyone would like to add a memory before we do that, please see Brother Idris or me.'

As Nell listened to the congregation murmuring to each other, an icy draught hit her ankles and crept under her skirts. Shivering, she looked down and saw wisps of white mist inching across the floor.

'As this is my last blessing,' continued Father Emlyn, 'it is my great honour to perform this final act for the lost maidens.'

Sister Winifred had told Nell that up until six months, when severe headaches and occasional fits began to afflict Father Emlyn, he'd still been hearty for his great age, managing to walk five miles a day and row his boat down the Eel to his favourite fishing spots.

'Age, it seems, has caught up with me over the last few weeks,' Father Emlyn continued. 'It is time for me to stand down and let a younger man nourish your souls. Brothers Caddock and Idris will lead the blessings for the next month, while the brethren and the town's elders decide on my successor. May God's love sustain you all until our new abbot opens the blessing box on the next full moon.'

Brother Idris rose and embraced Father Emlyn as he turned away from the lectern. Keeping one arm around the old man's shoulders, he led him to a pew set along the sanctuary wall with such tenderness that Nell wondered why she'd thought him faintly sinister. Once both monks were seated, Idris wiped his face on the sleeve of his robe, then stared at the floor. Father Emlyn put a comforting hand on his back.

After a few moments of contemplative silence, Brother Caddock stood and signalled to the choir.

Nell bowed her head, trying to enjoy the uplifting harmonies of the plainsong, but the white mist seeped up her nose, coating her tongue with the taste of river mud. It was unlike any mist Nell had seen before; it looked alive, as if it was moving with purpose. Her throat constricted, and an invisible band tightened around her chest. She muttered a hasty amen, grasped Eben's hand and vacated the pew.

The porch, she saw with dismay, was now a sea of billowing fog. Eben leaned forward into it, scooping it up with his hands.

As she braced herself to step into the mist, Julian Simms scooted into the aisle in front of her. He handed her a piece of parchment.

'I must apologise for my odd behaviour earlier,' he said. 'I've had a trying day. Here, I sketched this for you.'

She had to let go of Eben's hand to stop the parchment curling inwards, and was surprised to see a charcoal drawing of her own face. Julian Simms was certainly a talented artist – he'd skilfully captured her likeness in a short time – but perhaps one without scruples, going by the scroll she'd shoved into her pocket.

Nell thanked him and reached down to take Eben's hand. But he was nowhere in sight.

She ran out to the porch and yelled Eben's name, but the fog swallowed her words as soon as they passed her lips. She felt her way carefully down the steps and onto the path, aware that she needed to move faster in case he found his way down to the river at the bottom of the hill.

She stubbed her toe on one of the rocks edging the path. When she crouched down to feel for the cobblestones and get her bearings, she was surprised to see Eben at the end of a white tunnel. The fog seemed to be curling aside to let him pass, as if it was leading him somewhere. Icy shards of fear pricked along her spine.

'Stay where you are,' she shouted.

Eben glanced over his shoulder at her, but instead of stopping, his little legs moved faster.

'Eben, stop!'

He stumbled over a wonky cobblestone and toppled face first towards the ground. The unnatural fog smothered his cry and billowed inwards, preventing her from lunging into the tunnel after him.

With arms stretched forward like a blind woman, she blundered into the mist but couldn't find the spot where he'd fallen. Her teeth chattered with cold as she muttered the same prayer over and over: 'Please do not let him fall into the river.'

After a few panicked moments, her sweeping arms struck the stone wall surrounding the churchyard, which she followed until she reached the lychgate. This, she knew, was the entrance closest to Holy Apple Row. She peered through the shifting gaps the stiff wind made in the fog and finally caught a glimpse of Eben trotting through the maze of headstones. He seemed unhurt from his fall. It was only once she knew he was safe that she realised she'd been sobbing aloud.

Darting through the lychgate, she hurried along a well-worn grass path. Dew dripped from the yew trees and the grass was slippery underfoot. Needing to cut Eben off before he reached the river, she left the path and wove through the jumbled graves.

She'd almost reached the place where their paths would cross when an eerie humming filled her ears. It sounded as if a choir of girls was singing, but their voices were coming from somewhere above her. The effect, when added to the swirling mist, was disorientating.

Eben was only a few feet from her now, but when she tried to intercept him, her legs became cumbersome, as if they were made from wet rags, and her head spun so fast she could have sworn she'd just drunk a jug of elderflower wine. As she stumbled like a sot between two wonky crosses, Eben trotted right past her. Blood trickled from a graze on his cheek, but he seemed quite unworried about being lost in the fog. She called his name but he didn't even look her way. Instead, he glanced up to his right and smiled and nodded, as if someone was talking to him.

Only a border of yews now stood between Eben and the river. Not trusting her wobbly legs to move, Nell flung herself through the air, hoping to latch onto him. But her foot snagged in a hole and she slammed to the ground, winding herself badly. Her elbow struck a decorative iron grave border, causing her to cry out in agony.

When finally she lifted her head and came up onto her knees, she saw that Eben had veered away from the river path and was now standing on one of the graves belonging to the murdered girls, the fourth one along – Phoebe Butterball's. Sister Winifred had told Nell that they'd been buried side by side in the same order they'd been found in Shymer Forest.

Just when Nell thought things couldn't get any stranger, little Fleur Simms ran past her, as light-footed as a fawn, and caught up to Eben. She turned her back to him and placed her hand on the hilt of her wooden sword, as if ready to guard him. Nell was dumbfounded to see her serious expression. What on earth was going on?

Scrambling shakily to her feet, Nell stepped towards the children. The surrounding fog immediately rushed to a point just in front of her and pushed her back. Before she could catch her breath, a girl emerged from the whiteness. She hovered about two feet above the ground, almost transparent, and looked frail, as if one breath could blow her away.

Nell almost fainted with shock. She blinked and shook her head but the apparition didn't disappear. When she looked closer, she saw that the girl's dress had once been white and her hair brown, but now she looked grey, as if she'd walked through a cloud of ash. The two faded yellow ribbons at the ends of her plaits provided the only splash of colour. Nell remembered Brother Godric wiping dirt from the yellow ribbons he'd found in Gracie Alcorn's grave on the day of the disinterment.

Nell was frozen with fear, but one clear thought flitted through her mind. Was she seeing a ghost because she was close to becoming one herself?

The ghost pointed over Nell's shoulder and seemed to be speaking to her, but it was hard to distinguish words amid the loud humming in her ears. Nevertheless, she could tell from the girl's distressed expression that she was trying hard to impart something important. Her look of desperation and determination was so insistent that Nell overcame her own fear and turned around.

She was surprised to see that the mist had cleared from the rest of the churchyard, as if Gracie had breathed it all in to give herself form in the earthly realm. A number of folk were standing just outside the side entrance of St Clement's, which led to the churchyard. Nell reasoned that if she herself was a ghost and able to appear to the living, the first thing she'd do would be to point out her murderer. Was that the message Gracie was trying to impart?

Lex Alcorn broke away from the group and walked down the path towards Nell and the graves, no doubt intending to visit his daughter's final resting place now that it'd been filled in and covered with flowers. Suddenly he shouted and waved his arms in the air. Nell had a terrible feeling that he'd just spotted Eben and Fleur.

When Alcorn picked up a stick at the side of the path and charged towards them, Nell was sure of it. She tried to rush forward to stop him, but found she couldn't move.

Julian Simms suddenly sprinted out of the church and weaved erratically through the crowd, no doubt looking for Fleur. In his blue cape he looked like a peacock gone mad, Nell thought. After speaking briefly with his mother, he darted down the path towards the river. Cook Simms hurried after him, her fat arms pumping back and forth.

Alcorn's angry cries attracted the attention of Sheriff Birch, who took off after him, the hem of his cloak knocking heads off dandelions as he ran. He was followed by Brothers Caddock and Idris, their sandals making a slapping sound on the grass. Something about this strange procession made Nell think of tiny birds being blown by a wilful wind into a thicket of brambles.

She imagined that Eben must be terrified by seeing so many grown-ups charging towards him. She forced her eyelids closed and felt into her numb limbs, trying to break the spell Gracie had cast. It was her desperate urge to see if the sheriff had stopped Alcorn before he reached Eben that finally enabled her to turn around so she could look beyond the ghost, though she was still stuck to the spot.

Fleur had drawn her wooden sword and was standing between Eben and Alcorn, who was almost upon them.

He shouted, 'Get away from there, you fucking brats.'

Fleur bent her knees slightly, wrapped both hands around the hilt of the sword and swung it up towards her left shoulder. She was ready for battle.

Eben, on the other hand, had his back to Alcorn and seemed oblivious to what was coming his way. His head was tilted to one side, as if listening intently to something, and he was holding his cupped hands in front of him.

Julian Simms left the path, hurdled a grave or two and overtook Alcorn by a whisker. Just as he was about to reach his daughter though, he tripped on a tussock of grass and sprawled face down upon the grave beside the one Eben was standing on. Disturbed petals from the many garlands of flowers adorning the grave, wafted in the air before settling on Gracie's resting place.

Alcorn came to a standstill, stunned, then let out an anguished roar. He kicked Julian in the hip and pushed his face into the dirt with the heel of his boot.

Cook Simms, panting heavily, came to her son's aid. Grabbing a hank of Alcorn's hair, she tried to pull him off her son, who was pleading for mercy and spitting dirt.

Mary and Arnod Butterball from the Merry Monkey, both carrying flowers, appeared from the opposite direction. When Arnod saw what was going on, he thrust his flowers at Mary and raced over to stop his cook from pounding Alcorn on the back as if she was tenderising a lump of tough beef.

Mary backed away slowly, as if she couldn't comprehend what was happening in the place where her niece now lay, and found refuge on a bench seat. The flowers fell to the ground, and Nell could see the woman's hands shaking as she pressed them over her mouth.

Sheriff Birch twisted Alcorn's arm behind his back and hauled him upright by the scruff of his coat, away from Julian. Brother Idris lifted Fleur out of harm's way, while Brother Caddock yelled something about the desecration of the churchyard.

Eben was still gazing steadfastly at his cupped hands. He appeared to be in some sort of trance, unaware of the commotion around him.

After a brief scuffle with the sheriff, Alcorn held his arms up in a gesture of surrender. As soon as Birch let him go, he stumbled to the end of his daughter's grave, crouched and buried his face in his hands.

In that moment, the sun suddenly shone fiercely through the clouds, brighter than a flash of lightning, to illuminate Eben's hands. He dropped to his knees and stretched his arms forward, and it seemed to Nell as if the clouds and the ground pressed closer to each other, as if condensing the folly of man into a tight ball, one that it would be easy to squash flat or throw away. She was unable to breath for a moment, as if the strange motion of the world had stopped time altogether.

Against a backdrop of legs and gesticulating arms, she saw something catch the light as it fell into Eben's open hands. The fact that he'd been standing on the same spot for at least five minutes suggested to her that he'd been waiting for whatever it was he was now holding so carefully against his chest. How was that possible?

Gracie was still barring Nell's way. The girl's form had faded considerably during the last few moments, and her hands now clawed the air in front of her, as if trying desperately to hold on to the earthly realm.

She disappeared, taking the mist with her. Finally released from the ghost's spell, Nell's legs buckled and she fell onto her back.

She quickly rolled onto her stomach, now facing St Clement's, and stood, eager to get to Eben. And then she saw why Gracie had been trying so desperately to stay in this world. Meryl Alcorn was lying on the damp ground at the bottom of the steps at the church's side entrance. Father Emlyn had removed Meryl's boot and was inspecting her ankle, while Sister Winifred rubbed her back and helped her to sit up.

Nell pushed her way through the crowd around the graves, and grabbed hold of Eben. A frayed leather lace was dangling from his fisted hand. When he opened it to show her, Nell saw a crescent moon made from shell tied to the lace.

Irma Linke slid off Phoebe's back and collapsed against the trunk of the oak the moment they landed back in the hollow. She could barely breathe and felt as if she'd never have the strength to move again. But it was Gracie's appearance that scared her the most. Her face was the colour of old cobwebs and Irma was sure she could see through Gracie's form to the ferns behind her. She was afraid that Gracie had drained her store of moondew doing what the angels had asked of her, and would be too weak now to replenish it.

'Nell could not hear me,' Gracie cried as Maye sat her on the ground among the bluebells. Her hands fluttered weakly against her chest as she looked at her friends. 'I tried to make myself brighter, but passing through the veil made me so tired. I could not stay there for long enough to do any good. I'm sorry.'

Maye held her as she wept.

Aware that they'd probably never get another chance to lead the townsfolk to the truth, not now that they'd exhausted themselves, Irma stuffed down the anger and curses threatening to erupt heavenward, and turned to Phoebe.

'How did you make your necklace fall into the boy's hands?'

Phoebe shook her head. 'I didn't. I just did what Gracie told me to and led him to my grave. It happened when the flash of light pierced the clouds.'

Irma wondered if the angels had finally lent them a helping hand and if it would help the townsfolk to solve the murders before Gracie faded forever.

Chapter Twenty-Four

A Thorn and a Rose

'Where did Eben get that?' asked Sister Winifred as she and Nell sat on a seat in the Garden of Tranquillity. She indicated the necklace that Eben was swinging back and forth as he stalked a sparrow along the path.

'Someone dropped it during the scuffle in the churchyard,' said Nell. 'I saw him catch it.' As she breathed in the lavender-scented air, she could scarcely believe that less than half an hour earlier she'd experienced one of the eeriest moments of her life.

Sister Winifred walked over to Eben and bent down so she was at eye level with him. She said something that Nell couldn't hear, and he placed the necklace into her outstretched hand. He then pointed at the clouds and said, 'Girl fwy sky.'

The nun took a sharp, shocked breath. 'What?'

Nell pretended not to hear. She wanted to think more about what she'd experienced in the churchyard before sharing the strange tale. She was finding it hard to believe that she'd seen a ghost and that it had tried to communicate with her.

Sister Winifred sat beside Nell again. 'This necklace belonged to Phoebe Butterball,' she said, her voice shaking. 'Her mother, Medwelyn, had two crescent moons fashioned from pearl shell when

Phoebe was born, each one engraved with a four-pointed star. She wore one, and gave the other to Phoebe once she was old enough to look after it. Phoebe never took it off. She always wore it, even to bed. But when Mary asked Brother Idris to remove the necklace from Phoebe's body so she could return it to Medwelyn, he could not find it.'

Sister Winifred inspected Phoebe's necklace. The crescent of pearl shell had been polished clean by Eben's fingers, but the ends of the brown lace it dangled from were frayed.

'It looks as if it was torn from her neck during her last struggle,' she said.

Nell couldn't help touching her own throat. 'Do you think that Phoebe's killer kept it for himself?'

'It's possible. How else could it have ended up in the churchyard?'

A disturbing thought popped into Nell's mind. If the ghost of one of the other murdered girls had led Eben to the place where the necklace could fall into his hands while Gracie was preventing Nell from moving towards him, did that also mean she had lured him to find the graves in Shymer Forest? But why choose Eben? Was it because he was young enough not to question what he was seeing? Would any child have sufficed or had she chosen him specifically?

And had the ghost Eben saw managed to bring the person who had dropped the necklace to the churchyard as well?

'But that would mean that one of –' Nell began, then stopped as the full significance hit her.

Once they had stopped reeling from the implications of Eben's find, Sister Winifred asked Nell to name all those who had been present near the graves when Phoebe's necklace fell into Eben's hands.

Nell counted each name off on her fingers. 'Brother Idris, Brother Caddock, Sheriff Birch, Arnod Butterball, Cook Simms and her son, Julian. When Eben caught the necklace, Lex Alcorn was crouched at the far end of his daughter's grave. He was too far away.

'And Arnod was on the mainland when Irma disappeared,' Sister Winifred said. 'He went with his brother-in-law to look for Phoebe's mother, Medwelyn. They haven't heard from her in nearly two years and Phoebe was beside herself with worry. Arnod was gone for at least a month.'

Arnod and his wife Mary, Nell recalled, had come towards the graves along the lychgate path, not the one leading from the church. They hadn't been standing among the folk milling about outside the church when Gracie was pointing that way. But the other five had. Nell had seen each of them begin their pursuit of Lex Alcorn from there.

'So, five people who could have dropped the necklace,' Nell said, hoping she wasn't leading anyone astray with her reasoning, but it was impossible to ignore what she imagined Gracie had been trying to tell her, especially if it gave those investigating the murders the only clue found so far.

'I must hand it over to Sheriff Birch immediately,' Sister Winifred said, gazing pensively off into the distance. Nell assumed the nun was concerned because two Greenfriars had been present at Phoebe Butterball's grave.

Nell was more concerned about the nun giving the necklace to Birch. 'Are you sure, given that he could have dropped it himself?' *And torn it from Phoebe's throat.*

'What choice do I have?'

Nell shut her mouth, remembering what Jack had told her about Birch lying to give him an alibi, but at the same time also giving himself one for the time of Irma's and Maye's disappearances. If her were the killer, then that would explain why no progress had been made on the investigation.

As Sister Winifred hurried away, Nell wondered if the list of suspects could be shortened by finding out where each of the five were the night Phoebe died. After hearing that the burial ground had been discovered, the killer had acted fast and perhaps carelessly. He

– or she – would have needed a couple of hours at least to strangle Phoebe and bury her in Shymer Forest.

She looked around for Eben. He had trampled some of the garden bed in his pursuit of the sparrow, and was just about to chomp on a yellow flower. She snatched it out of his hand and picked him up, ignoring his protests. He needed a good wash and something to eat before visiting his father later.

On her way back to the convent, she passed the Alcorns. Meryl, her left ankle bandaged, was sitting side-saddle on a brown horse, which her husband was leading. When Nell was almost level with them, Alcorn lifted his head and his gaze went directly to Eben. She saw his hands tighten on the reins before he angled his head and spat on the ground.

Nell picked up her pace, and only glanced back when she arrived at the beginning of the path through the orchard. Lex Alcorn was standing in the middle of the road, watching her retreat.

As Nell washed Eben's hands and face, she wished she could talk to him about what they'd experienced in the churchyard earlier.

Had she really seen Gracie Alcorn's ghost? If so, she should be overjoyed to discover that folk lived on after death – but Gracie hadn't looked like she was blossoming in the afterlife. The desperation she'd seen pouring from the girl's eyes would haunt Nell for a long, long time.

She shivered, as if someone had run sly fingers down her back, remembering the moment when that blinding light had pierced the clouds to shine upon Eben's hands, and the way the sky had seemed to press against the earth, stopping time altogether. Was Gracie's ghost responsible for creating that phenomenon? Or had something greater set it in motion – the hand of God, perhaps?

After attending the women's gathering with Poppy and Flannery Goodfield, Nell had been hopeful that the unseen force they had talked about was benevolent. Poppy had told her that the experience

of feeling heaven on earth gave her comfort and guidance, but that
didn't fit with what Nell had seen in Gracie. What sort of God would
leave a murdered child crying near her own grave?

Tears rushed into Nell's eyes. She swallowed hard, not wanting
to upset Eben, and began to sing to him as a way of comforting
herself.

> '"*Touch me with your finger,*" *said the mother to her little boy,*
> "*It's a joy for me to watch you grow.*
> *And today, I saw you*
> *Smile at a frog,*
> *Jump in a puddle*
> *And put on your own pants.*
> *Until we meet again,*
> *Remember the ways I loved you.*"

Eben looked at her quizzically and said, 'Not night, Wee. No
stars.'

'The stars still shine even when we can't see them,' she said,
hoping it was true.

He screwed up his face and looked at the ceiling as if trying to
decide if she was telling him fibs.

'Eben,' added Nell, 'what did your ma do to make you smile?'

'Um, make me cake, played hidey, tickled toes. This little ducky
went wee, wee, wee!'

She smiled and sang again.

> '"*Whisper, whisper, whisper,*
> *Close your eyes,*
> *Our love shineth bright.*
> *I'll watch over you this night and all nights to come*
> *Whisper, whisper, whisper …*"'

~

On her way to the castle to see Jack, Nell stepped through a stone archway in the convent's walled garden, covered in vines and moss, and almost bumped into Sister Winifred who was with little Fleur Simms and tossing scraps of bread to some ducks in the stream. Eben let go of Nell's hand and ran to join Fleur, swordless now and tugging at the ribbons threaded through her hair as if they were an irritation. The girl handed him a crust of bread.

'Did you find the sheriff?' Nell asked the nun.

Sister Winifred nodded. 'He asked that we keep our find to ourselves for now.'

'Of course,' Nell said, wondering if the sheriff had made that request to take advantage on the quiet of the mistake the killer had made or to protect himself. 'And it should be an easy task now for Birch to discover where each of the five were the night Phoebe was killed and how they could've heard so quickly about the graves being found.'

Without responding to Nell's comment, Sister Winifred delved into the bag she was holding and gave the children some more bread. Eben shoved a chunk into his mouth and began to sing, 'This little ducky went wee, wee, wee.'

'We know already,' continued Nell, 'that Cook Simms and Brother Caddock were at the Merry Monkey when I was giving the serjeant directions to the graves, so I was wondering if Brother Idris could've heard about them that night also.'

'Brother Caddock would've told him, and then Idris would've helped Godric prepare for the disinterment,' Sister Winifred said a touch brusquely. 'They would've been run off their feet, I imagine, as Father Emlyn suffered a fit that afternoon and had such terrible pains in his head that Brother Godric sedated him heavily. The brethren, who feared that he might not make it through the night, held a dusk-'til-dawn prayer vigil at his bedside. Both Caddock and Idris would have attended that at some point as well.'

'Perhaps you could find out a bit more about their movements and if they were absent from the abbey for any length of time.'

Sister Winifred pressed her lips together, as if stopping herself from crying, and nodded as she half-turned her face away. Nell felt guilty for upsetting her, but ignoring the obvious wasn't going to make it go away nor lead them to finding the killer of four girls. Thinking about the others who were present at the Merry Monkey during the discussion about the graves, Nell realised that not only could Cook Simms have done the deed herself, she could've left the Merry Monkey and told her son, Julian. That just left the sheriff. If he had been sheltering from a storm on his way back to Bellayne from Archstone, as he'd said he'd done, then it was unlikely that he'd have heard the tidings in time to act before dawn. Nell wasn't ready to let him off the hook just yet, though.

Fleur interrupted the awkward silence between Nell and the nun when she stopped an overeager Eben from tumbling headfirst into the stream. The two children then held hands and giggled as Fleur taught him to count ducks. Seeing a way to change the subject, Nell commented on the strange way Fleur had drawn her wooden sword and bravely defended Eben's back as Lex Alcorn charged towards them wielding a stick.

Sister Winifred, whose shoulders relaxed slightly, seemed relieved to discuss something other than the victims and their killer. She began to tell a tale about Simms – the odd painter of murals and of things less savoury – and the night his daughter was born. 'According to her grandsire, Hammond Carpenter, who's a stickler for facts and precise measurements, not to mention his rigid following of the commandments, Fleur came into the world three-and-a-bit years ago on a frosty, star-bright night at the moment when one day passes into the next.

'As her first cries drifted out the window, Julian and Hammond saw white flakes drifting down to the earth while they sat together on a garden seat, united for the first time in their acquaintance as they awaited the outcome of what was proving a difficult birth. At first, they thought that it was snowing, an unusual occurrence for these parts even in midwinter, but, when Julian caught a flake upon his fingertip, they were surprised to find that it was a petal. Both of them, Hammond told me, then looked up and saw that the pear tree they were sitting under had suddenly burst into blossom, when only moments before, its boughs had been bare and that they'd barely time to glance at each other in astonishment before the whole tree quivered and countless buds burst forth. The tiny pears then swelled and ripened before either of them could blink.

'According to the midwife who bustled into the yard to dump an armload of bloodied sheets on the ground and who witnessed the miracle for herself, both men had then fallen to their knees and cried silvery, pear-shaped tears.'

'Fleur is, I believe, a gift from God,' continued Sister Winifred, 'sent to earth to remind us that heaven's light is always shining upon us, even during the darkest of times.'

While Nell didn't believe that the miracle that'd apparently accompanied Fleur's birth was possible, even taking into account the strange happenings she'd witnessed over the last few days, she agreed that Fleur did have an otherworldly air about her, and wished that she could find as much comfort in that tale as Sister Winifred obviously did. Rather than making a pear tree blossom and bear fruit in midwinter, Nell wondered – confused as to how God's mysterious ways made sense – why had he not stayed the hand of Gracie's murderer?

'A son for a rose,' said Nell, reading the message that had been shoved under Jack Lea's bedchamber door just a couple of hours after she and Eben had encountered Lex Alcorn. 'What the hell does it mean?'

'A threat. One that I'm sure Lex will follow up on if he's not stopped soon.'

'What's the sheriff doing? Is he going to lock Alcorn up now?'

Jack shook his head. 'He reckons that'd only make things worse, considering how many folk have now joined the Red Guards. It could start a riot. Birch has called for aid to get the town under control, but the soldiers who could have come are busy tracking the person who murdered the King's agent. Apparently, if the rumours are true, he was tied to a stake and burned.'

Bile rushed into Nell's mouth as she recalled the flames licking Lord Bente's scalp as he ran towards the river. She was relieved that Doreen Wilkes hadn't yet named her as Bente's assailant and the soldiers didn't know who exactly they were seeking. On the other hand, she was horrified to realise that Eben's safety partly depended on the soldiers coming to Bellayne to restore order. Would handing herself over to the sheriff help keep him safe? She tossed that question around her mind – aware that her fear of being tried and hanged for Bente's death was tainting her reasoning. The Red Guards might be disbanded for a time if its members were rounded up, but if the identity of the killer of the four girls wasn't discovered, the vendetta against Jack was likely to resume as soon as the soldiers left town.

If there was a chance that the sheriff was responsible for disappearance of the girls then he was unlikely to find proof of his scapegoat's – Jack Lea's – innocence. If Nell was locked in the castle's dungeon for her part in Lord Bente's death, she wouldn't be able to make sure that the sheriff followed up on the person who had dropped the necklace. She couldn't watch over Eben from there either.

'Besides, there's no proof that this threat has anything to do with Lex,' continued Jack, unaware of Nell's dilemma. 'Although Gracie's middle name was Rose ...'

'Who put it under your door?' Nell asked.

'I know not. But given that the castle's locked up tighter than a nun's –'. He quickly caught what he'd been about to say. 'It must have been delivered by someone already within these walls. One of Lex's cronies, no doubt.'

Nell told Jack how Alcorn had chased after Eben with a stick in the churchyard, and then spat on the ground when they'd next seen him. 'I am worried that he knows Eben is your son. I saw Cook Simms talking with Alcorn while we were sitting in the church. Perhaps it was she who told him.'

'Humph, it would not surprise me. Leticia Simms had a thing for my father many years ago, before and after he married my mother. He admitted to having to be quite nasty with her the last time she tried it on.'

Eben dived under the table Nell and his father were sitting at, and wrapped his arms around the leg of her chair. She wasn't sure if he was hiding because Jack's battered face scared him, or if he was just feeling shy. She noticed his head tilting slightly from left to right every time they spoke his name. If ears could flap, then Eben's were just about ready to fly away.

'Maybe Eben should stay here with you now that you're out of the dungeon,' she said. 'It's not safe for him out there.'

'Nor in here, not any more. Lex's man might poison our food, or light a fire outside the door, just like they did at the farm.'

'I could take him away from Bellayne then – somewhere north of here perhaps – until your innocence is proven.'

'I considered that,' said Jack, 'but Lex could organise for someone to attack you on the road. Birch has offered to put a guard on you and Eben at the convent – assuming of course that you're willing to stay in town until this mess is sorted. I've been assuming a lot of you, and I'm sorry. Sister Winifred could arrange for Eben to stay at the orphanage if –'

'I can stay,' said Nell, hoping she sounded braver than she felt.

There was no way she could leave Bellayne now, not while Eben was in danger. If she left, she'd forever wonder about his fate. And if something bad befell him because she'd lacked the courage to protect him, she'd never forgive herself.

The strange birdmen's prophecy had come to pass, she realised:

this wasn't the end of her time in Bellayne. It dawned on her that Eben wasn't the only one perhaps being led down murky paths by otherworldly creatures. Could she trust where the Crows were leading her?

'I've more tidings,' she said, and quickly told Jack about Eben finding the necklace and who was present at the time, including Sheriff Birch. She didn't mention the ghost.

'Jesus, you think one of them is the killer?' said Jack, shaking his head as if dumbfounded. Then he frowned. 'Birch didn't mention the necklace to me.'

Nell was glad to see that he was now questioning his friend's motives.

'Only Sister Winifred and I know that Eben found it,' she said. 'And when she handed it over to Birch, he said that he wanted to keep its discovery secret until he'd had time to investigate further. Maybe he should tell the Alcorns on the quiet though. That way, Lex Alcorn will know that you can't be the killer.'

Nell realised her last suggestion was idiotic as soon as it left her mouth. Alcorn was unlikely to keep such tidings to himself.

Jack shook his head thoughtfully, though not in a way that made her feel stupid. 'Lex and his Red Guards would go after all five people, and then still come after me just to make sure.'

Eben peeked out from under the table. Jack saw him, and reached for a bag hanging on the back of his chair. He pulled out three wooden toys: egg-shaped and ranging from chick-sized to the length of Nell's hand, and painted in various combinations of red, green and white stripes.

'My father got a friend to retrieve these from our cottage and cleaned them up. They used to be mine,' said Jack, grasping the handle of one and setting it spinning across the table.

When all three were spinning at the same time, Eben stood on tiptoes and peeked over the lip of the table. He waited until one of the tops neared him, then shot out his hand and flicked it with his finger. The top wobbled drunkenly to the other side of the table.

Jack stood and rocked from side to side, his tongue poked out comically, making it appear as if catching the top would be touch and go. He grasped it, dived to the ground and held it triumphantly in the air.

Eben squealed with excitement and tried to poke one of the other tops, which had come to rest just out of his reach.

'I feel useless,' said Jack, getting to his feet and bouncing the top from one hand to the other. 'What sort of father cannot protect his own son?'

'It's hardly your fault.'

'I'm going mad in here, knowing there's nothing I can do to stop them hurting my boy.'

Anger surged up Nell's legs and along her spine, infusing her with a strength she'd not felt for some time, if ever. How dare Alcorn and his fucking mob threaten Eben? Grief from losing a daughter didn't excuse such devilry. Those men wouldn't get within an inch of that beloved little boy.

If Sheriff Birch couldn't – or wouldn't – prove Jack's innocence, then the fastest way to keep Eben safe was for Nell to find the killer herself and prove his guilt. And she knew just where to start.

Chapter Twenty-Five

A Not so Merry Monkey

Just before dawn, Nell crawled out of her bed at the convent's guesthouse, lit a candle and retrieved the scroll she'd stolen from Julian Simms and hidden beneath the mattress.

The drawing, mostly rendered in black ink, was both exquisite and appalling. A naked young woman lay upon a single bed in a narrow room with a low raked ceiling – which would have been the cause of more than a few bumped heads, Nell thought. There was a crucifix made out of shells on the wall. The woman's long black tresses flowed over her pert breasts, and her delicate hands rested upon the inside of her parted thighs. A glistening smear of ruby ink framed the entrance to her maidenhead. Her dark blue eyes were fixed upon a hooded monk who stood beside the bed, his face partly concealed by shadows and his stiff red member poking from beneath his lifted robes. Another man was peeking into the room through a diamond-shaped window.

Nell remembered how Julian Simms had nearly jumped out of his skin when she caught him looking into the urn at St Clement's. No wonder if he'd been hiding more of these obscene scrolls in there. Was that why Fleur had put a scroll into the urn too, because she'd seen her father do exactly that?

The young woman in the picture looked very much like Hester Hannigan – Nell had seen her at the funeral – who was Maye's identical twin. Which sister's face was this? If it was Maye's, did that mean Julian could have been involved with her as well as with Phoebe – and had he killed both girls so they couldn't expose him?

Nell placed the scroll in the bottom of her bag. It wasn't something she could show Sister Winifred, but she could ask Jack Lea for his opinion.

'Folk are saying there was blood on her thighs,' said Alice.

Cook Simms threw fat into a hot pan and added sliced onions while she soothed her aching gums and teeth with her tongue. 'What are you babbling about?'

'A friend of mine heard from Serjeant Oswald that there was blood on Miss Phoebe's thighs. It seems that her baby fell from the womb sometime before or after she died.'

'Humph.'

'And I was just wondering if maybe she'd sought help to get rid of her shame,' Alice added slyly.

'Well, we've no way of knowing that now. Phoebe and her shame have gone to their grave.'

'Along with any tales she might've told.' Alice dropped quartered potatoes into a pot of water, then scraped their peels into a bucket and wiped her nose on her sleeve. 'I've heard that forcing a babe from the belly often ends with the death of both child and mother.' She snorted. 'Silly me, I'm telling you something that you already know much about.'

Cook pressed a palm to her throbbing jaw. She'd never imagined Alice challenging her. The bony, limp-witted dishrag was getting too big for her boots.

'Fetch me three turnips and some carrots from the cellar,' she said.

Alice just perched her bottom on the table and crossed her

ankles. 'Before Sheriff Birch went upstairs to speak with the mistress and Master Arnod, he asked me if I knew anything about Phoebe's secret beau.'

Even though it was her pet hate, Cook didn't order Alice to get her arse off the table. All she could muster was, 'Turnips.'

'I told the sheriff that I didn't know who Phoebe was seeing, but now my conscience is getting the better of me.'

Cook diced and rolled the meat in flour, hoping Alice didn't notice that her speed and rhythm were off. 'Turnips,' she repeated.

'I still find it disturbing that your dearest Julian painted all of the dead girls,' said Alice, curling limp strands of her mousy hair around her chafed fingers.

'That's no secret. Julian's used half the town as models for his murals. The sheriff will think you a fool. Besides, my son had naught to do with Gracie Alcorn. He never painted her likeness.'

'Mmm, but she liked to look at his mural. Little girls like to stick their noses into dark corners. Maybe she saw Julian kissing Phoebe … or more.'

Cook stabbed the knife into the table. 'Get me some fucking turnips before I slice –' She stopped herself with an effort.

Alice slid off the table and clacked her teeth together. 'Methinks I've touched a sore spot.' Sidling towards the cellar, she added, 'I *should* tell the sheriff that your Julian came looking for Phoebe late afternoon on the day she died, just a few hours before she snuck out to meet her killer. He seemed annoyed that she wasn't yet home, though he tried to hide it.'

'You're a fool and a twit.'

'A twit who could also tell the sheriff that your bed was empty for many hours that same night.'

Cook slammed her hands onto the table and immediately regretted it as pain flared in every inch of her mouth. 'My stomach cramped. I was out on the privy for most of the night.'

Alice tapped the side of her nose, mimicking Cook's favoured all-knowing gesture. 'I saw the most beautiful crimson gown at the marketplace the other day. I've never worn a new dress and I'd very much like to have it.'

Nell tiptoed away from the ajar kitchen door and picked up the tray of refreshments from where she'd stowed it at the bottom of the stairs. After listening to that conversation between Cook Simms and Alice, she was glad that she'd only offered to help out at the Merry Monkey for a couple of days. It wasn't quite mid-morning and she already felt like cracking their heads together.

Nell had lain awake for hours last night pondering her plan to find the killer. It seemed to her that if he'd kept Phoebe's necklace as a morbid keepsake, it was likely that he'd taken something from each of his victims. If that was the case, all she needed to do was search the belongings of the five folk who could have dropped the necklace in the churchyard. The pickpocketing skills she'd learned at the Boar's Den would come in handy for that task. This morning, after making sure that Eben was well-guarded at the convent, she'd arrived at the inn and offered her services – which were welcomed as the chambermaid wouldn't return to work for weeks.

Cook Simms was first on Nell's list, especially after hearing Alice's accusations and that Cook was absent from her bed on the night Phoebe died. She was hoping to go through the woman's room at the back of the inn sometime today. Was Julian Simms really the father of Phoebe's baby? Perhaps Phoebe had threatened to tell his wife? Had Cook Simms left her bed in the middle of that night to help her son out of a nasty predicament? Nell made a mental note to ask Jack Lea if he'd heard any rumours about Cook Simms helping girls rid themselves of unwanted babies.

She paused at the top of the stairs, just outside Mary and Arnod Butterball's private quarters. Sheriff Birch was in there with them, running through Phoebe's movements on the day she died. She could hear that he was carefully picking his way around the possibility that she'd been with child, and hoped that his concern for Phoebe's aunt and uncle was heartfelt.

'Phoebe left the Merry Monkey just after the seventh hour of the morning,' said Birch. 'She was spotted wandering around the marketplace a few times that morning and Sister Winifred saw her crossing Monk's Mill Bridge and heading towards Maiden's Well just before midday. It seems likely she had a tryst with a beau. Did you know of one?'

Mary answered. 'Nay, but Phoebe was troubled about something. She was not herself.'

'Do you know what was bothering her?'

'She was worried because she'd not heard from my sister, her mother, for two years. But I could tell there was something else. Oh, God, we argued on our last morning together …' Mary broke down. 'Harsh words – I slapped her – my sweet girl.'

Nell tapped on the doorframe and entered the cosy parlour, the tray in her hands. She skirted around Sheriff Birch, who was seated on a straight-backed chair with his back to the door – until she'd discovered who'd dropped the necklace, it'd be hard looking him in the eye – and placed the tray on the low table between him and the Butterballs. Even without looking at him, she could tell he was annoyed at the interruption.

She bent over the tray and poured hot lemon balm tea into three goblets. Birch's bag was looped over the back of his chair, sparking ideas in her mind of how she could get a look inside it.

'Phoebe returned home just before supper,' Birch continued. 'How did she seem then?'

Mary was sitting very close to her husband on the settle. Her face was drawn and she'd not combed her nut-brown hair since she'd thanked Nell three hours ago for coming to help them during this difficult time. Phoebe's necklace was cupped in her hands. Nell wondered if Birch had told the Butterballs that one of only five people could have dropped it. And if so, had he included himself in the tally?'

'She was sorry that she'd argued with me and gave me this scarf.' Mary stroked the emerald silk scarf around her neck. 'She picked it because it's the same colour as a gown I'd made for her. It was her way of saying that she forgave me for slapping her, but that does not make me feel any better now.'

Mary reached across and took one of her husband's hands, which up until then had been clasped tightly against his chest. Arnod sat hunched over his knees, and looked as if he couldn't wait for Birch to leave so that he could curl up in a dark room and sleep his troubles away.

'Phoebe said she had something to tell me,' Mary continued, 'but I was in the middle of serving supper to our guests. And then Nell arrived a short while later with the sad tidings about the graves in Shymer Forest, so Phoebe never got the chance to tell me what was on her mind.'

Arnod fished a clean handkerchief out of his pocket when Mary asked him for it. She wiped her eyes, then rested her head against the side of his upper arm.

Nell wondered if Phoebe had been going to tell her aunt that she was with child. Had her lover sweet-talked her into another tryst at midnight, so he could strangle her under the cover of darkness?

Nell handed Mary a goblet of tea and a napkin, then passed around a plate of sweetmeats. Birch waved her away with an impatient flick of his hand.

'Did Phoebe say anything to you?' he asked Arnod.

'Nay, she was already abed when I returned home that night. And earlier that morning, when I walked in on her and Mary arguing, I was annoyed with them, impatient. I had a long, tiring day ahead of me and wasn't interested in listening to their woes.'

His handsome face contorted and his shoulders slumped further, as if weighed down by the many things he could have done differently that morning. Going by the way he clamped a fist over his mouth to smother a sob, Nell had no doubt that he'd contemplate that mental list for a long time, if not the rest of his life.

Nell stepped towards Birch with a full goblet of tea in her hands, and pretended to catch her foot on the table leg. Lemon balm tea sloshed over his bag and the floor. She apologised, and kneeled to mop up the mess with a napkin. Her left hand pressed down on some small, sharp stones that looked as if they'd come from the sheriff's boots. One of them pierced her palm, which started to bleed.

As Nell stared at Birch's empty goblet, something stirred in the very back of her mind. The sodden napkin dripped onto her skirt as she tried to drag the memory forth, though she knew already, deep in her belly, that it wasn't something she wanted to acknowledge.

Birch glared at her, and she recalled herself and asked if she could take his bag to the kitchen to dry it by the fire – an opportunity for a sneaky peek inside it.

He shooed her away, saying, 'Leave it. It'll dry.'

Arnod raked his fingers through his short, dark hair. 'If I'd taken the time to listen to Phoebe that morning, she might have shared her troubles with us and be alive still.' He got up and walked over to the window. 'I waved to her, but she did not see me because the sun was in her eyes – or that is what I tell myself. Perhaps she turned away from me because I'd failed her.' He bowed his head and wept. 'I should have gone after her.'

Nell leaned against the wall in the kitchen passage, not ready yet to join Alice and Cook Simms, who were still at each other's throats. Each time she looked at the empty goblet on the tray, she felt breathless, as if her past was able to put a stranglehold on the present.

'What the hell are you doing now?' Cook was saying to Alice.

'I'm off to St Clement's to confide in Brother Caddock.'

'Not while there's cheese and bread to slice for the midday meal.'

'Do it yourself,' said Alice. 'I'm going to tell Brother Caddock all about you and your precious Julian. That way, if something unfortunate happens to me, like a wrung neck perhaps –'

'Caddock, Caddock, Caddock,' shouted Cook. 'You sound like a sick crow. Well, I'd watch yourself with him, missy. He's not as pious as he pretends. He's more likely to wring your neck than I am, and that's saying something.'

Taking a deep breath, Nell pushed open the door and entered the kitchen. She didn't have time to waste on the past; not if she was going to find the killer and keep Eben safe.

The kitchen was steamy and overly warm, the air thick with the smell of frying lard. Nell put the tray on the table, and washed the empty jug in a tub of water, her mind ticking over with ideas about how she might get on Cook's good side and find out more about the skeletons in Brother Caddock's cupboard.

Alice tucked her hair into an unbecoming mustard-yellow scarf, stuck her red-tipped nose in the air, and slammed the door behind her as she went out into the yard.

Nell rounded her shoulders to appear more docile and turned towards Cook Simms. 'In the last inn I worked at, the cook would've hung that scullery maid from a butcher's hook for a whole day for being so rude.'

Cook sniffed. 'Alice comes from a family of imbeciles. We don't take much notice of her ramblings. We can't get rid of her because she has a deft hand with dough.'

At Cook's request, Nell fetched bread and cheese from the cellar and began slicing them.

'Um, I don't want to pry,' she said, 'but I heard what you said about Brother Caddock …'

Cook dropped the wooden spoon into the stew and spun around with such an aggressive expression that Nell was reminded of a time she'd spotted the rotten part of a plum just as she'd been about to put her lips around its juicy, ripe flesh. Hanging her head, she fiddled with the corner of her apron while she made up a tale about the possibly innocent monk.

'It's embarrassing, but I thought I should tell someone about what I saw at St Clement's.'

Cook relaxed her wide, mannish face. 'No need for embarrassment here. I'm a woman who knows much about the sins of men.' To Nell's horror, the squat woman rounded the table and put an arm around her shoulder. 'Come, come, dear, and tell me all about that wicked Greenfriar.'

'Last night,' said Nell, still thinking about that rotten plum, 'I went into the Lady Chapel to pray while the church was empty. When I came out, I saw him standing in front of the mural of Eve. He was … His sleeve was empty and his hand was inside his robes. He was …' Nell forced a sob and edged out from under Cook's arm.

'Pulling his pizzle?'

Nell nodded and sobbed louder. 'I crept back into the Lady Chapel so he did not see me.'

'Nothing that man does would surprise me. Believe me, there's more than one sticky mess on the floors of St Clement's.'

If the scroll Nell had stolen from Cook's son Julian was anything to go by, then she'd no doubt that was true. Pretending to dry her eyes, Nell gave Cook a weak smile. 'Have you heard something like this before?'

Cook tapped her nose. 'The monks killed my Albert. He went into their hospice with a cough and came out in a box. He saw things there that meant they couldn't let him live.'

The woman was loopy with a mean streak a mile wide. Nell hastily changed the subject. 'What do you know about Brother Caddock?'

Cook poured two mugs of ale and pointed at some chairs. Complaining loudly about a toothache, she kicked off her woollen slippers and sat upon the cushioned seat. 'Once upon a time, Caddock had a much younger sister named Lorraine. She was raised in the orphanage along with handsome Brother Idris.' Her shrewd light-grey eyes looked slyly over the lip of her mug. 'Have you seen him?'

Nell nodded. 'Most handsome indeed.'

'Lorraine and Idris were friends all through childhood, until Caddock put a stop to it. He dreamed of the day when his sister would take her vows and enter the convent, and he wasn't going to let a dark-skinned urchin get in the way of that. But lusty Lorraine had other ideas.'

Nell leaned closer, widening her eyes.

Cook slowly sipped her ale and scissored her legs. 'My feet are aching too. My Albert used to rub them three times a day.'

Taking the hint, Nell sat on the floor and lifted one of Cook's surprisingly clean but rough feet into her lap. She ran her hands over the cracked heels and cursed herself. She'd overplayed the role of an enthralled underling.

Groaning with pleasure, Cook said, 'Where was I? Ah yes, fourteen years ago, Lorraine fell in love with the stonemason's son and arranged to run away with him, far from Bellayne and out of her brother's clutches. Idris helped Lorraine sneak away from the convent, and escorted her to the Maiden's Well, where he farewelled his childhood friend. He ran back to attend the midnight blessing before he was missed, while Lorraine waited for her betrothed. Alas, he did not come.'

'What happened?' Nell asked.

Cook lifted the hem of her skirt. 'My knees need some attention.'

Nell ran her hands up Cook's veined calves and kneaded her pudgy knees. She hoped the woman didn't get a sudden cramp in her thigh.

'Unbeknown to Lorraine,' continued Cook, 'her lover had broken his leg on his way to Maiden's Well. They found her the next morning, floating face down in the reeds at the edge of the river. Some said that she'd drowned herself to escape a broken heart, but I did not believe such twaddle.'

Nell sat back on her heels. 'What do you think happened?'

Cook tongued her gums. 'Caddock wasn't at the midnight

blessing – said he was unwell. I think he got wind of Lorraine's plans and drowned her. If he couldn't have her himself, then no one else was going to defile his precious sister.'

Nell recalled Cook's comment about Brother Caddock wringing Alice's neck. 'And you think he has something to do with the recent murders?'

'No doubt at all.'

'Why would he wait so long between killings though? It's been fourteen years since his sister died. It does not make sense.'

Cook's eyes narrowed. "Tis fortunate then that I'm wiser than you are.'

Looking as humble as possible, Nell lifted Cook's other foot onto her lap.

'You've seen little of the world,' the woman said, 'and do not know that St Clement's is a haven for fallen girls from all over our isle of Squinte. Some mothers take their babies with them when they leave, but most dump their newborns at the orphanage and flee straight after giving birth. Selling babies to unblessed couples is a profitable business for the Greenfriars. My Albert believed that some of those mothers who did not want to part with their children are lying in unmarked graves all over Bellayne.'

'And you believe that Caddock is involved?' Nell prompted.

'Since his sister betrayed him, Caddock loathes young women. And he certainly has the pick of Squinte's fallen strays.'

Snatching her hands from beneath Cook's skirt, Nell wrinkled her nose. 'Methinks your stew is burning.'

While Cook sweated over the scorched pot, Nell scrubbed her hands in a basin of water, thinking that the woman's hatred of Brother Caddock had blinded her to another possibility.

Brother Idris could have drowned his darling Lorraine in the river, instead of escorting her to her lover at Maiden's Well that night.

Chapter Twenty-Six

Without Merriment

While Eben gazed in awe at the boars and deer in the longest hunting scene tapestry that Nell had ever seen, his father leaned over the table in the sheriff's draughty great hall and looked at the scroll that she'd taken from Julian Simms.

'Ah, it certainly looks very much like Maye or Hester Hannigan,' said Jack, shaking his head as if he couldn't comprehend what he was seeing. 'As for the monk, he has dark features like Brother Idris, but I cannot say for sure if it's him.'

Clenching his jaw, he quickly rolled up the drawing. His cheeks were as flushed as Nell's felt. She'd seen much worse during her years at the Boar's Den, but she'd never had to discuss such things with any man, let alone Eben's father.

'And you say that Julian had many scrolls just like this?' Jack said.

'At least a dozen, but this is the only one I've actually seen. He must be raking in bags of silver selling them.'

'Jesus! If he was doing that here in Bellayne, he'd not keep this secret for long. Someone would talk, especially if the local lasses are somehow … Well, you know what I mean.'

'Maybe he sends them with a merchant to the mainland,' Nell said. 'I do not know. But I got the impression that he's been hiding them in the church.'

Jack laughed wryly. 'If Julian's very pious father-in-law catches him with these, he'll hang him upside by his you-know-whats. Julian seduced Hammond's daughter some years ago and wormed his way into the Carpenter fortune. As punishment, Hammond keeps his purse strings tightly knotted and makes Julian paint those murals at St Clement's to earn his keep.'

'Which explains why he might want to make money on the sly.'

'Although 'tis hard to imagine this sort of thing going on at St Clement's,' Jack said.

'According to Cook Simms,' said Nell, who had a thumping headache, no doubt brought on by a day of listening to Cook and Alice bitching at each other, 'there's a lot more going on at the abbey than monks posing for obscene pictures. She could be inventing stories to divert attention from herself or her son, but I cannot dismiss her accusations just because she's a rancid crone.' Nell paused, unsure how to word the next delicate subject, and decided there was no pretty way of saying it. 'I overheard Alice accuse her of ridding girls of unwanted babies.'

'God help any lass needing to go to her for that sort of help, but yeah, I'd say that rumour is true, sadly.'

'And her husband Albert reckoned that Brother Caddock was disposing of some of the young women who come to St Clement's to give birth to their illegitimate babies. I imagine he'd think of them as harlots, or worse.'

'He has never supported Father Emlyn's policy of giving aid to girls in trouble and makes no bones about stopping that practice if he wins the abbotship. Whether he'd go as far as to kill them, I could not say. From what I've seen of him, he tends to stew on matters that displease him and is prone to odd outbursts.'

Nell wondered what Brother Caddock might do if he discovered that one of the Hannigan twins had sat for Julian Simms's drawings, and if any of the other victims had also featured in the scrolls? She decided against mentioning that possibility to Jack for now. He'd be loath to consider the idea that Irma Linke might have posed naked for such a drawing.

'I heard Caddock singing the other night,' continued Jack, 'about a lost lover while sitting by the place his sister had drowned. He sounded heartbroken, forlorn.'

'Creepier and creepier,' said Nell.

Suddenly realising that it might be a good idea to speak with Hester, Nell snatched the scroll out of Jack's hand. 'Before you suggest it, I'm not giving this to the sheriff yet. He might be your friend but I do not trust him.'

'I cannot believe that Hester or Maye would have taken off their clothes for Julian,' he said, clearly agitated. 'Or that Birch would ever harm any of those girls.'

'There are many things that you do not want to believe or even consider,' said Nell.

'Would you be over the moon if I accused one of your friends of murder?'

'I do not have any friends,' Nell said, and immediately wondered about the welfare of her one remaining friend – Emily – and kicked herself for making such a thoughtless statement.

'I'm beginning to see why. You're like a dog with a bone. A bone that no one asked you to sink your teeth into.'

Jack was wrong about that, but Nell wasn't going to tell him about how Gracie Alcorn's ghost had tried to point to her killer.

'Whether you like it or not,' she said, 'Birch was there when the necklace fell. And may I remind you that he covered his own hide too when he lied and told everyone that you were with him when Irma Linke disappeared.'

He didn't respond, instead making a big show of upending a basket of toy soldiers and wooden horses onto the table. Eben, his interest sparked, ran across the room and climbed onto the heavy chair that Jack had pulled out two places away from where he sat.

Nell was surprised and grateful for the gentle way he tried to bond with the son he must be aching to hold. He never forced Eben to come closer than he was comfortable with, nor did he insist on a response to his questions.

Clacking his tongue, Jack *clip-clopped* a horse and its armoured rider over the toy castle's drawbridge. When Eben tried moving his tongue in the same way, his spit sprayed the table, which led to the first giggle Nell had heard from him in a long while. Each time the two of them interacted, she memorised every detail so that she could imagine their life together once she was no longer there to see it.

Suddenly feeling overheated in the large room, she pulled off the unbearable weight of her cloak, and fanned her face with both hands. She'd so much to do and a short time to do it all in. She had no idea where to start. She did her best to ignore the hammering pain behind her temples and think clearly. The threat to Jack and his father needed to be removed before they could truly bond with Eben as a family. Jack knew the townsfolk better than she did, and so she needed his help. They didn't have time for games.

'You cannot pretend that I'm not here,' she told him.

'I can try,' he said, assembling the soldiers on the castle walls. The red welt across his neck appeared to darken and stand out more, perhaps inflamed with irritation.

Nell glanced around the hall. Finding anything incriminating among the sheriff's possessions seemed a hopeless task. The castle had many rooms, each containing countless chests and cupboards.

'You could at least search Birch's bag and work chamber for anything else that might have belonged to the victims,' she said. 'If he is the killer, he's unlikely to keep anything damning at home, where his wife and daughters could find it.'

'Arundell's my friend,' Jack said again.

'Still, you could do more than sit there like a tub of lard,' Nell said crossly. 'I've had to listen to Cook and Alice screeching at each other, *and* had to rub that horrid woman's knees while she rattled on about her dead husband and fallen girls. And after all that I did not get a chance to look through her things.'

Jack chewed his bottom lip thoughtfully, then looked her in the eye. His hair was hanging loose about his shoulders, and his shirt sleeves were rolled up, revealing tanned, muscly forearms. Although he had a scruffy look Nell realised, to her surprise, that she found it appealing. He was lean and agile, and his movements were quick and smooth, even though he was obviously agitated about her continued presence.

'I give you leave to journey home then,' he said. 'I'll make sure that Eben is safe with Sister Winifred.'

'I cannot turn my back on Eben,' she said. *Or Gracie.* She couldn't forget the look of desperation she'd seen on the ghost's face.

Jack crossed his arms over his chest, making it clear he wasn't going to give in to her demands. Frustration flared in her mind. Could he not see that Eben's safety might depend on his cooperation? She felt guilty about her next words before she uttered them, but it was better to open a fresh wound now in the hope of preventing the infliction of a much deeper one – the loss of his son.

'Sister Winifred told me about your friendship with Irma Linke, that you'd grown close to each other over the last couple of years.'

A shadow crossed his face. She felt bad for upsetting him, but at least she had his attention.

'My father – and my mother, when she was alive – loved Irma like a daughter. She whiled away many of her childhood years on our farm.'

Nell touched his shoulder. 'You must miss her very much. But someone strangled Irma, your dearest friend, and now someone else has threatened your boy. Yet you won't search Birch's belongings to find out more.'

Jack pushed Nell's hand off his shoulder, his eyes flashing with anger. An image came into her mind of harsh sunlight glittering on emeralds.

'My feelings for Irma are none of your flaming business,' he said. 'And I *will not* betray a friend.'

Shaken by his outburst, she stood, determined to goad him to action. 'Can you not see that by keeping you here, the sheriff is making you look guilty?'

'Go home.' His voice was cold.

'Would you prefer to see Jack hanging from a tree?' asked Sheriff Birch from the doorway.

Nell turned too quickly to face him and pain shot up the side of her neck. He was leaning against the doorframe with one leg crossed in front of the other, and looked as if he must have heard her last comment at least.

Even though he'd passed his fortieth year, he had an imposing charm that some young women might find tantalising, or foolishly wish to tame. Had Phoebe Butterball run her hands through his wavy hair and over his tall, well-muscled body? Had the other victims felt safe with him because he had four daughters?

Eben interrupted the silence by edging off his chair, bum skywards, then trotting one of the wooden horses into the space behind where his father was seated. 'Giddy up,' he shouted.

Birch entered the room and hung his black coat on a peg just inside the doorway, but stowed his bag under a chair at the head of the long table. Nell wondered if it was his usual habit to keep the bag close, or if he had something to hide.

Suddenly coming up with another plan for getting a look inside it, she sat in the chair next to Jack. He immediately leaned away from her, his hitched shoulder sending her a frosty message. Pretending to scratch her leg, Nell squeezed her fingers inside her boot and wrenched a small silver bell from her anklet. Once upon a time, Eben had liked to tinkle it with his finger to wake her in the mornings.

When a serving maid entered the hall and placed a plate of bread and cheese in front of Birch, Nell clicked her fingers behind the back of her chair to get Eben's attention, then rolled the bell towards the sheriff's feet. After cocking his head quizzically, Eben crawled under the table after it. She was hoping that he'd up-end the bag, or bring it to her so she could 'accidentally' do it herself.

'Jack tells me that you came here from Stonhard,' Birch said. 'A rough town for a petite young lady.'

Had he deliberately drawled the last word? Nell's hackles – and headache – spiked.

'I managed to survive there for seven years without being strangled,' she replied.

Birch swallowed a piece of bread, then flicked crumbs off his beard. 'Two soldiers arrived here this morning. They're enquiring about any strangers who've recently come to town, particularly women.'

Nell was disturbed that the soldiers knew they were looking for a woman, but Doreen Wilkes couldn't have given them a full description or a name as yet, otherwise Birch would have dragged her off to the dungeon. She mentally kicked herself for not asking Jack to keep to himself what little of her story she'd told him. She hadn't realised she'd be staying in town this long.

'Lord Bente and his companion set out from Stonhard too,' continued Birch, not taking his eyes from Nell. 'Which way did you come?'

She almost lied and answered Coastway Road, far from where Bente had fallen into the fire, but changed her mind. Better to stick as close to the truth as possible in case he could tell she was lying.

'The Flegg Road. For much of the way we tagged along with a large group of Travellers. It was safer that way.'

'You may have seen something that could point the soldiers in the right direction,' he said. 'I'll be sure to mention your name to them.'

Though she was quaking on the inside, Nell wasn't going to let Birch's threats interfere with her hunt for the killer. 'Someone within your castle threatened Eben,' she said, hoping to show that the soldiers were of no consequence to her. Although if Birch were the killer, the fastest way to stop her would be to accuse her of Lord Bente's death.

Eben prodded the bag and Nell quickly drew the sheriff's attention back to herself.

'Cook Simms told me that her husband had proof that something terrible was going on at St Clement's that might be connected to the latest victims. Apparently some young women who came to Bellayne to give birth to their illegitimate babies disappeared not long after. What say you to that?'

'Ah, Leticia Simms.' Birch carefully dabbed the corners of his mouth with a napkin. 'What can one say? I do not wish to speak ill of the dead, but Albert Simms was as silly as a wet hen. I did, however, look into his accusations and found nothing amiss. The girls most likely went back to where they came from.'

Eben poked his hand into the sheriff's bag. With a loud scrape, Jack pushed back his chair, crouched and lifted Eben out from under the table, away from the bag.

Without looking at Nell, he said, 'Sister Winifred will be wondering where you are by now. I'll walk you both to the gate.'

Although Nell was upset that Jack wanted to be rid of her so abruptly, she noticed that it was the first time he'd held his son and Eben didn't seem too troubled by it, at least not once Jack had given him a knight and horse to take away with him.

Jack put his hand firmly on Nell's back and steered her towards the door. As she passed the sheriff, she said, '*You* could have dropped the necklace.'

'I could have,' Birch said, and popped a piece of cheese into his mouth. He seemed unperturbed but she noticed that his leg was jiggling.

She wondered how he'd come by the scratch on his face. She'd first noticed it when he and the other men were recovering the dead girls' bodies the morning after Phoebe Butterball had been murdered. It had looked fresh and inflamed then. Had Phoebe inflicted the wound with her nails as she tried to fight him off?

As they crossed the courtyard, a droopy-eyed Eben resting his head on his father's shoulder, Jack said, 'You dropped something.' His tone lacked warmth. He opened his fist to reveal the silver bell that Nell had thrown towards the sheriff's bag. 'Upon the morrow I will ask Sisters Winifred and Agnes to care for Eben at St Clement's until it's safe for us to go home,' he added. 'So you can be on your way.'

'I ...' The words caught in Nell's throat as sadness coursed through her body.

Jack placed Eben into her arms, then turned and strode back towards the castle without a word of farewell. He was dismissing her, after all that she'd done for him. Angry that he doubted her love for the boy, she hurled the silver bell after him, hitting him in the back of the neck.

When his pace didn't slow, she shouted, 'I risked my life to bring Eben home.'

With one foot on the bottom step, he swivelled his torso. 'And I thanked you. But can you not see that your foolhardy delving into folks' affairs is putting him in danger? Any attention drawn to you is also drawn to him. He is not your plaything and this is not a game.' He stabbed the air twice with his finger. 'Go home.'

Before Nell could respond, he bounded up the stairs without a backward glance.

She felt an inexplicable pang of loss. If Jack could understand why she was so desperate to find the killer, then maybe he'd see that she wasn't acting recklessly and that Eben's safety was foremost in her mind.

'I saw Gracie Alcorn,' she called after him, before she'd really thought through what she wanted to say.

He paused at the top step, then turned to face her. For a long while he just stood there watching her. Though he was quite a distance away, she could feel him touching the air around her with his thoughts. Could he smell her sadness? Could he taste her loneliness upon his tongue? Could he see that she'd let down her defences because she was weary and no longer had the strength to hide from who she was? Or to hide herself away from what she truly wanted? The latter was becoming more apparent daily; she wanted to belong, to feel safe, to love and be loved.

As she stood there, slightly hunched from showing her vulnerability and trembling as she resisted the urge to protect that softness with folded arms, the urge to keep showing herself overtook her. What did she have to lose?

'Eben saw something too,' she said. 'A girl in the sky who led him, I think, to the place where the necklace fell into his hands. I'm not sure if it was another ghost … or something else.'

Jack loped down the steps and crossed the courtyard towards her. Nell shrivelled inside, wondering if he'd spit in her face and snatch Eben from her arms.

'I cannot walk away while Eben is in danger and a little girl is begging for help,' she said. She felt tears on her face, but left them there.

Jack pulled a cloth from his pocket and tucked it into her hand. 'And Irma?' He could barely speak.

'Nay, I did not see her in the churchyard … but I heard them, all of them … singing a cradlesong about swans.' He'd certainly think her mad now, if he didn't already.

He looked down to hide his anguished face and scuffed a flagstone with his boot. Then, wiping a hand over his eyes, he wrapped his cloak around her shoulders and ushered her towards the castle gates. She was grateful for the warmth. She hadn't realised that she was shaking from head to toe, and she'd left her own cloak behind in the castle's dining hall.

Jack signalled to Serjeant Oswald, who was lounging against the wall, and waiting to escort Nell and Eben to the convent.

Sighing in irritation, Oswald handed his jug of ale to another guard, hoicked and spat on the ground, then unbarred a narrow door beside the castle gates.

'What are you doing?' asked Nell as Jack followed them through the door. Looking back at the castle, she saw Birch watching them from a shadowed balcony.

'I'm coming with you,' Jack said.

'Nay, you cannot risk the Red Guards capturing you again. Eben needs a father.' So the serjeant wouldn't overhear her, she whispered near his ear, 'And you're the only one with access to the sheriff's work chamber and bag.'

He frowned.

'If I promise to stay with Eben within St Clement's walls, will you look through his things tonight?' she pressed.

Jack ruffled Eben's hair but kept his eyes on her. 'You promise?'

Nell nodded. 'I'll ensure he is safe.'

As she and Eben walked away with the serjeant, Jack stuck his head through the door and called after her, 'Nell, drop the bone before you break your teeth.'

It was the first time that he'd spoken her name.

In the cellar of the Merry Monkey, Cook Simms clamped her aching gums around the stem of Albert's old pipe, dipped a quill into a pot of black ink and applied the finishing touches to her final message to the folk of Bellayne. It showed Sheriff Birch's black stallion, with the man himself draping the body of a young woman with yellow hair across the horse's back. It was far from her best work, but she needed to point the finger in another direction quickly, before someone listened to Alice's vicious ramblings.

Cook was saddened to give up her favourite pastime as the Stirrer of Truth, but she didn't need any more unwanted attention. Julian, the ninny, was creating enough trouble for the both of them, and she couldn't risk losing her job at the inn, not at her age.

Once the scrap of parchment had dried, Cook tiptoed along the passage and into the room that she shared with Alice. Thanks to the sleeping draught she'd purchased at the marketplace, the girl was snoring loudly. She rummaged through Alice's battered chest of belongings and hid the quill, ink and parchment in a tin of keepsakes. Then she pulled from her cleavage the emerald scarf that Phoebe had given to Mary and stuffed that into the tin as well. Upon the morrow, when it was missed, she'd whisper her suspicions of Alice's pilfering into Master Arnod's ear.

She blew out the candle and climbed into bed. No one would believe anything that Alice said about any of the Simms family once they discovered that the scullery maid was the poison-monger of Bellayne. There'd be no crimson dress for Alice now.

Sighing loudly, Cook tucked Albert's pipe into her underdrawers. Her toothache had almost disappeared.

Chapter Twenty-Seven

Against the Grain

'A feisty lass,' said Sheriff Birch as he finished his supper and wiped his beard.

Jack Lea chewed on a strip of juicy beef a moment longer than necessary as he decided how to respond. 'She had a difficult journey to bring Eben to me and I cannot thank her enough.'

About an hour later, after they'd finished discussing tactics for beating their opponents in the upcoming rowing race – an annual and fiercely fought event – Birch yawned and pushed back his chair. Just as he bent to pull his bag out from under the chair, one of the soldiers searching for Lord Bente's attacker appeared at the door and announced that he had a number of urgent matters to discuss. Obviously irritated given the late hour, Birch followed him out the door.

Jack settled back in his chair, preparing himself for a long wait before he could search the sheriff's work chamber. He knew that Nell wouldn't believe him if he claimed he'd not had a chance to do as she'd asked.

Thinking of Nell took him back to Birch's earlier threat to tell the King's soldiers that Nell had been travelling on the same road the lord was attacked on. He'd only known her a short time so couldn't read her reactions with any certainty, but she'd seemed to become agitated upon hearing mention of the soldiers. Her insinuation that Birch himself could have dropped Phoebe's necklace had come soon after, perhaps as a deflection. Did that mean she had something to hide herself?

Drumming his fingers on the table to stay awake, he turned his mind instead to contemplating the fact that he was now a father. How wonderful would be the moment when he carried his son back to Lea farm and made him a cosy bed in their cottage. He was pondering how old the boy would have to be before he could learn to fish and ride and gather mushrooms when he noticed that Birch's bag was still lying on the ground at the end of the dining table. Should he? Shouldn't he?

Jack whacked the table with the flat of his hand and cursed himself. He wasn't usually this indecisive. If there was any possibility that Birch was responsible for Irma's death, there was no doubt what he should do.

Standing abruptly, he made sure the passage outside the hall was empty, then dashed over to the bag and unbuckled its worn straps. Quickly removing several documents, a couple of cloths and a woollen hat, he tipped the smaller items gathered at the bottom of the bag onto the table. Loose coins immediately rolled hither and thither, making more noise than he wanted.

He opened the first of two small cloth bags and discovered a few strips of jerky. He pulled the drawstring on the second and tipped its contents into his hand. He frowned, and held the item closer to the candle flame to get a better look at it.

What the hell did this mean?

His stomach turned and he questioned whether he knew his friend at all.

'I'm fading into shadow,' said Gracie. 'There's a strange fluttering in my chest.'

'Nay, they cannot take you before me,' said Irma, who feared that this would happen soon. Gracie had not recovered from passing through the veil in the churchyard to the mortal realm and had been unable since then to gather moonlight and replenish her store of moondew.

Irma lifted heavy eyelids and squinted. Gracie was grey and almost transparent, as if she were made from ash and smoke and dust. Her yellow ribbons had slipped from the ends of her plaits and were lying on the ground.

'Nay, I will not let them take you further from the light than you are already,' Irma cried.

She crawled along the ground even though the ache in her ghostly bones was excruciating. She called out to Maye and Phoebe, who were slumbering amid the bluebells, but her feeble croaking didn't disturb their unquiet dreams.

When she reached Gracie, she didn't have the strength to stand, so pulled the girl onto her lap and held her tight.

'I'm afeard, Irma.'

'I will not let them take you.'

Irma quivered with distress and rage. Gracie had done what the angels had demanded without any thought for herself, and now they were condemning her to an eternity in shadow and taking away her last hope of ever reaching the gilded door and of ever seeing her family again once their time on earth ended. To Irma, that was beyond cruel.

A further niggling fear surfaced in her mind. Who would relay the angels' messages once Gracie left the hollow? She was their only link to the heavens. Irma had oft scorned the cryptic tidings from above, but now dreaded the coming silence.

'The Shadow boy is here,' said Gracie.

Irma looked up and saw Glynn standing an arm's length away. He squatted in front of Gracie and held out his hand.

'Take me too,' said Irma.

Glynn shook his head.

Irma kissed the top of Gracie's head and sobbed into her hair, which smelled faintly of pudding and flowers, scents from her old life.

'Let me go, dear Irma, it's my time,' Gracie said.

Irma loosened her embrace and said, 'Forgive me. It's my fault you are here. If only I'd let him be and hadn't forced my way into his dreams.'

Gracie stood and took Glynn's hand and walked with him into the shadows at the edge of the clearing. Her ghostly form became fainter with each step she took. If Maye and Phoebe – who had not faded enough to see the Shadowfolk as anything other than smoky, amorphous swirls – had been awake to witness Gracie's fading, they'd have seen her becoming more mist-like until she was nothing more than a lightless wisp.

Gracie's last words echoed around the hollow. 'Irma, you can hear the angels if you try.'

After leaving Jack at the castle, Nell had contemplated how she was going to search the belongings of Brothers Caddock and Idris for anything that might have belonged to the four murdered girls. If either monk had dropped the necklace, then it was possible they had other 'keepsakes' in their bedchambers. She'd studied the abbey from the outside and noticed that the latrines and dormitories were linked by an enclosed courtyard in the same way the convent's facilities were; and the latrines had an outside door accessed from the back garden.

As soon as Eben was asleep, Nell tiptoed out of the convent and made her way through the orchard to the abbey. She had to hide twice when she heard someone approaching the latrines, but finally she reached the passage that ran along the sleeping quarters. There was a curtained alcove just like the one in the convent used to store bedsheets and the like, and she tucked herself into it to wait for the monks to leave their bedchambers for the midnight blessing. Candles burned on a table further down the passage but their light barely penetrated the thick red curtains shielding her hidey-hole.

After half an hour, she felt as if her bones had turned to ice. She grabbed another blanket from the alcove shelf and tucked it beneath her bottom to stop the cold rising from the stone floor. The silence was thick and menacing, offering nothing to distract her. She concentrated hard on hearing the faintest sounds of life coming from beyond the alcove, but no snore or furtive scurrying reached her ears. Only her own shallow breaths touched the darkness pressing in on her. She tried imagining the curious noises Eben made in his sleep – faint whistles, murmurings and soft lip smacks – so that she didn't feel so alone and to distract herself from herself, but her thoughts turned inwards against her will and it was not long before her mind-shadows stirred and crept forth.

Showing her vulnerability to Jack Lea in the courtyard had reminded her of how she'd learned at a young age to show her mother only what she wanted to see and how she'd never found the courage to ruin her mother's idea of a perfect life and tell her that Elmer Long had begun pinching her tiny breasts and stroking her hand along his trousered thighs as soon as her father had died, long before her mother had walked in on them in the library.

A sharp pain clutched Nell's belly, as if someone had punched her there, and she acknowledged finally that she'd been holding onto that hurt and lying to herself for a long, long time. And that she couldn't ignore the truth any longer, not if she wanted to find the courage to stop hiding from her past and live a better life, one free of persistent despair.

It was time for her to face the fact that her beautiful but fragile mother had turned a blind eye to what was going on in Long's home. One winter's eve in Nell's ninth year, Elmer had been licking her face when she'd heard her bedchamber door creak open behind her and felt the draught chill her wet cheeks. She'd twisted away from his soft tongue, hoping to be saved from his attentions and taken away from that sickening home, and saw that the door was once again shut fast. Her mother's floral scent, however, had lingered in the room.

Nell pulled the hood of Jack's brown cloak down over her ears and wrapped her arms around her body to stop herself from crying. Her heart ached bitterly as she remembered how helpless and alone she'd felt all those years ago and how she'd longed for someone to hold her close and tell her that she was safe and loved. The smell of dried sweat on Jack's cloak, musky and woodsy with a hint of fresh-baked bread, was oddly comforting and helped her to hold herself tightly together – for the time being at least. She wished that he was there keeping her company.

A handbell clanged in the passageway. Nell crawled over to the curtains and peeked through them. Brother Caddock was closing the door to the room next to the alcove. He rang the bell again and tapped his large sandalled foot impatiently on the floor. She prayed that he didn't find a reason to inspect the alcove.

Twisting her neck to an uncomfortable angle so that she could see more of the passage, Nell searched for Brother Idris and finally saw him leaving the very last room in the row. While his brothers headed to the midnight blessing, he stopped outside the room diagonally opposite to where Nell was kneeling and gently rapped on the door.

When he received no answer, he opened it and said over his shoulder to Caddock, 'Father Emlyn's fast asleep and I've not the heart to wake him. Every moment free of the terrible pain within his head is a blessing.'

Caddock pursed his thick lips, then said, 'Leave him. Of late he makes little sense and his ramblings disturb our worship.' Brushing past Idris, he marched along the passage and turned sharply around the corner.

Once Idris was alone – or thought himself so – he slammed the heel of one hand into the stone wall, then held his arms stiffly by his sides as he looked up to the ceiling. The muscles in his throat tightened and Nell had the impression that he was working hard to contain a bellow of outrage.

Once the passage was clear, Nell ducked into Caddock's room, which lacked even the faintest of scents – no body odour, mustiness or lingering fart. There was a chest in the corner of the room, but when she bent down to open it she saw it was locked. She found no trace of a key or anything else – not even a stray hair – on the washstand nor in a small cupboard that contained spare clothes. At the bed, she ran her hand beneath the mattress, finding nothing, then lifted up the pillow and found a silver locket. She opened it and saw a lock of red hair.

None of the victims had red hair so she was fairly sure that the lock had once belonged to his sister who had mysteriously drowned in the Eel fourteen years ago. Had Lorraine walked into the river of her own free will, Nell wondered again, or had Caddock or Idris forced her head beneath the water?

She carefully placed the locket back where she'd found it and straightened the tightly tucked sheets, wondering all the while what was in the locked chest. She would have to find a tool to break the lock and come back later. Poking her head gingerly around the doorframe, she made sure the way was clear and ran to Idris's room.

She entered the cell and gasped as she noticed the diamond-shaped window on the other side of the rumpled bed. The room looked identical to the one featured in the scroll that she'd taken from Julian Simms. Had Julian peered through that window to witness an unholy coupling between Idris and a young woman who looked a lot like Maye or Hester Hannigan? And if so, was Julian now blackmailing Idris?

However, despite a thorough search, Nell didn't find anything else incriminating in the room. She peered into the three other cells to see if any of them also had a diamond-shaped window, but they didn't – at least, not that she could see.

She contemplated opening the door of Father Emlyn's room

but a nearby sound of something being dropped startled her. She fled down the passage towards the latrines.

Darting across the courtyard, she considered how what she'd just discovered put Idris at the top of the list of suspects. Had he killed Maye Hannigan to keep her quiet about their activities?

The only way to answer those questions was to ask more questions – which went against the promise she'd made to Jack to drop the bone before she broke her teeth on it. Nell resolved to find Hester Hannigan first thing in the morning to talk to her about the incriminating scroll.

On her way back through the moonlit orchard to the convent, Nell's belly suddenly began cramping again, although it was nowhere near her moon time. Pressing her hands against it to suppress both the physical pain and the wild emotions straining for release, she stumbled through a carpet of pink blossoms to the closest apple tree and rested her forehead against it.

Her mind flashed back to the day Pearl had opened the library door and seen her daughter sitting on Elmer Long's knee. Nell had wriggled free, followed her mother into the kitchen and watched her prepare the midday meal, waiting desperately for Pearl to see how afraid and confused she was.

Her mother, however, continued to pour wine into goblets and slice bread without looking Nell's way. And, with her attention fixed firmly on laying the tray, she'd then asked Nell to collect a brace of conies from Hairy Tom because she wanted to make a rabbit stew for Long's daughter who was arriving there that day. By the time Nell returned, her mother was dead.

Nell gripped the tree trunk so hard that its bark grazed the cuts she'd received on her hand the day she'd spilled lemon tea onto the sheriff's bag. Her mind immediately conjured the sheriff's goblet and she realised what had started to trouble her that day. Her mother had hated mulled wine. So why had she poured it into two goblets? Bile rushed into her throat as the sickening truth dawned upon her: Pearl had poisoned the wine and then drunk it herself. Had she intended to drink just a small measure to make herself sick so that no one would suspect her of poisoning Long? Or had she intended to die?

Nell considered the casual way her mother had bade her farewell as Nell had left to fetch the conies, not even kissing her daughter's cheek. If Pearl had intended to die, wouldn't she have hugged her daughter close and whispered words of love to her? Or given her some idea of how to survive once she was alone in the world? And why had she tried to murder Long in the first place? Wouldn't it have made more sense just to pack her and Nell's belongings and leave?

Tears flowed down Nell's face as she answered her own question. Pearl, who had pretended not to notice that Elmer Long was fiddling with her daughter, would not have had the courage to leave. The reason the sheriff's goblet had bothered her so much now became clear: it'd been empty. And so had Pearl's. She had drunk every drop of the poisoned wine; she had chosen to leave her young daughter alone in the world rather than face starting life anew.

And, to hammer home that painful truth, Nell remembered that when she'd crawled over to her mother's body she'd not gotten any bloodstains on the lower part of her dress because there had been no blood visible on the floor surrounding her – only vomit – making it more likely that Christiana Long had stabbed her father and not Pearl because Pearl was already dead.

Unlike her mother's goblet, a pool of wine had been present on the table beside Long's, which had been lying on its side. This most likely explained why he had still been breathing when his daughter found him.

Nell slumped to her knees, heartbroken, and clamped Jack's cloak over her mouth to muffle the cries of anguish that surged in waves from her aching belly.

She remembered the night she'd arrived at the Boar's Den, shivering, dirty and hungry from a two-day journey across the sea, and how she'd seen the leering faces of the men gathered in the bar room. As young as she was, she'd recognised those looks instantly for she had seen the same expression many times on Long's face, just before he touched her.

Her life flashed before her eyes – all the despicable things she'd done to survive since that day; all the times she'd looked the other way herself, not wanting to risk her own wellbeing to help someone in need.

Her mind raced and her thoughts fractured as she struggled for somewhere to hide from them. But there was nowhere. She was trapped. She could never escape the pain. Never. She had wished herself dead many times over the last seven years; had felt unworthy of life because her own mother hadn't loved her enough to stay with her. Could a mother bestow upon her child a more poisonous curse?

She was angry now, so fucking angry that her mother had left a broken girl of ten years to cope with all that. Thrusting her head back, she opened her mouth wide and screamed as quietly as possible so as not to wake anyone in the convent. The rush of air was like a fire roaring through the woods, and she forced it from her belly over and over again. Her heart was thudding so fast she felt light-headed and nauseous.

Between your heartbeats, silence whispers.

She latched onto the Crows' words even though she didn't really believe that they could calm or comfort her. To her great surprise, she saw within her mind an image of the Crows sailing across a turbulent sea in a small boat that somehow crested and rode the treacherous waves with ease.

Nell blinked, and suddenly she was sitting all alone at the bow of the boat. At the crest of the next wave, she frantically searched the horizon for a glimpse of land but only the pounding sea stretched ahead of her for mile upon mile. The boat gracefully sailed down the swell to a hollow at the base of three converging waves. Taking what surely must be her last breath, Nell waited for the cold green water to swamp her.

Instead, a deep silence surrounded her, removing all thoughts of drowning, and the water gently rocked her until she calmed enough to sense a subtle flow of strength and serenity in the darkness.

The little boat then left the sea and floated down the river, where she saw her mind-shadows standing on its banks. One by one, as she acknowledged them, they stepped into the water and swam with the ancient wisdom emanating from the earth. Feeling lighter, she softened, yielding to the dance with nature until the boat disappeared and she became part of that sacred flow. Her hips undulated in harmony with the earth's pulse, and wisdom and shadow became one seed that quivered to life in her womb.

As she sighed and let go, the seed's roots grew and strengthened, its tendrils climbed up and up, nourishing the parts of herself that she'd neglected and even loathed. She could see now that she was much more than the child who had been abandoned and who had experienced the worst of mankind's nature. She had grown into a young woman who could read the pain on a child's face and choose not to look away. The resilience and determination – not to mention the skills of stealing and spinning a yarn – that she'd gained from living through difficult experiences were strengths she could use now to keep Eben safe.

The river followed the path of silvery moonlight until it flowed back into the sea. This time, Nell embraced the expanse before her with open arms and whispers of truth touched her ears, reminding her of things she'd forgotten about herself. Finally, she perceived that she was at one with the seabed and the stars.

Chapter Twenty-Eight

Of Rings and Rats

'That's not my Maye,' cried Hester, stepping sharply backwards and closer to one of the two large boulders marking the path to Maiden's Well. Tears glistened on her dark lashes and her creamy skin blushed as she crumpled the scroll with both hands and threw it on the ground at Nell's feet. 'And it's not me either. I know not why Julian would … What do you want from me?'

Before Nell could reassure Hester that she just wanted to ask a few questions, the girl wrenched one of two identical rings off her little finger and threw it on top of the scroll. 'That should buy your silence. Now, leave me be.'

Nell, who'd left Eben eating breakfast in the refectory with Sister Agnes, so that she could catch up with Hester on her way to work, picked up the ring – Idris must have returned it to the twins' mother as he'd promised the sheriff he would – and handed it back to Hester. 'I want to find the person who killed your sister. Whether you posed naked for Julian Simms is not my concern. The safety of a little boy is at stake. Will you help me?'

Hester put the ring back on her finger, then nervously adjusted the grey scarf holding back her untidy black hair. 'That was my ring I threw on the ground, not Maye's,' she said. 'Julian paid me and two of my friends to pose for him in our shifts. That's all. I've never set foot in Brother Idris's room.'

'And what about the other victims? Did they pose for him too?'

'I know not, but I'm sure we weren't the only ones. Julian is charming when he wants to be.'

Nell thanked her for her honesty, then added, 'Irma Linke saw Idris crying in the chapel shortly after Maye disappeared. He was holding the altar cloth your mother made against his chest. Was something going on between him and Maye?'

Maye's lips parted and she sighed sadly. 'My sister loved him quietly, secretly, but not one word of affection passed between them, let alone anything else. A few weeks before she died, she told me that she'd decided to join the convent and that she'd be content to work alongside Idris for the rest of her life. I often teased her about her love for Idris, and have since realised that I did so because I was jealous that she had found someone who touched her deeply, even if she could never act upon it or speak to him about her feelings. I did not understand then how painful heartache could be. Now, I ache ... and wish ...' Hester broke off and stared at the ground, her fingertips pressed against her brow.

'Not long before she disappeared, I pretended to be Maye and flirted shamelessly with Idris. He avoided her whenever possible after that. She was devastated. I apologised to him, but she had not yet forgiven me before she died.' She wrapped her arms around herself and sobbed. 'And I cannot forgive myself.'

Nell's throat trembled with sadness as she witnessed the anguish on Hester's face. She waited until Hester was calmer, then asked, 'Did Idris return Maye's affection?'

'He was always courteous to her, almost aloof, but I sensed that stronger feelings smouldered beneath the surface. He often watched her when he thought no one was looking. Methinks he was as bewitched as my sister, though she insisted that he was not and had never given her any reason to think otherwise.'

Nell wondered how Idris coped with temptation, with fighting against his natural urges, denying himself a wife and family. Did anger and frustration overwhelm him sometimes? Had he lashed out and drowned Lorraine, his childhood friend, so that he didn't have to watch her with the stonemason's son?

'Are you sure that Idris and Maye never …?' asked Nell.

Hester shook her head. 'I'd have known. We never could keep secrets from each other, even when we wanted to.'

'Was she wearing any other jewellery on the day she disappeared?'

'She wore a locket most days. I had one the same but lost it a year or so ago.'

'Does your mother have Maye's locket now? Or is it missing?'

'I cannot say, but will ask her if you think it important,' said Hester. Picking up the crumpled scroll, Nell asked if she could hold on to it for a while longer.

'Burn it when you're done,' Hester said. Nell thanked her and had almost reached the river path, when Hester added, 'It should have been me.'

'What?'

'On the day Maye disappeared, she left Lambley Manor before I did. Usually it was the other way round.'

'Why would someone want to kill you?' Nell asked.

Hester shrugged. 'I know not. But it haunts me to think that Maye might have died in my place.'

'Even if you're right, you cannot blame yourself.'

'But I do.'

As Nell left Hester and returned to the river path, she wondered why Idris – if he'd killed Maye Hannigan – would have killed the others. Had he reached the point where he could no longer cope with denying his manly urges and, if so, was he now removing those temptations from his path? Before going to the refectory to collect Eben, Nell decided to confront Brother Idris with the scroll.

~

On her way over Monk's Mill bridge to the church, Nell realised that she was almost marching, stiff and jerky with anger and resentment, and the fear that her past would never cease to haunt her. Hester Hannigan's heartache and guilt had stirred up the bad feelings again. They had hit her as soon as she'd returned to the convent last night and climbed into bed. She'd wondered where her mother had found the poison she'd used – stirring it into the wine in her daughter's presence – within the space of a quarter hour, roughly the time it'd taken her to leave the library and begin preparations for the midday meal. The only answer Nell had been able to come up with was that Pearl had already stashed some in the cellar, knowing that the day she'd use it was soon coming.

The magical sensations she'd felt growing inside her in the orchard had disappeared instantly, leaving only a cold empty ache, and making her wonder if she'd dreamed or imagined that brief experience of being connected to something comforting and enduring. She was alone again now, both physically and spiritually, and feared she always would be.

As Nell had buried her face in the pillow, willing sleep to come, she'd then remembered clearly what she had done the day her mother had opened the library door and seen her daughter sitting on Long's knee, his last groan still tainting the air. Pearl had taken a step back then, as if she'd been about to close the door and walk away *again*, but Nell had held her gaze and had refused to obey the unspoken plea she'd read on her mother's face – "just close your eyes, sweet girl, and think about pretty things until it all goes away". Had Pearl killed herself because she wouldn't've been able to go on pretending that all was well after that? Had she chosen to punish her daughter for making her feel guilty or ashamed?

The church was almost empty, except for Brother Caddock, who was vigorously polishing the wooden altar, and Julian Simms. Nell saw that Julian's satchel was leaning against the wall at one end of his mural, while he was muttering feverishly to himself and scouring black ink off Eve's face. According to Sister Agnes, someone had defaced Julian's work sometime during the early hours.

She crept close, snatched up the bag and up-ended it. Brushes, pots of ink and a number of scrolls scattered over the floor. She rummaged through them, looking for anything that might have belonged to the murdered girls. Her hands came up empty.

'What are you doing?' asked Julian as he fell to his knees beside her and frantically gathered as many scrolls as he could. He stuffed them back into the satchel before Caddock saw them.

A spark of inspiration hit Nell. ''Tis not your scrolls I'm after,' she said, and before he could stop her, she'd picked up his book, *Simms's Nymphs of Wood and Sea*. She darted with it into the main body of the church and stood between two pews. 'If you come near me, I'll scream.'

'What on earth's going on?' Caddock's voice boomed across the church.

Julian looked like he was about to faint.

'Forgive me, Brother,' said Nell. 'A mouse startled me.'

'A mouse? I think not. You're stirring up trouble, not praying. If you cannot contain yourself, then leave.'

As Caddock stared her down, his thick lips pursed in a fish-like manner, she thought again of the lock of pale red hair coiled in the locket under his pillow. Julian's portrait of Eve had artfully woven locks of blonde, gold and red. Was it Caddock himself who'd splashed ink across such an enchanting work of art, because he didn't want his sister associated with Eve the temptress?

Caddock about-faced, apparently satisfied that Nell was back in her place. She dreaded to think what would happen to the townsfolk and the many desperate and destitute folk who came from all over the isle to St Clement's for help if Caddock won the abbotship. Sister Winifred had shared with Nell her concern that Caddock's lack of compassion and empathy would undo much of Father Emlyn's good work.

Nell turned her attention back to Julian Simms. While she would have loved to denounce him to Caddock, she was loath to shame Hester and her family – they'd suffered enough. Or any other of the local lasses, for that matter, whose likenesses might appear on the scrolls.

She waved Julian forward and whispered, 'Turn out your pockets.'

As he closed the gap between them, he had a spring in his step that she didn't like. She gave herself a mental kick in the behind. He must have sensed her reluctance to call upon Caddock for help. Mayhap he wasn't as dim-witted as she'd thought.

With one eye on the monk, Simms swept his cloak over one shoulder and pulled several items out of his pockets. He placed them with exaggerated care on the pew, until Nell was satisfied there was nothing more to come. She gritted her teeth. Nothing incriminating, but she couldn't eliminate him from her list. The killer could have hidden any keepsakes from the murders in a safe place, not on their person.

Why, she asked herself, hadn't Sheriff Birch searched the homes of the other four people present in the churchyard when the necklace was dropped? Sister Winifred had said that he wanted to watch the churchyard in case the killer came looking for the keepsake, but in Nell's opinion the most obvious action would have been to search each person in turn, then peer into every nook and cranny of their homes.

'What about my book?' asked Julian, putting his belongings back in his pocket.

Nell flicked through the beautifully illuminated and sensual drawings of exotic nymphs, unicorns and mermaidens. They looked alive and she could have gazed at the exquisite detail in each forest haven and underwater realm for hours. 'Twas a pity such a masterful artist had stooped so low as to create those obscene scrolls.

'Where were you on the night Phoebe Butterball died?' Nell

asked.

Placing a finger close to his lips, as if preparing to tell a secret, Julian said, 'Mmm, tucked up in bed with my sweet wife.'

'Did you sleep with Phoebe and get her with child?' Nell asked.

'My wife tends well enough to my needs.'

Nell doubted every word the shifty man uttered.

'What about your other models? Did you bed them too?'

Julian's eyes narrowed briefly, giving Nell a chill. Then he smirked and leaned forward. 'Are you offering yourself to me?'

Nell resisted the urge to step back. She had wanted to get Julian's reaction to the rumour that his mother was ridding girls of unwanted babies, but decided against it as he was unlikely to tell her the truth anyway. And he was giving her the creeps. She looked him slowly up and down, aiming to disarm his confidence while she considered her next move. She could destroy the scrolls, at least, to save Hester any more grief.

'Give me the satchel,' she said.

He handed it to her. 'Enjoy the drawings. Many others have.'

Nell's blood boiled. She wanted to hammer his smug and pretty face with her fist.

'Fish the others out of there,' she said, pointing to the urn he'd been peering into the other day. 'Bring them to me at the convent by suppertime.'

'My hand will not fit through the neck,' he said, confirming her suspicions that he had been hiding the scrolls in there the other day and making her wonder if perhaps he'd hidden any keepsakes in the urn as well. Given his stupidity, Nell couldn't see Julian killing and burying four bodies and remaining undetected for many months without assistance. If he were the killer, it was certain that Cook Simms would have had a meaty hand in the cover-up.

'If you don't, I'll tell Caddock and the sheriff about the scrolls and your models.'

'If I do as you ask, will you give me back my book?'

Nell recalled the snide way Julian had pointed out his father-in-law's face amid the hair and shading on the camel's rear end in the mural, and what Sister Winifred had said about Hammond Carpenter rigidly following the church's commandments.

'If you do not do as I ask, I'll give the book of nymphs to your father-in-law,' she said.

With great satisfaction, she saw that she'd finally rattled him. Panic rippled across his face and his eyes flicked frantically around the church, as if he was looking for a way out of a tight corner.

But as she hooked her arm through the strap and settled the satchel on her shoulder, she sensed a change in him. Looking back, she saw that he was now watching her closely, like a cat waiting for the perfect moment to pounce on an unsuspecting bird. He no longer looked dim-witted.

'By suppertime,' she said.

'I know where to find you.'

Was she imagining the dangerous glint in his eyes? She suddenly remembered her father once trapping a rat behind a cupboard and how it had fought for its life with tooth and claw. Had she just cornered a rat?

Chapter Twenty-Nine

Alibis and a Promise

Later that day, while Eben played at the orphanage in the care of Sister Agnes, Nell ducked over to the Merry Monkey, hoping to speak to Alice about the relationship between Cook Simms and her son. She thought it was unlikely that Alice had ever been asked to pose for Julian, so she might be jealous of the lasses who had and be keen to gossip. She might also have vital information regarding the occasions Julian had called upon his mother during the last month and whether those meetings had been heated or conducted in secrecy.

Nell had almost reached the inn's backyard when an almighty yell rent the air. She hurried towards the kitchen, and was almost bowled over by Cook Simms who suddenly burst through the door. She was clutching her head, which was bleeding, and cursing vilely as she ran on unsteady feet towards the front yard.

Now that the shouting had ceased, Nell peered inside the door. The kitchen looked as if ten hefty men had been brawling inside it. Over by the fireplace, amid scattered pots and pans and clouds of still-falling flour, Arnod Butterball was wrapping a cloth around a nasty gash on Alice's arm.

'She put them in there!' cried Alice. 'I'd never do such a thing.'

Arnod closed his eyes and rubbed between his eyebrows. 'Enough,' he said. 'Enough.'

Mary was kneeling beside a small overturned chest, its contents scattered over the floor. She held to her breast the green scarf Phoebe had given her. Nell saw it was splattered with blood.

'What's going on?' Nell asked, kneeling beside Mary.

Mary shook her head. 'Everything's broken. I cannot take any more.'

An hour later, Nell emptied a bucket of broken crockery onto the scraps pile at the back of the inn and arched her aching back. On her way back to the kitchen to help Mary with the supper preparations, she saw Sister Winifred and Eben coming down the side path. Serjeant Oswald was straggling along behind them.

After Nell had told the nun about Cook Simms accusing Alice of being Bellayne's poison-monger, Sister Winifred offered to help Mary prepare supper while Nell ran an errand for Mary. The bacon hock intended for breakfast the next day had been used by Cook as a weapon.

Before setting off for the butcher's, Nell took the opportunity to ask Sister Winifred about Brother Idris's whereabouts on the night Phoebe disappeared. She wanted to know if he'd been present at the dusk-'til-dawn prayer vigil the brethren had held at Father Emlyn's bedside after he'd suffered a debilitating fit that day.

'He was not there the whole night,' said the nun, sounding a little testy. 'But he freely admitted that. When Brother Caddock returned from the meeting with you at the Merry Monkey about your discovery of the graves, he and Idris discussed arrangements for the disinterment, then went about their separate tasks. They had much to do.'

Nell could see holes in Idris's alibi. He could have left the abbey and killed Phoebe, then hidden her body and waited until his tasks were done and the brethren were asleep before burying her in Shymer Forest. The same reasoning could also be applied to Brother

Caddock. None of the other three suspects had confirmed alibis either, so Nell couldn't cross any of them off her list yet.

'Your promise to me was not long kept.' There was anger in Jack's voice as he placed a hand on Nell's lower back and ushered her into a small room alongside the castle stables. Nell had stopped off at the castle on her way to the butcher's so that she could give the satchel of scrolls to Jack for safekeeping. She didn't trust Julian and feared he might try to steal them from her.

The room, empty except for a few hooks hanging on one wall, smelled of horse piddle and damp straw, reminding her of the stink that had wafted up from the stables below her room at the Boar's Den.

'Promise?' she queried.

A cloud of dust puffed into the air as Jack slammed the door and crossed his arms over his chest. 'To stay safe within St Clement's walls.'

'Forgive me, but all hell broke loose at the Merry Monkey this afternoon. I offered to help Mary and Arnod clean up the mess in the kitchen and prepare supper for the guests. I'm on my way to fetch a bacon hock for breakfast tomorrow.'

'Birch told me that Cook and Alice have each accused the other of being the poison-monger of Bellayne,' he said, raising his eyebrows.

'Alice clouted Cook over the head a few times with a frypan and accused her of planting the poison letter and stolen scarf in the chest in her room. Cook denied it and stabbed Alice in the arm with a knife. Alice is resting in the infirmary now, and Cook has disappeared – for good, I hope.'

She pulled the satchel off her shoulder and gave it to him. 'This bag contains more of Julian Simms's scrolls. Keep them well hidden until we have time to work out what we are going to do with them.'

'We should give them to Birch,' Jack said, dumping the satchel on the dirt floor.

'Maybe, but not yet. I need time to think. They are going to cause a stink all over town.'

Jack cocked his head and urged her to go on.

'The room in the scroll you saw is identical to Brother Idris's.'

'Shit ... but how can you know that?'

'Never mind that for now.'

Jack shook his head, clearly exasperated, and stepped towards her. 'Your tidings have not deflected me from your broken promise. You also promised to keep Eben safe. Where is he?'

She stepped backwards, away from him, and banged her head on one of the wall hooks.

'There,' she said, rubbing her skull, 'I'm punished. And Eben is with Sister Winifred. As a matter of fact, she and Eben arrived at the Merry Monkey just as I was leaving. We're having supper together at the inn and then Serjeant Oswald will escort us back to the convent.'

Jack looked crestfallen. 'Are you not bringing Eben to see me this evening?'

'Not if I'm under the strictest of orders not to wander about alone,' she said, irritation and a touch of frigidity lacing her voice. 'And to top it all off, I'm knackered. I'd rather put my feet up and sip a mug of camomile tea than butt up against your cold shoulder.' Even though Jack hadn't remembered to bring the coat she'd left in the sheriff's great hall, she thrust the one she'd borrowed off him into his arms and pushed past him to the door. 'I must away.'

As she grasped the doorknob, a bewildering thought popped out of nowhere: would he notice the scent of her hair on the cloak's hood the next time he wore it? Perhaps that would prompt him to think of her sometimes after she'd left Bellayne.

She shook her head, trying to dislodge such nonsense, worried that she'd banged her head much harder than she'd thought.

'Rosemary,' she said. 'I rinsed my hair with rosemary water.'

'What?' He frowned in puzzlement.

'Er, nothing, just thinking aloud.' She searched for an explanation for her odd outburst. 'I was trying to remember the name of a very demanding guest at the Merry Monkey.'

'I wish you'd put as much effort into remembering and upholding your promises,' he said.

'I've endured enough scolding for one day.'

Jack nudged her shoulder with his. 'I'm worried about you. If you persist with your prying, you could encounter the one who is disturbed.'

Fuming, Nell tugged at the door but it was stuck fast. She looked down and saw his foot jamming it shut. 'Open the door … please.'

'You may want to hear my tidings before you storm off.' There wasn't a skerrick of banter left in his voice now.

Letting go of the doorknob, she said, 'What troubles you?'

He pulled something from a pocket in his breeches and gave it to her. She moved closer to the narrow window and drew in a sharp breath as she ran her thumb over a piece of pearl shell with a four-pointed star scratched onto it.

'Has this something to do with Phoebe's necklace?'

'Look at the shape,' he said.

'It's oval. Hers was a crescent.'

'When Eben gave the necklace to Sister Winifred, didn't she tell you that Phoebe's mother had two crescents fashioned out of pearl shell at the time of her daughter's birth?'

Nell flicked her hand impatiently to hurry him up. 'So?'

'So, imagine two crescents on either side of this oval.'

'A circle. One piece of shell?'

He nodded.

'Might the three pieces represent a family?' she mused. 'The circle could belong to Phoebe's father?'

'Perhaps.'

'Where did you find it?'

'In Birch's bag.'

'Aah!' She poked him none-too-gently in the chest with her

finger. 'I told you that the sheriff had something to hide but you would not listen.'

Jack swept her fingers away with a sharp flick of his hand. 'Such glee, while another is heavy of heart.' Sliding his back down the wall, he sat on his haunches and stared at the dirty floor.

Nell let her hands flop against her thighs. 'I'm sorry. I did not stop to consider your feelings.'

'Do you ever consider anyone else's feelings?'

'That's hardly fair. You do not know me well at all.'

Tilting his chin up, he said, 'Knowing you a little is more than enough.'

A lump swelled in her throat. 'I could have left Eben lying in Maureen's lifeless arms.'

His eyes flicked away from her face.

'I wanted to walk away,' she added, 'but I did not.'

Blowing a stream of air through his lips, Jack stood again and faced her. 'Arundell's eldest daughter, Mariah, was born a few months before Phoebe.'

'So Birch was married when he slept with Phoebe's mother?'

'If we're right about him fathering Phoebe, then yeah, he was married.' He kicked the door, then paced around the room, stirring up cloudlets of dust. 'Medwelyn was just fourteen years old when she gave birth,' he added, barely able to get the words out.

'Ah, I see.'

She wanted to give his arm a comforting pat but thought better of it. It was unlikely to ease the distress he was feeling at discovering something unsavoury about his friend. He might be reluctant to think the worst of Birch, but she was certain that the two crescents and the oval of shell had once formed a circle. And there could be only one reason for that.

'Do you think that Phoebe knew Birch was her father?'

'I doubt it, otherwise we'd have heard rumours.'

'But if she did, maybe she asked him to help her confront

the father of her baby. Maybe she threatened to expose him if he refused.' She sucked in a sharp breath. 'My God, did Birch kill his own daughter?'

Groaning, Jack raked his hands through his hair. 'I know not.' He dropped his head and sighed long and loud, as if trying to blow away the things he wasn't ready to face. 'God, can this get any worse?'

Seeing Jack's distress made Nell rethink her churlish refusal to bring Eben to see him later. 'I'll fetch Eben from the inn and bring him to you this evening. I promise.'

Chapter Thirty

No Blessings

Irma Linke peered into the woods outside the clearing, desperately praying to see Gracie, who hadn't been seen since she'd become one of the Shadowfolk. Maye and Phoebe were no longer talking to Irma, not even to curse her, and she was struggling to deal with the terrible loneliness eating away her mind. Her ghostly form was virtually useless now, having almost spent her store of moondew, but that didn't stop her from trying to think of ways to mend the damage she'd caused.

Glancing into the woods again reminded her of how Gracie had been killed because she'd seen items belonging to Maye and Irma in their killer's possession that would prove his guilt. If, Irma thought, she'd been able to affect the mind of the man who'd killed her by invading his dreams with her thoughts of vengeance, would it be possible to picture those personal possessions in her mind, make their auras brighter and lead someone to them?

Irma closed her eyes and concentrated hard on bringing to life the locks of hair he'd cut from her and Maye's heads. Once she could imagine their colour and texture and the way they'd feel sliding between her fingers, she focused on the place where they were hidden.

~

At the end of Castlegate, as the sun sank beneath the hills surrounding Bellayne, Nell turned the corner and walked swiftly down the centre of Nun's Way, her eyes scanning the breaks in the hedges that fenced a cluster of well-kept cottages for signs of an ambush from any one of the suspects she'd alerted to her interest in their comings and goings and secrets. Images of Cook Simms suddenly looming out of the twilight brandishing the knife she'd used to stab Alice quickened Nell's footsteps to an awkward jog.

As she ran, she contemplated the implications of Jack's discovery. She'd no doubt that the three shell necklaces, all engraved with stars, had once formed a circle; and that the piece found in Birch's bag meant he was Phoebe's father. Was he also the killer? He'd made no progress in the investigation, and had created an alibi for himself when he'd lied for Jack. And Nell reminded herself of how he'd scoffed when she'd mentioned Albert Simms's concerns that young unwed mothers were being murdered after they'd given birth at St Clement's. The sheriff had dismissed those concerns as the ramblings of a man who was 'sillier than a wet hen'. Did the fact that he'd seduced – or raped, perhaps – Phoebe's mother, Medwelyn, when she was thirteen, indicate that he still desired young women? Had Birch killed Phoebe, his illegitimate daughter? But if so, why?

One reason sprang quickly into Nell's mind: was Birch, not Julian Simms, the father of Phoebe's baby? During her time at the Boar's Den, she'd known quite a few lasses whose fathers had fathered the child in their bellies. If that was the case, Birch couldn't risk the discovery of such a vile secret, not when he'd a rich wife and four legitimate daughters to protect from scandal.

And Sister Winifred, Nell hadn't forgotten, had seen Birch – and Julian Simms – heading towards Maiden's Well at around midday, shortly before Phoebe had crossed the same bridge on her way to meet with someone, a person who'd not yet come forward. In any case, Birch's alibi was unconfirmed for the night Phoebe died. He could have been the person she'd gone out to meet once everyone, including Nell, was asleep in the Merry Monkey.

Nell passed the convent, opened the squeaky gate to the orchard and walked quickly but carefully down one of the blossom-scented avenues. When a stitch gripped her left side, she leaned over her knees to catch her breath. Straightening her back, she saw with dismay that a light fog was rolling in from the Eel, partially obscuring her path through the fruit trees, and that the dusk had thickened considerably in the last few minutes. She turned around, deciding to head back to the safety of the convent, but the squeak of the gate she'd just passed through stopped her in her tracks. Was someone following her?

Caught in a panic of indecision, she looked this way and that, trying to decide the best way to go. When a dark silhouette loomed out of the fog several yards away, her feet made the choice for her, taking her onwards through the orchard. She ignored the thought that if whoever was behind her caught up with her, she'd be even further away from help.

Resisting the temptation to look over her shoulder, she reached the gate on the opposite side of the orchard, fumbled with the latch for a heart-stopping moment, then leaped onto the grassy verge of Holy Apple Row. She raced across the road and up St Clement's porch steps, dreading the moment when someone grabbed her shoulder and pulled her down.

Panting heavily, Nell came to a halt about halfway down the nave. She suddenly realised that the church was deserted. Most folk, including the Greenfriars, would be sitting down to their supper by now. Not wanting to go back outside, and reluctant to take a pew because she'd not be able to watch her back, she imagined herself spinning slowly on the spot for the next hour or so, until she collapsed from dizziness. The empty space surrounding her, the great expanse between the top of her head and the rafters, overwhelmed her, making her feel as insignificant and worthless as a speck of dust. She was alone now, in every sense of the word.

Urging her tired feet to keep turning, she squinted into the half-light to make sure no one had crept through any one of the two entrances. She wished now she hadn't told Julian Simms to bring her the scrolls that evening. Surely this quiet time would be the perfect moment to retrieve them from the urn.

As her gaze drifted past the candles and constant lamp on the altar, a trick of the eye caught and entranced her. If she kept her gaze steady upon the lamp's flame, its light miraculously bloomed like a flower opening its petals. The silver candlesticks glinted, the white altar cloth shimmered, and the wooden cross on the wall glowed golden.

Even though she knew the phenomenon was enhanced by her imagination, tears streamed down her face as she stepped a little closer to the halo. She wanted it to touch her, to help her enter again the *flow* that she'd experienced in the orchard. She wanted it to ease her fears and help her to know for a few moments that she was a unique and intrinsic part of something greater than herself.

A draught swept down the aisle, making her shiver, more from fear than cold. Terrified that Julian Simms would appear at any moment, she looked around the church for somewhere to hide. Without caring that entering the sanctuary was forbidden, she ran up its three shallow steps and huddled behind the altar. The blessing box, which was sitting on an open shelf at the back of the altar alongside two large tomes, drew her attention. While tracing with her fingertips the carving of a lithe male angel, she remembered Father Emlyn telling the parishioners that the box wouldn't be opened again until the next full moon, after his successor had been named. If Caddock or Idris had murdered the girls and kept morbid keepsakes, the box would be the perfect place to hide them in case the sheriff decided to search their belongings.

Nell lifted the blessing box off the shelf and settled it in her lap, then held her breath as she unlatched and opened the lid. It was empty. The pieces of parchment bearing stories about the four murdered girls had been removed in preparation for their placement in the Lady Chapel.

She was about to close the lid when she noticed a tiny piece of ribbon, almost the same colour as the dark red velvet lining, sticking up from the join near the bottom left-hand corner of the box. Pinching the ribbon between the tips of her finger and thumb, she pulled. After her third attempt, a false bottom lifted out of the box. Her belly gave a sickening lurch. The box wasn't empty, after all.

With trembling fingers, she picked up a frizzy straw-blonde curl and cupped it gently in the palm of her hand. A red thread was knotted around the middle of the curl to stop the hairs from drifting apart.

Nell's sigh trembled with sadness, and she wished she could close the lid and walk away. But the truth couldn't, and wouldn't, stay hidden. Sister Winifred had pointed out Irma Linke's cheery face and curly blonde hair among the angels at the top of Julian Simms's mural. Nell had no doubt that the killer had cut the curl from Irma's head.

Dipping her fingers back into the box, she pulled out a thick coil of what was most likely Maye Hannigan's sable hair.

A soft footfall touched her ears, but before she could turn around, something struck the side of her head. Stars exploded in front of her eyes as she fell forward and hit the altar shelf with her forehead.

'I've been watching,' said a voice.

And then all went black.

Someone grasped Nell's shoulders and pulled her away from the back of the altar. Her head was swimming. Her body was limp. She couldn't defend herself. It was over. She'd failed Gracie Alcorn, who would likely haunt the churchyard for eternity; and she'd failed Eben, who would never be safe while Lex Alcorn continued to believe that Jack had killed his daughter. Her heart ached at the thought of never again holding Eben in her arms nor hearing his sweet, husky voice.

Someone lifted the blessing box off her lap, awkwardly uncrossed her legs and lowered her back to the floor. Cold, strong hands pressed the sides of her throat.

The vision she'd seen in the well at Larke-upon-Eel was about to come true. But there'd be no desperate lunge across the room and attempt to escape her assailant tonight. She was incapable of fighting off the hands about to claim her life.

She forced her eyelids apart and looked up at Brother Idris. For Sister Winifred's sake, she had hoped to see Leticia or Julian Simms. The nun's fears had come to pass: poison had leached into St Clement's, the heart of Bellayne.

Idris was panting, almost whimpering, and looked tormented. She could see that her death would stay with him, haunting his prayers, his sleep.

'Is she dead?' asked someone behind him.

'Her heartbeat slows. It'll not be long.' Idris pulled his hands away from Nell's throat, then put a finger to his lips and gently closed her eyelids with the palm of his hand.

What was he saying? Her heartbeat wasn't slowing. It was thumping quite loudly and painfully in her head. Straining, she lifted her head off the floor and tried to sit up, but he pushed her back down and bent close to her ear. 'Shhh! Be still. I'll help you soon.'

The other voice said, 'She would not let you be. By night and by day, she watched you. I could not let her ruin your life.'

Nell gasped when she recognised the speaker. *Father Emlyn?*

Idris's troubled face was still only a few inches above her own. He shuddered and slowly shook his head as if he couldn't believe what he was hearing.

'She came to me, Idris ... she came to me and asked to enter the convent. She would have tempted you every day. I saw the way your face softened whenever she was near.' Father Emlyn started to cry. 'And one day, my son, you'd have given in and all that we'd worked for would be lost, wasted.'

Nell was sure that Father Emlyn was referring to Maye Hannigan. Hester had told her that Maye had loved Idris quietly and would have been content to work alongside him at St Clement's. She didn't sound like a temptress to Nell, but Father Emlyn had obviously thought otherwise. Nell hoped she would get the chance to tell Hester that she wasn't to blame for her sister's death; that the killer hadn't mistaken one twin for the other.

Idris sat back on his haunches, then slowly stood and walked over to Father Emlyn. Through lowered lashes, Nell could see the old monk sitting slumped against the wall near the door to the sacristy, an entrance she hadn't accounted for or watched.

He swiped away tears and held out a hand to Idris. 'I could not let that happen.'

Idris crouched beside him, positioning himself so that Nell's view of Father Emlyn was blocked. That meant he couldn't see her either. She coaxed her limbs into action and rolled onto her side as quietly as she could. She wasn't sure what Idris had meant when he'd said that he'd help her, but she wasn't waiting around to find out.

Coming up onto all fours, she saw the hefty silver candlestick that Father Emlyn must have struck her with, lying on the ground beside her. She was thankful that he was frail otherwise he could have crushed her skull with it. His blow must have glanced off the side of her head and hit her shoulder though, because it throbbed as she readied herself to crawl away.

'Hark, Idris, is she moving?'

Nell immediately flopped back onto the floor and watched the two men through slitted eyelids.

'Nay,' Idris said soothingly. 'She is still unconscious.'

'I used the alms cart and a handbarrow to take the others to Shymer Forest, but we cannot go there now,' said Father Emlyn.

'You'll have to throw her body into the river during the evenfall blessing. Go through the back gate of the churchyard. The yews are thick there. No one will see you.'

Idris turned to look at Nell, his expression unreadable. Was he weighing up his options for getting rid of her corpse?

'Irma Linke came sneaking around. She told Sister Winifred she'd seen you crying over that girl in the Lady Chapel.' The wheedling tone was gone from the old man's voice. He sounded matter-of-fact now, justified. 'She began prying into your whereabouts on the day I hid the first one in the forest and I knew I'd made a mistake. I'd sent you out to the villages to get you out of the way, instead of keeping you here where everyone could see you.'

'And Gracie?' Idris asked in a whisper.

'Gracie?'

'The little girl, Father. I saw her …' Nell could hear that Idris was crying now. He leaned closer to the man who'd raised him from a baby. 'Oh, dear God, I saw her in her grave with what I know now to be *your* belt around her throat. Why? Why did you bury her face down in the dirt?'

'Her eyes wouldn't stay closed, my boy. She came into the chapel late one afternoon to give me an egg. I did not hear her come and she saw me with the blessing box. She wanted to know if I was giving a lock each of Maye's and Irma's hair to the angels. I told her nay, and that I kept their hair so I'd remember them, for often now I forget.'

'Oh, God, she was an innocent child.'

Father Emlyn wrapped his arms around Idris and rested his cheek atop his head. 'Oh, my boy, tell me you understand. Please tell me.'

Idris bowed his head and gave no answer.

While Father Emlyn was focused on Idris, Nell pushed up onto her knees again, ignoring the queasiness in her belly. She crawled around the altar towards the sanctuary steps, but the ground swam sickeningly beneath her.

'I forgot to take the rope from her neck. Her hair was covering it,' Father Emlyn continued. 'And Caddock, the canny devil, started asking about the Hannigan girl and watching you too. I was worried that he'd try to blame it all on you. Forgive me, son, for getting it wrong.'

Nell slid down the sanctuary steps and got shakily to her feet. She recalled Father Emlyn handing her the olive rope on the mortuary chapel stairs, and realised that she'd misinterpreted what she'd overheard him saying to the other monks in the undercroft. He'd been distressed because his mistakes might lead to Idris being blamed for the murders, not because he'd seen something that pointed to Idris having killed the girls.

'She's gone!' Father Emlyn cried. There was no frailty in his voice now. 'Idris, stop her!'

Chapter Thirty-One

While He was Sleeping

Using the pews for support, Nell ran unsteadily down the nave. She screamed but nothing came out of her mouth. She'd almost reached the porch when Idris latched onto her shoulder and pulled her backwards.

Wrapping his arms around her, he held her back against his chest. 'Be still, I'll not hurt you.'

She didn't believe him. She clawed at his arms and kicked backwards into his shins but to no avail.

He held on tighter, hunched his body over hers and lowered his head so that his mouth was near her ear. 'I just want to talk.'

Father Emlyn cried out, 'She cannot go free.'

Idris's chin dug into her shoulder and his body shook as he rocked them both from side to side. He was lost in a world of his own, one that no longer made sense.

'Maye … God … oh, God, make him stop speaking. I do not want to hear any more.'

Nell's knees buckled as she tried in vain to hold him up. They both sank to the floor. He sagged against her back and cried into the hair at the nape of her neck.

'I thought I saw her … her ghost … in the Lady Chapel. I waited every day for her to come, for her to comfort me.'

Nell couldn't help but cry with him as the unbearable truth ripped through his heart, tearing faith and love asunder, boring swift and deep into his soul. If he could see the terrible state Gracie Alcorn was in now, Nell wondered if he'd still want his beloved Maye to appear to him.

All of a sudden, he opened his arms and released her. She scrambled away, spun around on her knees and lashed out at him. Holding his arms out to the sides, he let her thump his chest.

'I will not let him get away with it,' he said.

Nell sat back on her heels. 'What do you mean?'

'Idris?' Father Emlyn was leaning against the lectern, watching them.

Placing a hand over his heart, Idris said, 'I will not let him go free, but he is old and sick ... A sickness grows inside his head. He knows not what he does or has done. He is no longer the man that I and others have loved.'

'That's no excuse,' Nell began.

'I know. Oh God, his sins are terrible, but I'll not see him hang. I beg you for some time ... not long ... before you call upon the sheriff. Let me take him to his bed ... Brother Godric will help me ... a poison. And I'll stay with him until the breath leaves his body.'

'Why shouldn't he suffer for his sins?' Nell said. 'Gracie Alcorn is suffering still.'

Confusion, grief and disbelief showed raw upon Idris's darkly beautiful face. 'I will carry his sins for the rest of my life.'

Nell agreed to keep quiet – out of fear that Idris would not let her go if she did not – until he and Godric had helped Father Emlyn to a peaceful death, but she didn't intend to keep that promise, not if Sister Winifred thought that he should suffer before he hanged. Serjeant Oswald was guarding Eben and the nun at the inn, which was a lot closer to the church than the castle, so he could hasten there to stop Idris if that was what she wanted.

~

Nell stumbled along Holy Apple Row, away from St Clement's and back towards the Merry Monkey, where she would have to tell Sister Winifred that Father Emlyn, her oldest friend, had strangled Irma Linke. She dreaded that moment and feared that the shock would strike Sister Winifred to the ground.

She glanced over her shoulder to make sure that Idris hadn't changed his mind about letting her go. She was utterly spent and wouldn't have the strength to fight him if he did come after her. The egg-shaped lump above her ear throbbed, her shoulder ached, and blood trickled from a cut on her forehead.

As she made her way along the dimly lit road, avoiding potholes, she considered what Idris had said about carrying Father Emlyn's sins for the rest of his life. How would he do that? Perhaps he would punish himself by carrying out the most menial and toilsome tasks around the abbey until he drew his last weary breath. But no amount of suffering on his behalf would bring Maye, Irma, Gracie and Phoebe back to life, nor would it soothe the hearts of their grief-stricken kith and kin. And why *should* he carry someone else's sins? His hidden love for Maye had inadvertently led to her death, but he couldn't be blamed for Father Emlyn's deeds.

Nell wondered how much Father Emlyn's illness had contributed to the killings. From all that she had seen and heard of him during her time in Bellayne, his deeds certainly seemed out of character, but she'd also witnessed cunning beneath his frailty of mind. Only moments ago, he'd whacked her over the head with a candlestick and then dispassionately discussed dumping her body. He had fooled Sheriff Birch, moved four bodies to Shymer Forest in the alms cart without getting caught, and, despite his apparent forgetfulness, his tongue hadn't slipped once in five months. He'd also been clear-headed enough to keep on killing to cover up Maye's murder. Despite his supposed afflictions, he'd removed with ruthless determination all obstacles and temptations from Idris's path so he might fulfil his own dreams for Idris.

And he'd failed. Idris, Nell guessed, would never accept the abbotship of the Greenfriars now, even if the brethren supported him. If it hadn't been for Father Emlyn's wishes, would Idris have handed back his olive robe and taken Maye Hannigan into his arms? A huge part of him must wish now that he'd declared his love for her long before winter came to Bellayne.

At the corner of Holy Apple Row and Hitchhorse Road, rage surged through Nell as she recalled what Father Emlyn had said about Gracie Alcorn. No illness, no frailty of mind, could excuse his strangling of a child.

Nell had already made one mistake by misinterpreting what Gracie had been trying to show her in the churchyard. Gracie had been pointing to St Clement's, where Father Emlyn had just given his final blessing to the townsfolk, and then to Father Emlyn himself, once he was outside the church, not to any of the folk milling about the churchyard, which included the five who'd then followed Lex Alcorn to the graves. Nell would not make another mistake now. Turning quickly, she headed back to St Clement's so she could raise the hue and cry.

She ran hard, determined to stop Idris before he handed the cup of poison to Father Emlyn. Was she already too late?

The image of Father Emlyn lying peacefully on his deathbed reminded her of what Sister Winfred had told her about the night Phoebe disappeared. Brother Godric had given Father Emlyn a sleeping draught and the brethren had held a dusk-'til-dawn prayer vigil at his bedside. Father Emlyn could not have killed Phoebe Butterball.

Now that she thought about it, he'd not mentioned Phoebe's name when telling Idris why he had killed the others. And considering his current state, she doubted he'd have had the strength to dig another grave. From what she'd heard, he'd gone rapidly downhill over the last month. And, realised Nell with a painful mind-jolt, Father Emlyn had not been near the graves when the necklace was dropped. He and Sister Winifred had been tending to Gracie's mother, who had fallen down the church steps and twisted her ankle on the other side of the churchyard.

The discrepancies Nell had noticed at the disinterment between the way each of the girls had been buried made more sense now. She remembered that someone had placed bluebells into Phoebe's hands and covered her with sackcloth, while Gracie and Irma had been buried carelessly, one dumped face first into a hole, and the other barely covered with soil. And Phoebe had fingermarks on her neck, not rope patterns. Nell had assumed Father Emlyn had strangled Phoebe with his bare hands, but why not use a rope as he had with the others? He had one with him always, tied around his waist, as did all the Greenfriars.

It couldn't be coincidental, however, that all the bodies had been found together in Shymer Forest. Someone must have heard about the graves Nell had found and seized the opportunity to bury Phoebe alongside the other victims.

The Crows' earlier message to her now made sense: *The end is not the end. You must look beyond.*

Swirling dark clouds fractured the twilight, making it appear as if tricksy goblin lights were flickering beneath the mist touching the ground. Disorientated, Nell stumbled in a pothole and landed hard on all fours. Small, sharp stones pierced her left hand and the throbbing in her head increased.

She sat back on her heels, her mind ticking over the puzzle of who could have killed Phoebe. That person needed to have heard almost immediately about the discovery of the graves *and* have been present in the churchyard when the necklace was dropped.

Cook Simms could have killed Phoebe, or slipped away from the inn to share the tidings with her son, Julian. Or Brother Caddock, who'd then returned to the abbey after the meeting at the Merry Monkey and discussed the arrangements for the disinterments with Brother Idris.

Of the five who'd been present in the churchyard, Sheriff Birch was the only one who hadn't heard about the graves that night, or so he claimed. But it was possible that he'd lied about sheltering from a storm on his way back from Archstone. He could have returned to Bellayne much earlier than he'd stated, and if Phoebe had gone to meet him that night, he could have heard about the graves from her. Had he seized the opportunity to get rid of his illegitimate daughter? He might have worried that she would hear one day – if she hadn't already – the truth of her parentage from her mother.

Nell brushed the stones from her bleeding hand and realised that she was shaking badly. Tremors of shock no doubt, brought on by Father Emlyn's attack on her, and then listening to the callous way he had justified his killing of the three lasses. Wishing that she could curl up on the ground and sleep instead of running the short, remaining distance to St Clement's, she stood, wavering slightly until she found her feet.

A crow cawed. Looking up, she saw three of them silhouetted on a branch in the orchard. She turned her head left and right, wincing as pain shot through her neck. There didn't seem to be anyone nearby.

'What now?' she whispered, afraid of what they'd come to warn her about or what they were going to make her face. She'd had enough of looking into her own and others' secrets and just wanted to be left alone.

As Nell pulled a cloth from the pocket of her skirt, wrapped it around her hand and tied it off, something niggled at her. After some thought, she realised it was sparked by the stones she'd cut her hands on. They were sharp like the stones that had come off the sheriff's boots in the parlour at the Merry Monkey, when he was questioning the Butterballs about Phoebe's movements on the day she'd died.

Nell closed her eyes to recall the scene. Mary had been crying quietly on the settle beside her husband while Birch urged them not to blame themselves for not knowing what was going on in their niece's life. As Nell asked Birch if she could take his bag down to the kitchen fire to dry it, Arnod had stood and walked to the window overlooking Hitchhorse Road. He'd cried as he told them how he had waved to Phoebe the last time he saw her, but she hadn't seen him because the sun was in her eyes. What was so troubling about that detail?

The three crows cawed once more, swooped low over her head and then disappeared into the sky. She longed to call them back.

Dusk had fallen early, owing to the heavy clouds, she suddenly realised, its chill settling around her shoulders, and the moon had not yet risen. She needed to move now, before something frightening stepped forth from the shadows, but her feet were rooted to the spot. As she peered at the creeping cloudbank, hoping to see a patch of guiding light, tingles of urgency shot up her legs. She realised what she'd been missing.

Arnod had told Birch that he'd left for Stout shortly after the seventh hour of the morning and hadn't returned to Bellayne until later that night. But the sun couldn't have blinded Phoebe at that time of the morning because it needed first to rise above the hills surrounding Bellayne, which it did at about the tenth hour. Nell remembered seeing that for herself on the day that Lex Alcorn had tried to hang Jack Lea and again on the morning of the funeral, when the sun had bathed Holy Apple Row with golden light and she'd thought it too beautiful a day for mourning.

Arnod was either mistaken or lying about his last sighting of Phoebe. Nell thought the former unlikely; he'd been so distressed by the thought that she might have turned away from him because he'd failed her in some way. But if he had nothing to hide, why would he lie? Instead of going to Stout, had he followed Phoebe to her tryst at Maiden's Well? Had he seen or heard something there that had enraged him enough to kill her when he arrived home later that night?

Nell's heart skipped more than one beat. Arnod had been in the churchyard the day the necklace fell into Eben's hands, but Sister Winifred had discounted him as a suspect because he'd been on the mainland looking for Phoebe's mother when Irma Linke disappeared. In the case of Phoebe's murder, however, that alibi was no longer valid.

St Clement's bell tolled, and continued to do so, not stopping at the eighth hour. Was Father Emlyn dead?

Nell's heart hammered in her chest. The tidings would spread around Bellayne like wildfire. If Arnod was guilty, how would he react when he heard that Father Emlyn had confessed to killing only three of the four girls?

She ran down the road towards the inn – in the same direction, she realised with a sudden jolt of panic, that the Crows had just flown. She needed to get Eben and Sister Winifred away from there before Arnod realised that his plan to blame Phoebe's death on the other victims' killer had failed.

Chapter Thirty-Two

A Gift

Nell saw with a frisson of alarm that Serjeant Oswald wasn't guarding the back of the Merry Monkey. She ran across the yard and entered the kitchen, quickly closing the door to muffle the dreadful tolling of St Clement's bell, and steeled herself to lie in answer to the questions Mary Butterball was bound to ask.

Neither Sister Winifred nor Serjeant Oswald was sitting at the kitchen table as Nell had hoped. But neither, thank goodness, was Arnod Butterball. A quick sidelong glance at the coat-pegs reassured her that no green garment was hanging there. It didn't rule out the possibility, however, that he'd return wearing a cloak of that hue.

'What's happening out there? The bell?' Mary's face was pinched with concern as she lifted Eben from a tub of water sitting on the table. She hastily wrapped his dripping body in a blanket and walked across the spotless floor to Nell.

'I know not,' Nell said.

She felt bad about deceiving the woman who had already suffered so much, but until she learned otherwise, she was going to heed the Crows' warning and assume that Arnod Butterball was guilty of killing Phoebe. And get Eben out of there as soon as possible.

Mary drew Nell to sit in Cook Simms's chair. 'What happened?

You're bleeding and look fit to collapse. Did someone hurt you?'

'Um, I thought someone was following me and I tripped and fell. It's nothing.' But she was grateful to sit, if only for a moment. Her vision was blurry and her legs were shaking.

Eben lifted his head off Mary's shoulder and looked at Nell with drowsy eyes. 'Wee's head broked?'

Nell felt like bursting into tears.

'Where's Sister Winifred and Serjeant Oswald?' she asked, hoping they'd just stepped into the dining hall, or out to the privy.

'Old Widow Winters collapsed while eating her supper so Arnod and Sister Winifred took her to the infirmary in our cart. I promised to look after Eben until you returned. Arnod should have been back by now. He must know I'm beside myself with worry.'

Panic set Nell's head spinning even faster. If Arnod was at St Clement's he would more than likely hear why the bell was tolling. Would he discover also that Father Emlyn had confessed to only three of the four murders? Whatever his private reaction to those tidings, he was sure to rush home to share them with Mary. He could burst through the door at any moment.

Still carrying Eben on her hip, Mary walked back to the table and dipped a cloth into the tub of water, then returned to wipe blood from Nell's face and hair with gentle strokes. 'I pray that another girl has not …' She audibly swallowed the lump in her throat and kissed Eben's damp head.

Eben nestled contentedly against her chest, too tired perhaps to sense the tension in the room. Nell thought it sad that Mary had never had a child of her own, and couldn't imagine how she'd deal with the grief if it turned out that Arnod had murdered the child she had nurtured.

'Serjeant Oswald can walk me back to the convent then,' said Nell.

'Oswald scuttled off to the Pickled Eel as soon as Sister Winifred was out of sight. Arnod will take you when he gets back, and I'll look after Eben for tonight. In truth, I'll be glad of the company.' Mary walked back to the table. 'I'll just dry and dress him, then fetch you a blanket, and warm some milk and honey to soothe you.'

Fighting the urge to give in to the dizziness, to close her eyes and sleep, Nell planted her hands on the arms of the chair and stood. The room lurched. Her stomach churned.

'For goodness sake, lass, sit down,' Mary said. 'You're as pale as the moon and shivering.'

'Nay, I promised Jack Lea I'd take Eben to the castle. I must leave. I can't break my promise. He'll be fretting.'

Nell could barely string two thoughts together and was vaguely aware that her argument was jumbled.

Mary dried Eben's back and clacked her tongue. 'You cannot carry a child in that condition. Please, just wait for Arnod.'

'Jack will hear the bell and think that it's ringing because of me.'

'Oh, my dear, I did not mean to distress you. We've a young lad staying here with his father. I'll ask him to run to the castle and let Jack know that you're safe.'

'Nay, do not trouble him. St Clement's is just around the corner. I felt a bit faint but I'm quite recovered now.'

Straightening her back, Nell carefully planted each foot on the stone floor as she headed to the table and held out her arms for Eben.

Grasping Nell gently by the shoulder, Mary steered her back to the chair. 'We do not know yet why the bell tolls. This town has lost four girls, and I'll not let you walk into the night alone. Jack would not –' Suddenly letting go of Nell, Mary stumbled towards a chair herself and sat, her hand at her mouth. Eben squirmed on her lap. 'Oh, my God, you know why the bell tolls but you're afraid to tell me. That explains your haste to be away.'

Eben wriggled out of the blanket, climbed off Mary's lap and ran to Nell. He buried his face in her skirt.

Mary wrapped her arms around her body and leaned forward.

'Please, tell me what's happened. Not knowing is cruel. Is it Arnod? Is that why he's not yet returned from St Clement's?'

Nell put a hand on Eben's head and cleared her throat. 'Nay, 'tis not Arnod. Father Emlyn is dead.'

'Oh.' Mary looked confused. She rubbed her temples. 'Why would you be afraid to tell me that? Such tidings are sad but not unexpected.'

Even though Eben was naked and damp, Nell picked him up and backed towards the door. It was time to go. She'd apologise to Mary later for her strange behaviour.

Mary lurched from the chair and clutched Nell's arm. 'For pity's sake, tell me what you know.'

'I did not fall and hurt my head,' Nell said, giving in. 'Father Emlyn attacked me.'

Mary's eyes widened and she clapped a hand to her bosom. 'Father Emlyn? I do not understand.'

'He killed them ... Maye, Irma, Gracie ...'

'Nay, there must be some mistake.' Sinking to the floor, Mary buried her face in her hands.

Nell put Eben on the ground, then kneeled and put her arm around Mary's shoulders. 'I found their hair in his blessing box. Brother Idris stopped him from killing me too. When I realised that Sister Winifred was not here to comfort you, I decided to hold my tongue. I'm sorry my cowardice has hurt you.'

Mary lifted her head and looked at Nell with red-rimmed eyes. 'He cut their hair?'

Nell nodded, but didn't tell her that Father Emlyn couldn't have killed Phoebe. Someone else could do that later.

'Did he say why he killed my girl?' Mary asked.

'Not to me. Now, let me help you to St Clement's so Sister Winifred can tell you what Father Emlyn has confessed to Brother Idris.'

'He had time to confess his sins?'

'He was still alive when I –. That's all I can tell you.'

Nell bit her lip, hoping that Mary hadn't noticed her blunder. She didn't want to have to explain how she knew that Father Emlyn would die *after* she'd left the church.

Hooking her arm through Mary's elbow, she said, 'Come, let me help you up.'

'I must wait for Arnod.'

'If he's already left St Clement's, we'll see his cart upon the road.'

Nell pulled a cloak from a peg near the door and draped it over Mary's shoulders. Something flared in her mind and she looked back at the coat pegs. Her heart thudded. A green shawl hung there. The cloak had been hanging on the same peg, concealing it. She instantly thought of the green garment that she'd seen in the vision at the well and knew that the Crows had indeed foreseen the danger heading her way at the Merry Monkey. She needed to leave post-haste.

Darting around the table, she grabbed Eben's tunic off a chair by the fire and, without putting on his undershirt, quickly shoved it over his head and pulled his hands through the armholes. Plonking him on the floor, she squatted beside Mary.

While Nell was dressing Eben, Mary had pulled Phoebe's necklace out from the neckline of her dress. Tears streamed from her eyes as she pressed it to her lips. Nell held out her hand and helped her to stand. Mary wiped her eyes and lifted Eben into her arms.

'I'll carry him for you,' she said and took three slow steps towards the door. 'Sister Winifred told me that you found Phoebe's necklace in the churchyard.'

'Eben was the one who caught it. It must have fallen out of someone's pocket.'

Mary came to a standstill, shrugged the cloak from her shoulders and let it fall on the floor. Her shoulders slumped. She looked lifeless, worn out.

'I must wait for Arnod,' she said again.

'Please, come with me. I cannot leave you here alone.'

She cocked her head. 'Why not?'

Nell's mouth went dry.

'Why not?' Mary repeated. 'What aren't you telling me?'

'You're upset. I do not think you should be alone, but I must take Eben to Jack.'

Mary put Eben over her shoulder and stroked his back. He yawned and rubbed his eyes.

'You know that Father Emlyn was not near Phoebe's grave when you found her necklace,' she told Nell.

'That's true, but what —'

'Then you already know that he could not have torn it from her throat.'

'My head hurts. I'm too tired to think.' Nell's tone was harsh, but she was past caring what Mary thought of her. She just wanted to get Eben and herself away before Arnod returned.

Mary walked over to the fireplace, picked up Eben's undershirt and sat him on the table. 'I told Arnod to bury the necklace with Phoebe, but he could not bear to let it go.'

'What are you saying?'

'If he'd listened to me, no one would have ever known.'

Chills raced up Nell's spine. Her thoughts bounced wildly around her aching head. 'You knew … you knew that Arnod strangled Phoebe, yet you did not speak?' She stumbled back against the wall. 'Oh, my God … you knew!'

Mary pointed to the stairs near the corner of the kitchen. 'Go down into the cellar and shut the door. You can wait there until Arnod comes home. I need to think.'

Nell considered screaming for help, but doubted that the guests would hear her. The door to the service passage was made of sturdy oak, and the guests' parlour was at the front of the inn. And Mary had Eben. She couldn't lunge for the back door either until he was safely back in her arms.

'You're frightening Eben,' she said. 'Please, give him to me and I'll go into the cellar.'

Mary turned sideways, snatched a knife off the chopping block and put it on the table. 'Eben stays with me.'

'Sister Winifred and Jack will be wondering where I am.'

'I'm wondering too. You should have returned with the bacon hock long ago.'

Nell shook her head in disbelief. Mary's warmth and gentleness were gone and she was cold-heartedly protecting her nest. Her love for Arnod was unnatural. He'd strangled her niece but she remained loyal, helping him to keep the truth hidden.

Nell knew that if she went into the cellar, she'd not come out alive. She'd not be able to protect Eben from there either. He was in danger because of her, because she'd made a mistake at the churchyard. She'd assumed that Gracie pointing to her killer and the dropping of the necklace were connected, but it was obvious now – far too late – that they'd been separate clues. Gracie had been nowhere near the graves when the necklace fell from Arnod's pocket; she hadn't even glanced that way when her father threatened Eben and Fleur with a stick. Her attention had been focused on St Clement's and Father Emlyn, her killer.

Sliding her back down the wall, Nell tried to appear smaller, non-threatening. She needed to keep Mary talking for as long as possible. And make it clear to her that getting rid of Nell wouldn't stop the sheriff from putting two and two together.

'Oh, Mary, your heart must be bleeding. But Sheriff Birch will soon realise that it was Arnod who dropped the necklace. He slipped up the other day when he was telling Birch about the last time he saw Phoebe. The sun could not have been in her eyes at the time he left for Stout. He must have seen her again, later in the day. Did he follow her to her tryst at Maiden's Well?'

'There was no tryst with a secret beau.' Mary laid Eben's undershirt on the table, flattened some wrinkles with firm sweeps of her hand, then took off his tunic. 'Arnod and Phoebe met at Maiden's Well to discuss a gift for me.'

When Sheriff Birch had questioned Mary about Phoebe's demeanour, Nell remembered that Mary had told him that Phoebe had wanted to tell her a secret, but never got the chance because Nell herself had arrived shortly thereafter with tidings of the graves in Shymer Forest.

'What was the gift?' Nell asked.

'A baby – the greatest gift of all. Arnod and I have waited for so long.'

'Phoebe met secretly with Arnod to tell him that she was with child?' Nell frowned. 'Why did she not confide in you?'

Mary finished dressing Eben, then held him firmly against her bosom and rocked from side to side. He squirmed and tried to turn his head but she was holding him too tightly.

'It happened only once, but our heavenly father blessed us with a child of our own.'

A child of our own. Nell was stunned. '*Arnod* fathered Phoebe's baby?'

Mary slammed one palm down onto the table. 'It's not what you think. Phoebe was upset about her mother's whereabouts one night when I was not here. Arnod held her in his arms and it happened.'

If the baby was such a blessing, Nell wondered why Arnod had killed Phoebe. Had he changed his mind about becoming a father after he arrived home from Stout and heard about the graves in Shymer Forest? Had he seized the opportunity to rid himself of a problem? Bellayne was a small town. Folk would forever speculate about the father of the child, especially if it looked like him.

But she held her tongue. Mary was agitated enough, and seemed unaware of how tightly she was holding Eben against her breasts. His whimpering was muffled and Nell was afraid that he couldn't breathe properly.

Still swaying from side to side, Mary closed her eyes, perhaps lost in her own warped world. She seemed to have forgotten all about Nell. As quietly as she could, Nell stood, judged the distance to the table and wondered if she could get to Eben before Mary held the knife to his throat. A few moments ago, she'd have scoffed at the notion of Mary harming a child, but she knew now that Eben wasn't in safe hands. Yet she was terrified of what Mary would do to him if Nell failed to grab him.

Mary opened her eyes. 'It was over so quickly … so quickly.'

Nell felt sick. She didn't want to hear about Arnod's and Phoebe's coupling. Arnod had murdered their niece and Mary had forgiven him. Nell wondered which of the two had concocted the plan to bury Phoebe alongside the graves in Shymer Forest.

'Arnod wanted Phoebe to wait until he'd returned home from Stout before she told me about the baby,' Mary continued. 'But Phoebe could not keep the tidings to herself a moment longer. After you'd gone to bed, she left her bedchamber and followed me out to the privy. It happened so quickly. My hands were not my own.'

My hands were not my own. The words rang in Nell's ears until she thought her head would burst. Mary had killed her own niece. And she knew there was no way now that she would let Nell walk freely out of the Merry Monkey.

Mary looked across the kitchen, as if expecting to see her niece walking in the door. 'She told me that Arnod thanked her. At Maiden's Well, my husband … my Arnod … thanked her for giving him a child and begged her not to tell me that he was the father.' She made a choking sound that was somewhere between sad laughter and a cry of pain.

Eben strained back against her arms and let out a short, stifled cry. Nell stood as still as possible so that she didn't alarm Mary, or give her cause to grab the knife off the table and hold the blade against Eben's throat.

'But Phoebe ignored Arnod's wishes,' continued Mary. 'She told me what she'd done with no hint of guilt or shame. Nay, she was dressed as if for a special occasion and was smiling when she told me that Arnod had thanked her, as if that could somehow take the sting out of her words. As though I should rejoice at the tidings. Before I knew it, my hands were around her throat. I closed my eyes and hung on, and she slipped to the ground.'

Nell's skin crawled. Mary's voice was calm and even, as if she was reading aloud from a dull book. It frightened Nell more than a display of hysteria.

A log shifted in the fireplace. Nell nearly jumped out of her skin, fearing that Arnod had opened the door. Once he arrived home, there'd be no hope of getting Eben safely away. Arnod could have taken Phoebe's body to the sheriff and denounced his wife as a murderess, but he'd chosen instead to take his niece's corpse to Shymer Forest and bury his wife's vile deed. There would be no help from that quarter.

She contemplated running down the service passage and screaming for help, but was afraid of what Mary would do to Eben in her absence. Terrible images of him drowning in the washtub or stumbling into the fireplace flashed through her mind and kept her feet frozen to the spot.

Mary gouged her forehead with her fingertips and sighed. 'I'm tired ... so tired. Go down into the cellar now.'

Nell stepped back towards the stairs in the corner of the kitchen. If she went willingly, Mary might let Eben live.

But if she went down into the cellar, she'd not come out alive.

Chapter Thirty-Three

Eben

Overwhelming fear exploded in Nell's belly and surged up to block her throat. She didn't want to die. Panic benumbed her limbs. All outer sounds disappeared as the pounding of her heart filled her head. There were no discernible spaces between the last heartbeats of her life.

As her knees turned to jelly and she thought she might faint, Eben squirmed and kicked his little legs against Mary's belly so that he could turn his head to look at her. There was confusion and fear in his eyes but also something else, something softer, stronger and enduring that went beyond the bounds of blood, time and earthly senses. She felt that he was gently placing the gift of his life into her hands with complete trust and understanding, though he was nowhere near old enough to do such a thing. As their gaze deepened – perhaps for the last time – and they stayed connected to each other despite their fear, a silvery light, bright like a tiny star, appeared at the centre of his chest. It pulsed with his every breath, opening the way between them, and she had the impression that she was seeing into his soul. His inner beauty took her breath away.

Her fear dispersed long enough for her to feel again the subtle *flow* between the heavens and earth. It stretched the space between her heartbeats and, as a forgotten part of herself awakened, she perceived that she too was a bearer of sacred light, as were all folk who walked upon the earth. Ancient memories of where that light had originated and why she'd been unaware that she was carrying it stirred and unfurled and brightened. She couldn't quite grasp them, not while her attention was fixed upon the knife Mary was holding, but knowing that those answers existed inside her helped her to see her fate through older and wiser eyes. She knew what she had to do.

Every instinct urged her to stay with Eben, no matter the outcome for herself. She could not trust Mary to return him safely to Jack Lea. Though he was too young to speak of the wickedness in the Merry Monkey this night, in her madness Mary might fail to see his innocence. Nell couldn't take that chance.

But as she prepared to give her life in an attempt to save him, a part of her was still crying. She'd glimpsed and felt the magical *flow* and now knew that she was more than flesh and blood, but was afraid to take that first step towards death.

As if sensing that Nell had no intention of going quietly into the cellar, Mary suddenly swung Eben from her hip and plunged him into the washtub. He screamed Nell's name as Mary clamped a hand against the back of his head and forced his face into the water. His gurgled scream was echoed from Nell's mouth as she leaped towards the table.

As her front foot touched the ground, she slipped in a small puddle of water and landed hard on one knee. Her link to the *flow* shattered and vanished. These were her last moments of life. She yearned for someone to hold her close before she died, to tell her that she was beloved and to help her face her approaching death with courage.

The air suddenly warmed and curled around her, as if moulding itself to her body, and an unseen hand touched her back, just behind her heart. Somehow, she recognised that holy touch from long ago and the being who was watching over her now. Crying tears of gratitude, she leaned back and melted into the arms of the one who had tenderly lifted her from the wellspring of life, who had held her close as she took her first breath in another time, another realm. Indescribable sweetness welled within her heart and flowed through her whole body, quenching her parched spirit. Her essence, she sensed, was as beautiful as Eben's and always had been. Fear vanished, her trembling body stilled and her soul ears attuned to unspoken words from the one who had first given her a name.

I am with you.

She wasn't alone.

With a guttural roar, Nell leaped to her feet, skirted the table, swung her arm sideways in a wide arc and backhanded Mary across the side of the head. As she cried out and stumbled backwards, Nell thrust her hands into the washtub and lifted Eben's face clear of the water. His body was limp. No sound did he make.

As Nell pulled his body over the edge of the tub, Mary grabbed a hank of her hair and wrenched her head backwards. Nell screamed and held on to Eben's arms as Mary clamped strong hands around her throat. The room darkened and swam before her eyes. As she fell to her knees, her grip on Eben's arms weakened and he slipped partway back into the tub. The pain of not breathing was unbearable but Nell fought the urge to let go of his hands so that she could claw at Mary's fingers.

I am with you.

Nell silently screamed Eben's name, urging him to wake up, to move, but she couldn't hear any sound from him over the roaring of blood in her head.

Mary slammed Nell's chin into the edge of the table. As pain sliced through her jaw, she knew that her time had come. She was spent. Her last plea for Eben to wake up drifted out of her mind. Her heart stopped beating. In the silence between life and death, she cried. She'd failed to save Maureen's child. She felt the coldness of a new shadow emerging, one that would darken Jack Lea's life.

Mary let go of Nell's throat.

Something crashed, and she heard shouting. Blessed voices that belonged to the sheriff and Jack.

Eben curled his hand around Nell's finger. And let go.

'I've got him.'

'Is he alive?'

'Oh, God!'

'Put him over your knee. Press on his back.'

'Nothing.'

'Harder. Faster.'

'He's breathing. Oh, God, he's breathing. My son lives.'

Nell's inner eye closed. She slipped to the ground.

'Nell, can you hear me?'

With one arm keeping Eben safe against his side, Jack kneeled and pressed his ear to her chest, hoping to feel it rise and fall against his cheek, hoping to hear her heart beating faintly. Nothing.

'Quiet,' he shouted at Mary Butterball, who was wailing for her husband as Birch tied her murderous hands to the leg of the table with his belt.

Eben, perhaps frightened by the anger in his father's voice, began to scream and thrash about, making it impossible for Jack to detect any signs of life in Nell. He was finding it hard to breathe himself. Panic was a lead weight on his chest and a raging torrent in his head.

'Give me your boy,' said Birch, 'while you take her to the infirmary.'

'Just hold him for a moment.'

With his arms free, Jack lifted Nell into a sitting position, then hoisted her over his shoulder and stood. He held out his free arm for Eben, silencing Birch's promise to keep him safe with a look that could have killed two wild boars at twenty paces.

Jack made for the door, with Eben secure on his hip, just as

Arnod Butterball arrived home. Arnod's eyes flicked around the kitchen, then settled on his wife. As she fought against her bonds, straining towards him, he dropped to his knees and buried his face in his hands.

'Oh, God, what have I done?'

Jack didn't wait to hear more. Desperate to revive the young woman who had brought his son to him, and then defended him with her life, he ran from the Merry Monkey with Eben's cries spurring him on.

'So it's my fault,' Nell said to Jack, a couple of hours later at the infirmary, 'that the King's men weren't here to stop the Red Guards from threatening you and Eben. They were too busy scouring the isle looking for me.'

She could hear that her voice was slurred because of the tonic Brother Godric had made her drink shortly after he'd revived her. She gripped the rim of the stool she was sitting on to stop the room or herself – she wasn't sure which – from swaying.

Jack was sitting with his back against the bedhead and rocking Eben in his arms. He made no comment when she finished her account of how she'd been falsely accused of Bente's murder.

Eben lay face down on his father's chest and belly, asleep but still hiccoughing occasionally because of the way he'd been screaming earlier. While Brother Godric had been tending Nell's wounds and bandaging her head, she'd heard Eben's wails and had felt so helpless that she couldn't comfort him. And guilty because she was in some way to blame for his distress. She'd insisted, quite hysterically, on seeing him before she'd let the nuns put her to bed. Brother Godric had finally relented and allowed her to sit by Eben's bed for a brief quarter-hour. She longed to touch him, to tell him a story, to tell him she was sorry, but didn't want to risk waking him now that he was calm.

Jack stroked his son's back and whispered a poem about the

song the river sang – one that Nell had never heard before. He kept his gaze away from her and she couldn't blame him for being angry that she'd kept so much from him, things that had affected the safety of his son. But she'd rather he yelled at her and even banished her from Eben's side, rather than sitting there in such fraught silence.

Brother Godric, flanked by two stern-looking nuns, marched into the room and flicked his bald head towards the door. As one of the nuns gripped her under the armpit, Nell tried in vain to get her sluggish tongue moving. She still hadn't apologised to Jack for ignoring his advice to keep Eben safe within the convent.

Jack finally looked at her as she was led towards the door. 'I'll speak with Birch,' he said.

Whatever that meant, she could not tell.

But as Brother Godric herded her out of the room, Jack added, 'I believe you', which uplifted her spirits more than she could say. Especially as he had only her word for what had happened and not one shred of proof.

Chapter Thirty-Four

The Past

Long before dawn, the cart carrying Mary Butterball to a gaol nor-east of Bellayne where she would await trial for the murder of her niece juddered to a halt. Serjeant Oswald poked his head through a flap at the side of the canvas canopy to tell Mary and the young nun accompanying her that he needed to move a fallen branch off the road.

The nun muttered something about answering a call of nature and alighted from the cart.

Mary closed her eyes and gouged her thighs with the fingers of her bound hands. While she lived, she'd never stop seeing the look on Arnod's face the night he'd opened the privy door and seen Phoebe's lifeless body on the floor. Mary had no illusions about Arnod's feelings for her now. He'd buried Phoebe in Shymer Forest out of guilt rather than love, and had turned his back on her for good when he'd arrived home to find Jack Lea attempting to revive a lifeless Nell and his half-drowned son. She never should have let Arnod see what she'd done.

Mary had no illusions about herself either, but at the back of her mind a question still niggled. Would she have lashed out and killed Phoebe if she'd not already heard about the graves in Shymer

Forest? She had no reason to lie to herself any more, but try as she might she couldn't remember if she'd planned to bury Phoebe there before she'd fastened her hands around the girl's throat.

The cart rocked as someone climbed aboard. She pretended to be asleep. She was tired of listening to the nun's nervous prattle.

Cool air wafted against the back of her head.

The back of her head?

There was a nick of pain as someone wrenched her head back, cut Phoebe's necklace from where she still wore it around her neck, and dangled it in front of her face.

Mary closed her eyes. She couldn't look at what she'd done. Where had it all gone wrong?

Her assailant leaned close, whispered in her ear and ran a knife across her throat.

Without Arnod, Mary was too afraid to open her eyes in the afterlife.

'Why are you helping me?' Nell asked Sheriff Birch as they walked together along a meandering path through the woods behind the convent. She was grateful that Jack had insisted on speaking to the sheriff on her behalf, but now, in the daylight, with her secrets laid bare, she wished she could hide again.

Birch waited until they'd passed two young nuns, tittering and chirping to each other with as much enthusiasm as the flock of tiny birds they were feeding, before he said, 'Because you did what I could not. You stopped Father Emlyn from killing again. I am in your debt.'

'But Doreen Wilkes will never change her story and tell the soldiers that it was Elmer Long's daughter, not me, who stabbed him. Nor will she tell them it was she who accidentally knocked Lord Bente into the fire. Her legs were badly burned and I left her sitting helpless in the woods. She'll not care if I hang for crimes I did not commit.'

'Wilkes stands to lose more than half a leg if it becomes known that she protected her cousin, a murderess, for seven years and also helped her to blame Long's death on you.'

'But it's *Lady* Christiana Hammerton's word against mine now. My word will carry little weight against such wealth and standing.'

Nell had not been surprised when Birch told her that Elmer Long's daughter had married Lord Hammerton, the witness to Christiana's supposed discovery of her father's body. Nell wondered if she had married for love or to protect her own interests.

She had often asked herself why Christiana had chosen to give her 'a second chance at life' as she'd put it – not giving her up to the sheriff and then helping her to get away from the mainland. That reason was now blindingly obvious: she had wanted a scapegoat for her father's death, one who wouldn't regain her senses in time to deny killing Long. A young girl whom she could point a finger at and say, 'That jealous, wicked girl has run from her terrible crime.'

After killing her own father and changing out of her bloodstained clothes, Christiana must have hastened to find a witness – Lord Hammerton – to her 'discovery' of the bodies. In the meantime, Nell herself had returned home and very helpfully picked up the knife.

Christiana's maid, who had sailed for Squinte with Nell that very night, had given Pearl's betrothal ring to Doreen Wilkes to pay for Nell's upkeep and to ensure, no doubt, that Doreen remained silent. Nell recalled how old Nancy Wilkes had thwarted Doreen's plans to sell Nell on the sly-market, which would have been the best way to ensure that a ten-year-old witness didn't live for long enough to tell any tales. Despicable bitches, all of them.

'That's where Wilkes comes in handy,' Birch said. 'Life for a one-legged woman will be hard. Why should she beg for every penny when her cousin is living high on the hog in the royal court of Lanbricke? In exchange for her help, I'll make sure Lord Hammerton pays her a small fortune. All Wilkes need do is detail all she knows about

Long's murder. When I present my findings to Lord Hammerton, I'm sure he'll settle the matter quickly and quietly. He won't want to test our fickle King's affection for him. If he does not retract the letter he wrote chronicling your "evil deeds" and accept our terms, I'll investigate the death of Elmer Long further, with much ado.'

Nell was about to thank him again when he held up his hand. 'To settle the matter once and for all, I'll insist that now a missing witness has reappeared – you – and new information has come to light, all parties must sign an amended declaration about how Long met his end. Bear in mind that Hammerton is more likely to accept our terms if we absolve his wife of all guilt. Are you certain that your mother attempted to poison Long?'

Nell nodded.

'Well, if you, Hammerton and Lady Christiana are all willing to say there was blood on your mother's clothes and hands, the record will state that she also stabbed her betrothed prior to drinking the poisoned wine.'

Nell's throat trembled as she recalled the way her mother had looked the last time she'd seen her – lifeless and defeated. And she acknowledged how close she'd come to giving in to that same despair herself; the many times she'd nearly let it take her. She put a hand over her heart, not caring if Birch thought her a fool, as she finally understood a little of what the vision in the well had meant. She had faced death in the Merry Monkey last night and thwarted it, but a part of her had been destined to die. She had an opportunity now to throw off the heavy cloak of her past, straighten her shoulders and look up at the sky.

'I will sign,' she said.

'Then I'll do my best to see it done.' Birch wiped a hand over his face, which was haggard from lack of sleep. 'In regards to Lord Bente's accident, perhaps you and Doreen Wilkes could agree that he was drunk – a regular occurrence, by all accounts – when he tripped and pitched headfirst into the fire. And that Wilkes herself was burned when she tried to save his life.'

'I thank you, Sheriff, but how do you know I'm speaking the truth about Long's death?'

'From the amount of blood you say had pooled on the floor, the wound in his upper back must have been deep. I doubt a girl of ten years could have delivered more than a glancing blow, especially when his jerkin was fashioned from leather. If it turns out, however, that you're lying, I'll come after you myself.'

Without a word of farewell, he turned and walked back the way they'd come. His stride lacked its usual vigour and pace, not just because he was exhausted, Nell guessed, but also from having to keep his heartache hidden. Phoebe, his secret daughter, was dead and he could not openly grieve.

As he disappeared from view, Nell wondered who had slit Mary's throat in the early hours of the morning. Did Birch have her blood on his hands?

Nell sat down on a bench beside the sparkling, breeze-ruffled Eel and took off her worn boots. She drew her bare feet up onto the seat and hugged her knees while she thought about Gracie Alcorn. Now that her murderer was dead, was she free to run with other ghost girls across the meadows of brilliant green and splash about in the clear forest pools that Nell hoped existed in a heavenly realm?

She'd wonder about the girl's wellbeing for the rest of her life, and couldn't understand why she'd been left to haunt the churchyard in the first place. Since feeling the *flow* and the presence of the mystical being who had embraced her in the Merry Monkey's kitchen – both experiences so beautiful they made her cry just to remember them – Nell couldn't comprehend why folk had to endure so much suffering on earth, and in Gracie's case even after death.

Questions queued in her mind. If the Crows and that mystical being had helped her through her recent crises, why hadn't such beings come to Gracie's rescue and stopped Father Emlyn from strangling her? And why, when Nell had prayed for help so many times as a child, had she to wait until now to receive it?

While she'd been in the *flow*, it had felt natural, and there'd been no sense of having to work hard to feel it or that it was being withheld in any way or only bestowed on those who deserved and had earned it. Quite the opposite had been true, which made Nell wonder why she and most folk she knew were unaware of the magic surrounding them.

Were the terrible things that happened in life, such as the murder of a child, really heaven-sent opportunities – or invitations, perhaps – for people to look deeper for meaning and purpose, and for a better way of living and treating each other?

When Mary had been holding Eben captive, Nell's desperate need to save him had forced her to go beyond the locked doors she'd constructed in her mind to keep herself hidden and safe from harm, and to step into a clear space where she could hear the hum of life, a place where guidance and inspiration dwelled. Instead of giving in to that primal urge to run for help and safety, to leave Eben and get away from the kitchen as fast as possible, she'd trusted, despite her fear, the strong intuition she'd felt to stay with him no matter the outcome for herself. It had given her the courage she'd needed to stand her ground and do what needed to be done. Her love for Eben had been the key that opened her up to sensing what had always been there, just beyond what she thought she knew about herself and life.

Nell wondered how her own self-hatred and view that life was little more than a cruel cycle of hardship and endurance might have kept her from feeling that holy love long before now.

She'd often felt unclean and ashamed as if it was her fault that Long had touched her, and she'd repeatedly told herself that she was a bad girl because she'd been unable to make her mother happy. Perhaps her feelings of unworthiness and shame had blocked any sense of the truth reaching her.

Now that she knew something greater existed beyond anything she could ever have imagined, she was afraid to ask herself the most frightening questions of all. Did she have to wait for another crisis and the strong emotions it would trigger before she could experience the *flow* again? Was that connection dependent on the consent of some divine being?

She began to cry, silently, deeply. If she could have one wish for herself right now, it would be to feel and follow that guiding whisper for the rest of her life. She had glimpsed that mystical wonder only briefly, but had felt so alive during those moments. It made the emptiness she was feeling now worse than ever, as if every anguished thought had intensified. It was a state she could no longer bear.

Resentment hissed and spat like a feral cat in her gut as she cursed her mother for her neglect and abandonment, for making her feel small and worthless, for leaving her without anything to hang on to. Nell held her bended knees so tightly that they jutted painfully into her breasts. Her shoulders hunched automatically and pain shot up from her rounded back to her head as she clenched her jaw and willed the memories of her mother's uncaring face away.

When she reached a point of breathlessness, she suddenly understood how such thoughts had been constricting the growth of love within her, cutting her off from the *flow*. Unwilling to live a half-life any longer, she quickly cast her mind back to the moment in the Merry Monkey when the cloak of despair had been lifted from her shoulders and she'd felt the holy touch upon her back. Just thinking about melting into the arms of the one who had first lifted her from the wellspring of life helped her to deepen her breath and unclench her throat and her belly.

Placing her bare feet on the lush grass, she let her hands fall into her lap and closed her eyes.

I am with you. Breathe me in.

Each time she whispered the blessed words, they flowed inwards, smoothing jagged memories and turning to sweet water the mire of dread … eventually touching the well of aliveness deep within her heart. As she dipped her mind into the well and allowed her breath to undulate through her body, her senses expanded and she slipped gently through the spaces between her heartbeats.

The most exquisite sensation she'd ever experienced bloomed within her chest, evoking an image of sun-warmed nectar in a flower cup, and she began to quiver on the inside, as if her body was shaking free a dusty shroud and waking up for the first time.

A shaft of light appeared in her mind's eye, beckoning her to look deeper, to follow it. An intense longing to do just that grew within her until she could bear it no longer. She cried out her willingness to embrace the unknown and surrendered to the *flow*. Her awareness immediately soared skyward at such a pace that she gasped with surprise but not one ounce of fear. Her flight felt natural and familiar, as if she had done it before.

Way above the unquiet clouds, she streaked past stars to the source of the light: a creamy-gold orb that looked as if the moon and sun had become one in the violet sky. Though it was bright beyond any measures of man, she gazed with ease into its shimmering depths, and as its celestial murmurings touched her ears she remembered the many things she'd forgotten about herself. The quivering she'd felt earlier had been the stirring of her soul as she unfurled her wings, joyously anticipating the dance through the air that angels breathed to her eternal home.

'I can fly,' whispered Nell.

As can each earth-child.

The words came forth from the swirling core of the orb and the truth of them touched the crown of her head, sending a shower of delicious shivers down her spine, into the soles of her feet and then deep into the nourishing earth. She became aware then of the delicate glow emanating from her own soul, and that it was the same warm creamy-gold as that of the heavenly orb before her and had always been there.

'Dwagfwy!' It was Eben calling out excitedly from somewhere behind her.

Nell almost cried as her awareness of the heavens disappeared, for she only understood a little of what she'd seen and knew there was much more to discover.

But then she remembered that she'd found for herself a pathway to that place of bliss, and could find it again. If she quietened her mind and embodied the holy breath present in the surrounding air, there was a way for her to touch heaven while she was on earth.

Nell knew she had Poppy and Flannery Goodfield to thank for this revelation, and looked forward to the day when she could do so in person. They had shown her at the women's gathering that a connection to the *flow* wasn't only possible, but essential for living and loving wholeheartedly.

Chapter Thirty-Five

By the River

'There you are,' said Jack's voice.

Nell turned her head to see him stepping off the woodland path onto the grassy riverbank. Eben, pink of cheek and hale, was sitting atop his father's shoulders and making woofing sounds as he watched a dog running around further along the bank. The small bells on the liripipe hanging from his hat tinkled as his head moved. It was a miniature version of the hat his father sometimes wore.

'We wanted to give you these,' Jack added, pulling a posy of meadow flowers from his bag. 'I picked some for Irma too and laid them upon her grave just now. I can't believe I'll never see her again.'

With a lump in her throat, she stood and took them from his hand.

Nell knew that Jack had held Eben through the night at the infirmary, but this was the first time she'd seen Eben choosing to be so close to his father. They looked comfortable together, natural, and she knew the time had come for her to let Eben go so they could get to know one another better. It would be unfair to expect him to come back to the convent with her now.

'Brother Godric caught Eben smearing an old man's bowl of gruel all over the spotless infirmary floor while I was snoring,' said Jack. 'He shooed us both out the door faster than you can crack an egg.'

'I'm heartened to hear that he's well enough to make mischief,' said Nell, reaching past Jack's shoulder to pat Eben's bottom.

Eben squealed in what sounded like fright and kicked her arm, before burying his face in his father's hair.

To stop herself bursting into tears, Nell pressed her lips together and stepped back. She couldn't blame him for being afraid of her now. She'd led him into danger. Whenever he looked at her, he'd remember Mary Butterball's ruthless hands on the back of his head and the taste of soapy water as it rushed into his mouth and cut off his breath. Did he wonder why she'd taken so long to cross the kitchen and come to his rescue?

'And I see that you're just as contrary as this little man,' said Jack, reaching up to ruffle Eben's hair, pretending not to notice she was upset. 'Sister Winifred thought you were still tucked up in bed, but you've given the nuns the slip.'

'I couldn't rest. You may add another broken promise to my growing list of flaws.'

She sounded brusque even to her own ears, but couldn't forget that he'd only come looking for her at the Merry Monkey the night before because she'd failed to bring Eben to him, as promised.

Tilting his head to one side, he regarded her quizzically. 'I spoke in jest.'

Feeling foolish, Nell feigned great interest in the comings and goings across the bridge.

'Eben cannot even look at me,' Nell cried, when she could no longer ignore the guilt she felt. 'I frighten him, and it's no more than I deserve.'

It was unreasonable to expect Eben to remember how he'd curled his hand around her finger as she'd slipped towards death, but it was a moment that she would never forget. She'd never felt more close to anyone in her life.

Jack put his arm around her shoulders and tucked her against the side of his body. 'Given time, his memory of that terrible night will fade.'

'If you'd not come looking for us ...'

'But I did, and found you both in time. And you hung on to Eben until help arrived. I thank you, Nell, for bringing my son home. And one day Eben will thank you too. Take comfort from that thought.'

He held her close while she cried.

When her trembling eased, he said, 'I'd have trusted Mary with him too. I've known her all my life.'

He shuddered, and she stepped out from beneath his arm.

'What?' she asked.

'Birch told me that Mary stuffed Phoebe's body into the privy when she heard my bell that tells folk I'm approaching their yard.'

'Shit,' said Nell, shaking her head in disbelief.

'Phoebe was in there while I emptied the bucket of nightsoil through the trapdoor at the back. Mary seemed on edge and somewhat flustered while I was chatting to her, but I didn't think for one second ...' He wiped his face on his sleeve. 'If I'd arrived a few moments earlier, Phoebe might still be alive. I feel sick thinking about it.'

'You cannot blame yourself.' Nell's own thoughts on whether she should have told those in the Merry Monkey about the graves fluctuated between distress at the consequences and relief that she had done her best to help Gracie Alcorn's ghost.

They stood in silence until Jack blew his nose and stuffed the cloth back into his pocket. 'By the way,' he said, 'you look terrible.'

'What?' Nell didn't know whether to laugh, cry or flounce off in a huff.

'Your face is black and blue and there are big lumps on your forehead and chin. Methinks that's why Eben will not look at you. He's not sure if it is you.'

'I'm not sure about myself sometimes either,' Nell said wryly.

'You're puzzling, to say the least.'

'Wee yucky,' announced Eben suddenly.

'See,' said Jack, 'I was right about your lumps and bruises confusing him.'

'You look smugger than Julian Simms right now,' Nell told him.

'Not possible,' he said, lowering Eben to the ground and sitting on the seat himself.

'Dwagfwy, Wee!' Eben squealed.

When she saw the blue-winged insect zigzagging above the grass, she chuckled to herself and said, 'Birdie.'

Eben, his face scrunched with confusion, looked at the dragonfly then back at her. 'Dwagfwy?'

'Birdie.'

He must've heard the mischief in her voice for he stomped his foot and shook his finger at her. 'Dwagfwy!'

Laughing, she clapped her hands. 'Dragonfly.'

'Do not leave his life too soon,' Jack said, as Nell sat beside him. 'You're welcome in Bellayne for as long as you choose to stay. Besides, we need someone with unflagging determination to keep an eye on Julian Simms.'

'Is that a polite way of calling me stubborn?'

He smiled at her. 'Tenacious.'

'Mmm … but you're right about Simms. He's shiftier than a privy rat.'

Nell fished Maureen's shawl out of her bag and handed it to Jack. He laid it across his lap and traced with his finger the crooked angel that Maureen had stitched onto one corner.

He sighed. 'She'll not be forgotten. I'll tell Eben stories about the hard-working and kind-hearted young woman who cherished him for the first two-and-a-half years of his life. His laugh and rosy cheeks remind me of her.'

They sat in silence while they watched Eben rolling down the grassy bank.

'You did not doubt me,' Nell blurted out, 'when I told you that I'd seen Gracie's ghost in the churchyard.'

One corner of Jack's mouth twitched; he seemed to be enjoying her discomfort. She stared, intrigued by the dimple hidden among the stubble to the left of his mouth.

'You've my mother to thank for that,' he said. 'She saw an angel hovering over my cradle one night when I was ill. From then on, come what may, she had great faith that all would be well in our home. And anyway, I could hear the truth in your voice.'

'Well, I shall take more care then when I next tell you a fib.'

A crow cawed and Nell almost jumped out of her boots. What did the Crows want with her now? Had she not earned a rest?

Quickly scanning the riverbank and bridge, she finally spotted them on a boat floating upstream without any oars. The three men laughed and clapped their hands, then tossed their fishing rods overboard. They rummaged around on the floor of the boat and held up a large shell above their heads.

Nell's mouth fell open. There was an enormous pearl sitting on the shell. *Pearl.* Her inner light dimmed instantly as she was reminded of the way her mother had chosen to leave her and a feeling of helplessness overtook her. But instead of being carried away by that pain to a dark place, she breathed into the part of her that was untouched by her mother or Long. And, as her perception of her eternal self expanded, she let go of the things she couldn't change.

Although she still believed that Pearl had not done everything she could have to care for her only child, nor considered what would happen to that child after her death, Nell wished her mother peace in the afterlife. Instead of yearning for a different childhood, she would be grateful for the many lessons she had learned. And from now on, she would choose how she wanted to live in each moment. She'd found a way – at long last – to look at and learn from her past without getting lost in it.

Bringing their palms together over their hearts, the Crows bowed their heads. Then each sprouted wings and flew skyward.

'Friends of yours?' asked Jack as he watched three crows turn to black dots in the sky.

When Nell realised she was waving to the birds, she tittered with embarrassment. With as much dignity as she could muster, she said, 'As a matter of fact they are.'

'Bewildering,' said Jack.

'Methinks you mean "mysterious". And may I remind you that I received more than one blow to my head yester-eve, so cannot help it if I seem a little strange.'

'I'll let you use that excuse for one more day.'

Eben tired of rolling down the riverbank and climbed up onto the seat beside his father. Every now and again, he peeked out from behind Jack's arm to look at Nell. She wanted to shout 'Boo!', but kept her smiling lips shut. Sometimes patience was a virtue. In the meantime, she'd look forward impatiently to the day he once again climbed willingly into her open arms and laid his head upon her bosom.

Eben picked his nose again, then looked thoughtfully at his finger and said to himself, 'Ma-ma blowed nose. Honk, honk.'

Laughter drifted down from Monk's Mill Bridge. On days like this, when young lovers were frolicking in the sunshine and children were playing Leap the Witch's Toad on the towpath, it was hard to fathom how darkness wormed its way into the hearts of men and why mankind seemed to have been separated from the Light in the first place for it had felt like home to Nell. 'Why are we here?' she asked.

'Mmm,' Jack mused, leaning slightly towards her, 'my mother used to say that the "why" was a mystery, but we could bloody well help each other while we are here.'

Nell nodded thoughtfully, liking the truth of what he'd said, while fully aware that she'd never be able to leave that mystery alone, not now that she'd touched it and it'd touched her. Life was a conundrum she'd likely ponder to the end of her days … and beyond. For now, though, she wanted to bask in the soulful afterglow, grateful that she'd taken the first step towards living and to feeling more of the light within her.

Aaaah, Nell sighed contentedly. She'd a mind to stay in Bellayne just for a few days more, so that she could wander the woods and meadows with Jack and Eben and get a better idea of where the boy would grow up. After that, once Sheriff Birch had dealt with the soldiers and Doreen Wilkes, she'd head back to Stonhard and get Emily away from the Boar's Den. She'd knock her out and carry her if she had to. And after that ... well, who knew?

The midday bell tolled. Nell's stomach rumbled as she caught a whiff of the tempting aromas wafting down from St Clement's refectory.

Jack slapped his thighs and said, 'We'd best get a move on before Sister Winifred gobbles up all of Brother Peter's fish and cheese pies.'

'It's not fish and cheese pie day,' Nell said.

'Peter made them especially to warm the cockles of Sister Winifred's heart.'

Eben jumped off the seat and rubbed his tummy. 'Num nums, Wee,' he squealed, and ran off up the hill.

Nell wriggled her feet and yawned contentedly; the coming meal was going to be the most delicious of her life so far.

'Do you want me to carry you up the hill?' asked Jack.

'Nay, but I could use a hand. I'm quite worn out.'

He laid the back of his forearm on his thigh and opened his hand. She put her hand in his and shivered slightly when she felt the warmth and smoothness of his wrist against hers. He smelled of porridge and hay and peace.

As he walked her up the hill, he said, 'By the way, I *could* smell rosemary upon the hood of my cloak after you'd worn it.'

Nell feigned confusion but her cheeks flushed. 'I was talking about Rosemary, a very demanding guest at the Merry Monkey.'

'Methinks you're fibbing,' he said, and the smirk on his face was irritating to behold.

Chapter Thirty-Six

A Maiden's Grave

Sheriff Arundell Birch looked down at the knife that had slit Mary Butterball's throat. It was lying in a shallow hole alongside Phoebe's grave. He pushed dirt back into the hole with the side of his hand to cover the knife. He wished that he could go back in time and acknowledge his second-born daughter, embrace her and tell her she was loved. But it was too late.

'Wait,' said Medwelyn, the woman who had given birth to Phoebe seventeen years ago.

Even in the moon's gentle light, she looked well-used. She was only one-and-thirty years, but her waist-length fair hair was streaked heavily with grey, and her shabby but well-cut dress of beaded silk hung loosely upon her frail frame. When she had arrived in Bellayne secretly the day before, Birch had commented on her bedraggled and wan appearance. Without a hint of shame, she'd admitted to drinking too much wine over the last two years and dabbling with potions that brightened her soured life. Birch knew that some of the blame for her troubles rested heavily upon his shoulders. He'd have to go a long way back in time to make things right.

Medwelyn crouched beside the grave and placed the two crescents of pearl shell that she and Phoebe had worn around their necks into the hole next to the knife.

Birch grasped her wrist. 'Medwelyn, no!'

She pulled away from him and stood. 'I mistakenly – and selfishly – thought that Phoebe would have a better life with my sister. I did not deserve such a beautiful child. I could not even get here in time to see her laid to rest. I failed her in life. I'll not hold her to me in death. My guilt is mine alone to bear.'

She sprinkled dirt over the necklaces, then tucked her hair beneath her hood and briefly touched Birch's shoulder. 'We've done what we can for her. We'll not meet again.'

Laying his hands on Phoebe's grave, Birch bowed his head and cried.

As the almost half-moon rose above the hollow, Irma Linke clung tightly to the oak's aura as she climbed slowly up to her old sanctuary, crawled out along the bough that was directly over the pool of black water and stood. Her strength was all but gone and an intense sadness quivered through her whole body. It was time for her to make things right; something she should have done long ago.

Looking down, she saw that Maye was lying on her side near their empty graves, curled into a tight ball, her head tucked beneath her arm. She had been withdrawn ever since she'd returned from Bellayne with tidings of Father Emlyn's and Mary Butterball's deaths. Phoebe's eyes were ringed with dark circles, and her once glorious hair was matted and sticking out, as if she'd crawled through a hedgerow. There was still no sign of Gracie or Glynn.

Irma had expected all of them to feel relieved, if not euphoric, now that they'd achieved their aims, and for Maye to be happy that Hester was safe, but the pall of heavy emotions still hung over the clearing. She could see now how the Shadowfolk had become bound to the hollow.

Irma knew that even if some miracle happened and she crossed the threshold of the gilded doorway herself, she'd find no peace in that place beyond the stars. The thought of leaving Gracie behind, of the little girl wandering forever in the shadows, was unbearable. She didn't know whether casting herself into darkness would help Gracie or the others, but she had to try. Once she was gone and separated from all that she held dear, she hoped the poison she'd created would disappear with her and that the heavenly beings would have mercy on Gracie and lift her out of the hollow.

She called out to Phoebe, wanting to find comforting words for the girl, who was still desperately grieving the loss of her baby. 'Maye will help you to face … to find your way once you both fly to the gilded door.'

'How can I set foot in the heavens now?' Phoebe wailed. 'I lay with my aunt's husband and pushed that kind and loving woman towards madness. And my baby Lillian died because of me. Choosing to stay here in the hollow is my eternal punishment.'

Maye slowly uncurled herself and sat up. She and Phoebe looked at each other and then at the ground. Irma could feel the guilt and shame that was weighing heavily on their minds and holding them back from freedom.

'If you stay here, Maye, Hester will never see you again. And, Phoebe, your sweet Lillian will never know your touch. Does either of them deserve to feel that terrible ache?'

'Irma? I need to tell you something.' Maye was hugging herself, as if trying to stop the last of her warmth from disappearing. Pain was etched deep into her face. She fell to her knees and cried, 'Oh, God, I'm so sorry. It began with me. Father Emlyn saw that Idris loved me as I loved him. I would never have told him of my feelings … but you and Gracie died because of me.'

'We died because of Father Emlyn, not you,' said Irma. 'Hester is safe now. Be at peace.'

Maye shook her head and wept. 'How …'

'Please,' Irma pleaded, 'promise me that you will both open your hearts and forgive yourselves while you still can.'

Phoebe helped Maye to her feet, and both girls cried as they hugged each other. Then they placed their left hands over their hearts and held their right hands up to Irma in a gesture of thanks and farewell.

Irma shivered as she balanced on her pointed toes on the branch and opened her shaking arms wide.

'Sing to me as I fall into darkness,' she asked Maye and Phoebe. 'I'll carry your song with me until ...'

Their mellow voices drifted up to her as they sang her favourite ballad.

> *'Come hither fair maidens,*
> *Wipe away your tears,*
> *Give to us your smiles,*
> *Sweet promises and*
> *Kisses upon our swords,*
> *As we ride out to battle on*
> *The cold and lonely moors.'*

To give herself courage, Irma remembered the many times she and Jack had raced each other along woodland paths. As she wove between the trees and skipped nimbly over rocks, she'd liked to imagine that she was as fleet as the wind and at one with it.

She tucked Gracie's yellow ribbons into the bodice of her dress, close to her heart, and opened her arms wide. There would be no turning back once she leaped from the branch. And once she entered the darkness, she guessed there'd be no way for her to know if the heavenly beings had kept their side of this unspoken bargain to take Gracie home.

Pressing her trembling lips together, she closed her eyes, let go of her memories and tilted forward.

'For Gracie,' she whispered.

'Stop!' screamed Maye. 'Oh, my God, Irma!'

Throwing her outstretched arms backwards to stop her fall, Irma dropped awkwardly to her knees and dug her toes and fingers into the branch's aura to steady herself. She looked down at Maye and Phoebe, who were both standing with mouths agape and pointing upwards.

'Irma, look,' Maye called again.

Irma tilted her head back. The gilded doorway was a warm and lustrous shimmering glow amid the night sky. She blinked, not believing her eyes. Her scalp quivered as the glow bloomed and soft, almost palpable light filled the hollow. She wanted to lie on her back and wallow in it until every skerrick of grime and every petty thought washed away. Fresh, clean air moistened her mouth and sweetened the faint putrescence that had oft wafted up their noses. The hollow was waking up after a long, unwholesome sleep.

Then, with barely a whisper of sound, the doorway to the heavens opened. Sweet music purred through the hollow, spreading warmth and ease through Irma's body. The aches of mind and soul disappeared, and as she became lighter her feet lifted off the branch. The angels were calling her home.

'Irma! Look at us.' Maye and Phoebe were shouting excitedly over the top of each other.

With great difficulty, Irma tore her eyes away from the doorway and looked down. The hollow was aglow. It was breathing, undulating with life. Owl and mole, fox and hedgehog, and many other forest dwellers had gathered at the edge of the clearing to watch Maye and Phoebe dance amid soft-hued swirls of heavenly mist. With a bonny blush upon their cheeks and glossy hair streaming out behind them, they looked like merry faeries as they skipped and twirled through glittering cloudlets of mauve, green and silver.

Fresh, salty tears of relief rolled down Irma's face.

Phoebe lay upon a swirling turquoise bed and closed her eyes.

Maye languidly fanned her fingers through a puff of palest pink and said, 'Methinks this is angel-breath.'

Irma wasn't sure if the mist was angel-breath, but it certainly appeared to have magical qualities for it had bewitched her friends. Fearing that the door would disappear again before Maye and Phoebe made it safely home, she was about to clap her hands to break the spell when a crimson cloudlet drifted over her shoulder. She covered her nose and mouth with one hand; she'd not be so easily beguiled. Someone needed to keep a clear head and a close watch on the heavens.

She cautiously poked the cloud with a fingertip. It was surprisingly warm and creamy … tingly … sublime. She laughed with delight. It was time to dance on lightsome toes with her friends.

She was about to flop onto the cloudlet and drift down into the clearing when a terrible thought struck her. For a few giddy moments she had forgotten all about Gracie and Glynn. She jerked away from the mist and her tears soured. The opening of the doorway had come too late for some. No celestial light was shining upon the Shadowfolk.

The heavenly ones hummed as two ropes spiralled down through the air. As soon as their feathery ends touched the ground, Maye and Phoebe quickly grasped heaven's offer of safe passage out of the hollow. Irma wouldn't relax until they stepped over the door's golden threshold, but things were definitely looking up.

As they lifted off the ground and swung sideways towards Irma's tree, she saw a rope dangling just behind her left shoulder. It looked as if it had been spun from moon and sun. She reached a hand out to it … it was warm to touch and softer than the finest silk.

'It's time to go home,' said Maye as she and Phoebe each stretched out a hand to help Irma off the branch.

Irma smiled and touched their fingertips, then dived headfirst out of the tree. Maye's and Phoebe's cries of disbelief followed her as she plummeted towards the ground, eyes closed. Fear squeezed tight around her throat. She could feel the air tearing as she fell.

When frigid air buffeted her face and a terrifying roar filled her head, she knew that she'd passed into darkness.

~

'Irma, open your eyes.'

It was Gracie's voice. Tears seeped through Irma's lowered lashes. She'd fallen into shadow, rather than darkness, and was with Gracie. Now she could face whatever awaited her in the gloaming with a tremulous but peaceful heart.

'Amen,' she whispered, and opened her eyes.

She stared in astonishment at Gracie, who was rosy-cheeked and wearing a cloak of shimmering yellow mist and a pair of new ribbons. Irma was speechless. Far above her, she could see Maye and Phoebe still clinging to their ropes.

Gracie grasped her hand and helped her to stand. 'Light streamed through your heart and into the Shadow realm when you fell into that muddy puddle, my dear, brave, funny Irma.'

A puddle, not a dark doorway. Irma felt a little foolish.

'You saved me,' Gracie said, then pointed into the space behind her. 'And helped them too.'

Irma turned, then fell to her knees and cried. The Shadowfolk were standing in the middle of the clearing, all holding silver lanterns. Among them she could see the folk who'd watched over her as she faded: the young monk with scarred wrists; Glynn's mother, tearfully receiving hugs from six of her seven excited children. It was a blessed night for all dwellers in the hollow.

The Shadowfolk raised the lanterns above their heads and one by one the swirling mist lifted them off the ground and carried them up to the heavens.

Irma heard a familiar whistled tune and saw Glynn standing in the middle of the hollow, grinning at her. He was no longer grey and faded, but appeared to have thrown off one hundred years of misery in the blink of an eye: he looked as gangly, lively and ready for mischief as any other boy of twelve years.

His sky-blue eyes never left her as she crossed the clearing and stood before him. She could barely speak as she remembered the many times he'd sat with her as she withered.

'Thank you,' she whispered.

Glynn nodded. 'My mother and the others finally saw their goodness shining bright. They could not resist the call of the Light any longer.'

Three more ropes descended from the heavens.

'Irma,' said Gracie, 'it's time to go home.'

'Then let's go before the angels change their minds and shut the door,' Irma replied.

'They can hear you,' Gracie said, sounding cross. As they lifted off the ground, she added, 'I wish my mother and father could see me riding up to the heavens on a rope spun from angel-hair.'

'Methinks,' said Glynn, 'that the angels will help you call upon them in their dreams.'

Gracie contemplated his words for a moment, then wiped her eyes and turned to Irma. 'And I wish that Nell and Eben could know that they helped us leave the hollow.'

Irma looked back at Bellayne, which was bathed in moonlight, and saw something that made her smile. She whispered in Gracie's ear and pointed to the little girl sitting on the windowsill of a cottage that had a pear tree in the yard.

'Do you think Fleur will tell her?' asked Gracie.

Irma put a finger to her lips. 'I do … one day.'

Hundreds of silver dewdrops showered down as all five of them stepped onto a cloud of purest white and stared in awe at the doorway to the heavens. They'd made it home.

Without a backward glance, Phoebe walked quickly through the doorway. Heartening for all to hear was her cry of joy. It sounded as if she'd found her Lillian.

As Maye looked down at Bellayne, Irma heard the breath catch in her throat. Though they were about to walk into the Light, leaving behind their loved ones was hard to bear.

'You'll see your Hester again … and Idris too,' said Irma. 'And in the meantime, I'll gladly keep you company.'

'I'm not sure if that's a curse or a blessing,' Maye said with a smile. 'Now, with or without you, Irma Linke, I'm going home to put my feet up and drink cup after cup of angel-nectar tea.'

Irma linked arms with Maye and looked over to Jack Lea's farm for the last time. She cocked her head and sniffed. There was a hint of change in the air surrounding his cottage. It smelled of romance, laughter and many children.

She smiled and whispered, 'Fare thee well, my friend.'

Just before Gracie and Glynn stepped over the golden threshold, Irma caught some dewdrops in her cupped hand and winked at Glynn. 'Angel-breath, angel-hair, angel-tea … this had better not be angel –'

'Shut up,' whispered Maye. 'They can hear you.'

Irma dipped the tip of her tongue into the liquid and shivered. Angel-nectar tea was blissfully delicious.

As the angels ushered Gracie and Glynn through the door, Irma heard a lilting voice say, 'Our tea will render her insensible for hours.'

Maye's laughter rippled across the heavens.

The moon looked down on little Fleur Simms and smiled.

The girl was sitting on her bedchamber windowsill watching the angels welcome her friends home. Her face was alight with wonder.

She was unaware of the delicate wings fluttering gently on her back.

Epilogue

One-and-Twenty Years Later

Midsummer sunlight danced across the meadows as Nell, sitting on the porch of Lea Farm cottage, watched her family fishing in the stream at the bottom of the hill. The racket they were making would have old Father Caddock stomping down the road to berate them in next to no time.

Jack turned, perhaps sensing her eyes upon him, and waved his hat three times above his head: a sweet signal that it was time for them to give their brood of six the slip and find a secluded spot in the woods so that they could play together. Quivering with delightful anticipation, Nell waved back.

Just as she was about to skip down the steps though, Fleur awoke in the chair next to her. She snuggled her newborn against her chest and kissed her downy head. Little Ealinn-Rose, Maureen's grandchild, had kept Fleur and Eben up most of the night but was sleeping innocently now.

'You look flushed,' said Fleur, her lips twitching with mischief as she glanced at Jack striding up the hill towards them.

'Just a little warm,' said Nell, lifting the hair off her neck then fanning her face with her hand. 'It's time for a stroll through a shady dell.'

'A lovely idea. I might join you.'

'Um …' Nell began.

Fleur grinned at her. 'Tomorrow then, once I've had a good night's sleep.'

'Cheeky sprite.'

Keeping one hand on her baby's back, Fleur leaned sideways to rummage around in the handbasket beside her chair. She handed Nell a slim, leather-bound book. 'I've started a journal. I liked your idea of handing down to Ealinn-Rose and any other children we might have stories from my life. You can read it once you've returned from your jaunt if you like.'

'With pleasure,' said Nell.

She turned to watch Jack. He had stopped to pick cherries from the tree they had buried her friend Emily under almost nineteen years earlier. The lass had never recovered from the illness she'd been suffering when Nell had helped her escape the Boar's Den, but she'd spent the last eighteen months of her life surrounded by those who loved and cared for her.

Jack balanced his upturned hat, now full of cherries, on his head and performed a short jig, one hand on his hip and the other pointing at the sky.

'Someone's impatient to head off,' said Fleur.

'What? Oh, I had not noticed,' Nell lied. 'Anyway, anticipation makes ardour smoulder. It won't hurt him to wait a few moments.'

She opened the journal and ran her fingertips over the parchment, contemplating how her many talks with Fleur over the last couple of years about the similar and different ways they'd each experienced the *flow* had helped her to understand more of why she'd once felt no sense of the *flow* at all and why, once she'd glimpsed it moving through others, she'd believed that she was separate from and not part of that wonder and that was the way it would always be. When she'd first set out from Stonhard all those years ago, despairing and believing that life was nothing more than a cruel cycle of suffering and survival, she'd never imagined it could be possible to feel so nourished and alive, to experience such a deep sense of belonging, not just with kith and kin, but with the very heartbeat of the sky and the earth itself.

After her first direct experience of the *flow*, her inner journey into the mystery had begun, and she'd followed that path through upsets, troubles and good times alike, asking for guidance and understanding from above whenever the way before her dimmed. New insights had empowered her to look deeper, to hear and trust the soft hum of her intuition; and she'd awakened to the unseen a little more each day, until she could hear clearly the song of her soul. Its essence was a glorious reflection of the heavens, and a miracle that she could embody each day if she chose to. Whenever she slipped into the silence between her heartbeats, and her awareness soared across the violet sky to where she could see the light emanating from the birthplace of all life, she had a deep sense of coming home to its love and to herself. She felt held then, inspired and at peace; knowing without doubt that life went on beyond the earthly realm and that death was merely a lifting up, the sacred and complete unfolding of one's soul wings.

Nell's scalp shivered deliciously – something that happened whenever she felt light-hearted and brimming with life – and what she'd come to call 'a heavenly shower' touched her senses and tingled its way to her heart, which bloomed into the magical flower it was, to share with others its unique and precious radiance and perfume. Ah, it was a blessing to feel and to know that earth's garden and they themselves were part of the heaven they sought.

After another glance at Jack, who was now sprinkling the beginning of the path they'd take into the woods with the flower petals he must've ripped out of her garden while she wasn't looking, Nell read the first entry in Fleur's journal.

~

I saw the Light, my dearest child, one night when I was a wee girl. Upon my windowsill I sat, gazing at the moon, when a golden doorway opened in the sky and I heard angels sing. Moonlight bathed the ground, and even though I wasn't touching the frosty grass I felt the earth pulsing through my feet.

Then, above the distant hills, I saw the souls of four murdered girls soar into the sky. I should have been sad, because they'd often played with me while your grandsire created his paintings inside St Clement's, but only joyous tears splashed onto my cheeks. My friends had been lifted home.

Once the moon and I were alone again and all was quiet, the coldness of the world settled around my shoulders. I felt small and empty, as if something had stolen my smile and thrown it on the midden. Then unseen hands touched my brow and the back of my head, and soft breath wafted warm against my temples. My eyelids drooped and my mind drifted like a cloud while someone whispered an old story into my ears.

Towards the end of the Old Age, when the fertile darkness soured and evil slunk across our thresholds, we gazed in horror at the dead sprawled across our fields. We gave that evil a name, and allowed it to thrive until the very earth we'd tilled so lovingly began to quake and crumble and die.

To keep us from eternal suffering and despair, She *of the Mystery gathered us close and whispered memories into our ears, while* He *of the Light reached into his heart and gave each of us an ember of sacred starfire. Then, before our home burst asunder,* He *lifted us to safety and laid us gently upon the undulating sky-seas.*

But alas, the darkness sensed our leaving and spat its venom high into the air and a single drop stained every one of us. We looked at each other with frightened eyes for a dense shadow had been cast upon our light. We had been cursed with bitterness and jealousy, sickness and fear. In one terrible moment, as we watched our home fall apart, we saw that the darkness was a figment of our wrath and greed, a creature we'd conjured with our imaginations to excuse our foul deeds and to carry our shame. We'd cursed ourselves.

At the dawn of the New Age, when our new home was shimmering with radiance and peace, Mystery and Light reached down to lift us from the sky-seas, but we had grown heavy and blind with guilt and could not see their outstretched arms yearning to embrace us. We plummeted through our minds towards an abyss writhing with tortured thoughts and echoes; eternal reminders of all the terrible things we had done to each other.

Out of his great love for us, He fashioned a golden cord and anchored one of its ends deep within his heart. She grasped the other, then leaped from the heavens and plunged through the void. When She was beneath us all, She lay on her back and with his breath, He created Earth on her belly; a safe place for us to land and to heal our battered spirits. As each of us took our first breaths, She unwound a thread from the golden cord of life that linked us all and secured it to the ember of starfire within our hearts.

For a time, peace reigned among us, but then we forgot … And, almost imperceptibly, shadows began to inch across our lands.

Some said the coming of darkness began with one harsh word; others swore it was the discovery of a despoiled child. But most believed that the return of evil was inevitable and that there was little we, as simple folk, could do to halt it. The darkness that we imagined and then believed quickly obscured our view of the heavens with a rigid shroud, and fiddled with our destinies until our memories shrivelled and the ancient stain we carried secreted toil and trouble, heartache and fatigue. To keep us isolated and running in panicked circles, it gleefully scattered disease and temptation among us, rage and poverty.

He anointed each of our threads with courage and planted seeds of light within every disheartening and heartless thought. But the darkness cursed us with a grief so powerful that we lost all sense of our eternal nature. Fear of death and loss overpowered any vague sense of knowing.

Starlight birthed new earth-angels and He blessed us all with a celestial guide to help us open the ears and eyes of our soul and to answer our questions once we remembered to ask them.

Decay and Light both gave to us free will.

As his seeds of love sprouted within every kindness we shared with each other and sent their roots deep into her belly, we began to see glimmers of truth. Some folk glimpsed beyond their minds and remembered that we were linked to something wondrous, and as the starfire within their hearts kindled that message rippled over deserts, snow meadows, seas, woodlands and mountains, and others began to awaken and look up.

To keep the rest of us ensnared and from shattering its brittle illusion, the darkness lashed us with disaster and forced its underlings to bare their teeth at us. But those acts of destruction only encouraged us to stand together.

And some folk began to recall the last words She had whispered into our ears: "When enough of you join hands, the seven sacred beacons will flare within your souls and on earth, forever opening the door to the heavens for all to see." '

Once the sweetest voice I'd ever heard finished telling me that story, ethereal fingers stroked my brow until a glowing ring appeared around my head.

> *'From moondew and daystar,' sang angels,*
> *'A circlet of heavenly windows was forged*
> *For you and each earth child.*
> *Kindness and a willingness to look beyond what you can see*
> *Clears them,*
> *And when they open,*
> *The illusion of aloneness vanishes*
> *And your whole being fills with*
> *The nectar of the heavens and earth.'*

Nell closed the journal. 'When each of us shares our tales, a little more of the mystery is solved,' she said to Fleur.

And then she blew her impatient husband a kiss and skipped down the stairs towards him.

'We are with you. Breathe us in,' said Mystery and Light.

The End

Acknowledgements

Thank you to the following folk for your guidance, insights and support:

Nicola O'Shea, an amazing and patient editor, who streamlined *Whispers & Poison* and helped me to clarify what I wanted to create; and Keith Stevenson, who dealt with the file conversions and other technical stuff, both found at www.ebookedit.com.au.

Pauline O'Carolan (paulineprivate5@gmail.com), who proofread and gently polished my final copy, and helped me get to 'The End'.

Jen Mulligan (jenmulligandesign.com), the talented designer of my website and beautiful book cover.

My friends Joy Bells and Anna, my sister, Deb, and my daughter, Jack, who read many drafts and gave me frequent cups of tea and kicks up the bum.

It was a pleasure working with you all. With heartfelt thanks.

About the Author

Mandy Rae Wylie lives in Queensland, where she loves to play board games, swim, garden, watch sword fighting, and read thrillers and murder mysteries in bed. She also loves to walk in nature, gaze at the night sky, have at least one good belly laugh a day and as many hugs as she can get from loved ones and her dog, Daisy.

You can find Mandy Rae at her website

www.mandyraewylie.com

and on Goodreads

www.goodreads.com/mandyrae_wylie.